I0819563

THE LOST BOOK OF ELIZABETH BARTON

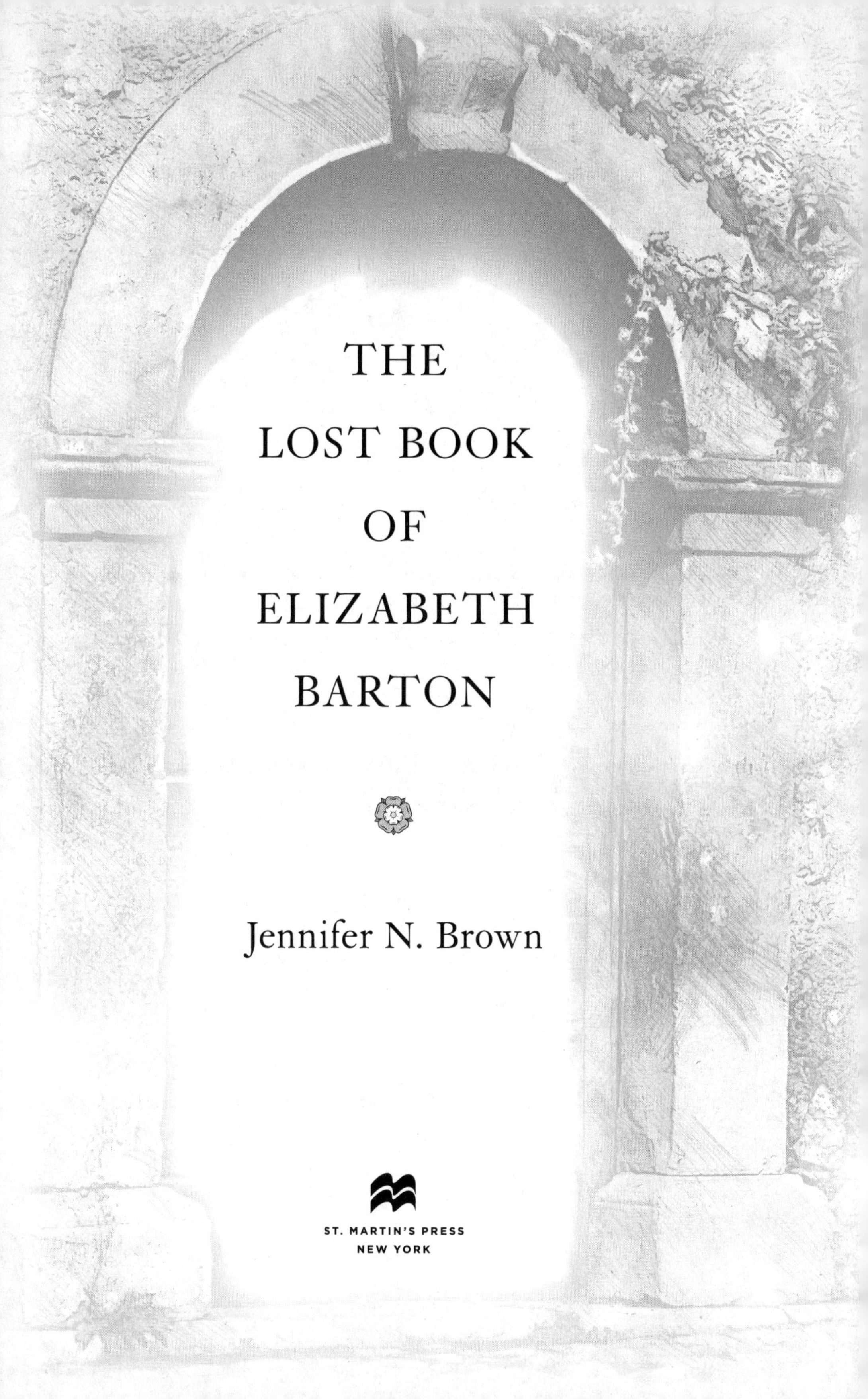

THE LOST BOOK OF ELIZABETH BARTON

Jennifer N. Brown

ST. MARTIN'S PRESS
NEW YORK

This is a work of fiction. All of the names, characters, organizations, places, and events portrayed in this work are either products of the author's imagination or used fictitiously.

First published in the United States by St. Martin's Press, an imprint of St. Martin's Publishing Group

EU Representative: Macmillan Publishers Ireland Ltd, 1st Floor, The Liffey Trust Centre, 117–126 Sheriff Street Upper, Dublin 1, D01 YC43

www.stmartins.com

The Library of Congress Cataloging-in-Publication Data is available upon request.

ISBN 978-1-250-38359-4 (hardcover)
ISBN 978-1-250-38360-0 (ebook)

First Edition: 2026

10 9 8 7 6 5 4 3 2 1

For Kevin Alban, O. Carm.,
friar, priest, medievalist, friend,
who would have loved this

TIMELINE OF EVENTS

1501 Arthur, Prince of Wales (b. 1486) and heir to the English throne, marries the Spanish princess Catherine of Aragon (b. 1485)

1502 Arthur dies of illness; Henry Tudor (b. 1491) is now heir; Henry is engaged to Catherine of Aragon

1506 Elizabeth Barton born

1509 Henry VII dies; Henry Tudor marries Catherine of Aragon; Henry is coronated as Henry VIII

1516 Mary, future queen, born to Catherine of Aragon and Henry VIII

1521 Pope Leo X names Henry VIII "Defender of the Faith"

1522 Anne Boleyn comes to the court

1525 Elizabeth Barton has her first vision at the farm of Thomas Cobb, on the property of Archbishop William Warham

1526 William Tyndale's translation of the New Testament into English printed in Cologne

1527 Around seven hundred copies of Elizabeth Barton's book *A marueilous woorke of late done at Court of Streete in Kent* printed in London

1528 Elizabeth Barton meets Cardinal Wolsey, Lord High Chancellor of England, and Thomas More

1529 Thomas More replaces Cardinal Wolsey as Lord High Chancellor of England

1532 Thomas More resigns as chancellor; Thomas Cromwell becomes chief minister to Henry VIII; Barton prophesizes that Henry VIII and Anne Boleyn will burn in hell if they marry

1533 Henry VIII and Anne Boleyn marry in secret; Henry VIII appoints Thomas Cranmer as Archbishop of Canterbury; Cranmer officially annuls Henry VIII's marriage to Catherine of Aragon; Anne Boleyn is coronated; Elizabeth I, future queen, is born to

Anne and Henry VIII; Elizabeth Barton is arrested and confesses that she has fabricated her visions

1534 The Treason Act, with punishments for speaking out against the king or his policies, is made into law; the Act of Supremacy declares Henry VIII as head of the Church of England; Elizabeth Barton is hanged for treason

1535 Thomas Cromwell assesses all the wealth of the Church in England in the *Valor Ecclesiasticus*; Thomas More is executed

1536 Thomas Cromwell begins the dissolution of the monasteries; Catherine of Aragon dies; Anne Boleyn is executed; Henry VIII marries third wife, Jane Seymour

1537 Edward, future king, is born to Jane Seymour (who dies days afterward) and Henry VIII

1540 Henry VIII marries fourth wife, Anne of Cleves, annulled six months later; Henry VIII marries fifth wife, Catherine Howard; Thomas Cromwell is executed

1542 Catherine Howard is executed

1543 Henry VIII marries sixth wife, Catherine Parr

1547 Henry VIII dies; Edward VI is coronated

1553 Edward VI dies; Lady Jane Grey (Henry VIII's grandniece) is proclaimed queen; Mary Tudor and her supporters imprison Lady Jane; Queen Mary I is coronated

1558 Queen Mary I dies; Elizabeth Tudor becomes queen

1559 Elizabeth I is coronated

1568 Mary, Queen of Scots (Elizabeth's first cousin once removed), is imprisoned in England

1587 Mary, Queen of Scots, is executed

1603 Queen Elizabeth I dies; James I ascends the throne

1606 Nicholas Owen is tortured to death by James I for his work building priest holes throughout England

Prologue

Tyburn, 1534

Elizabeth was at first unafraid at the Tree. Even through her exhausted, muddled mind, the searing pain in her shoulders and head, she believed that God would save her. When they first placed the chafing rope around her neck, she welcomed it.

Death would not yet come for her like it had for others. It may at last be her hour, but her bridegroom was waiting for her in heaven.

There were already corpses swinging and awaiting company, hanged earlier that day. Birds voraciously picked at the flesh despite the roar of the crowd.

The people gathered there were shouting and cheering for this ceremony of death. Her eyes fixed on a family up front, a small child on the shoulders of a man. A day out. To watch them hang.

She moved her gaze, for her head would no longer move as she willed it, to the hangmen who climbed onto the cart, making sure the nooses around their necks were secure. There were six of them waiting to die, but the crowd was there only for her.

"The Mad Maid of Kent! Did you foresee this?"

"Do the Tyburn jig for us, Holy Maid!" the man with the child spat out, laughing. The child clapped.

"What good are your prophecies now?" shouted another spectator.

And the chorus: "*Liar! False prophet!*"

Was she? Elizabeth no longer knew, with her weakened body and confused thoughts, what was real and what was not, what had been true and what was false. She closed her eyes tightly and tried to remember the voice of God. She had heard it once. She knew she had. But here, there was only the sound of the people demanding her death.

The horses took some steps ahead, frightened by the noise, and she felt the noose tighten. Through the fog in her head, she heard the cart driver shout to stop. It was not yet time.

She swallowed the bile that rose in her throat. It tasted like fear.

Then the executioner nodded to the cart driver, who whipped the horses to move. They followed their command, and as the horses galloped away, taking the cart with them, the six bodies stayed tethered firmly to the Tree.

As she felt her toes leave the cart, she was immediately desperate for breath, her body in its jerky dance under the Tyburn Tree. She tried to will her arms to pull the rope away, but they continued to hang useless at her side.

Some fell heavy, their necks breaking almost instantly.

The rest convulsed, kicked, clawed at their necks. Their feet were mere inches from the ground, taunting them.

But she was as light as air. No quick death for her. She felt her legs running as if they could escape her body.

She was gripped with terror, until the very last moment when it all went black.

Kent, 2023

I am not dead.

Someone will find me. Right?

Breathe. Calm.

I have never been a phobic—not afraid of flying or blood or heights or spiders or open spaces or public speaking. I can breathe myself calm, relax, slow my own pulse.

But now, as I sit in this dark and tight space for what must be the third hour (time is so blurry without a watch or a window that I can't judge how much has passed), claustrophobia is settling in to stay. I don't know if it's the smell of that dead animal, still lingering in the heavy air inside this place, the dust that I can feel crusting on my nostrils, or that my body is touching all four walls of this small, dark container at once.

I am so thirsty. The air is stifling and my mouth is sandpaper-dry. If I ever get out of here, I will never take a glass of water for granted again.

The researcher in me wants to think of all the others who have hidden here, holding their breath, hoping that they are not discovered and that their secrets are safe. But the practical me, the me whose throat is raw from screaming and whose hands are chafed and bloody from pounding on the door to this hole—that version of me doesn't care about the past. I care only about the future. As in, will there be one?

I try not to ask the question that is the only question worth asking right now: Is this how I die?

Part One

MISS MANUSCRIPT

Aldington, April 1525

This is how it began. Elizabeth was nineteen years of age and ever exhausted from working on the Cobb farm. She had worked there since her father had died five years prior (her mother having been long dead from childbirth), and her uncle found a place for her there. She still was not used to how tired she became by the end of the day, tumbling onto her pallet every night desperate to close her eyes, often thinking that the sheep were better cared for than the servants and farmhands.

She and the other indoor servants—Edith and Kate, village girls, sisters—all slept on the floor of the kitchen, which was warmer in the winter, with the embers in the giant hearth still burning, and cooler in the summer, with its stone floors. She knew that she was lucky to have work and a place to sleep and food to eat. Yet at night she would fall into the most powerful slumber, every muscle aching.

And then one Easter morning, she did not wake.

There had been three glorious days of less work at the farm as the servants attended mass on Maundy Thursday, Good Friday, and Holy Saturday. Edith was annoyed that she had to poke Elizabeth in the ribs to keep her awake at church, but the chanting of the monks and the heat of the place with the bodies inside and the damp spring air outside conspired to make them all sleepy.

Sunday mass would be the longest one, but it would be followed by a feast, so the girls were happy to arise early and do their chores, getting the kitchen ready before heading out. After forty Lenten days without any meat or eggs, the whole household was looking forward to the meal that would follow. Despite their habitual fatigue, Kate, Edith, and Elizabeth had been up late chatting excitedly about the milk and eggs they would eat the next day, and wistfully hoped that some of the chicken reserved for the Cobbs would remain for the servants.

But as the sun rose on Easter day and morning light streamed through the small window of the dark kitchen, Elizabeth was stiff and unresponsive.

"Elizabeth?" Edith said, still curled around her. "Kate is up. It's time." Edith nudged her lightly with her hand, and when Elizabeth did not even stir, Edith shook her more forcefully. Edith was scared but also angry—there was *always* something amiss with her. Would they not receive their eggs?

"Elizabeth!" she shouted, shaking her again, but the girl lay red-faced and immobile.

When Kate came back from her toileting outside, Edith was already in tears. "She's hot with fever," Kate whispered to her sister, her hand on Elizabeth's brow.

"Like Christopher," Edith whispered back. The strapping farm-hand who had caused them all to giggle whenever he passed by, hoping he would glance their way, had fallen ill with fever one day in January and was buried two days later.

"Get Mistress Cobb."

Cobb's wife was mostly kind, but she prodded Elizabeth with her toe a few times before bending over and feeling the girl's forehead with one extended finger. Later, she would feel guilty at being so irked at the inconvenience of such an ill servant on Easter morning, the long-awaited feast canceled.

Only when Cobb came in and tried to shake Elizabeth conscious, muttering, "Not another damned sick worker," did they send for the priest. Cobb wanted the last unction administered before her death; he did not want the state of that child's soul as his burden.

Elizabeth did not remember any of this; it's just what she was told. This is what she remembered: she was in a peaceful place with a soft bed like Cobb's, and a light that was warm, and she heard a voice. As the voice spoke it was as if her whole body was aflame, and she thought that she should be afraid, but she was not.

The voice said, *I am with you, Elizabeth. And so is my mother, the Holy Mary. You have been chosen. I will give you a showing.*

And then it was as if the world around her fell away and transformed from the cool kitchen into blazing great fires, the heat of which should have burned her to embers and somehow did not. She could smell the brimstone. There were strange horned men dancing, their unnaturally long bodies naked and their grins exposing jagged, sharp teeth. Demons. They were prodding a line of people as they danced, and when Elizabeth looked she saw that they were dead people she had known in life! Men and women of every rank. They screamed in agony like women in labor. And then she saw also those that she knew were still alive as if they, too, were burning.

"Is this what awaits me?" she asked the voice. *No,* she heard in her mind, *not if you recount what you have been shown.* Jesus—because suddenly she knew it was his voice—spoke again. *You must return and demand a mass for everyone you have seen here. For every prayer you say, a soul will be relieved of time in purgatory's fires. They will move ever closer to paradise where they will be washed in the oil of my mercy.*

And then Elizabeth woke up, drenched in sweat, to see the ring of a wide-eyed audience: dear Edith, Kate, Father Richard Master, the Cobbs. She told them what she had witnessed and whom she had heard. And then she turned to Cobb and said, "One of your children is wicked and I saw him there in those sweltering flames, his wrist clasped in the talons of a demon. He will be there soon if he does not repent."

Cobb replied, "What filth is this?" But he knew which child she was talking about: Julian, a boy of eleven whose cruel tricks on the servants and farmworkers were well known. Those assembled there saw the sweat on his brow, the recognition in his eyes. Julian, who had just that morning collected the mice the cats left on the doorstep and put them in Elizabeth's shoes, saw his father glance quickly at him before he fell into a swoon. The farmer ordered his household back to work and the priest to leave, hoping to put the strange incident behind them.

Within a week, though, the fever had swept through the house, and Julian lay stiff, pale, and cold.

All the village people spoke about how the servant girl had seen God and that she had predicted the hour of the Cobb boy's death. When Father Richard returned to the farm to pray over the dead body of the boy, readying him for burial, he realized he had witnessed a miracle when Elizabeth had spoken.

The vision had been not a fever dream but a real gift from God. After the boy was properly buried, the priest wrote quickly to summon his superiors who dealt with such things.

Elizabeth had become a prophetess. A seer.

Atlantic City, January 2023

Miss Norway almost steps on my foot as Miss Brazil pushes me and the other women deeper into the elevator and squawks out "floor fifteen" to the man charged with the buttons. I know the near-culprit is Miss Norway, and that Miss Brazil is Miss Brazil, and that the other women are Miss Mexico and Miss Luxembourg, because they are wearing their sashes.

Apparently, they wear them all the time because this is the second day I've had to cram myself into spaces with impossibly statuesque women with eyelashes that look like they could fly off their faces at any moment. And they always have their sashes.

I am not statuesque, have no extra eyelashes attached to my eyes, and I don't even wear much makeup. I also do not have a sash. Instead, I have a badge. A badge that in other venues I am happy to have around my neck identifying me as "Dr. Alison Sage, New York University, Department of History."

Not that it's a name too many people would recognize, but at least it shows that I belong when the Manuscript Society takes over a hotel in Cincinnati, or Providence, or Cambridge (either continent). But the unfortunate choice of Atlantic City (close to so many airports! easy for the Europeans!) and a hotel large enough to house not only a bunch of academics but also another big group has instead landed me in this hell: an unlikely confluence of the Manuscript Society—or "ManSock," as it is affectionately known—scholars' annual convention and the Miss Universe pageant.

Normally at ManSock, I would be doing my best to gamely hold court at the hotel bar with some of the old boys (if they are older than fifty, they are almost certainly men), but this conference is very different. I need to get to my room to prepare for this evening's keynote lecture. A talk I just happen to be giving. Down at the bar, meanwhile, many of those same boys (at least the straight ones) are sitting slack-jawed, making guesses as to the gold-lettered country on the sash before a woman turns around or trying out their genuinely terrible small talk with those same women.

Just as I was getting onto the elevator, I heard Jasper, the current president of the society, trying to impress ("Well, I speak Greek, you know. . . ."), followed by Siegfried pulling up photos from his semester in Egypt to show the bewildered audience of women they had cornered. It's all too cringey for me even to find slightly amusing.

Only a week ago, I held such high hopes for this conference. This is my first keynote talk anywhere, much less at the biennial gathering of ManSock, and I have a bombshell to unveil. A scholarly bombshell, to be fair, but one that could completely reignite my career. I've gone with the ambiguous "A Discovery in the Archive" as my title, but the discovery is giant, and I waited until all of my ducks were in a row (publication ready to drop, authentication completed, large venue) to let the work become public. But now I feel as if my excitement has been deflated, popped like one of the many pink helium balloons designating the pageant spaces.

Sigh. I have to shout my "Excuse me!" twice to get off at my floor, and somewhat unnecessarily let my elbow jam into Miss Luxembourg on the way out.

Back in my room, I drink some coffee even though at this late hour I know it means I will sleep poorly tonight. I feel ready. "Go time," I whisper to the mirror, laughing even as I say it since it seems so cliché. "GO TIME!" I say again with even more conviction. I stand with my legs apart and arms akimbo; it's a "power stance" I read about in some women's magazine. "You are the keynote speaker at ManSock," I tell my reflection.

* * *

Just before heading into the ballroom where the talk will be held, I decide to duck into the bathroom one last time (too much coffee, after all). Inside at the sink, a Beyoncé doppelgänger at least a foot taller than me, the gorgeous Miss Canada, wears a multicolored dress with sequins that shimmer like the scales of a fish, reminding me of a children's book that I used to read to the twins when they were small. The dress clings to every curve, revealing the toned (and, sigh, perfect) body underneath, with her sash slung over her shoulder. She holds a baggie of makeup and checks herself out in the mirror. I guess there is no room for pockets on that small strip of fabric she is wearing.

"How do you walk in those things?" I ask, pointing to her silver stilettos.

Miss Canada looks down at me, not unkindly, and says, "Well, it takes practice, but it makes your legs look longer and every little thing counts here. I guess it doesn't matter anyway; I was out in the first round. But I want them to see what they're missing." She applies more lipstick to her already-glossy mouth, mascara to the already-darkened fringe over her eyes. I watch the practiced ease of her hands.

"I'm sorry. For what it's worth, I think you look great," I say. It sucks to lose, in academia or Miss Universe. I know the feeling exactly.

"Thanks." Miss Canada turns and assesses me more closely. "You look nice, too. You could use some"—she shuffles around in her baggie—"eyebrow pencil, though. They're a little sparse. May I?" Before I can object, Miss Canada leans over and applies some makeup to my brows. When I turn back to the mirror, I have to admit that I look better.

"Wow. Thanks! I don't even own that stuff." I point to the pencil. "Guess I'll have to buy some."

"Take it," says Miss Canada, handing it to me as she turns away. "I have loads."

* * *

WHEN I ARRIVE at the Centennial Ballroom fifteen minutes before the scheduled talk (the grander Millennial Ballroom is the venue for the second round of the pageant), it is empty. Strange. I flip through the conference program to double-check the time and the room, even though I have committed both to memory and know I am in the right place at the right time. The sea of empty hotel chairs (gold, white, uncomfortable; pretty sure I've sat in the same ones at many a wedding) stretch out in front of me.

Could it possibly be that for my first (and I guess only) keynote, no one will come to hear it? A few friends told me that they would be here. And the moderator has to come, right? Was my title *too* vague?

Ten minutes to go. Still no one. I decide to just lean in to this panic. Isn't that what a woman my age is supposed to do? Lean in? I breathe in. Out. Breathe. Calm. I am taunted by the title glowing on the screen behind me, "Manuscript Society Keynote Lecture, 'A Discovery in the Archives,' Dr. Alison Sage." My paper illuminated on the podium is almost a punch line.

But just as I am about to tip over into total despair, I am saved by Jenny (Yale, lucky duck), who comes running in, her dark curls shimmering like a halo around her head. "Oh, Alison! So sorry! The evening panels started late because the guy who opens all the doors apparently got distracted by the, ahem, losers of the first round of the pageant and was nowhere to be found. We are running twenty minutes late. Didn't you get my texts?"

I dig around in my backpack for my phone, buried at the bottom under the flotsam and jetsam of my life. I triumphantly pull it out and realize I had left it on silent mode. Now I see that I have several texts from Jenny. And Frankie (the moderator). And Charles (who had invited me to do the keynote). And Pete (the ex-husband, father to my children, who manages to text me with queries for every possible detail when it is his turn to parent).

The first four were variations on a theme:

Starting late! Long story but
involves a drunk hotel employee
and Miss Trinidad and Tobago.

This bloody pageant.

Terribly sorry. Let's count on
starting at 7:30 instead of 7.

Can you believe this? Dying to
see everyone's faces when you
finally speak!

And then:

What time does G have ballet
tomorrow? What's the address
of T's tutor?

Alison? Are you there?
Alison?

I answer only the last one:

10:00. And then Lucinda's mom will get Georgina, so you just need to drop her off. Tristan KNOWS the address. It's the building next to the dentist he's been going to for 12 years.

I shut off my phone, returning it to the deep detritus of my bag.

"I didn't realize it was already time," I lie. "I just thought I was early." I feel to make sure my ever-necessary reading glasses are on top of my head. Deep breaths. Calm.

I turn to Jenny. "Okay. I'm ready to go when you are."

* * *

"Good evening, and thank you all for being here," I begin. "I am especially grateful so many of you made it despite the 'universe' of distractions in town this week." The light from the projector pretty much blinds me to the audience beyond the first row, but I can at least see that the auditorium, after all, is full.

"When I first received the invitation, I was deep in my sabbatical, happy in the archives. I thought I would be telling you about the origins of a few medieval lyrics. However, I'm sorry to disappoint those of you who were counting on that—all four of you."

I stop for the laughter that I am hoping will follow and am gratified when it does. Looking over my glasses at the audience, I clear my throat and say, "I instead want to tell you what I found, miscatalogued, damaged, in a Belgian monastery. But let me take you back a little first—I promise, it's worth the wait—since I know we come from many areas of interest, and I need to make clear the importance of what I have found."

I can tell I have the audience's interest now—an uncatalogued and forgotten manuscript worthy of a keynote is undoubtedly exciting.

Everyone is alert, leaning forward just a little bit. It's the body language I see in students sometimes when I know I have them.

They're hooked.

My next slide displays an image of a robust, opulently clothed Henry VIII, and some rumblings of excitement bubble up from the crowd. "Many of you know, of course, the story of Henry VIII, his marriage to Anne Boleyn and divorce from Catherine of Aragon, and the path it then set England on afterward.

"While you may know these famous figures of English history, not too many of you know the story of Elizabeth Barton, the so-called Holy Maid of Kent. There is not much known about Barton's early life, although she was likely a farm servant, and circa 1525 she began to have visions, interesting enough to capture the attention of the Church and later even the king.

"Women visionaries had a lot of political power once important men championed them, and this is what appeared to happen with Elizabeth at the start. She moved into St. Sepulchre's Priory, whose wealth grew with her residency, and she began to gather audiences. As with the visionaries who preceded her, Elizabeth dictated what she had seen to her spiritual advisor—Edward Bocking—who wrote them down. He helped to have them published in a small book, which detailed Barton's prophecies and predictions. It was widely distributed."

I am getting closer to the reveal. I have the audience now, eyes wide. I can see the prominent scholar Roger Shefield in the front row, literally on the edge of his seat. I turn to a manuscript image of a priest speaking at a pulpit.

"Although the men around Barton were politically savvy and understood what a tinderbox the country was religiously, she likely did not. Barton started saying the wrong things as far as some of these men were concerned, the *very* wrong things. As we might have predicted with the lens of history, it did not go well for her."

I turn the slide to a picture of Anne Boleyn, the famous image where her golden "B" drops from a gold chain encircling her neck, precisely where the executioner's axe would sever her head a few years after the portrait.

"What did Elizabeth say?" I ask the crowd, rhetorically. "Well, she said that Henry was making a gigantic mistake with Anne Boleyn. She said that the soul of both king and country were imperiled by his choices. She said he would die a villain's death within months of his marriage. She said that he would burn in hell."

I pause to allow the enormity of this to sink in. "Remember," I say, "people believed that her prophecies were true. Her claims about Henry suited many of the influential churchmen around her as they were trying, desperately, to prevent the king's turn away from what they saw as the one true Church. They, too, believed these things that Elizabeth said. What better mouthpiece than a visionary? What better admonition than that of God himself?

"I think we all know that Henry would not—could not—let Elizabeth continue speaking unchecked. The consequences of her transgressions were dire. Under what was likely torture at the hands of Cromwell's men, she confessed that she had fabricated her visions, that she had been directed in what to say by her confessor and spiritual advisor, Dr. Bocking. Whether her visions were real or whether this was a great and carefully crafted con job has been up for debate."

I pause and turn to a stock image of a gallows. "At twenty-eight years old, alongside several of her champions, Elizabeth was hanged at the gallows known as the Tyburn Tree. Nearly a hundred thousand people attended her execution, after which her head was removed from her body and placed as a warning to others on London Bridge, the only woman to ever receive that treatment."

Now is the moment. I breathe in, pause, ready to announce my discovery. I can feel my heart quickening, note the slightly nervous tremble in my voice in anticipation of what I am about to say. "Elizabeth's book was ordered banned and burned. It was heresy to own it. And Henry's men did a good job. They were completely erased, incinerated, destroyed. We believe—or should I say 'believed'?—there were no surviving copies of the possibly five hundred to seven hundred that once existed."

I move back to my initial slide, a page of my manuscript, but now they can see what I was showing them. "My esteemed colleagues, let me now reveal to you what I found, miscatalogued, mistreated, partially but not completely destroyed, among other monastic papers in Belgium. This cache of documents, clearly taken in haste during the dissolution of the monasteries when English Catholics read the temperature of their fickle king and fled abroad, seems to have sat untouched for centuries. And among them, I found a copy of Elizabeth's book."

Rochester, February 1526

After Elizabeth's vision, Father Richard Master wrote to the nearby Benedictine monastery, Christ Church, asking for spiritual guidance for the miracle of the vision he had witnessed. "My dear brother in Christ," he wrote, "I have been blessed by God to be present at a great miracle, where an unlettered girl, a mere servant, was granted a vision of purgatory and told by God that a boy's death was forthcoming. When his death did indeed come to pass, I undertook to write to you to come see what has transpired in my parish." He hoped that those at Christ Church would see that his presence at such an event could only be a sign of his own favor in God.

Father Richard's letter reached the monk Edward Bocking, who once studied at Oxford and knew that these rumors of prophecy were more often false than true. Women had fantasies and were more prone to the fake visions that the Devil sent than men were, as it was with Eve, who had committed the great original sin because she was so tempted by the serpent and his honey words. It is because women are ruled by the flesh and not by reason, like men—and the flesh is so weak.

But when Father Bocking and the other monks and priests had spoken to the farm girl and seen how fair and innocent she was, how overwhelmed at her vision and what it meant, and how awestricken to be in their blessed presence, they were convinced that she was no charlatan. The fate of the Cobb boy was the tangible proof of her holiness as two witnesses—and some women, too—heard her foresee his imminent death while in the bloom of health.

A visionary could not remain a servant, Bocking knew, and this was why he would take her to Bishop Fisher. He needed the Church's support for whatever was to come next. He was glad to have such an important errand, to bring a visionary and a prophet to speak to the bishop. He had been laboring for so long for advancement and now he was sure to get it.

It was the first time Elizabeth ever left the farm since she had arrived there, but she visited the town of Rochester more than once as a child, and its imposing cathedral and castle both loomed large in her memory. The whole town was blanketed with new snow and glowed with an otherworldly white light, as if the town itself were welcoming Elizabeth into her new godly role. She pulled the wool shawl, a reluctant gift from Mistress Cobb, tighter around her shoulders, not sure if the prickles of cold she felt were from the icy air or something inside of her rising to the surface. Bocking turned away from the path leading toward the stone towers of Rochester Cathedral and instead directed her toward one of the grandest houses in the city.

"Are we not to meet the bishop at the cathedral?"

"No. We are to go to the Episcopal Palace to see the bishop." Bocking stopped and turned to her. He believed that Elizabeth was special, important, and he was anxious for Fisher to think so, too. "Listen, Elizabeth. You shall kneel at his feet and kiss his ring. You must answer every question. Keep your eyes on the ground. Call him 'Your Grace.' He is the most important man you have ever met."

"Because he is a bishop." It was a statement, but Bocking took it as a question.

"Yes, and he was once tutor to the king and was a great friend to his father, King Henry VII, and to his grandmother, the blessed Lady Margaret Beaufort. He is an important defender of the faith."

"What do you mean by this?" She could tell he liked when she asked him questions, acknowledging his authority. She had been so used to taking orders from her father, then her uncle, then the Cobbs, that she got so much pleasure from having someone speak to her with goodly words, with learning.

"I mean that there are people among us who do not believe England should be loyal to the pope. They want to follow that excommunicated heretic, Martin Luther, as many across the sea have done. Praise God that men like Fisher and our great King Henry are loyal to Rome. That is what I mean by 'defender of the faith.' God speaks through him." He paused. "I believe he speaks through you, too, Elizabeth. You may also be his mouthpiece in this battle."

"These Luther men, they are not Christians?" asked Elizabeth, shocked at the thought.

"Not as we are, although they believe themselves to be so," answered Bocking gruffly. "Our faith is in the one, true Church. They are blasphemers."

The Cobb farmhouse always seemed gigantic to Elizabeth, but the three-storied Episcopal Palace was much, much bigger. When they arrived at the door, a quiet priest led them past a big hall into a smaller room where Fisher was sitting at a table, papers and books before him.

Elizabeth did not raise her eyes off the floor to meet Fisher's and instead concentrated on the fire behind him, which offered a warm contrast to the icy wind outside; heavy tapestries hung on all the walls to insulate the room. Although Elizabeth had seemed calm as they walked into the palace, once they were close to Fisher's chamber, she felt as if her heart would fly outside of her breast. He was seated at a table and silently slipped his glasses to the end of his long nose with one hand, glancing up, and with the other hand first beckoning in Bocking and then waving away the priest who had led them there.

Bocking knelt next to the desk, pulling Elizabeth down with him, and kissed the ring as Fisher turned over the same hand that had beckoned them. Fisher moved his hand over in front of Elizabeth's face, his bright ring—which she could see was emblazoned with a scaly fish—glinting under her chin. She kissed it quickly and then scurried behind Bocking as he stood and moved them back behind the table so that it separated them from the great man.

Elizabeth noticed that there were books everywhere, not simply piled on the table but also in stacks around it. She did not know there could be so many books. The Cobbs did not have any, although she thought that maybe Cobb could read as he sometimes had some papers in the house.

She brought her eyes up to the bishop. The black of the bishop's hat and robe accentuated his sharp, hawklike features. Around his neck hung a gold chain and a crucifix, with Jesus twisted in pain. She could see that the stitching at his collar was especially fine and wondered what women had been tasked with embroidering it. He was looking at her in a way she recognized. It was how she looked at a chicken before she slaughtered it for the Cobb dinner: *Is this one ready to go?* Her breath caught in her throat. With the fire behind Fisher, he looked sinister. Elizabeth's mind flitted back to her vision of purgatory, flames all around. She quickly moved her eyes back to the floor.

He peered at the small, skinny girl sternly. Her greasy dark hair slipped out of her white cap and nearly covered her face as she bent her head forward, willing herself to disappear.

"Elizabeth?" he said.

"Yes, my lord bishop," she barely breathed—and then, remembering, added, "Your Grace." She could feel that her face was as hot and sweaty as when she was overcome by the fever that had nearly killed her. She watched the flames flicker and reflect on the floor tiles, the books, the tapestries.

Fisher looked down his nose at her. He seemed to be growing even taller, elongated, as he spoke. He was pale, gaunt, and she felt his dark eyes bore into her. "I understand you had a vision in a fever."

She nodded.

"I want you to tell me exactly what you have described to Father Bocking. This could be a great gift. This could also be a visit from the Devil." He drew out the last word, "Deeee-viiiil," his voice laden with malice. "However," he intoned, extending a bony finger toward her, "you would do well to remember that lying is a grave mortal sin. Lying to me, who speaks with the voice of Jesus himself here on earth, is even graver." With this, he reached under the table and pulled out an object. "Look on this."

Elizabeth tentatively raised her eyes again and was horrified to see that the item in his hand was a weathered human skull. Fisher placed it on the table in front of her. "This is a powerful memento mori. I would like you to speak in front of it when you describe your vision." He stood and walked around the table until he was standing next to her. He pushed the skull toward her face. "Look on it as you speak."

Elizabeth summoned all her courage to gaze upon the fearful thing. Animal skulls did not bother her, but human skulls, with their permanent grin, made gooseflesh pucker along her arms.

"Your Grace, I know those are a man's bones. But I do not know what is this thing you say it is." The bishop leaned close to her mouth to hear her near whisper and she could smell him: wool and blood. Like sheep being washed to shear. Like sheep being slaughtered. He turned to consider her face carefully before he responded.

"A memento mori," he explained. "A reminder of death. Of what is waiting for you. You do not know when or where it will happen, neither the hour nor the day, but you can be assured that it will transpire. Will you be ready? Will you have reconciled yourself to God? A lie will send you to hellfire. Even uncertainty will lead you to purgatory, where you will burn just as surely as in hell until you have served your penance for your worldly sins. Only the truly clean and honest will have a seat in front of our Lord Jesus Christ. Before you speak, consider this. And then speak from surety."

His frown seemed to deepen, and his eyes darken, looking so much like the skull in front of her. There was no humor in his face. No love. Only a scolding voice full of accusation.

Bocking, his roundness in body and face a stark contrast to the bishop's skeletal boniness, took her hand. She sensed that he was as cowed by Fisher as she was. She knew he wanted her to speak. To say the right things. Bocking said, "Your Grace, I have examined her. She is so unlettered; how could she have known those contours of purgatory?" He knew that God had chosen Elizabeth to speak and, more important, God had chosen *him*—Edward Bocking—to be her guide. He would be the St. Raymond to her St. Catherine of Siena, whose visions had influenced the pope himself. He had already undertaken the role as her spiritual teacher.

He turned toward Elizabeth and, in a voice slightly above a whisper, said, "Answer the bishop, child."

She closed her eyes to erase the skull's empty stare and spoke. "I am clean. What I told Father Bocking is true. I saw the fires of purgatory. I heard a voice telling me I was special." She paused, searching for words.

"The voice was the Son of God! Our Lord Jesus Christ," cried Bocking. Fisher glared him into silence, but Bocking's interruption had reminded her of what she needed to say.

Her voice became louder and surer. "Yes, Jesus spoke to me. I heard his voice in my mind. I beheld the vision in my mind's eye. He told me that he would bless me like he did the holy women St. Catherine and St. Bridget, great visionaries both. He said the Cobb boy, Julian, would die—and he did! I am chosen among all his children." She then started to say things she did not quite remember, but that she had heard Bocking tell others—she so wanted him to approve of her words. "Jesus told me heretics would burn, not in purgatory but in hell. He said there are many enemies in England and that we should find them and make sure they do not spread their poison."

Fisher shifted, walked back to his seat at the desk, and moved the skull closer to the edge of it so that the firelight made the shadows of the empty eyes move as if they were looking into Elizabeth's own imperiled soul. He leaned forward, considering. "Our Lord spoke of heretics? Here? Luther's men?"

Elizabeth knew that the voice, Jesus, had said nothing about Luther or heretics, but she sensed that this was what Bocking wanted her to say. Her vision made it clear that there were bad people and good people. She now knew the bad ones were "heretics," and Fisher was telling her they were with Luther. She nodded.

The bishop seemed content. She knew she had said the right thing. He leaned back and swept the skull into its bag, removing it from Elizabeth's sight. She sighed in relief, noticing for the first time that her legs had been shaking.

"Bocking," he said, "I believe she is true. Let's encourage some more visions. Perhaps we do have a new St. Bridget here. Take her to a convent near you, so that you may continue to tutor her."

Bocking folded his hands in pleasure across his ample belly, his arms lost in the folds of his black habit. "St. Sepulchre's is very close to my monastery."

The bishop nodded in approval. He pulled a piece of parchment from a small stack and picked up his quill, scratching something out onto it, folding it closed. Elizabeth watched curiously as he picked up a squat red stick and held a candle to its end. It dripped drops of vermilion blood onto the paper. He removed his ring and sealed the note by pushing it into the red pool of wax, his fish on a line seemingly shimmering there as it hardened.

Fisher handed the letter to Bocking. "For the prioress," he said, standing up and then leaving the room without looking at Elizabeth or Bocking again. Elizabeth felt the beats beneath her ribs slow, her heat cooling. She looked only at her feet until Fisher's footsteps disappeared and she could raise her eyes again to her smiling confessor.

"Elizabeth," Bocking said, gently raising the letter to her eyes, "you shall now leave the farm. You will be a nun."

* * *

On her final night at the Cobbs', Elizabeth could barely sleep for excitement, anticipating the promise of a new and holy life. Poor Edith spent the same night crying. She did not understand what had happened to take her friend so far away from her. And, in truth, she was jealous of the attention and the fresh start that Elizabeth would have. Cobb and his wife, for their part, were glad to see her go. Ever since Julian had died, they thought Elizabeth responsible and would have turned out the strange girl long ago had she not the consideration and care of the priests. Finally, they could be rid of her for good.

"Do you know the story of the virgins and the oil, child?" Father Bocking asked as they walked the long miles to St. Sepulchre's Priory. He took her silence as a reason to continue. "A parable from the Gospel," he said, his voice rising as if he were preaching to more than an audience of one. "There were ten virgins awaiting their bridegroom. Five were wise and five were foolish." He splayed out his ten fingers in illustration. Elizabeth noticed for the first time how clean his nails were, how soft his hands.

"The wise ones had oil in their lamps, ready for whenever the bridegroom arrived. The foolish ones did not. When the bridegroom came, the foolish ones cried and asked the wise ones to share their oil. They refused, and instead went to meet their bridegroom. The foolish ones were left behind, crying to be brought along, but the bridegroom said, 'I know you not. Watch ye therefore, because you know not the day nor the hour.'"

Elizabeth's face betrayed her confusion at his words.

"The foolish maidens are like souls who are not ready to die," he explained. "They have not confessed. They are in a state of sin. They will go to hell. The wise ones are the holy ones. They are ever ready for their deaths. When the bridegroom comes, they are lifted up to heaven."

She did not understand his meaning but knew that what he was telling her was important. "There is only one bridegroom?" she asked in barely a whisper.

"Yes, God is the only bridegroom. And you shall soon be betrothed to him at the priory. No earthly bridegroom can compare."

She briefly thought of the farmhand Christopher and his smile, and the times—before he died—that she and Edith would imagine their lives as his betrothed. When they brought clothes to launder out by the river, they would make crowns from daisies and pretend to dance at their weddings. Was this bridegroom a better one than in her fantasy? At least she would not die in childbirth, as her mother had.

The priory's imposing position on the top of a hill meant that she could see it for quite a long time before they arrived at the doors. Even though there was still a winter chill in the air, the day was sunny, and Elizabeth was warm with their brisk pace. They carried no bags. Elizabeth had few items of her own, and Bocking told her that at the convent she would be allowed none. He said, "All will be provided," a thought that thrilled her.

Right before they ascended the final small hill to the priory gates, they walked past a house that was not quite as grand as the Episcopal Palace where they had met with the bishop but still reflected the substantial wealth of its inhabitants.

"Is that a castle?" Elizabeth asked.

"A manor house," Bocking answered. Elizabeth had more questions, but she could see that Bocking was no longer in the mood to talk. He was walking quickly toward the priory and soon they reached its gate.

A nun who must have seen their approach came out to the entrance and nodded silently to Father Bocking while gesturing that they follow her. She was dressed in a habit that was entirely black except for the white linen wimple framing her face under her veil. Elizabeth could never manage to keep her hair from escaping the white cap she wore, and she wondered what color hair the nun had.

The air inside the convent seemed as cold as it was outside and, now that they had stopped walking, Elizabeth began to shiver. She suddenly longed for the company of Edith, curled up on their pallets next to each other after a long day's work. The nun left them at the door to the prioress's receiving room and then sat on a bench outside.

Bocking pushed Elizabeth gently ahead of him and told her to kneel at the feet of the prioress of St. Sepulchre's. She was sitting at a small table, not an imposing one like the bishop's, but it conveyed authority just the same.

Philippa Jonys, prioress of St. Sepulchre's, took in the drawn girl before her, unwashed and too thin, as so many of the farm servants in those parts often were. Not enough sleep. Not enough food. Certainly, not enough prayer. At least she was dressed warmly, the prioress thought. More local children than usual had died with the winter fever that seemed to travel with the frigid wind from village to village.

The prioress walked over, gently touching the girl's shoulder, motioning for her to rise. Elizabeth stood slowly. The top of Elizabeth's head came only to the prioress's chin. "Please pray here in this other chamber, while the good father and I discuss your admittance."

Elizabeth nodded, unsure whether to stand or possibly crawl on her knees. The hushed coldness of the convent was frightening, and the curious stares of the sisters as they moved around in silence felt like heat on her cheeks. At some unseen signal from the prioress, one of those sisters appeared, took Elizabeth's elbow, and navigated her through the entry to the next room, where a small altar beckoned.

"Father." Philippa gestured toward a seat for the monk. The room was suitably austere, barely hinting at the books and art that gave the priory its modest wealth. She had long ago decided this one public-facing space, the meeting area attached to her lodgings, should emphasize poverty and piety, so other than a small statue of the Virgin carved out of rosewood—a gift from a patron—the room merely had places to sit and to pray. The ceilings were magnificent, though, as they were throughout the priory: vaulted, reaching up to heaven.

"Father," she said again, before he was even fully seated, "I know you believe this matter settled, but we do not want a seer among our sisters. Visionaries are ungovernable. They bring attention. We are a small priory and are very much in balance here." She held her hands out evenly, palms up. "And to have a girl so poor and unlettered? She will find no place. There must be a more suitable convent." She pursed her lips into a small frown.

"Mother P-Prioress," Bocking stuttered. He could not help it. She terrified him even more than the bishop. These nuns always did, with their tight white wimples and black veils tucked around their heads, leaving only peering eyes and stern, disapproving mouths. And Philippa was especially terrifying. She was so tall for a woman, taller than he was, and her low voice resonated with each word she spoke. She turned her gray eyes angrily toward him, remaining tight-lipped as he cowered. He pulled Fisher's letter out of the folds of his habit and handed it to her, speaking while she opened it and read the words written there. "I do not believe you have a choice in the matter," he ventured, clasping his hands in what he hoped was supplication. "I have, as you know, been instructed to bring her here by Bishop Fisher himself. I have examined her with a commission and the bishop agrees. She is true. And her visions! They are most holy. She urges us all to attend to our sacred mother, Mary. She tells us to go to Canterbury or Walsingham and to make our penance in pilgrimage. She has seen the fires of purgatory and knows who is there and who will go."

Philippa drew in a breath as if to speak, laying the letter aside. She wanted to warn about the dangers of false visions. Twice she had seen it happen—a young novice reads about one of Bridget's revelations, then has a dream and believes she is blessed. Or worse, the Devil himself tries to convince her that she is hearing God's voice instead of the demon's. But those visions fall apart under scrutiny.

"And yes," Bocking continued, with more strength in his voice. "She is unlettered, you are right. But I am undertaking her spiritual instruction. I have brought with me here"—he gestured to the satchel at his feet—"many holy books that I have read to her since she has been entrusted to my care, examining her truthfulness and holiness all the while. I have the holy hermit Richard Rolle's words here, and those of Walter Hilton, and Sts. Bridget and Catherine, and of course St. Benedict himself as befits this holy place. These books will be gifts to you and your sisters."

Philippa shifted forward, the satchel next to the fat priest suddenly more interesting. That many books, all by important spiritual writers, were a treasure indeed. St. Sepulchre's was not one of the wealthiest or most educated of the convents—not Dartford or Barking or Syon, whose libraries, it was said, rivaled those of many monasteries. Most of the lettered sisters had exhausted their small closet of books and so few of the novices came in with their own these days.

"She needs a woman's house, Mother," he said quietly, seeing that the prioress was softened by the sight of the books. "A respite. We have tested her. She is true. I believe her words are important for others to hear." He then leaned forward, lowering his voice to a near whisper.

"The danger of heresy is very strong right now. The Devil is at work throughout England. God has spoken through Elizabeth."

Philippa shifted uncomfortably. She had heard that some close to the king had turned toward Luther but felt that Henry would keep England true to Rome. If the maid would aid in that holy war, she supposed it was her duty to help her do so.

"And will she be enclosed? As is proper for a Benedictine nun? As we all are here?" She knew the answer to this question. But she wanted to hear him say it aloud, so she could tell the sisters that she had no choice in this matter.

"Not entirely, no. We—that is, the bishop and I—believe that the country should hear her holy words. She will be allowed to travel, under our care, to speak about what she has seen." Still not looking at the prioress, Bocking delivered what he hoped was the most convincing of his arguments. "She may make St. Sepulchre's a site of pilgrimage," he said. "People will come to hear her, to see her. They will make generous gifts to the priory. Gifts better than books." He was not so certain about that last part, though he had seen it happen before. A monastery would get a relic and soon enough the pilgrims would trickle in bearing donations in gratitude. Would not it be more so for an actual person? A possible saint?

The prioress raised an eyebrow at his prediction. "Very well," she consented, reaching for the books. Although she knew she had little choice. She had long defied the oversight of the local priests who tried to meddle in their affairs, but it was harder to oppose the bishop's power. She prayed the girl was obedient.

She also hoped the girl's prophecies were true—and that the Devil was not at work here.

* * *

WHILE BOCKING WAS in with the prioress, Elizabeth prayed. She prayed that she would be allowed to stay at the priory. She prayed that Jesus would speak to her again. She prayed that she would make a friend. Bocking came to retrieve her from her prayers after his meeting was finished.

"Come, Elizabeth," he said, beckoning her up from her knees. "I will walk you through the cloister to the church where we can speak our farewells."

"I thought this was the cloister?" Elizabeth said, looking at the space around them.

"Ah, yes, I see your confusion. Indeed, the priory is called a cloister, but the cloister is also a holy space inside the priory." He led her through a door leading to an interior courtyard. Elizabeth took in the tranquil walkway whose stone arches turned toward the middle, a small, square garden inside. The garden was still bare from winter but Elizabeth could see some greenery starting to peek through.

"The cloister is the center of the priory," Bocking explained, taking her into the middle of the space. "From here, facing north, you have the church." He pointed, then turned her by softly pulling her arm. "The chapter house is east, where you and the sisters will come together to discuss items of importance to the convent." He turned her again. "The refectory, south, and"—they turned one more time—"the dormitories are west. The walkway is covered so you can get to all of these places without trouble even when it rains or snows, but this is also a place where you can walk in the square and pray."

As he was speaking, two sisters left the church and headed toward the refectory. Their heads were bent together and there were some smiles as their downcast eyes flashed up and noticed a monk. They quickened their step. Elizabeth felt a pang of longing for Edith. There was a peacefulness at St. Sepulchre's, she decided. A peace that she could do with.

Bocking turned her again toward the church and, taking both of her hands in his, said, "We will pray together, sister. Then I will leave you here." Seeing her eyes widen with apprehension, he assured her, "I will be back soon for more tutoring and to write down anything you see in a vision. Mother Philippa knows how to send me a message if I am needed."

Much smaller than the cathedral, the church reminded her of the village parish near the Cobb farm that the family members and their servants attended. One door led to a path that continued outside the priory walls; Elizabeth supposed the members of the village used this door to enter for mass. The door she had come through led to the cloister, and it was reserved for the nuns. She felt proud and special, walking through that door with Bocking. She was not a servant anymore.

But when they turned into the nave of the church, Elizabeth stiffened and swooned; she almost felt as if another vision was coming on. Before her was a monstrosity, its obscene mouth stretched across the entire wall, sharp, pointed teeth bared, fire licking between them. The reds and oranges of the flames and the green of the creature's menacing eyes swam together, making her woozy. The monster had in its maw kings and bishops, bakers and butchers, monks and nuns, marked only by their hats and items of their trade, for otherwise—if their bodies were still whole—they were naked. They were being chewed up, prodded by devils, spending eternity burned and panicked. She knew immediately that she was looking at hell. At least the souls in purgatory had some chance of eventually reaching paradise. Hell was hopeless.

"Elizabeth," said Bocking with concern. He helped her to kneel. "Are you quite all right?" He nodded toward the bestial image on the wall. "I know. The mouth of hell. It can be startling the first time you see it. It has been here as long as the priory. It is meant to be frightening, but it is also an important memento mori." It was the second time she had ever heard the phrase, and every time it was uttered, she was faced with something dreadful.

Bocking pointed to the people among the devils, the ones impaled on teeth and screaming as the fires licked the clothing off their bodies. "It does not matter if you are a king or a pauper, a prophet or a farm girl," he said, looking at her closely. "What awaits you is the same in death. Only you have the choice whether God will send you to heaven, purgatory, or hell. You must always act as if Doomsday, the day of judgment, is upon you. You must have your oil lamp ever full."

Elizabeth swallowed and looked away, training her eyes on the images of saints painted on the giant wood screen that divided the nave from the altar, hiding the latter's mysteries from the congregation. She recognized St. Catherine of Alexandria there, the wheel of her torture behind her, a book in her hand. "Can women read?" she asked Bocking, shaking the image of the hellmouth from her mind with the question.

"Some," he said. "You will find that many of the nuns here can do so." He noticed where her eyes rested. "God gave St. Catherine the gift of much knowledge," he said. "He spoke through her, and she bested the greatest pagan scholars." He put his hand on her head as if to pronounce a blessing. "Elizabeth, God is speaking through you, too. You are chosen." Elizabeth closed her eyes. God had chosen her.

New York, February 2023

From: RShefield@oxford.edu
To: ASage@nyu.edu
Subject: Codex Consortium Invitation

Dear Alison (if I may):

I am sorry we did not get a chance to connect more at the Manuscript Society conference last month. I was very impressed with your keynote. Forgive the rather late notice, but I am writing to invite you to the eighth meeting of the Codex Consortium, to take place this June at Vale House Manor outside of Canterbury. Each participant of the Consortium gives a 45-minute talk. An abstract should be circulated one month in advance. As this week-long consortium is limited to seven people, please let me know as soon as possible whether you will be participating.

Sincerely,
Roger Shefield, Professor Emeritus, Oxford University

I read and reread the email, sipping my coffee. The Codex Consortium! Even more than the keynote lecture at ManSock, this seems to me a sign that I have "made it." I own every one of the seven volumes that the Consortium has published after their seemingly secretive and irregularly scheduled meetings. It is unlike any other conference—invitation only, intensive, and taking place in a manor in the English countryside.

There are some usual suspects whom I know attend regularly—Roger, of course, the organizer and a past president of ManSock; Marla Shultz, whose books have won every award; and likely Charles Madingley, my onetime mentor, whom I suspect is behind this invitation.

I have never been invited before, and I already feel nervous energy in my stomach just from reading the email.

Jenny, holy shit! I got invited to the C.C. Should I go? I don't think I have enough tweed.

An immediate reply pings back.

Amazing! You're a big shot now. You must go. You don't need tweed in summer. Just wellies.

I'm not sure I can secure the funding so late—they've been so stingy lately! But I'll try.

From: ASage@nyu.edu
To: RShefield@oxford.edu
Subject: RE: Codex Consortium Invitation

Dear Roger (if I may),

Thank you so much for inviting me. I will first need to see if I can secure travel funding from my department, but I would very much like to participate if I can. Can I let you know in a month? It usually takes that long to get through all the steps at work.

Best,
Alison

I send the email and continue to respond to panicked students and angry deans and all the other items that have piled up overnight. It's only a few minutes before I receive another email from Roger.

From: RShefield@oxford.edu
To: ASage@nyu.edu
Subject: RE: RE: Codex Consortium Invitation

Dear Alison,

I should have made it clear that we will pay for your travel and that room and board are provided. We may even be able to manage a small stipend if that helps convince you. I can't stress enough how much your presence would be appreciated. In addition, you may be interested to know that the manor is adjacent to the ruins of St. Sepulchre's Priory, where Elizabeth Barton was housed. I believe you will find much there of interest.

Sincerely,
Roger

I admit, I am very flattered at the invitation and also at Roger's insistence that I join. I've dreamed of being invited to the C.C.—and to have it paid for, too!

* * *

MY MIND STARTS to race as I allow myself to envision accepting this invitation. I start to feel a vague panic about all that this entails: a new paper on Barton, and a juggling act of epic proportions regarding the twins with Pete, whom I suspect will be an asshole, since lately he's just an asshole about everything that inconveniences him in the slightest.

And my reward for this? A week trapped in a remote manor house with God-knows-whom. Although I am intrigued to be so near to where Elizabeth lived. What secrets did she leave there?

It's too good an opportunity to pass up. Jenny's right. I have to go. Before I can overthink it, I hit "send."

From: ASage@nyu.edu
To: RShefield@oxford.edu
Subject: RE: RE: RE: Codex Consortium Invitation

Dear Roger,

Well, it's hard to say no to that! I am honored to accept.

Sincerely,
Alison

St. Sepulchre's Priory, May 1527

Sitting at Philippa's table, as had become his custom, Bocking held the quill and was writing something down, even though Elizabeth was not speaking. She trailed her fingers back and forth across the worn wood, scratching her nail when it hit a splinter, thinking about the nun tasked with cleaning the prioress's quarters. She liked these sessions with the monk, and not only because they excused her from the normal work required of the other novices. The prioress had tried assigning her priory chores, but when she told Bocking that they exhausted her too much to speak to God, he made sure she was exempt.

The prioress had set aside her meeting room for the spiritual instruction of the Holy Maid of Kent—as she was now known outside of the priory; it was out of the view of the other sisters who did not like to see a man, even a monk, inside their walls. The meetings had a familiar rhythm: first, Bocking would read to her from a book of spiritual instruction—her favorite so far was St. Mechthild's book, where she wrote that the humblest among them can sing God's praise; she hoped he would read from that again. She did not like the story of the holy St. Catherine of Siena, who sucked the pus from lepers' wounds as an act of penance. She was quick to retain the stories and lessons that Bocking told her, and she repeated them confidently to the pilgrims who had started to come see her.

"What do you write?" Elizabeth asked, watching as the words appeared before him, bored with the silence.

"I write of your revelations," he answered, pausing for a moment, taking in the girl. He was pleased to see that she had grown sleek with sleep and nourishment. She looked more holy in his eyes than the feeble thing he had brought only two months prior. "I am describing how you look when you speak, what words of the Gospel or the psalms you echo.

The great visionaries have books, and you shall have a book as well. Like St. Catherine's book. Like St. Bridget's. Their confessors heard them and wrote down their words. They explained what was meant by them. And now those holy men sit at the right hand of God for their good works." The quill continued to move across the page and, for the first time, Elizabeth really wished she could read.

"And the sainted women? Where do they sit?" she asked.

"They are surely in heaven. God used them as mighty instruments in his plan. They were blessed to be his mouthpiece," he muttered as he dipped the pen into the pot. He held it up. "God was the quill and they were the ink, as it is with you, child." Elizabeth thought she would rather be the one writing.

After the readings, Elizabeth would relay her most recent vision to the monk, and he would write it down, asking questions or clarifying what she had seen. In truth, she had not again had the same kind of vision that she had during her fever. She somehow understood, though, that her position here—one of learning, respite, pilgrims, meat and ale—depended on her always having something new to tell Bocking when he came to see her. Her new life at the priory, and the bishop's protection, felt too precious to lose.

"Father Bocking, can you read me what is written there?" She pointed to the page he had just completed.

He waved his hand across the page several times to make sure the ink was dry before he picked it up to read. "'This Holy Maid lies still as if dead and upon awakening will say that she has been "home," even though her body has not moved its place,'" he read. "'And she will ask how long the chapel bells have been ringing even though there is no sound from the chapel. And then she falls before a statue of Our Virgin as if she is diseased and in great pain and says the Lady bids us to confess our sins. These miracles have occurred at St. Sepulchre's Priory and have been witnessed by me.'"

Elizabeth felt her back straighten and a rush of pleasure hum through her body as she heard the words that made her sound like one of the famous saints. Even the sunlight coming in through the open window seemed a bit brighter, as if God himself was blessed by her presence.

"Can you teach me to read?" she asked, so quietly that Bocking had to incline his ear toward her mouth to hear the words in their entirety.

"No, no, my child." He dismissed her with a vehement slice of his hand. "You—as with most—need a priest to interpret the words of God. That is why I read to you and explain what the meaning is there. This is one of Luther's heresies, you know, that people should be able to read holy words without God's earthly representative to guide them." He gathered his papers into the satchel he had brought with him. "Well, that's enough for today. You will be needed for the prayer hour of nones very soon."

The thought of standing in the church singing with the other nuns made Elizabeth feel queasy. Even now they looked on her with suspicion, and some with outright anger and jealousy. She had found no friendship inside these walls. She grasped at ways to make Bocking stay, to extend these precious hours of companionship. "Should I have a vision now?" she asked hurriedly. "While you can witness it?"

He looked at her curiously. "Can you call it upon you at will?"

Elizabeth looked down and very slightly nodded yes. As she did when she recounted a vision to the monk, she closed her eyes and remembered that febrile state and that voice, and then spoke the things that she was sure the voice had wanted her to say.

Bocking seemed most interested when she spoke of illness and hell, of whom she saw there and who God told her would go there if they were not confessed and shriven of their sins. Now she tried to see hell in her mind's eye, and to describe what she saw when she did as if she were in a visionary state.

She closed her eyes, willing herself into the trancelike state that allowed her to hear the voice, however faintly. She searched her mind for prayers and words that had been read to her in the priory. She imagined she saw the hellmouth. She stiffened and fell to the ground.

"Behold the demons!" she shouted to Bocking. "They are before you. Do you not see them?" Bocking wrote frantically as she spoke. She screamed in terror. And then she sighed in relief.

"Our Lord Jesus is here, seated next to the Godhead!" Then she turned to what she knew he wanted to hear. "He speaks in one voice and says, 'Beware the sickness in this land.'"

Bocking wrote faster. "What sickness? Luther?"

Elizabeth's eyes shifted. She focused on Bocking, noticed his interest, his eager encouragement. "Yes," she answered, satisfied to see him nod in agreement. "And his followers among us. There are many. We are in grave danger."

Bocking smiled as he continued to transcribe. *Indeed,* he thought, *this holy maid has been sent to save us.*

Part Two

GHOST STORIES

Vale House Manor, June 2023, Day 1

On the train from London to Canterbury, I review my notes one last time. Reading them over repeatedly is the only thing keeping my nerves at bay. I am starting to regret the third espresso I had at the station in an attempt to wake up after a very restless night's sleep on a flight where I tried my best to origami myself into a somewhat comfortable position. The ride is a little over an hour, just enough for one last look.

I need to have some talking points on hand for the relentless social interactions I know are about to happen, so reminding myself of the details of each Codex Consortium participant will help. Pete is an extrovert—he loves parties, the hobnobbing with parents on the soccer field, and skips off to conferences with a joy I never understood. I prefer a close group, with smaller, quieter interactions—one-on-one dinners with colleagues, my morning runs.

A grad-school professor once told me that writing a dissertation would feel "monastic," which he meant as a warning about loneliness. But I thrilled at his words. *That's perfect,* I remember thinking. Is it any wonder that I ended up studying nuns?

I'm told that the C.C. projects inform one another, and that the papers intertwine after a week of discussion. Time is set aside during the week for research and rewriting, readying the essays for the newest C.C. volume. My paper, written frantically in between classes and on the weekends when Pete had the twins, explores Elizabeth Barton's visions more closely. I speculate how much was actually Elizabeth and what was influenced (or manipulated) by the powerful men around her who were happy to have a new weapon in their arsenal for what they saw as a holy war against the Protestants.

"This is Selling." The automated voice comes over the speaker as the train pulls into the station. "This is the Southeastern Service to Dover Priory. Next stop, Canterbury East. Canterbury East station is the next stop." I look at my watch. I have about ten more minutes—one last chance to go over my notes, gleaned from faculty bios on their schools' websites and colleagues' gossip:

- Roger Shefield: Retired from Oxford. American but lives in the UK. Last book w/Oxford: *Chaucer: His Enduring Legacy.* Wife Janine. Loves wine. Horse racing. Paper: local patronage of poetry.
- Charles Madingley: English. York. New book next year? On animal marginalia? Husband Dicky. Gardening. No kids. Two greyhounds. Former president of ManSock. Paper: illuminated manuscripts owned by monasteries.
- Marla Shultz: Austrian. Birkbeck. Supersmart. Won the M.S. Award for her last book, *What They Left Behind*, on wills and estates. No partner. No kids. No pets. Paper: wills of the local gentry.
- Calista Craig: Scottish. Saint Andrews. New book on women scribes. Four (!!) kids. One of Roger's former students. Runner. Paper: letters between a pair of Stuart-era sisters.
- Arjun Devi: Anglo-Indian. Cambridge. World's expert on medieval lyric poetry. New book on same almost done. Ex-wife. Adult children. Shouldn't he be retired? Paper: lyrics. Always lyrics.
- Brian Jackson: American. Book: *Sports of Kings: Hunting, Hawking, and Whoring.* Princeton. Married to a former student (barf). Paper: falconry (yawn).

It looks like the usual group of scholars that Roger tends to assemble, but Calista and I are new, making it a record number of women this year.

Charles was an early mentor, although I haven't seen him much since graduate school. Brian and I are both involved with New York–area scholars and events. He gets handsy when he has too much to drink. Arjun and I were on a panel once and he seemed nice enough. Marla intimidates me because everything she does is brilliant. Finally, I am excited to catch up with Calista, whom I have always really liked and with whom I seem to have much in common. She's also the only one there who will be my generation; everyone else is at least fifteen to twenty years older.

The world of manuscript studies is small, maybe a thousand scholars spread across North America and Europe, and the areas get even smaller as you telescope in: England (maybe a hundred people), the Reformation (maybe thirty), women (maybe ten), Barton (me?). The process of becoming an academic was exhilarating, as I watched that circle narrow around me until I was at its center, the expert. But sometimes it feels more like a noose, leaving little room to explore something new. So here I will be with people who intersect at various spots, people I know or should know, and the pressure to perform is intense.

* * *

By the time I get in the taxi to the manor house, I am fighting utter exhaustion. The taxi driver tries desperately to make conversation with me, but I am both too tired and too nervous to engage much. "The Vale manor, huh? That's an interesting old place. Odd owners, though. Business or pleasure?"

"A bit of both," I say. "I'm a scholar of Tudor England and am here for a small conference."

"Will there be a fair?" he asks, hopefully. For some reason when I tell people I study the medieval period or the Renaissance, they expect me to come out in full dress, eating a turkey leg. Medieval Times is the public's view of my work. I'm pretty sure that Victorianists don't have this same problem.

"No fair," I say, smiling indulgently. "Just scholarship."

"Ah, too bad," he says. "Well, here we are."

The manor looms before me as I walk up the gravel path from the road, where the taxi has left me next to a small blue sign declaring VALE HOUSE MANOR. I have to carry my bag rather than roll it because the gravel is too loose. The house is larger than I pictured—no Downton Abbey but still a rather impressive manor home. My very meager architectural training allows me to at least notice the varying periods represented here—a Tudor core, white with pointed gables and brown beams; a Victorian medievalish round tower with a turret to the left;

a squarer, early-twentieth-century addition to the right. Six different chimneys announcing the promise of many fireplaces inside.

Even with my untrained eye, I notice that the house is in some significant disrepair: bricks are missing, cardboard covers several windows, and the overgrown pathways through the garden contain broken stepping stones. Miss Havisham is not about to greet me at the door, but the manor is more dilapidated than I anticipated. Steps lead from the path up to what was once a grand entrance, I can tell, although it, too, has fallen into decay. There is a fountain, a many-layered Victorian affair covered in vines that have overgrown and spilled out like water must have at some point. And some scaffolding off to the side indicates a restoration work in progress, although even the scaffolding looks like it's about to collapse.

The overall gloom of the place dampens my enthusiasm considerably. This place does not seem as glamorous as it was in my imagination.

I try to smooth down my increasingly unruly hair, which has just been cut into what I thought was a chic bob but now seems to be sticking out at all angles (the drizzly rain doesn't help), before I press the bell beside the large wooden door. I hear nothing when I press it. Broken. I knock, loudly.

After about a minute without anyone coming to let me in, I decide to shuffle between some hedges and knock on the window, which is slightly ajar. It's a bit undignified but less so than standing out in the rain all night waiting for someone to answer the door. I'm prickled by the hedges behind me and enveloped by the smell of honeysuckle and pine while I snake my body in between the greenery and the manor. As I get close to the window, I can hear two men's voices and see their outlines through the light curtains.

"It took some manipulating to make it happen," a low American voice says. "So let's not squander this opportunity."

"I hope you're right. I'll do my best this week," answers a vaguely familiar voice I can't place. British.

A third, slim outline of a body joins, another English accent. "Excuse me, sir. I believe I saw some headlamps and heard a car departing outside, so perhaps our last guest has arrived?"

"I'll go . . . ," the second voice says as he moves away from the window. I hustle back to the entrance, knocking again as if I've been standing there the whole time, feeling as if I've heard something I shouldn't have, though I'm not sure what. My reading glasses fall off the top of my head and I am bending over to pick them up when the door opens.

"Alison," that distantly familiar British voice says above me. Not Roger. Not Charles. I scan slowly upward. Converse sneakers. Jeans. A dark-blue T-shirt. Stubble.

"Westley?" Fuck. "I . . . I didn't know you would be here." How? Why? He wasn't on the email list.

"Alison. It's good to see you. It's been a while." He steps aside so that I can come in and shake off the water, pull in my bag. He doesn't offer to help. I suddenly am keenly aware that I look more drowned-rat than renowned scholar and brush my hand over my hair, removing a few stray leaves as I do so.

"I didn't really know I would be either, but Calista fell rather suddenly ill." He moves the dark hair that has fallen forward out of his very blue eyes. "Covid, I'm afraid. We can't seem to rid ourselves of it. And Roger knew I had something to offer and was nearby, so he asked me to take her place. I trust you aren't unhappy to see me?" With this, he leans forward and gives me a quick kiss hello, just a suggestion of his lips on my cheek. I breathe in his faint scent of whiskey and tobacco while he is close.

"Of course not," I say, pulling away, trying to swallow my disappointment at losing my ally in Calista and my shock at being unexpectedly reunited with Westley. Westley, whom I haven't seen in . . . let's see . . . twenty years.

"I've kept up with your work," he is saying as I try to compose myself. As if I don't know. As if I haven't read every critical review of my books. There had once been a time when he thought my work was good. That our work was good together. That we were good together. God, he was still so handsome, though. That hasn't changed, even if he has.

I say nothing but smile and turn away from him, busying myself with putting down my bags and taking off my raincoat. Trying to hide the combination of surprise and dismay I am sure is plain on my face, I take in the scene. The entry hall feels like a step back in time, with dark wood paneling topped by a rich, burgundy-colored silk wallpaper (peeling in several places, with a few water stains from a long-ago leak), a low coffered ceiling, chandeliers with candelabra light bulbs. There is a bench upholstered in a deep-blue velvet and etched yellowed-glass sconces that look like they once held gas lamps, although now bright electric bulbs are the only things that burn inside. The entry hallway leads straight ahead to stairs (more dark wood, more burgundy) and there are doors on either side, leading to what must be the central living areas of the home: the library and the dining room.

Just as I fully collect myself, Charles comes out of the library, a glass of red wine in hand. As I have come to expect with my former mentor, he is smartly dressed, trim in a pale-pink shirt with his trademark bow tie and tailored gray pants. His white hair and wire glasses scream "distinguished professor." I fight the urge to grab the glass out of his hand and drink it outright.

"Alison! Darling!" he bellows. Charles pulls me into a warm hug. "Our victorious champion returns! Restoring Elizabeth Barton and her naughty visions to our history." He must be close to seventy, but he is fit, and with his sharp clothes, always seems younger.

I hug him back. "Hello, Charles. So honored to be here!"

He whispers into my ear, "I vouched for you with Roger. I know you won't let me down." The compliment feels a bit like a warning, and I don't know how to respond.

Fortunately, I don't need to do or say anything other than give a quick smile because immediately behind Charles is Roger himself, also with a glass in hand. Plump, mostly bald, bearded, and actually wearing a tweed jacket over a crisp white shirt (I'll have to text Jenny later), Roger is clearly the captain of this ship. "Dr. Alison Sage," he says, extending his hand, a stern look on his face. "So very glad you can join our little think tank this week. I hope the travel was not too arduous. The trains are such a mess these days and we are utterly dependent on them. Welcome to Vale House. And I see you have met Westley Charney, a folklorist that we have added to our group." I recognize his voice as the one I heard behind the window, American but clearly inflected by his years in England.

"Oh, Alison and I go way back," says Westley, whose eyes I avoid as he speaks.

"Yes," I mumble, "when I had a postdoc fellowship at Oxford one summer."

"I was her student!" Westley says pointedly, and at this, my eyes meet his briefly.

"*Graduate* student," I emphasize. "He helped me with some research."

In spite of my exhaustion, the shock at seeing Westley, the damp clothes, the foul smell I can detect is definitely exuding from me, I force myself to smile. "I'm so very happy to be included, Roger. Give me twenty minutes to shower and change from these traveling clothes and then please put one of those in my hands." I move my chin in the direction of the glass he is holding, a brown liquor shimmering enticingly inside.

"Yes, yes!" he says. "Alex will show you to your room." A tall and very thin man steps from the shadows as if he is part of the manor's very architecture. A butler? Do they still have butlers? He is dressed entirely in black and I find something about him instantly repulsive: the way he moves, the way he leers at me when he leans down and picks up my bag. He is oddly ageless: I can't tell if he's twenty or fifty. He strides ahead of me up the beautiful staircase, with its dark, carved-wood newel post at the bottom that rises up through the railing, and the same burgundy shade from the entry on the carpeted steps. Although the carpet is threadbare, it still all feels rather grand. I run my hand along the smooth wood of the banister on the way up, thinking of the generations of hands that have done the same.

When we reach the top of the stairs, Alex points to the left with long, skinny fingers. "At the end of this hall is the main bedroom, where Dr. Shefield is staying. Four rooms are in that direction, and there are three on this side."

He turns to the right and beckons me to follow. "Your room is here on the end, Dr. Sage. I believe you have Dr. Charles Madingley and Dr. Westley Charney on either side of you." Alex opens the door at the end of the hallway, revealing a room much larger than mine in Brooklyn. Even with the light on, it still feels dim, with a vaguely musty, sour smell that Alex seems to notice, as he quickly walks over to the window and opens it. Gauzy white curtains flutter with the breeze, and the honeysuckle scent I detected when I arrived does what it can to mask the mustiness. This room, too, has the dark wood low ceiling that seems to run throughout the manor. At least it has its own bathroom.

"No air-conditioning," Alex says. He pauses and looks me in the eye, a disconcertingly intense stare. "Americans always ask. I suggest you keep your windows open at night. You cannot tell now, in the dark, but your room overlooks the property's garden. It is quite beautiful in the sunlight." It is indeed unnervingly (for this city girl) pitch-black outside—no streetlights to illuminate anything, the moon and stars hidden by storm clouds.

Alex moves a step closer to me, too close, and I take a step back. His paleness, even down to his blond hair and eyebrows, makes him appear ghostly, as if he has very rarely seen the sun. He continues to stand there as if waiting for more from me.

"Um, yes. It's a very nice room. Very comfortable. Thank you." I am unsure what he wants me to say, what magic words I need to dismiss him. The room *does* actually look very comfortable, if a bit fussy and badly in need of an update. All of the furniture is painted white—sleigh bed, nightstand, window seat, small desk—which contrasts with the pale-green (and fraying) fabric wallpaper.

"I look forward to exploring tomorrow," I finally say, hand on the bathroom door, hoping Alex will get the hint that I do not need him anymore.

"Yes, you should. There is much hidden here. A house full of secrets. Let me know if you have any questions about the place that I can answer." And with this he gives almost a little bow and backs out of the room. I am somewhat distressed to note, as he closes the door upon departure, that the only way to lock the door is with a push button on the knob.

* * *

SHOWERED, CHANGED, AND with makeup reapplied, I feel more human when I make my way downstairs to the library. Roger puts a drink in my hand as soon as I walk into the room: scotch on the rocks, which is not my drink at all, but I am so grateful for its soothing burn down my throat. "This is the heart of Vale House," he says. "A gem within the gem."

And it is. If there is anything I like more than a well-appointed library, I would be hard-pressed to name it. Although the fireplace is empty, the room has a smokey, woodsy smell. There's the same coffered ceiling as in the entry hallway but with more beautiful and complete chandeliers. I am really too tired to take in all the details but see that the room's walls are lined with bookcases that will definitely require a closer look later. There is a grandfather clock and a bar cart parked on the side with every conceivable liquor, crystal glasses on a shelf above. Chairs and tables are arranged around the room to allow for pockets of conversation. In the center of the library are three couches (worn blue velvet, like the bench in the entryway) in a kind of semicircle, currently occupied by Charles, Westley, Roger, and Marla. As I scan the rest of the room, I am acutely aware of Westley's eyes on me.

One corner of the library holds a game table, a faded chessboard inlaid on top. Brian and Arjun are deep in conversation there, intermittently moving pieces as they talk. There is a lot of gesticulating and laughing, and I assume they are swapping stories of younger, wilder days together.

"Alison!" Brian says, holding a hand out to an open chair near them. "Join us!" He laughs as I sit down and places a hand on my shoulder, shaking it gently. "I told you that you should have taken that earlier flight with me from Newark. I know it's closer to Princeton than to you, but the flights are more reliable. I've been here for five or six hours already. And dinner was delicious. Welsh rarebit! Do you know Arjun?"

Arjun and I signal our mutual acquaintance. "You're right, Brian," I say. "I unfortunately had kid-related duties that I needed to attend to first. I would have much preferred to have eaten here rather than the Cornish pasty I grabbed at the train station. Those things always *sound* like they're going to be delicious, and then . . . not. I am looking forward to the food here. Charles said it's one of the best features of the place. I take it you both have been before?"

They nod in unison. Finally removing his hand, Brian says, "It's not every year—basically at Roger's whim when they are held, and honestly this invitation was strangely late in the game since we usually have a year's notice, but I always try to come when he calls. I missed it once when Princeton needed me to run a summer course. This is my third." I play a game with myself whenever I see Brian: How many times can he work the word "Princeton" into the conversation? *We know where you work, Brian. Very impressive.*

Arjun holds up a palm, four fingers up and his thumb folded in.

"My fourth. You will see that much work gets done. And much play, too! The evenings here are very collegial with the brilliant group that Roger assembles." He laughs again and gestures to himself and Brian. "Sometimes, we even play billiards."

"There's a billiards room!" says Brian. "Isn't that fantastic? I love thinking about the conversations that took place over the centuries in that room. It's the same feeling I get in some of the older spaces at Princeton." That's three. I imagine many generations of cigar-smoking men preening over a pool table, the women elsewhere, so I myself am not too interested in what conversations were had.

Brian stands up to refill his drink, places his hand again on my shoulder, and points at my glass, which I am somewhat surprised to see is already empty. "A refill, Alison?" I start to nod and almost immediately realize how flattened I really am by all the travel.

"Thanks, Brian. I think it's actually time for me to turn in. But I look forward to catching up more with both of you tomorrow." Brian stands as I do and, without warning, kisses me on both cheeks.

"Nice to see you again, Alison. I heard you made a splash at Man-Sock. The Barton book. Quite a feat," says Arjun, reaching out his hand, "I'm looking forward to your paper. Sleep well."

"Likewise," I say, shaking it. "See you both tomorrow."

Lastly, I walk over to the four sitting in the center couches. Their conversation seems to stop abruptly as they note my approach, and they sit in silence until I reach them.

"Thank you again for having me," I say to Roger, squeezing Charles's shoulder as a way to show that I heard him earlier, that I know I am being tested. "I'm headed to sleep so I can be in form tomorrow."

Marla stands, gives me a dazzling smile, and takes both of my hands in hers with a firm grip. "Oh, Alison, I'm sorry we didn't get a chance to talk tonight. I hope we find some time to do so tomorrow. You're working on some very exciting things. And very impressive work, too!" I smile despite myself; any praise from Marla is high praise indeed.

"Thank you. I can't wait to hear your suggestions for it." Even though I was just saying it as a courtesy, I realize I mean it.

Westley looks like he is about to say something, too, but to avoid him, I feign an exaggerated yawn, wave, and quickly turn around to go upstairs. I decide my best plan is to steer clear of Westley as much as possible—the summer we shared is decades behind us, and I'd rather it just stay in the past.

Alex is standing by the door of the library, again in the shadows, as I exit the room. He says in a near whisper, "Sweet dreams, Dr. Sage." Ew.

The Consortium has begun.

St. Sepulchre's Priory, July 1527

Elizabeth sat with Bocking in the prioress's study and marveled at the small book she held in her hands, amazed that her words—her *words*—were written there. She couldn't read them, but she knew they were hers. Even more astonishing than the book itself was the fact that Bocking had a whole case of them. Each the same, copies of her words that he would send across England. She brought the book up to her nose and inhaled the paper and the ink. If Bocking hadn't been watching her, she would have extended her tongue to taste the page. She would have eaten it to make it a part of her.

"Can you read me the first page?" she asked, again wishing that she could unlock the mysteries of the letters before her. Each time she saw a sister carrying a book from the library to her chamber, she wanted to cry out and beg for that nun to teach her to read. But they all kept their eyes on the ground and walked faster when she was in their path.

Bocking placed a finger on each word of the title as he slowly read aloud. "A marvelous work of late, done by a holy maid in Kent, and published for devout people and their spiritual consolation." With the help of a local patron, the good, pious Agnes Vale, he had commanded copies of the work and planned to bring them to many holy readers.

He was very pleased with it, thrilled to think that it was his observation of Elizabeth's visions about devotion, prayer, penance, and pilgrimage that could move those seduced by Luther back to the right side of religion. There were men in the country who were dangerously speaking against the pope, and this Holy Maid's revelations were a warning of that peril and a reminder of true faith. She was warning the king, too. Bocking had heard of some grumblings among many nobles about having any allegiance or money tied up with Rome. He believed the king needed constant reassurance that his loyalties were correct. To that end, he had ensured copies of the book had been placed in the hands of Henry's advisors, including the chancellor Cardinal Wolsey and the king's friend and advisor Sir Thomas More.

The book began with the story of Elizabeth's first vision about the farmer Cobb's dead child, proving her power.

Elizabeth had turned the page, and Bocking pointed out some of the words. "Here, daughter, is your vision of purgatory as you described it to me. Three giant fires, demons fornicating, offending your pure soul." Elizabeth did not know what "fornicating" meant but she trusted that the monk had conveyed the horror of what she had seen that day.

"Are all the pages my words?" she asked hesitantly. It seemed many pages for what she had told him she had seen.

"No," he answered, "some of the words are mine. I wrote what you have seen or said that can be read in scripture. I wrote, too, that although you are a woman, I have witnessed your miracles and can vouch for them. That God often chooses the weakest for his words. See, here I have written, 'As the apostle Peter has said, *quasi infirmiori vasculo muliebri impartientes honorem*'—that is, 'give honor to the female as to the weaker vessel.'" He smiled as he read back his words, imagining how well they would be received by Wolsey, More, and the other important readers for whom they were intended.

Am I weak? Elizabeth wondered. Not now that she was eating meat most days, that people listened when she spoke. She thought of the prioress, who was stronger certainly than Bocking himself. *The power is not just in the reading,* she thought, *but who did the writing.* "What scribe wrote all of these words?" she asked, marveling at the neat script, page after page.

"This book was not written with hands," he said, realizing that Elizabeth could not recognize the difference between a book from a press and one from a scribe. "It was printed. I have had some seven hundred of them made. They are each the same." He picked up another book to show her.

"Look, Elizabeth," he said, taking the book from her and turning to the final page, "it is an image of you receiving a vision from the Holy Spirit." The picture on the last page showed an image of a woman dressed as a Benedictine nun. Her hands were in prayer and her head tipped back, looking toward the heavens where a dove surrounded by fire was drawn. In the style of a saint, she had a jeweled halo around her head—a nimbus.

"Who drew this?" she breathed. It was beautiful. She shone with the light of the Lord.

"Our patron, Lady Vale, requested it especially," Bocking said. "She commissioned the woodcut for this volume. So everyone knows what a jewel you are. Your words are like gemstones." He had once read about a miracle of a saint, in a convent much like St. Sepulchre's. Many of the sisters there had had the same dream, in which perfect white pearls fell out of the mouth of their holy companion when she spoke. Bocking supposed that Agnes Vale knew this story and had asked for the gemstones in the nimbus. Although it had not been his idea, he was pleased with the effect. It made Elizabeth's virtue clear. Her value.

The Holy Maid was a weapon of the faith, and he was its wielder.

* * *

A WEEK AFTER Bocking showed Elizabeth the books, he began traveling with them in hand, taking nearly fifty at a time with a determination to distribute every one. He would walk into a village, make a public sermon in the town center and speak of Elizabeth's holiness, and then sell the book to those who wanted it. Luther had made so much progress with his heresy in just this way, by putting his so-called theses in the hands of easily influenced people who were swayed by his misguided arguments.

It was time for the Church to fight back. When Bocking first heard that King Henry was going to seek an annulment from Catherine of Aragon, he did not think it could be true. Bocking himself was not fully aware of the goings-on at the court, but the bishop, who knew the king well, angrily explained at his last visit that Henry wanted to marry another woman. A lady-in-waiting at the court who did not deserve his attentions, whose upbringing had been in the Low Countries and, even worse, in France—heretics' nests both.

Bocking knew full well how weak the flesh of man was, having many times broken his vows of chastity and repented sorely for it, but he also knew it was the woman who was most at fault. Is it a dog's fault if he falls into a hole that has been hidden? Women dig the holes; men just trip unsuspecting into their snares. This Anne Boleyn had trapped Henry in such a way. She had not only led him astray from the good Spanish queen but was also trying to tempt him away from his faith.

The narrow sea between England and the Continent was not strong enough to block out the heretical ideas fermenting in Germany, Switzerland, and even Flanders under the banner of "Lutheranism," prompted by that apostate Martin Luther. And while the printing press had made it easier for books like Elizabeth's righteous one to find many readers, Bocking knew that each ship bringing goods also brought hidden heresies just as surely as it brought rats and other vermin aboard.

Even at his own monastery he had discovered a monk with a copy of Tyndale's New Testament. The Bible! In English! For anyone without Latin to read. Bocking promptly had the heretical book burned and the monk severely punished.

Bishop Fisher had revealed that, more and more, Henry was surrounding himself at court with heretics, men who believed that Luther was right about many things, that Rome had too strong a chokehold on the kingdom, that English priests and monks were more loyal to the pope than to the king. Bocking could not help but feel that this bid for divorce was going to tip the scales for the royal household. He urgently hoped the Holy Maid could bring things back into balance.

There was much work to be done. And fast.

Vale House Manor, June 2023, Day 2

I groggily open up the email from Roger while still in bed, seconds after my phone rudely tells me it is time to get up. It's 2 A.M. in New York. I've never easily adjusted to a time change.

From: RShefield@oxford.edu
To: ASage@nyu.edu, arjundevi2000@gmail.com, charlesmadingley@york.edu, mshultz@birkbeck.edu, bjackson@princeton.edu, wcharney@canterbury.edu
Subject: Codex Consortium: Welcome & Schedule

Welcome to Vale House! How delightful to email all of you when you are down the hall, but I know you like to have our schedule laid out ahead of the day, so here it is. In the future, we will simply discuss the day's agenda at breakfast.

Some housekeeping before we begin: I have a master key to all of your rooms as does Alex, so grab either of us if you lock yourself out. Alex will lock the manor doors at ten, but if you're going to be out for a late night at the pub (which closes at 11:00), let us know and we can keep it open for you.

Speaking of the pub, the King's Head is just a short jog down the road toward the village (the pub and a few houses actually are the village). Once the sun sets, it is extremely dark, so bring a torch (that's a flashlight to the Americans—no flames involved).

Our schedule:

Monday (today)

8:00 Breakfast in the Dining Room
9:30 Small Group Discussions
11:00 Break
12:00 Lunch in the Dining Room

2:00 Small Group Excursions
3:00 Tea in the Library (optional, but who doesn't want a cuppa?)
4:00 Writing and Research Time
5:00 Libations (other than tea) in the Library
6:30 Dinner in the Dining Room
8:30 After-Dinner Drinks and Discussion in the Library
9:30 Onward Billiards? King's Head? Bedtime?

The mealtimes and drinks will stay much the same all week, although we have some specials for you after dinner on some of the days. You know when you are presenting your work to the group. There is plenty of time for exploration of the grounds, the village, Canterbury and more! Just let me (or Alex) know how we can help you.
Roger

Fortunately, I am already dressed when the knock comes at my door. Overnight, the musty, sour smell I noticed upon arrival hasn't dissipated—in fact, it's become more intense. It smells rotten, like someone left a piece of cheese or an egg somewhere in the room and it has become spoiled. I search the bathroom for the origin of the smell—mold, maybe?—but can't find anything that could be the source.

So, despite my instinctive dislike of him, I am somewhat relieved to see Alex, the manservant/butler (what *exactly* does he do here?), at the door.

"Good morning, Dr. Sage, I trust you slept well. I have been dispatched to tell you that breakfast is served in the library."

"Ah, yes, thank you, Alex. I'll head down shortly, but while you're here . . . There is a strange smell in this room. I can't seem to find where it's coming from. Maybe the last occupant left some food somewhere or something? Surely, you can smell it, too."

Alex folds his frame as he enters my bedroom, bending down a little to get through the low doorway, like Alice after she drinks the potion that makes her too big. He exaggerates a sniff, almost sarcastically, but I can see his features change and his nose wrinkle in disgust. "Ah, yes. A dead mouse, I think. We get them here sometimes."

He walks the perimeter of the room, sniffing as he goes, which looks ridiculous to me although I had been doing essentially the same just moments before. Then he stops in front of the window seat. "I think I can solve your mouse problem and show you the most unusual feature of your room at the same time. I doubt you would find it on your own."

"The window seat?" I reply.

"No. Not that." He presses a panel in the bottom right part of the seat, almost where it joins the floor, and a small door swings inward, revealing what looks like a large hidden cupboard. "Take a look."

"Wow! What treasures did they stow away in here?" I say, kneeling down.

"Priests," answers Alex.

Once I am on the ground, the smell is so overpowering, my follow-up questions stick in my throat. It's all I can do not to gag. It's really dark inside, so I pull out my phone and turn on the flashlight. I feel Alex looming behind me.

My light scans the space: it's bigger than a cabinet, with space enough for a person to sit comfortably inside. The light lands on a sight that truly does make me recoil and retch—an animal much bigger than a mouse, an unrecognizable pile of bones, flesh, and fur, seemingly alive with writhing maggots.

* * *

ALEX USHERS ME quickly out of the room, promising that the animal (a mouse, he says, but by its size it must at least be a rat) would be cleaned up and the room aired out while I am at breakfast. I wasn't that hungry beforehand—jet lag—but now the image of the mass of maggots makes bile rise in my throat every time I think about it. I try not to dwell on the implications of there being rats in the house, especially in my bedroom. I feel like the smell is stuck onto me, following me down the stairs, and I find myself rubbing my arms as I walk as if I can shed it.

Since I'm a new kid here, my place at the C.C. already feels somewhat tenuous, and after Charles's comment yesterday I am even more aware that I am on probation, so as I enter the dining room I tell myself not to make a fuss and send up a silent prayer that Alex will take care of the carcass. As with all the other rooms in the manor, the ceiling here is relatively low, but this one is white with wooden beams; the walls, too, are white, and the windows open onto the garden to let in the breeze. A stone fireplace covers one entire wall, with silver (a plate, a pitcher) dotted along the mantel. The opposite wall holds a sideboard where pots marked COFFEE and TEA await their cups. There are faint outlines where pictures had apparently once hung, but now the walls are mostly bare. The center of the room is dominated by a long, shining wood table that I quickly calculate was meant to seat sixteen. As there are only seven of us, Roger is at the head with three settings on each side. I take the only empty seat, on the end, with Arjun next to me and Marla across the table.

I still feel nauseous as Alex carries a full English breakfast to each of us. (I wonder: How is he possibly cleaning my room at the same time? And should he be touching food?) There are eggs, what the British call bacon—more like a thick ham to me—sausages, cooked tomatoes, baked beans, mushrooms, and buttered toast. I take a few tentative bites.

"So," I announce to the group, "circumstances led Alex to show me the priest hole in my room. . . . I had no idea they were so tiny! I mean, I have read about them but never seen one. Gosh, it is so well concealed, I can see that it was effective. No one would know it was there."

"Ah, yes, it's quite a good example," says Marla, again flashing her brilliant smile at me. "I have stayed in that room before. In fact, I wrote my last book there. A great room for your first time here," she adds, putting some of my nerves at ease. I can't help noticing how impeccably dressed Marla is, as if the clothes have been tailored exactly to her body. My off-the-rack clothing always leaves pants a little too short or too long, shirts too large in the bust or shorter than I would like. But Marla's fitted button-down seems bespoke, with sleeves falling exactly at her wrists, the fit flattering her figure until it tucks smoothly into light-gray slacks that do the same. She has a silk scarf tied around her neck in a way that makes her look even more chic (rather than like a flight attendant or a cowgirl, as it would on me).

"Priest holes are beyond my area of research," I say, "so I don't know much about them. It seems incredible that anyone could hide in there for any length of time. It just seems cruel."

"It's hard for us to imagine what people would have done for their faith," says Roger. "When Henry VIII broke with the Catholic Church and started the Church of England, many Catholics continued to practice their faith in secret, but he wasn't going to kill them for it as long as they gave lip service to the C of E." He takes a big bite of sausage before continuing, waving his fork. "But the stakes got very high when the Protestant Elizabeth became queen. It was a shadow civil war. Many of the nobles were still Catholic and were putting money and support into getting Elizabeth's cousin, the Catholic Mary, Queen of Scots, onto the throne. Elizabeth saw that the only way out was to deal decisively with anyone showing Catholic sympathies. She executed Mary. She hunted down the priests. Both the priests and the people who housed them were subject to imprisonment and even death." I feel the hairs on the back of my neck prickle at the thought.

Roger continues, delighted. "The priests were soldiers in this war. And the stakes were real. You don't have priest holes unless there really were priest hunters, the pursuivants, as they were called, and you wouldn't hide yourself in such a space for hours on end unless the consequences of not doing so were dire."

"Was this hole the work of Owen?" Westley asks, his voice so suddenly familiar to me again after two decades of silence. "I grew up quite near here," he says to the group, "and have seen a few examples of the ones he made." I can't help feeling that this display of knowledge is for my benefit.

Roger nods, punctuating his words with his hands. "Yes, we think so. As you know, Westy, he's responsible for most of them around here." I bristle involuntarily at the nickname. Roger seems the type to make them up for people. How many times have I had to firmly correct men from trying out "Allie" or other versions of my name, usually diminutive, that they feel suit me better?

He turns to me. "Nicholas Owen—St. Nicholas Owen, actually—had a real genius for these hidey-holes. People think there are some still waiting to be found in these old houses, he hid them so well. Some houses had two or three that were connected so that the priest hunter would find one, but it would be empty, with the priest safely concealed in the adjoining—and better hidden—one."

"Was Owen canonized?" Arjun asks. "I suppose hiding priests is as good a reason as any to be made a saint."

Westley jumps in. "Yes," he answers. "He was eventually captured and tortured to death at the Tower, so really a kind of martyr." He looks around the table, clearly enjoying having an audience. "People have found all sorts of things hidden in the holes, though. Everything from sixteenth-century heretical texts to jewelry to a twentieth-century teen's hidden erotica. Lots of stories around here of finding long-dead bodies in these things, from starvation or lack of air. Nothing I know that's verified, although I keep looking. Would make a marvelous article." I think of the dead animal upstairs. Did it suffocate? Starve?

"What an awful way to die," says Marla, "rotting away inside a priest hole. Do you reckon with your faith as you run out of air? Or is it worth it to die for a cause?" At these questions, a silence descends over the group. In this shifting light, and in this house, I can see the dangers of the Reformation and the bodies (both institutional and corporeal) that were destroyed. Elizabeth Barton walked these very grounds, or at least the adjacent priory ones. She was really a kind of human shield in the holy war that Roger described. A pawn. A casualty. My thoughts turn again to the priest hole, but all I can evoke are the maggots writhing therein.

"Well." Roger claps his hands together, snapping me from my gruesome reverie. "On to cheerier topics. Today and tomorrow are days to discuss, collaborate, find points of connection between your work. You've already read the abstracts—except Wes's—so this part should be easy, pleasurable. You each have a presentation time allotted in the next few days where you can bring in some of the discussion points."

He says "schedules" in the British way. I wonder whether this speaks to how long he has been in England or a pretentious affect. My money is on the latter.

He continues. "Today I have paired you all according to interest. I have also set aside some time this morning for Westley to give an overview of his project since he was unable to send an abstract beforehand, so you know what to expect when he gives his full presentation. Then, this afternoon, weather permitting, I invite you and your partner to continue your discussion while you explore the area on foot or by bicycle—Alex can help you with these. The priory ruins are especially beautiful, and the chapel is still intact and occasionally in use. I have arranged for it to be open to you this entire week."

"Is the priory that close?" I ask, genuinely excited to see St. Sepulchre's.

"Yes," Westley blurts out before Roger can answer. "The manor is built within its actual grounds. With its very stones and timber!" He waves his arms up at the roof.

With its very stones and timber? Westley was always a bit of a showman, and I see that has not changed. I have a flashback to one of the last times we were together, a short trip to York. Westley talking loudly to me about some of the folk remedies tied to the cathedral, gesticulating, and quickly finding himself in the center of a tour group that had been pulled over by his magnetism, wanting to hear what he had to say.

"Oh, I knew they were closely related to each other, but I didn't realize they were truly adjacent," I say a little defensively. Westley needs to know I am not impressed with his act.

"Indeed," Roger says with a nod, "after the priory was dissolved, all the land that had belonged to the Church suddenly belonged to the Crown. And the Crown always needed money. Cromwell took the land from the Church and sold much of it to the neighboring gentry. Blood money, I'm sure many of them thought, to ensure that they didn't raise too much of a fuss. The royals were always terrified of rebellion." He pauses. "Not without reason, though. And this family was Catholic, so it must have been bittersweet to buy the land from the Crown."

"Of course, taking the land makes the manor susceptible to the curse!" laughs Charles, who is spreading jam on what must be his fourth croissant.

"The curse?" I ask, interested despite myself.

"Yes!" Brian says, sipping his coffee. "Do tell. I love the English and their myriad curses. We lack them in America. Although there are a few rumors of some at Princeton." *Of course there are, Brian.*

Charles smiles. "Legend has it that a curse visits the families who bought or were given monastic land because they basically took sacred Church land and made it secular. Probably started because Hampton Court Palace, which had been Cardinal Wolsey's, was where Henry VIII's wife Jane Seymour died in childbirth. So, whenever anything bad happens to these post-Reformation families on formerly Church grounds, it gets chalked up to the curse." Charles's eyes flit over to Roger. "Of course, as with so many things, it's just a Victorian ghost story."

"I love a good ghost story!" pipes up Arjun, who has been following the conversation with interest. "Are there any that have to do with the house? Should we be looking for encounters with old ladies dressed in Victorian garments?"

Roger shrugs. "Of course. Several. Let's see . . . Some guests have reported items moving around their rooms when no one was at the house." He raises his eyebrows dramatically.

Marla declares, "I have never believed in ghosts. But I do think, as historians, we are haunted by urgent questions of the past. Sometimes long-dead people are reaching out to us through books or wills or items they have left behind."

Roger turns his penetrating eye toward me. "Would you agree, Alison?"

I feel the way I did when a professor cold-called on me in graduate school. Is this when I fail to measure up? "Yes, Roger, I do indeed feel that way." I look at Marla to see if I have won her approval with my answer, and she is smiling.

"Of course she does, Roger," she chides. And then, turning to me, "I have read your work, Alison, and you endeavor to recover the humanity behind the records. Elizabeth should rest easy knowing her story is in the hands of such a capable scholar." I mouth a gratified "thank you," not sure I deserve such lofty praise.

"*Pfft*, I don't know," scoffs Brian, "this feels a flimsy interpretation of history. My work is more concerned with facts. Not with mystical connections to dead people."

"Yes, well, this may be why you only work with kings and nobles who leave so many records behind. It's much easier to follow those giant breadcrumbs," Marla says. A scarlet hue creeps into Brian's cheeks. I can't help but admire this evisceration.

While the meal feels collegial, I can see that the undercurrent of academic competition will be just as acute here as at any larger conference, and the pang of Calista's absence hits me even more keenly. I wish I had a true accomplice here, someone I could have giggled with later about the exchange. Just then, Alex comes in to clear the plates. I turn to Roger. "I'll email Calista this morning," I say, "see how she's doing. Tell her we miss her."

Roger looks up quickly. "No, no," he says sternly. "She's quite ill. It will just make her feel bad she is not here." He reaches a hand out toward Westley. "And aren't we lucky we found such a suitable replacement?"

* * *

"THIS PROJECT," WESTLEY says, giving the preview of his paper once we have taken our seats in the library, "has been greatly enhanced by the recent discoveries of Dr. Sage." *What? Shit. What a dick. He's working on Barton?* He smiles at me. I can't tell if it's an I-will-take-you-down smile or a genuine one. I've forgotten how to read him. I'm not sure I ever knew.

"I have long been working on the folklore of this area. Not the 'once upon a time' myths, although there are many and they are wonderful, but the more recent legends concerning the Reformation. When Henry VIII's divorce was not granted by the pope—thanks to the pressure from the Spanish, who did not want to see their own Queen Catherine of Aragon humiliated in such a way—he was convinced the only way to marry the object of his desire, Anne Boleyn, was to break completely with Rome." I try not to roll my eyes. Of course we all know this already.

"His advisor Thomas Cromwell saw how this change could accomplish another goal and help replenish the royal coffers. Imagine what it meant to take the convents and monasteries out of the hands of the Church and into those of the Crown. Cromwell closed—or 'suppressed' or 'dissolved,' choose your euphemism—the religious houses and took their land . . . which leads us here, to St. Sepulchre's."

He points out the window where the very tip of the church bell tower is visible. "The priory was dissolved shortly after Elizabeth Barton was hanged—it had a certain notoriety for housing her. I am sure Cromwell took a special pleasure in closing it down."

I kind of stopped listening at the history lesson but am brought right back to the room at the mention of the priory, which makes me feel somehow possessive. It's *my* priory, I think, where Elizabeth Barton had lived until her arrest.

Westley continues, and I work to contain my growing anger. "As many of you know, I grew up around here and am delighted to be able to study some of the legends I heard as a child. The local legend that I plan to present and study this week concerns real treasure—gems, I believe, although the exact nature of the treasure changes depending on the source—that was possibly given to the nuns in exchange for audiences with Elizabeth Barton and to keep her protected by them. They were supposedly hidden after Elizabeth's hanging, when the priory was sacked and the sisters had to leave in such haste. Many around here believe they are still hidden, waiting to be found, and that the sisters left clues regarding where to look when they returned." He seems to be looking only at me. I look everywhere else to avoid his gaze meeting mine: at my feet, at the back of Marla's head, the fireplace, my notebook. My eyes keep flickering back to Westley to see if he's still looking at me. He is.

"Of course," Westley adds, "they thought a return was imminent. That Henry would come to his senses, or that Catherine of Aragon's daughter Mary would become queen and restore the rightful church. No one anticipated that her rule would be so short, and I don't think any of them could have predicted that Anne Boleyn's daughter, Elizabeth, would ever rule. Yes, the future that unfolded was not one they expected. So, the treasure, if there was one, may still be here." He grins and actually tips an imaginary hat in conclusion. Roger literally claps.

It's not just Roger—everyone else seems rather pleased with Westley's stupid project. Based on what? Folklore? Small-town gossip? And pulling Barton into this? I have a *real* project about Elizabeth, about how Bocking inserted himself into the book, about how her words were manipulated and used to the ends of powerful men. This History Channel nonsense—"THE LOST TREASURES OF ST. SEPULCHRE'S"—that Westley is proposing gives authentic scholars a bad name. And yet, I look down at my notepad and realize I have covered it in interesting notes.

". . . you may move into your groups now," Roger is saying. Charles, Brian, and Arjun head into one corner of the room, Roger and Marla another. That leaves . . . shit. Westley walks over to me.

"You and me, Alison," he says, his blue eyes staring directly into mine, that half smile that once made me swoon. "The Bartonites!"

Hampton Court, March 1528

Everywhere she looked there was color: red and gold and tapestries and jewels. It smelled of cooking meat, making Elizabeth's mouth water. Lent was only days away and she assumed that the cardinal was getting all the meat he could before his forty days of fish. Although the priory had some riches, they looked dull compared to the palace that was the cardinal's home. She did not even know buildings could be so big. That this place was not a king's castle made no sense. How could the king live in any place grander than this one?

Elizabeth was glad that Bocking was with her, but less glad that Bishop Fisher was. The bishop continued to be stern and disapproving, and when she described a vision that she thought he would want to hear, he kept asking questions and describing it differently until it was something else entirely. When she spoke, he corrected her. He also told her to speak more quietly, if at all, and to cast her eyes downward. Bocking did none of this, although when he read her own book of visions aloud, he did embellish what she said she saw. Her advisor was cowed by Fisher, too; he was more deferential, quieter, when the bishop was with them.

An attendant greeted them at the door, a coat of arms on his sleeve. Elizabeth pointed it out to Bocking as they followed him down a corridor, asking, "Are even the servants nobles here?" He smiled in a way that she recognized was acknowledging her ignorance, a smile that she had seen many times in the three years she had been in his charge.

"No, daughter," he said, "that's Wolsey's livery. It's to show that they are in the employ of the cardinal-chancellor." The coat of arms depicted a red lion's raised paw and blue birds. Elizabeth imagined she saw the one ripping the other to shreds.

"Is that a special kind of cardinal?" she asked. "A cardinal-chancellor?"

Fisher, as usual, appeared annoyed at her questions. He preferred when she was silent. But Bocking smiled. "He is both cardinal and chancellor," he explained. "He is the chancellor of England, the most important advisor to the king. And as a cardinal, he is more important than even a bishop—"

Elizabeth glanced at Fisher to see if he was upset by the slight, but the scowl on his face remained unchanged.

"—and he is one of the many cardinals who are advisors to the pope and—"

Fisher held up a hand. "Enough of that prattle," he said coldly. "The only matter you need to know, sister, is that the cardinal is a powerful man. He speaks for the king. He can be a great ally or a great enemy. And he wants to examine you. You must only speak the truth."

They followed the attendant in silence, down yet another corridor, lined with paintings of scenes from the Bible or the martyrdom of saints. Many were saints that Elizabeth recognized from her Book of Hours, the prayer book that Bocking had recently given her with an image and a prayer for each day. One of the few kind sisters would read the prayer to her if Bocking was not there, but she spent many hours looking at the pictures, staring at those holy men and women who died for their faith. As they passed an image of St. Sebastian, she shuddered at the sight of arrows piercing his flesh, blood staining his white skin and running in rivulets down his body to pool at his feet.

The attendant stopped at an open door and gestured the three inside. *He* was standing there. Cardinal Wolsey: almost as powerful as the king, with a name that made many cower with respect and fear. His torso was dressed in the deep bloodred that displayed his position in the Church; he also wore additional signs of his status around his neck: a medallion the size of a plate and an ornate gold cross. Wolsey was a giant man, so tall and broad that he reminded Elizabeth of the hellmouth in the priory church.

"Here is our Holy Maid of Kent," Wolsey said in his deep voice, his jowls shaking. Ignoring Elizabeth and Bocking, he addressed Fisher. "She is gaining quite a name for herself. We must use her in a prudent way. Luther's heretics are multitude." As he spoke, he moved to a seat that Elizabeth assumed, by its heft and central position, was a throne. He made no motion for his guests to sit. There was not any place for them to do so, anyway.

"She speaks of this illness here, spreading like a fever," Fisher said flatly, pointing his fingers to the ground as he spoke. Although Bocking had shrunk into himself, the bishop did not seem afraid of the great man. "She sees it in her trances. The poison is spreading through the court—especially in the king's desire for annulment. The remedy is in prayer to the Virgin Mary. She is the intercessor we need right now, and this Maid can see her."

Elizabeth was startled by the words. Had she said she had seen the Virgin? She recalled describing to Bocking the image of Mary in her Book of Hours, bathed in light, a book open in her lap, the angel Gabriel coming to tell her that her life was forever changed.

"The solution is in penance, Your Eminence," Fisher continued. "We must bring these sinners back to us."

"The king's matters are not yours, Bishop Fisher. They are between the king and God." The cardinal nearly growled the words. "I agree, however, that we are imperiled. The king is pious. He may listen to a visionary if she be true. I would like to speak to the Holy Maid alone." Wolsey flung his hand toward the door, dismissing the men. Both Fisher and Bocking bowed and backed away, avoiding Elizabeth's eyes.

She felt too afraid to meet Wolsey's gaze as he addressed her. "You need to speak more of your visions against the heretics," he said in a voice that sounded almost bored. "The bishop tells me you have seen them in hell? Burning for their sins?"

She allowed herself to look up, just slightly, so she could see his chin. She wondered at the legion of maids who had to launder and press those red garments, at the servants who polished the gold glistening on his thick fingers and around his neck, at the cooks who prepared food to feed such a household. Their quiet whispers and light footfalls could be heard outside the room: an invisible army for a palace of one. She looked back down at her hands and marveled at how soft they had become since she had joined the nuns at the priory.

"Elizabeth?" The edge in Wolsey's voice brought her back. Now his voice was more gentle, as if speaking to a babe. "Have you seen heretics burning in judgment?"

She nodded. This was Bocking's favorite part of her first (and the clearest, most powerful) vision—that she had seen people she knew on earth suffering in purgatory. Every time he saw her, he immediately inquired about any new visions since their last meeting, and if she could name anyone she saw. The hellmouth in the priory church told her in its great image who was suffering in hell: kings, queens, cardinals, nuns, merchants, butchers, farmers.

The Devil came for everyone no matter their degree.

She had learned to listen carefully for the talk between Bocking and Fisher, or other priests that she had traveled with throughout England, and, when prompted, to speak the names they mentioned with clear contempt. Here, in front of Wolsey, she suddenly felt emboldened. Surely, God wanted her to speak these names if he had elevated her to meet with the cardinal-chancellor. God, who had plucked her from her lowly state at the Cobbs' and made her a living saint. She lifted her chin and, for the first time, met Wolsey's eyes, which she saw were rheumy and red. Tired eyes.

"Yes, Your Grace. I have seen the heretics in hell. The Lutherans."

"Speak more. Who have you seen? Do you know of secret heretics among us? I will say some names, and you may nod if you have seen them in your visions of hell."

She nodded slowly, repeatedly, as he began his recitation.

* * *

THE PATH TO the river was filled with carriages, as nobles came in and out of Hampton Court Palace, seeking the king's favor through his chancellor. As usual, Fisher and Bocking spoke mostly to each other, and Elizabeth remained silent. She didn't mind. She enjoyed watching the people around her and knew that the quieter she was, the more they would speak. As if she were not there at all. Her years on the Cobb farm had taught her how to be invisible. She could not understand all of what they were saying, but it was clear that neither of them liked Wolsey. Once in the boat, Fisher started to speak about the cardinal as if they had already been in the middle of discussion. "It's true, Wolsey has only cared about Henry. And power. He's never fully listened to Rome, even though he owes his position to them, and he will not start now. The pope, appropriately, has said no annulment. Catherine is the king's rightful wife. They have a daughter. Just because some hussy has captured the king's attention does not mean the marriage is void."

Bocking knew much of theology but not much about politics, and he frequently used these times with Fisher to fully understand the court.

Elizabeth, too, was learning what a tangled world existed outside of the priory walls—and it was a realm wherein she might have a role. The men were taking her around because the king's marriage was somehow entwined with the idea of heretics. How, she did not fully understand. She would have to ask Bocking later when Fisher was not with them.

"How can he claim a marriage of nineteen years is invalid? A marriage that produced a living child, albeit just a girl? A marriage that has secured our allegiance with Spain, our important ally in this holy war against the Lutherans?" Bocking rolled out his questions quickly, as Fisher, although angry, seemed in a talking mood. Bocking once told Elizabeth that Fisher had refused grander posts even though he had been so close to the king's father and especially his grandmother, for whom he had served as confessor. He believed in humility and detested opulence.

"He claims that it is consanguineous," Fisher answered, his voice darkening.

Bocking must have seen the confusion in Elizabeth's furrowed brow, because he whispered to her, "Of the same blood, like brother and sister." Turning to Fisher, he asked, "But how?"

"Because she had been married to his brother, Arthur, first. Everyone knows that marriage was unconsummated at his death, and the pope annulled the marriage, so it is all utter nonsense. Catherine is not Henry's sister. There is no sin there. The sin would be in annulment now." Fisher's voice was rising in pitch, his complexion reddening. "But Henry will not stop until his marriage is annulled, and Wolsey will continue to help him. He has opened the door to all this heresy." Elizabeth could not follow all these details, but she understood that the king was trying to argue that his marriage had never happened. That he was free to remarry whom he pleased.

"Perhaps the Holy Maid has convinced Wolsey otherwise," said Bocking, more quietly. "He would not go so clearly against the word of God. Wolsey will rein in the king." Elizabeth felt the glow of that deadliest of sins, pride, inside her belly. These powerful men needed her to do their work.

Fisher waved his hand angrily, as if to slice through her reverie. "The cardinal lives in a palace. He has two children. His home and his court were bought at great expense, emptying the coffers of the people who need it. Wolsey cannot rein *himself* in, much less the king." His voice grew louder as he continued. "It's not just that the monarch's soul is imperiled if he falls into Lutheranism, but if he does not have Rome to check him, his power will be unbridled, the abuse of that power assured. He already has dismissed the word of God, spoken through our holy pope."

Elizabeth gasped at what seemed to her a double blasphemy. To speak so easily against the cardinal! To speak against the king! It suddenly occurred to her that all these men were on different sides—meaning she would have to choose hers very carefully.

Bocking did not seem surprised to hear Fisher's words. "Yes, yes," he said, "we know this. But hear me, Your Excellency, the Holy Maid is the key. Elizabeth's visions will set the path rightly."

"It's not so simple," said Fisher. "The Maid has not swayed Queen Catherine of Aragon. She refuses to see her. We should try to get her to the good Sir Thomas More. He may listen and he still has much influence with the king." Fisher's eyes glanced up at the waterman, rowing with his eyes ahead but his ears open. He lowered his voice. "The Maid does not have everyone's support. It is ever thus with those who speak the truth. For now, she has the support of the cardinal and the king, but they are also frightened of her. We must temper her words. Make sure her visions are true."

Elizabeth contemplated silently as they settled into their boat back to the abbey where they were staying the night, the swampy, fishy smell of the Thames filling her nostrils. She considered all that she had heard and witnessed. The cardinal and king, afraid of her? Queen Catherine knew who she was and refused to see her? People would listen to her. She could save the king. She could save the queen. She could save the country. She bowed her head and prayed for more visions to come. And—assuming they may not—began to plan what she should say next.

Vale House Manor, June 2023, Day 2

Westley stays in the library with me while the groups set off to different corners of the household—Marla and Roger are in the room with us, but the other three go to the dining room to settle in and discuss. It's only an hour of this forced camaraderie, thank God, and then independent work until lunchtime.

"May I see your images of the Barton book?" Westley asks as we sit down at the game table. I scoot my chair slightly away from him as I turn the computer in his direction. I try not to look at him, try to pretend that I am not acutely aware of every inch of his body and the way he leans toward me. I can almost feel the heat coming off of his skin.

"Sure. Let me pull them up."

Even as I open the images on my laptop, I can't help but worry that Westley is using me to get what he needs for his own project. This is *not* collaboration. But what can I do? Hide them? Now that the book has been discovered, it is being conserved and will be placed in the royal library in Brussels, the Bibliothèque Royale de Belgique, for any qualified scholar to see. Despite his many faults, Westley would certainly qualify.

Anyway, before the ManSock speech, I sent my findings to *English Manuscript Studies*, the premier journal in the field; there is no way Westley could get anything out before my piece, "What Elizabeth Saw: The Discovery and Contents of Elizabeth Barton's Lost Book" will be published in the fall issue.

"It really is an extraordinary find, Alison," Westley says as he scrolls through the PDF I had made of the book. "That was a lucky right-place, right-time, wasn't it?"

"Or I could be a good researcher," I reply testily. "I knew this monastery had housed English recusants very soon after the dissolution. I guessed there were some important items among their documents, and no one had ever gone through them. It took months of back-and-forth with the archivist there before they would even let me in to take a peek. And then it was at least three weeks of sorting through papers, books, documents, trying to catalogue as I went along, before I finally found the book." Three weeks away from my family, while my marriage was falling apart. I look Westley directly in the eye. "I didn't just trip and fall into a box that happened to have Barton's book in it."

"Oh, of course," Westley says hastily. Is he blushing? "I'm sorry, I didn't mean to imply otherwise. You know I think you're a brilliant researcher." He lowers his voice so that Marla and Roger cannot overhear and leans even closer to me. "I learned so much by working with you. I've missed it. I've missed you."

"You were an excellent student, Westley." I ignore what he said about missing me. I can't let my guard down here. Too much is at stake, and not only my professional reputation.

"You can call me Wes, you know. You used to, Alison." He almost whispers my name and it triggers something buried deep in my subconscious. I can't help softening at his voice in that register, saying my name.

"I think it's a good idea if we just keep everything professional here, Westley." I firmly stress both syllables of his name. "That was a lifetime ago." Even saying it, I feel a clench in my heart. It took so long to release him the first time and I don't want to go through that again.

"Okay, professional, then. I'm very impressed with your work on Barton."

"Thanks," I say tightly, relieved to be moving out of what I can sense is dangerous territory. "It will come out shortly in *EMS*." I pause to let the prestige of the publication sink in. "It's an expansion of the Man-Sock talk. And the project I'm doing here is adjacent, as you know. I hadn't originally intended to do such a deep dive on Barton, but here we are, and I think I am onto something good."

"Sometimes the project finds you," Westley says softly. "I admit I was working on something else—ghost stories in the region—but when I heard about your paper, I realized that I needed to pick up on the Barton legends that had been floating around here. I thought they were all dead ends, but the book may change things. I hope you don't mind."

"Why would I mind?" I grit my teeth. "I don't own the topic."

The grandfather clock rings loudly enough that the four of us in the room stop our conversations. Eleven tones. We're done. Westley looks like he wants to say something more so I speak quickly before he can.

"Oh, too bad, collaborative time is up. I'm going to just type up some of my notes for my paper presentation, if you don't mind." Although Roger and Marla seem unwilling to finish their deep conversation, heads bent together in a way that recalls the kind of collaboration I once had with Westley, I lie to myself that I am all too happy to have an excuse to end our talk.

* * *

LUNCH IS AS delicious as breakfast, more so since the nausea inspired by the maggot-filled rat has subsided as long as I don't allow myself to think about it. I haven't been back to my room, and I hope it's well cleaned out by now.

Alex brings out several local cheeses (a cheddar, a Stilton, one I have never heard of called a "Merry Wyfe"), charcuterie, salads, some pickled vegetables, and another still-warm bread that smells amazing. Chutney, mustard, mayonnaise, all laid out. I opt for a little bit of everything and big slabs of the bread. The pale-cream china has intertwined letters in faded gold, V&P.

Although there is a little small talk as everyone serves themselves and tucks into the food (I start with the Merry Wyfe, since I no longer am one. If Jenny or Calista were here, I would make a joke about it), everyone is waiting for some kind of pronouncement from Roger to set the tone for the group luncheon conversation. And Roger, in turn, seems to know that this is his role and readily obliges. "When we first started having the C.C., we used to have ale with lunch, remember, Charles? When that was allowed?"

Charles laughs as he fills his plate with at least double what I have on mine. "Sure, I do. If I remember correctly, it was followed by a fairly long siesta to sleep it off and get ready for the evening talks and libations. Not sure we could get away with it these days, those three-martini lunches, so to speak. Dicky would be furious with me, for one." Dicky, Charles's husband, was a dancer in his youth and has been a fitness enthusiast all his life. The way Charles describes it, he keeps a close eye on what Charles eats at home, so he always happily indulges when away.

Brian pipes up. "There's no reason not to make a stop at the King's

Head in the village this afternoon. I think an afternoon pint is pretty much required when in England." Charles, Arjun, and he exchange glances and sheepish smiles, apparently already having made such plans.

I turn to Marla, whose face seems to be marked with disapproval at the whole conversation, but as soon as she meets my eye, she turns on a bright smile. "Charles tells me you have children, Alison. How charming. What are they doing while you are here?" I see Westley turn with interest in our direction.

"Um, they're with their father now." I look down at my watch and make a quick calculation. "And headed to camp for two weeks in about an hour. I'll call them to say goodbye before we do the afternoon excursions."

This is how you let people know you are divorced. You refer not to "my ex-husband," which seems a more logical label, but the strange linguistic contortion of "my children's father," as if he has always been entirely separate from you, tethered only by shared progeny.

Conferences have always allowed me the few days to just be a scholar—nobody's wife, nobody's mother. Especially in the early days of the twins' childhood when everyone, oddly, referred to me as "Mom": the pediatrician, the kids' babysitters, later their teachers. I felt erased. Entering the classroom would magically transform me from "Mom" to "Dr. Sage," and I would regain a bit of my own identity. But now, with no one who sees me as "Mom" at all, I wish Calista were here, so I could share just a bit of that other part of myself.

"If you all will excuse me," I hear myself say to the group, "I have to make that phone call. I'll be back down in time for the excursion. Give my compliments to the chef, Alex," I say as he clears my plate.

He nods back, unsmiling, then says, "Your room has been cleaned. I hope you find it satisfactory."

The room still definitely has eau de dead rodent hanging oppressively in the air, although it is overlaid with a chemical, bleachy smell and a gross floral one that definitely came from a spray can. The windows are wide open and the priest hole in the window seat is again concealed. Even knowing it is there, I can't see the outline of the door. It really is masterfully done. I sit on the window seat and practically hang out of the open window to breathe the fresh air. The morning fog is lifting, and the sun is trying to break through the clouds. I see Alex and Roger walking in the garden in what appears to be an intense conversation, judging by Roger's gesticulations. I suppose since Roger has rented out the space, he's in charge of all the logistics with Alex.

The twins can't bring their phones to camp, so a call to Pete is the only way I can talk to them. Pete hands me to each child and I get to say a quick goodbye before they board the bus.

Another shuffling, and then Pete's irritated voice. "Well, that's done. They're on the bus. You should have called earlier." *Thanks. Noted.*

"It's hard to time it right with the time change and the schedule here. I'm sad to miss seeing them go."

His voice softens just a tick. "I hope this summer is drama-free and we don't have a repeat of the spin-the-bottle incident of 2022."

I laugh. "More like the spin-the-bottle massacre." It wasn't funny at the time, but I'll never forget last summer's phone call when Georgina locked braces with Linus Stewart and they both had to go to an emergency orthodontist near the camp to be separated and then have their respective gear repaired. The call came while Pete and I were in a marriage-counseling session. Of course, the camp called me; I doubt they even had Pete's number. It was the perfect illustration of one of my complaints, that the twins' lives were *my* responsibility, that I had filled out every form, paid every bill, received every phone call for the last fourteen years. That I had fit my work in between drop-offs and pickups and during naps, while Pete was off at the lab all day. He never understood my frustration, although he didn't hesitate to point out when my academic productivity was lagging.

I force another laugh. "I don't think she will be getting anywhere near Linus's mouth this summer. And if Tristan can manage to keep all his bones intact, we should be good to go." Is the conversation over? I can never tell anymore. We have not really found a rhythm of speaking to each other again.

"I'll let you know when I hear that they've arrived."

"Thanks, Pete."

"Bye, Alison."

I click off the call and draw my knees up onto the window seat. Talking to Pete always makes me a bit melancholy. We were good—at least I thought we were—until suddenly I felt like I had woken up, and all at once I was middle-aged, and the last decade of my life had been just Georgina and Tristan and work. I had forgotten about myself.

But Pete? Pete hadn't forgotten about himself. Pete was a physicist at the same college, but his work was collaborative, in a lab. Mine was often solitary, enclosed with my books. I had allowed him the luxury of parenting without all its burdens: the homework, the heartache, the late nights and early mornings. And he had let me take all of that on.

And then the pandemic came, and we were closed up together. I realized that I could no longer speak to him. We had no shared vocabulary other than the language of the twins. And in that, I was a native speaker, and he was not even fluent.

* * *

WHEN I COME back downstairs, Westley is waiting by the door, sitting on one of the benches in the entrance hall. I feel my heart lift slightly at the sight of him. As if my body is telling me I want him even though my mind is saying I do not.

"Ready for our excursion?" he says cheerfully, standing up, stretching so that a strip of skin between his jeans and his T-shirt is tantalizingly visible.

Westley, despite looking like he just rolled out of bed and grabbed the nearest clothes, is still undeniably hot. Twenty years hasn't changed that. The sunglasses atop his head are holding the hair out of his eyes, which I realize match the blue of his shirt—and I'm annoyed at myself for noticing.

"Oh, have you already planned it? Where are we going?" I affect a smile.

Screw him for planning our outing. How does he know what would be of interest to me? He already knows this area, so shouldn't it be my choice?

"I thought you would want to see the priory grounds. I know them well—I grew up a stone's throw from here and spent a lot of my youth wandering these fields. You can see where our girl Elizabeth spent her almost-last days." He reminds me of a Labrador retriever, bounding up and down on his heels, his dark hair flopping, ready to chase a ball, show what he can do. He is already halfway out the door.

"Hardly a girl," I say. "Why do men always do that? Call women girls?

She was twenty-eight when she died. You're just fifteen years older than that, Westley." Twenty-eight seems so young. Two decades younger than me. A lifetime.

"Please," he says, ignoring my jibe and winking, "call me Wes. Especially since you remember exactly how old I am."

I am *not* going to call him Wes. We aren't friends anymore. That door closed a long time ago when I took the job in New York. We aren't even really colleagues. He opens the door and bounces off toward the priory. Finally, in the sunshine, I can see how green this place is, how the June flowers dot color through the countryside. Up close, the garden looks much like it had from my window: beautifully laid out but overgrown. There are flowers everywhere, but the vines and bushes near them threaten to crowd them out.

The path from the front door curves around to the side of the manor and joins another one coming from a side door. Together they form a wide walkway that meanders over a small hill to the priory, where you can just see a bell tower peeking above.

The hedges that may have once held topiary shapes are now just green blobs, crowding into the pathway and forcing me to walk closer to Westley than I like. England's damp June air seems to be exactly the recipe for greenery, and the garden has a good mix of cultivated but neglected flowers (so many roses and hydrangeas) and what look like native wildflowers, dotting the lawn and strangling some of the planted ones.

"Valentine's Day," he says, as we get close to the ruins.

"What?"

"Your birthday. It's Valentine's Day. You're forty-eight."

"And?" I'm not sure where this is going.

"I just wanted to let you know I remember how old you are, too. And your birthday. And that you love calla lilies and hate dark beer."

"Excellent memory, Westley," I say, although I can't help but be charmed that he remembers. Although he always had historical dates at his ready recall. Maybe he's just good with them. Time to change the subject. "How much of the priory survives?"

"As soon as we crest this incline you will see the whole of it. Or at least the whole of the ruins. Not much left other than the church, but from the top of the hill you can see the outlines of some of the other buildings." He stretches out a muscular arm to point out where we are headed.

We see Charles, Brian, and Arjun leaving the manor on bikes, cycling somewhat shakily over the gravel toward the village on their own excursion. I give them a wave.

* * *

THE RUINS ARE like so many others that I have walked before: vague outlines of walls in the grass, a few places where half a wall remains but not much else, a trace of a walkway around what would have been the cloister. A broken place. Haunted still by the ghosts of the Reformation.

It's not a destination for tourists, and there are no maps or signs to help situate what was the chapter house, broken walls which once held the cells, the kitchen, the infirmary, the prioress's quarters. Only the church remains intact. But the layout of these places is always the same, so I walk the footprint confidently and imagine how the sisters themselves paced these spaces in what was a silent choreography, knowing their places, their chores, finding time for prayer and reading.

". . . and then over here this path eventually connects to one of the Roman roads, so I think that's how and why the priory was placed here . . ." Westley is saying behind me. The busy hush of a working convent would be a welcome distraction just about now. "Did you know Anselm himself started this priory?" he asks.

"Yes, Westley." I face him with my hands on my hips. "I know that. I know all about it. Founded in the twelfth century. Benedictine. The land gifted to the nuns by Henry III in the thirteenth century. Lots of records of naughty nuns and prioresses, running off with men, badly governing, quarrelsome sisters. The church and manor house join the property in the fifteenth century. And"—I move my arms while circling around in a Julie Andrews in *The Sound of Music* pantomime—"I guess the church and the manor are all that survive. The priory was dissolved along with all the other houses by Cromwell in 1536. Two years after Barton was hanged." I can't help the annoyance creeping into my voice. How can he act like all is fine between us decades later?

He claps slowly. "I wasn't giving you an exam," he says with a laugh. "But well done. Top marks! Let's go see the church and the treasures inside it. It is truly something special, as you will see."

* * *

THE CHURCH IS still in excellent condition and indeed something special. I assume it survived because the family of the manor house worked to keep it intact even as the rest of the priory was dismantled. From the outside, the most distinguishing feature of the church is the bell tower, which would have been seen from afar to help locate the priory for those coming to seek out Elizabeth or to see the sisters. It also has a clock, which I make a mental note to ask about later. Clocks began to appear on churches as early as the fifteenth century, but I can't tell if this one is original or perhaps a later Victorian addition.

The temperature drops as soon as we cross the threshold. The church smells musty, like a cave, but that is overlaid with the scent of candles. It is dark inside, lit only by the sunlight that streams in through the stained glass windows, refracting colors onto the stone. The stained glass itself is a hodgepodge of images—some fragments of medieval glass, some images that look more Victorian, some modern pieces. This is not unusual in England, where the ruthless destruction of the Reformation, or later, bombs in one of the world wars, targeted the easily destroyed glass in most churches. It is rare to find intact medieval stained glass anywhere in the country, and the collages of reconstruction that most churches put together serve as a visible reminder of the violence of times past.

I turn to take in the whole church, breathing in the damp, cool air that signals both the place's age and its neglect. One wall features a giant painting, a hellmouth, but it is hard to make out its details in the shadows. At my feet there are brass grave markers, which are repeated throughout. Many seem to bear the name VALE, although the majority are worn into illegibility or smooth sheens of brass, their words forever lost.

My curiosity finally overrides my better judgment. "What do we know about the family of the manor? Are they the Vales? What was their connection to the priory?"

Westley squares his shoulders. "*Well,*" he says dramatically, "the manor house used to be part of the priory, but they were really suffering for a while for money. The more prominent families sent the daughters they didn't want to marry off to more prestigious convents—Dartford or Syon or Barking—and substantial moneys went with them. So, St. Sepulchre's had mostly local families, and the donations they brought with them were fairly meager."

He points in the direction of Vale House. "In order to gain more financial support, the prioress negotiated away what was then the manor house to the Crown—and some of that original house is incorporated into the grander house that has been added to over the centuries. The house, a title, and the adjacent lands were given to the Vales, who had served Henry VII well and needed a reward." He takes a big breath, as if he is trying to get all the information in while I am willing to listen. "At some point the house had a huge fire, so it was rebuilt after the Reformation, using stones from the then-dissolved priory, and the Vale family bought the priory lands from the Crown then, too. Although the family was obviously Catholic, they must have kept that fact private to continue to own the land here. There aren't any records proving that they were plotting against the queen or anything like that, but many of the family records were burned in that fire."

He pauses for another breath, but I put my hands up to stop him. "Got it!" I say with a laugh. "That's enough for me to get the gist of it. I don't need your dissertation on the place. Thanks." I am smiling, though. Westley knows exactly what details would interest me.

I walk down the center aisle, running my fingers over the smooth wooden ends of the pews. "How many hands touched these? What joys and sorrows were celebrated and mourned here?" I mumble half to myself, but Westley is looking intently at me as I speak.

"You've always looked for the people behind the objects, the papers, Alison. It's what's made you such an interesting scholar." He reaches out and I think he's going to touch my hand. I almost want him to. Instead he points to the small side chapel, the chantry, which would have been built for use by the family of the manor. "My favorite feature is in there. It's the tomb of Valentina Vale, the matriarch of the family, but most of the information about her was, as I said, burned in the manor fire. It's a shame to think what's lost. One of the legends about Elizabeth is that her most incendiary—no pun intended—prophecy was burned in it as well."

Now *this* is interesting information. I turn to ask him more just as he puts his hand on the small of my back to guide me toward the tomb.

Suddenly it feels as if his hand is electrified; I am acutely aware of every finger, of every shift in pressure as we walk. There is a memory in his touch: holding my hand the night before I left to go back to the States, leading me up the winding stairs to his flat. I open my mouth to speak but nothing comes out and I close it again.

Relief—at least I think it's relief—floods through my body when he removes his hand. It has been a long time since a man touched me. I bury the memory. Surely, this is just my body overreacting.

Breathe. Calm.

St. Sepulchre's Priory, July 1528

At refectory, Philippa had read aloud all the passages she knew about pride. She had exhausted all the treatises about *discretio spirituum,* the discernment of spirits, making sure that the sisters in her care knew how to tell if a vision had come from God and not from a demon trying to ensnare their souls or their own sinful minds. (There were at least one or two girls she was worried about having "visions" now that they saw the notoriety afforded Elizabeth.) She had admonished the Maid for overmuch pride both privately and in the chapter meeting. It was all to no avail.

In the years since Elizabeth had arrived, bishops and archbishops and even the cardinal himself had seen her usefulness, and Philippa suspected that the girl was too easily swayed by the men in her orbit to understand how she was being used to their ends. She had visions almost daily. They seemed to be getting increasingly dangerous, too, drawing more attention from the public when Philippa wished they were drawing less. She cautioned Elizabeth to stop naming specific people she had seen, which only fanned the embers of conflict between the Catholics and the Lutherans, whose numbers and voices were increasing by the day. Elizabeth did not heed her warnings. These were dangerous times. The prioress could feel it the same way that she could feel dampness in the summer air.

Philippa would have been more insistent about turning this Holy Maid out, but Bocking was right in his prediction that her presence would bring pilgrims and their wealth to the priory. Nearly every day some traveler was praying at the chapel, leaving alms for the Maid, asking to see her or hear her speak. When Elizabeth was at the priory, she did come out and warn those pilgrims about the dangers of hell, and what she had seen of purgatory, and the importance of confession to a priest before one dies. "Keep your oil lamp full! No one knows the day or the hour!" she would shout, almost in a state of madness. "Not even the angels in heaven." And the pilgrims would hurry to the priest to be shriven, confessing all their earthly sins, and leave behind their gifts of food or coins.

The sisters were growing fat on this bounty and as much as Elizabeth was a burden, Philippa knew the nuns preferred their better diet of meat and ale to the herring, eel, and small beer on which they had subsisted before.

"Mother?" One of the novices was at her doorway, eyes downcast.

"Yes, Sister Maria?" Philippa said, closing her book.

"Lady Vale is here to see you."

Philippa startled. The lady had never sought her out before.

Maria continued. "She says it is of utmost importance." This novice barely spoke above a whisper and flinched when touched. Philippa did not know what the girl's home had been like, but when a girl like this came to the priory, she was always happy that they had found sanctuary at St. Sepulchre's.

"Thank you, Maria. I will go to her."

Vale House Manor, June 2023, Day 2

I try to shake off that electricity attached to Westley's hand. I can still feel the place he touched me as if his handprint were somehow branded onto me. What the fuck was that? Twenty years disappeared in a second. I remind myself of how publicly critical he has been of my work in that time and how he never once wrote or called when I was back in the States. With effort, I turn my focus to what he is saying (is his voice quavering?), trying to sneak a glance at him to see if he is also feeling somehow a little shaken. ". . . a fine example of a fifteenth-century transi tomb and a thirteenth-century hellmouth," he concludes.

The transi tomb, sometimes called a cadaver monument, is horrifyingly beautiful. I've seen only one before and it was not nearly so grand or so finely carved.

From far away, a transi tomb almost resembles a bunk bed. But up close, you see that the top section looks like many grand medieval tombs, with an idealized marble representation of the dead person buried inside. A man could be wearing his armor, decorated with signs of nobility and bravery. A woman could be in expensive dress, a sleeping dog at her feet signaling that in life she was known for her obedience to God and, as important, to men.

This tomb's top features a woman, tightly wimpled, wearing a dress that once was painted and decorated; there are small flecks of paint still visible against the white of the stone. Her hands are clasped in prayer and the details of her dress—buttons, lace, folded cloth—are carefully carved in the marble. This top slab is held up by a team of sculpted marble angels, three on each side and one on each end, their hands above their heads holding up the effigy, each with eyes turned toward heaven.

But it's the bottom part of these tombs that makes them remarkable. The lower slab of marble, with the angels' feet atop it, also depicts a body. Here, though, you find the corpse as it was imagined buried, decomposing. A sculpture of a body in full decay: emaciated, shredded sinew, skeletal bones.

The transi tomb in this church is particularly gruesome, a sculpted worm crawling through one eye socket, the grinning skull open in a kind of scream. The exposed ribs also crawl with vermin, shreds of expertly chiseled cloth and papery strips of skin clinging to the bones. I bend down and shine my phone light in between the angels to see the cadaver up close. Carved in the bottom it reads REQUIESCAT IN PACE, VALENTINA VALE.

"'Rest in peace, Valentina Vale.' Quite the memento mori for her." My voice comes out in a whisper. I am both repulsed by and drawn to the tomb and its double statue—the sleeping woman in life, the buried, decomposed body in death.

"Yes," Westley replies, also hushed. "Most people want to remember their loved ones as they were alive, but these monuments do not let you forget what happens after they die. They remind you that is also your inescapable fate."

Goose bumps run up my arms at his words. "The hellmouth reminds you of the same," he says, pointing to the wall. On it I can just make out a giant beast's mouth, filled with bodies and surrounded by flames. "It's hard to see in this light, though, the paint has faded so much over the centuries. It's worth coming back in the morning for that."

"It would have been difficult to come here and pray and not remember that death awaits us all," I say.

He stands and looks at me meaningfully, "It's really a reminder to live while you can."

* * *

AT DINNER, I make sure not to sit near Westley, choosing instead a place between Roger and Marla, with Arjun and Charles—discussing scholars whose work they find vastly overrated—across from me. Roger seems a real bon vivant, and whatever funds he has access to that paid for this weekend also apparently pay for copious cocktails, wines, and damned good food (although I have yet to see the cook). So far only the coffee leaves something to be desired—why can't the English get that right?

"Wait until you try the meat pies here, Alison," says Charles, practically salivating. "They're Mrs. Bunch's specialty."

"Mrs. Bunch?" I ask, aware that I seem to be the only person not nodding in agreement. This conversation, like so many, keeps reminding me that I am an outsider here. Even though Westley is also new to the conference, no one treats him that way. It's a boys' club. I wonder how Marla successfully broke into it.

"The longtime cook of the manor," says Arjun. "I've tried to replicate the recipe at home but no luck. She must have left something essential out when she gave it to me so that it would never be right."

"Do you like the wine?" Brian asks me. "There's still a fairly stocked cellar here from the glory days of the manor house."

I take a sip and make an appreciative nod. It's unlike wine I have ever had. It might be the first time I understand what wine snobs mean when they say things like "balanced" and "notes of dark fruit." This wine is layered, offering different things to all parts of my palate. "Delicious. What are we drinking?"

"Pomerol," says Roger. "No one does wine better than the French, in my opinion. It's a 1985 Trotanoy." This means nothing to me, but Charles nods appreciatively from down the table and raises his glass in salute. "One of the only things that gets better if it's just allowed to sit without any attention," Roger adds. "If only the rest of the house improved by being left alone. Then this place would really be a gem."

It is true that the closer I look at things here, the more threadbare they clearly are. Although scaffolding covers a good part of the manor, there doesn't seem to be any work being done. No workmen; no one other than Alex, for that matter. Doors squeak, stair treads groan, splinters threaten from every surface. It is as if the house is just holding itself together on the strength of its past grandeur.

Roger reaches over his belly and refills my wineglass, crystal with the entwined initials V&P etched into it in the same manner as the china. I notice a menacing chip on the lip of my glass and turn it away from me. "So," Roger says, "tell me about your excursion this afternoon, Alison. It must have been strenuous since you didn't leave your room the rest of the day. You missed a somewhat heated discussion about repatriation of precious objects at our cocktail hour." Alex starts placing the dishes in front of us as Roger speaks. The meat pies with gravy are so fragrant that my mouth literally waters. Charles pulls Alex close and whispers something into his ear when the servant places his dish down. Alex nods briskly before walking away.

"And then we had a game of billiards," adds Brian. "At least Westley, Arjun, and I did."

"Oh, I'm sorry about missing that," I lie, sipping my wine more judiciously now that I realize how hard it will be to keep track of how much I am drinking if Roger remains generous with the refills. "I went for a quick lie-down and jet lag got the best of me. Thank you for sending Alex to wake me." Alex had, I think, lingered just a minute too long at my doorway, looking around before he shut the door. "The excursion was lovely," I say. "Westley took me to see the priory grounds and the chapel. He was also thoroughly informative about the history of the place." Heat rises to my face as I say his name. I try to change the conversation by turning toward Marla. "What did you and Roger do today?"

Impeccably dressed in a formfitting red sheath dress, her dark hair pulled back tightly into a bun, Marla turns her unwavering eye toward me. "We spent the afternoon going through the village archives. I am working on wills right now and some of the local ones are kept there, going back to the fifteenth century. Who knows what's been lost to fires, floods, time . . . but they do have a nice collection of wills. They tell you so much about what people valued. Roger, too, is working on local documents."

"What are you finding in the wills? Is this the start of another book?" I ask, searching for something that will keep the conversation going. Befriending and impressing Marla would be a great outcome of this trip.

Marla flashes her blinding smile (seriously, how are her teeth so white and perfect?). "Yes, a new book. I am looking at bequests before and during the Reformation; I am really interested in whether the wills can tell us what side of events people were on. What people felt was worth leaving behind and passing on, especially outside of their families." She signals to Roger to refill her wine by lightly tapping the glass with her finger and catching his eye, raising an eyebrow. He obliges without a word. "Not that it matters much." Marla lowers her voice, confidingly, and I lean in to hear her. "The university is closing its department of medieval and early-modern studies. They are, believe it or not, opening a department of video-game design with that money. I'll be made redundant by this time next year."

I am both sad to hear Marla's news and delighted she has taken me into her confidence. "I am sorry," I say. "That is happening in the States, too. Administrators deciding that history is unimportant. Every week there's an article about the death of the humanities, usually next to an article bemoaning our citizens' inability to think and read critically."

"It is a few years earlier than I had hoped or planned to retire," Marla continues, "but maybe I can travel a bit. Perhaps I can come visit you in New York, Alison."

I nod enthusiastically and feel a rush of pleasure at the thought of shepherding Marla through the city, already noting which restaurants and museums she should see. Marla may be the best thing to come out of the C.C., I think.

"Welcome to the retirement club," says Roger, who has apparently been listening in, with a raised glass. "Start saving your pennies!" he adds bitterly.

"Indeed." Marla meets his eyes for a longer-than-normal beat and takes an extended sip of wine.

Roger abruptly shifts his attention to Charles, Brian, and Arjun. "And what of your excursion today? Did I see you headed toward the river?"

Charles nods. "Brian, Arjun, and I took a bike ride along the towpath, mostly discussing poetics in a new location—we may have had a pint at the King's Head. Also, I promised Dicky I'd get my ten thousand steps a day while I am here." He waves his wrist, fitness tracker clearly visible. "I'm close. I'll have to march in place before bed," he says with a laugh.

By dessert—"pudding!" Charles exclaims, clapping his hands like a happy child—we are all a little tipsy and a lot chattier. My frustration and annoyance with Westley (and that strange moment between us) has been if not forgotten, then mostly pushed away, and I am looking forward to the next day when we will begin giving our papers to the whole group and spending careful time discussing each one. I can see why this process produces such excellent work. Roger's first full day functions as a kind of bonding exercise, a way to see who will help your work be its best. I am especially looking forward to hearing Marla's thoughts tomorrow.

* * *

Most of us retire to the library after dinner, where jazz music plays softly and after-dinner drinks are served, and we all fall into informal chitchat, underscored by the inevitable one-upmanship of academics in a room (which collective noun for academics? a contention of scholars? a rivalry of critics? an antagonism of professors?).

Charles bows out, saying he needs to work a bit more on his paper after some of the discussion he had with Brian and Arjun today. I see him speaking to Alex at the door and then heading to another part of the manor house, no doubt needing some supplies for his work.

Maybe my nap has been *too* restorative because I am wide awake, and happily accept a drink (this time a Negroni, absolutely my drink of choice) before I wander over to talk to Arjun, who is looking at some of the books on the library shelves, beer in hand.

Like Charles, Arjun always appears to be well-dressed with just a bit of humor, an edge, unlike Roger's tweed, which he apparently wears without irony. Today, Arjun sports white tailored shorts and a deep-purple golf shirt, with cool-looking white-and-green sneakers that I can just as easily imagine on my more fashion-forward students.

"It's quite a good collection," he says, barely glancing at me, unable to take his eyes off the books in a habit that I understand all too well. People's bookshelves are the most telling thing about them—often more interesting than the people themselves.

"A few of these have never been cracked, I'd wager. Some nineteenth-century manor-house gentleman who bought them for show. I bet some of them have entirely uncut pages," he adds, referring to the early printing practice where pages were sealed together, then separated with a letter opener as the book was read.

"It's all of the bestsellers," Arjun continues as he picks up a slim volume of Edgar Allan Poe's short stories. "Ooh, this is quite a good one," he says as he flips through, "'The Cask of Amontillado.' You know it?"

"I read it a long time ago, but if it was written after 1600, it's a little late for me," I answer.

"It was 1846," says Arjun, looking at the inside of the book. "I can't remember all the details, except of course the horror of someone being drugged and walled in alive and left to rot." He shudders and tucks the book under his arm. "Maybe I'll revisit it tonight. This is as perfect a place as possible to read such a thing."

I smile. "How many times have you attended the Consortium, Arjun?"

He looks thoughtful. "Five, perhaps? They aren't yearly, as you know, not even biennial, so I'm not exactly sure. Just when Roger feels like assembling some luminaries. This year Roger is really shaking things up with the addition of you and Westley Charney." I can't tell if that's a compliment or a dig. He pauses before adding, "Although the year Marla and I showed up was the first time things were rattled here. Not all old white blokes. My kids were so little that first year and my wife was furious I was leaving for a week, but I couldn't pass up that opportunity."

"How old are your kids now?"

Arjun gestures to the empty settee, and once we are seated, he pulls his phone out to show me photos. "My daughter is twenty-six, a detective in Birmingham, and she now has a daughter—here is Reva; she just turned two. And my son is twenty-two. He is like me and a scholar, studying at King's College in London. Mathematician. So maybe not too much like me. He has a girlfriend and I tell him he needs to marry her, but he doesn't listen to me. How old are your children?"

"Boy-girl twins. Fourteen. Reva is lovely. It must be nice being a grandfather."

"It is. I will move close to them when I retire. I am sorry about the divorce. Academia does it to you," he says with some bitterness. "You spend so much time establishing and defending your turf that you no longer know how to trust people." He pauses and says almost to himself, "Even here."

Uninvited tears spring to my eyes and I simply nod. I feel like my problem was being too trusting of Pete, that we would weather the storm. I was the last to recognize that the marriage had crumbled. Even the twins looked at us with something like relief when we sat them down to say that Pete was moving out. And the extraction of him from my life has been painful, like pulling shards of glass out of one's skin.

Arjun allows me to compose myself while he takes the last sip of his beer. I am hopeful that he will stay and talk to me, especially when I am so clearly in need of some camaraderie, but instead he stands to go. "Speaking of retiring, I think I am ready to turn in for the night and to frighten myself with this book." He grins and holds up the book of Poe stories that includes "The Cask of Amontillado."

* * *

FORTUNATELY, NO SOONER has Arjun vacated the spot on the settee than Marla, as if she has intuited my loneliness, comes and joins me, carrying a glass of port. She turns her smile to me and lays a hand softly on my elbow, giving it a reassuring squeeze. "How are you finding this all so far? I suppose it can be a bit overwhelming the first time." Her kind voice holds the vestiges of an Austrian accent. I can't help assessing Marla's clothes. They are so beautifully tailored and smart, and the small studs in her ears are almost certainly real diamonds.

"So far, so good!" I chirp.

Leaning in, she says, "I'm very impressed with your work, Alison. I am glad we are finally meeting. I've been watching your career with interest from afar."

I can't help the genuine smile I feel spread across my face. "Oh, Marla, I am so impressed with yours. Your last book was such a masterpiece. I've consulted it a hundred times and each time learn something new."

"Thank you, Alison," Marla continues. "It's nice to have another woman here. One time Joanne Buringham came, but Roger was not impressed and did not invite her back. He can be finicky about those things. This session was thrown together a bit quickly after ManSock—it has been harder for Roger to find the funding he needs, so the C.C. is meeting less and less frequently. But something at ManSock made him decide to do it this summer. I suggested Calista when he asked us who to have here, and he had already decided on you, so I was looking forward to a group of three. Maybe next time we can make up half."

"I was looking forward to seeing Calista," I tell her, slotting away the information that Roger is likely auditioning me for a future Consortium. "I plan to email her and check in. I'm sure being here would have felt like a vacation without all her kids around."

Marla shrugs. "That is why I never had them. I did not want a distraction from the work. Although less work than a husband. They are the ones who need the most."

I laugh out loud before realizing that Marla is dead serious. "Well," I say, "I have two kids and an ex-husband, so I didn't learn my lesson."

"Ex-husband is better than husband," Marla says. She pauses before adding, "By the way, I wouldn't email Calista. You will simply remind her what she is missing here."

She takes one last sip, finishing her port, and leans over me as she stands up to leave, whispering, "Now, just keep finding lovers. That is the way to do it." A beat. "And some more advice from one woman to another," she says. "Let them underestimate you. Then you can get them when they least expect it." I am so surprised at these last comments that

I can't even answer. I see Marla anew as the elegant woman strides out of the room.

* * *

I'M CONTEMPLATING TURNING in just as Westley appears in Marla's spot. I wish he would leave me alone. Don't I? I am—annoyingly—deeply conscious of exactly how much space exists between us, as if my body deliberately ignores what my mind thinks.

"You look like you've seen a ghost," he says. "Did a headless nun walk by the window?"

I shake my head, so he offers, "If it was a man, there's also a story about a long-dead Victorian gardener."

"No ghost, although this place could use a gardener, ghostly or not. Just somewhat surprised by Marla is all," I reply, scanning the room for an escape. Everyone else seems to be deep in conversations that would involve awkward interrupting on my part. "She's spicier than I thought."

"You mean her and Roger?" Westley winks, then sees the total shock in my face. "Watch. He will excuse himself soon to go to his bed. But it will be her bed. Or she will already be waiting in his. As if we all don't know." He emphasizes this point by butting his shoulder gently into mine. Again, I feel the heat of the connection.

"What? I didn't know! He's still married, though, right?" Sweet, stuffy Roger, a philanderer? Argh. Although an affair hadn't been the cause of my own marriage's destruction, the fights that began its full breakdown were precipitated by Pete's close relationship with a colleague, his declaration that he had more in common with her than he had with me, that she *got* him in a way that I no longer did.

"Long married, but I reckon they have some sort of understanding. Her family needed money to keep up the house, his family had it, although apparently not enough. It helped for a while. Only recently have they started letting other people use it for retreats like this, weddings and things, although of course Roger has always held the Consortium here. I think his wife wants to sell it now, but Roger would never let it go. They've dismissed most of the staff—you noticed the gardener is gone, once upon a time there was a housekeeper. It's just Mrs. Bunch and Alex doing all the upkeep and whatever Roger can put a bandage on."

I look at Westley, sure that my expression betrays my deep confusion. “Wait, what? This is actually Roger’s house? I thought it was just rented out for the conference.”

Roger stands up across the room and waves good night to us. “Early day tomorrow!” he calls on his way out.

Westley winks at me again. “Told you so. Almost ten minutes after Marla to the second. They’re not fooling anyone.” He scoots in closer to me and says conspiratorially, “But no, this isn’t Roger’s house, it’s Janine’s—his wife—and her brothers’. She was Janine Pitlock before she became Janine Shefield, and this was the Pitlocks’ home after it was the Vale family’s. But the family haven’t lived here since maybe 1980. It was sitting in disrepair until Janine’s marriage to Roger, whose family made a lot of money in America. Pittsburgh, maybe? I can never remember. Since his retirement, he spends more time here than he does at his home with Janine. He’s desperate to save the place.”

I finish my drink, taking this all in. Taking him in. “Well, Westley,” I say, standing up, afraid of where the conversation will turn if I stay any longer. “You’ve been very informative today. See you in the morning.”

He reaches up and grabs my hand, and his eyes meet mine. “I’m counting on it,” he says slowly, meaningfully. I don’t know how to respond to that, so I say nothing and am saved by the soft buzz of his phone indicating a message.

“I’ll walk out with you,” he says, looking at his phone and then up toward the door. I rehearse in my mind how to gracefully say good night at the top of the stairs, since our rooms are adjacent, but am saved the awkwardness, because as I turn to climb them, he heads down the hall, where I can see Alex waiting for him.

Hampton Court, June 1529

Elizabeth had grown used to being with Bocking and a few other monks, friars, and priests who were part of her traveling group: Father Henry Gold and the brothers Hugh Rich, Richard Risby, and John Dering. These were men who, like Bocking, firmly believed in her holiness and the power of her visions to right the country from its ill-chosen path. Bocking liked being the head of this band. If they were near Rochester, Fisher would sometimes join them, which Elizabeth could see that Bocking liked less. She did, too.

They frequently traveled to abbeys and priories in new towns, and with little urging she would shout her visions out in the street. She preferred walking than traveling by boat; as they walked, with a packhorse from Bocking's monastery kicking dust up alongside them, the word would spread that she was coming, and people would run to the road to see her, to give her small gifts or to ask for her blessing. She would lay her hand on theirs and, if the person pleased her, she would say, "I bless you." If she did not like the look of a person, she would sometimes say, "Your time is short for penance," and watch as the alarm on their face betrayed their secret sins.

The crowds were growing larger as more learned about her powers. She loved the throngs who wanted nothing more than to touch her, as if she were a saint, as if she were Jesus. Her days on the farm, at her father's mean house, these all seemed so far behind her. The calluses on her hands were entirely erased. So, too, the quiet, meek voice she had always spoken in. These masses of people called her "holy" and "a living saint," and she pushed down any feelings that told her that was not true. She had been blessed by God with a vision. What did it matter that there had been only one great one? Bocking's lessons had included so many visions from so many holy women who preceded her that she knew what Bocking wanted her to say. What God wanted her to say.

On this day Fisher was with them and they were headed to Hampton Court for an audience with the king—he had taken over the cardinal's former home. The three were walking the last mile together so that the people of Richmond upon Thames could see that the Holy Maid was to be received by Henry at the court.

Her habit weighed heavily on her in the warm summer air. They had been nearly two weeks without rain, and dust billowed up around them in great clouds as they walked, getting into Elizabeth's mouth and bringing tears to her eyes. One of the townspeople cried, "Look! She weeps to approach the palace!" and excited voices followed. "She knows what sin festers there," shouted one woman, and the crowd murmured its assent. Elizabeth bowed her head to the crowd and allowed the tears to spill down her cheeks.

As they approached, Fisher spoke to Bocking, quietly. "Wolsey's position is rather compromised since you last brought the Maid to this palace. He has still not secured the annulment and the king is enraged." Elizabeth noted this news. Wolsey, diminished? Even a cardinal-chancellor is subject to Fortune's wheel. She tried to imagine the great man as anything less than he had been on her last voyage to Hampton Court. She conjured one of the naked figures in the priory's hellmouth, a red cardinal's biretta on his head, the chancellor medal a noose.

Bocking's voice interrupted her thoughts. "Surely, taking his home was enough of a punishment? I am certain that Henry will realize he and the cardinal cannot defy the papal decision, that it is a binding word of God."

"I am not so certain," responded Fisher. "These are tenuous times. Henry has asked to see the Maid and she must tell him to be true to the faith. Until the pope has sanctioned it, the king must stay married to the queen. And if Pope Clement does not—he is under tremendous pressure from Spain and King Charles V for the marriage, and thus the alliance between Spain and England, to continue—then the king must abide by this decision."

As they arrived, it was immediately clear to Elizabeth that Hampton Court was much changed since her last visit there. The crowd now was so loud that the voices of the men were drowned out, and some of their small retinue had to forge a path through the bodies of people trying to touch Elizabeth, so that the Maid, the monk, and the bishop could make their way to the palace. The path cleared only when they reached the gates, held open by two royal guards, halberds with their menacing axe blades in their hands, ready to protect His Majesty. Elizabeth recognized their Tudor livery: red coats with the crest of a crowned, shining Tudor rose, gold thread expertly stitched. She imagined rooms full of women whose job it must be to keep the livery pristine, to clean and stitch and mend until their raw fingers bled Tudor red.

Everywhere there were men working: in the garden, on the roof, crawling all over the exterior of the palace like ants drawn to a dropped piece of bread. The inside was filled with builders and laborers as well. As they were led through the palace, with sawdust swirling in the air, Elizabeth noticed that walls she knew had been there the last time were now gone, as the former rooms seemed to have transformed into large open spaces and courtyards. Hampton Court had been opulent, but since Henry assumed occupancy, it was resplendent. Fit for a king. Every inch that was not covered in workers or scaffolding was already swathed in gold or rich red silks or gemstones.

Emblems of the Tudor rose, its five petals of the House of York nestled in the five petals of the House of Lancaster, were everywhere: carved into the wood, the focal point of the tapestries, painted on every item she saw. Men hauling timber logs hurried through the hallways, and servants carried vases and paintings and folded silks. Servants dressed in the livery of other noblemen were there, too, adding to the hubbub of the royal household and the many courtiers who were part of it.

There were so many people bustling about, bringing items from one room to the other, that Elizabeth could not imagine where they all slept or how they were all fed. There must have been ten servants to every person in the household. She watched a chambermaid rush by, carrying a tray with remnants of a meal, cheeses and fruits, sawdust clinging to her white apron and cap. The dishes were golden and the goblets glass; Elizabeth did not know such things even existed.

She was now far from her life as a servant on the Cobb farm, but it was not hard to remember what it felt like to labor for someone else. She knew that the maid and her friends would eat those scraps once they were out of sight, the way she and Edith would take what was left at the end of the day from Cobb's meal, hoping for some meat. She wondered if these women would later drink from those goblets of glass, far from their employers' eyes.

Now all her labor was for herself. And God.

Cardinal Wolsey met them in the hallway. He was still tall but had lost much of the heft that Elizabeth held in her memory. He had declined in other ways, too—his eyes were less fierce, sadder, almost as if a milky film had settled along their perimeter. And his posture now curved forward in the manner of an older man. Although she had not liked him the first time they met, she still felt a pang of pity at seeing him so changed.

"How does the king find his new home?" asked Fisher. It was clear that even he was impressed, or appalled, his eyes widening and jaw hanging slightly open as he took in the enlarged surroundings.

"He likes it well. There are new courtyards. New gardens. He is adding to the kitchens. And building a tennis court," Wolsey said gruffly, just a trace of sour anger underneath. "There are some thirty lodging suites now. He is building apartments for Anne Boleyn." Elizabeth startled at the name of the king's concubine said so plainly; she had heard people say that the woman was a witch and a heretic. "Come, we are meeting him in the Chapel Royal. We will pray together." Wolsey led the way, with Fisher and Bocking behind him, trailed by Elizabeth, as they exited the palace and walked through a small cloister before entering the chapel. As they reached the door, Wolsey turned to her, pulling himself straighter so that his height was somewhat replenished, and held up a warning finger. This was the Wolsey she knew.

"Do not speak," he warned, staring into her eyes. She stared back. Turning around, he said over his shoulder, "Also, do not look at His Majesty the king. Kneel immediately. Eyes to floor always."

She opened her mouth to respond, still floating from the energy of the crowds outside, filled with her own import, but then she thought better and closed it again, following the cardinal into the chamber.

The king was a giant of a man, in width if not in height, and the rich fabrics swathing his form made him seem even larger: the white silk frill of his shirt around his neck, the black velvet doublet decorated with pearls and other gemstones, trimmed in white ermine. Elizabeth had only ever seen the fur on the animal itself and never when it had its white coat. Although she knew to keep her eyes on the ground, she bent her head down but tried to look up and see the man. Sweat dotted his head underneath his jeweled cap, pearls and rubies between glinting silver thread. As she knelt, she was fully engulfed in his shadow, the sun streaming in behind Henry's back. She had never felt so small.

"Our Maid of Kent," said Henry, in a deep, resonant voice that hinted at his famed musicality. "You have visions of purgatory?"

She nodded, eyes to the ground.

"Is Our Majesty, King Henry VIII, in your visions?" Another deep voice. Hoarser. Wolsey. Fighting the urge to lift her head, she studied the yellow Tudor roses in the red tiles that lined the chapel floor.

She knew that the king was a great sinner, that he was putting the country in peril. What would God want her to say? What would Bocking? She spoke in a rush. "I see everyone who has offended God, Your Grace. Surely, our king would not offend him." She paused, remembering what she had heard her advisors saying as they had walked together to the court. How could she warn him of his peril? "These are tenuous times. Stay true to the faith."

"Do we not remain in God's favor?" Henry's voice.

She heard Bocking inhale as if he were to speak and saw the king put up a hand to silence him. He wanted to hear from her. From Elizabeth. A king wanted to hear what Elizabeth had to say.

She could feel her voice catching as she repeated her words, hoping that what she said was what was needed. "Stay true to the faith and you shall remain so."

Wolsey spoke up then. "Very well," he growled. "Let us pray together. Pray for the soul of His Majesty, Henry VIII, by the Grace of God, King of England, France, and Lord of Ireland, Defender of the Faith." Elizabeth could not fail to notice that Wolsey's voice grew loudest at "Defender of the Faith," which was the honor bestowed on the king by the pope.

The four men joined Elizabeth and knelt to face the altar. She closed her eyes and prayed as she was told, holding her position even as she heard the others standing and speaking around her. She could not make out the words fully, but it sounded as if Wolsey was admonishing her guardians. She heard the word "reckless" more than once in his deep, hoarse whisper. She kept her eyes closed as she heard footsteps leaving the room. When she finally opened her eyes, there was only Bocking, who took her somewhat roughly by the elbow and led her out.

Vale House Manor, June 2023, Day 3

The next morning, I somehow manage to wake up and run at six o'clock, avoiding the dreaded knock from Alex, who never fails to startle me. I slept fine although I was woken up twice by Charles's door, which slammed when it shut around midnight and again at one. Late-night billiards? Who knows. The run wakes me up and I follow the worn looping path that circles the priory grounds twice—about two miles each time around—and stop at a half-standing stone wall not far from the church to stretch.

The sky is already fully light, although white with clouds. It feels good to move my body, to breathe the cool and damp morning air. From this vantage point atop a hill, I can take in much of the surrounding area. A narrow, winding road leads from the priory to the village, curving past the manor and a handful of other houses until it reaches the pub. Because I arrived that first night in the dark, I haven't yet seen the village up close. But from where I stand, it doesn't look like much. Farther on, the spires of Canterbury Cathedral rise into the sky. My taxi ride was maybe thirty minutes from the Canterbury East train station, so it would have been a walkable distance to the cathedral for Elizabeth and the others who lived here, but a long one.

Etched into the stone wall are years of graffiti: from medieval crosses and daisy wheels, meant to ward off evil spirits, all the way to FOR A GOOD TIME, CALL NIGEL, followed by a phone number. Poor Nigel. I doubt he was that good a time. I decide to see if I can get into the church, hoping to experience it alone before what promises to be an intellectually exhausting day. Just as I am about to reach it, I see Roger leaving from the church's side door.

"Roger!" I call, waving, wondering when he left Marla's bed.

His eyes widen and his voice seems unnaturally loud as he replies, "Alison, hello. I was just coming by to make sure the church was unlocked in case any of you wanted to explore today. I believe you said you wanted to do a further study?"

"Yes, thank you. I was going to pop in right now before my shower. If you don't mind a sweaty companion, do you want to go back in with me? Westley showed me the transi tomb, but we didn't have time or good enough light to really take in the wall painting or the rood screen."

Roger gestures inside as he holds the door open. "Of course. It's quite remarkable. The church had few repairs over the years, so that's another item on the property we need to fix eventually. Preserving the past is a full-time job—the present keeps relentlessly rolling over it."

"I understand this property is in your wife's family?" I venture.

Roger nods. "Yes. For now. She and her meddling brothers are always fighting about it. They want to turn it into some goddamned Airbnb nightmare or sell it to the highest bidder—some London financier—and I, or *we*, rather, would like to keep it as it is. A family retreat that can also serve for small groups like this one. But the upkeep of a place like this is murder, as you can imagine."

He stops in front of the remains of the immense wall painting; Roger is a tall man, but he is dwarfed by the image, whose once brightly colored pigments are faded to pale pinks and grays. "It's fascinating to imagine this place was once completely covered in color," he says. "What a horror to sit here and think of hell swallowing you whole. Surely, it inspired many a penance."

I take the whole of the image in.

"A few churches throughout England still have these hellmouth wall paintings," Roger continues, "although in the Middle Ages there were many more. They all feature a giant beast." This one looks like some kind of cat-bear-wolf hybrid to me, with fangs, glowing eyes, and mouth agape with flames inside. "Among the flames, as you see, are the damned people interspersed with devils who torture them in various macabre ways."

The hellmouth covers the entire north wall of the nave, depicting thirty or forty doomed souls, many naked and bloody. Some give clear indication of their earthly lives through their headwear—there is even a bishop with his mitre and a king with his crown, reminding the viewer that no one is immune from the punishments of hell. Six horned demons are impaling the condemned, throwing fire at them, fornicating.

There are several nuns, all in Benedictine habit, a nod to the priory and the women who would have prayed in that place. One of the nuns has her mouth open, with flames coming from it, eyes wide in horror. Another holds a flaming book. The images are *terrific* in its truest sense—inspiring terror and awe both.

Above the hellmouth in gothic letters is written *DE DIE AUTEM ILLA ET HORA NEMO SCIT, NEQUE ANGELI CAELORUM, NISI SOLUS PATER*. "But of that day and hour no one knows, not the angels in heaven, no one but the Father alone," I translate aloud. Roger looks at me closely.

"You have been warned," he says, laughing darkly. "We are lucky the whole mural has survived."

"The letters are fairly clear, if flaking a bit. Has this been restored? The Victorians?"

"Oh, thank God, no," he says. "The Victorians were whitewashing everything they could get their hands on. The remoteness of this place seems to have saved it, as well as the church's other interesting features. But the original wall painting is probably early thirteenth century, and at least the words and some of the images were touched up in the mid sixteenth. Just around when your Barton was here. Maybe they gussied it up for pilgrims wanting to see the Holy Maid." He seems to draw closer, studying me again. It's unnerving. "Actually, I wonder if this portion here"—he points to the image of the nun breathing fire, then the one holding the burning book—"may be alluding to Elizabeth. A warning against the dangers of prophets and prophecies."

I look more closely at the nuns. The one breathing fire is twisted in anguish, her hands splayed, reaching for aid that will not come, her unseeing eyes wide open. The nun with the book is also contorted in pain, her hands seemingly unable to relinquish the flaming pages she holds. Although she wears a disheveled habit, she wears no veil, and the prominent white streak in her hair mirrors my own.

"It's somewhat different from the rood screen," he says, keeping his eyes on me as he ushers me to the wooden barrier that separates the small choir and altar from the pews. "Here the bottom half is intact, and the images remain."

Rood screens, sometimes called choir or chancel screens, served the purpose of enhancing the mystery of the mass. The chancel and the nave of the church are separated by it, so the religious activities of the priests on one side remained hidden from the laypeople in the congregation. "Rood" was the Old English word for "cross," and the screen usually contains a giant crucifix near the roof. These structures were largely dismantled during the Reformation, leaving only the bottom half in many churches, as it is here. They are often decorated with images of saints or stories from the Bible—ways for an illiterate audience to engage with the lessons from the pulpit.

Each panel in the priory rood screen still has a saint painted on it, although some of them are so corrupted or defaced, undoubtedly scratched out during the Reformation, that it is hard to tell who they were.

"These were also touched up—if not entirely repainted—at the same time the words painted on the wall were," Roger says, moving along the width of the screen and pointing out a few of the surviving images as he does. "There are quite a few women, which makes sense, given the church's attachment to the priory. St. Barbara with her tower, St. Catherine with her wheel . . ." Each image contains a halo, indicating sainthood and martyrdom. "And here's the Virgin herself."

The image of the Virgin Mary is the most beautiful, with faint traces of blue, red, and gold pigment clinging to the wood. Her face is the only one fully intact, and she holds an infant Jesus in her arms. "Then we have St. Thomas Becket, St. Francis, St. Benedict, of course, given that the priory was Benedictine. This last is unidentified, but in exquisite condition."

I kneel down to look at the unnamed woman saint, who holds a book in one hand and a skull in the other. She wears the habit of a Benedictine nun, and her eyes are cast upward toward heaven rather than demurely down, as the others' are. Her arm is outstretched, as if half in an embrace. Her gold halo is encrusted with jewels: rubies, diamonds, pearls. "How curious. I have never seen a saint with this image," I say, turning to Roger, who is still watching me so closely; I again feel unsettled. Above the saint's head, in small golden letters but in a style similar to the inscription above the hellmouth, are the words *CUMQUE ISSENT UT SEPELIRENT EAM NON INVENERUNT NISI CALVARIAM.* This time, I keep the translation to myself. "And when they went to bury her, they found nothing but the skull."

* * *

As we head out, Roger says, “Come this way around the church. I’d like to show you one more interesting feature. You will like it.”

We walk to the side of the building, where there is a kind of peephole, about six inches square, that opens into the church. With its elaborate stone frame, the hole was obviously built into the brick. Roger peers in, then steps aside for me. “Take a gander.”

I don’t need to bend down far to look into the church. From this vantage point, I can see the altar and virtually all of the hellmouth; if I move slightly to the side, I can make out the transi tomb.

“A leper’s squint,” says Roger. “There aren’t too many around here. This was part of the original church in the thirteenth century, and when they rebuilt parts, they kept it.”

“I’ve never seen one.” I look through again. “These were positioned so that lepers could take part in the mass and be blessed without interacting with any people?” How would that feel, I wonder, to be such an outsider to a community?

“Yes, that’s right,” Roger says. “They were considered dirty and cursed and were more or less excommunicated from society, but the squint is a charity extended to them. They had been members of this parish once, after all. They assumed one’s sins caused the illness.”

“I think it’s quite sad, in its way,” I say. “To think that there were exiles standing here, seeing the community in which they had once participated come together for mass.” I shiver thinking about it. “And then to look in and see the hellmouth devouring the damned and knowing you were one of them.”

“And you, Alison,” asks Roger, “do you have faith?”

“I believe in the archives,” I say, smiling. “In uncovering the past to understand our present. But if you are asking me whether I have religion?” I shake my head, slowly. “I do not.”

Roger smiles and shrugs, stepping toward the winding, overgrown path that leads to the manor. “Faith and religion are not always aligned. That is often the root of the problem.” He smiles. “We should get going or we will miss breakfast. And it is hard to think on an empty stomach.”

We walk side by side up the path toward the house. As we approach, my gaze goes to my bedroom window, right above the garden. Just as I look, the curtain on my window closes abruptly.

"Roger, would anyone be in my room? I'm quite sure I saw the curtain move."

He stops in his tracks. He looks up at the window, then at me. "No, no, it must be the wind. Quite drafty in this old house." But as we enter the front door, I note how still the air is this morning.

St. Sepulchre's Priory, January 1532

Elizabeth lay in her cell, listening to the wind howling outside and the murmured prayers of the sisters around her. She had a fever and kept shrugging off the blankets they wrapped around her. Sister Maria was blotting the Maid's brow with a cool wet cloth; someone whispered to Sister Catherine that she must summon the prioress.

And then the dream came, tinged with fire like the fever that burned within her.

She saw hell. A place without hope. These souls were not waiting for release; they were resigned to everlasting turmoil. She saw the giant beast of the hellmouth devouring its prey. Burning in the center of that mouth was that woman—Anne Boleyn. The concubine. The woman behind the king's request for an annulment of his marriage to Catherine of Aragon. Next to Anne was Henry himself. They were burning. And if the king burns, England burns.

Suddenly Elizabeth sat upright, terrifying the sisters, who had assumed she was near her last breath. "Heretics!" she shouted, unseeing, as Philippa hurried to her side. "I have been to hell, and I have seen the heretics. The king! The king! And his whore. When they are married, he will die a villain's death. I have seen the king at mass, and an angel is giving the host to all assembled. The angel stops in front of the king and tells him there is no Eucharist for such a man. No salvation for that adulterer." And then she swooned, collapsing back onto the bed and falling into slumber.

Philippa looked around at the startled sisters. "Tend to her," she told them, dread settling like a shroud on her shoulders.

* * *

PHILIPPA WROTE TWO short letters, her eyes straining to see the paper and pen properly in the weak candlelight of her quarters. Elizabeth's statement was unsettling and seemed to her to have the quality of a fever dream rather than a true vision, but she had to report it, especially since there were so many witnesses. She feared that the girl's words would galvanize both her supporters and detractors. This would lead to no good end. If her words became widely known, it would enrage the king. And then punishment would rain down on the priory.

Father Edward,

I am summoning you to the priory today to meet with your spiritual charge, Elizabeth. She has been gripped by a terrible fever and has had a new, violent vision or dream concerning the king. I witnessed it, as did four of the sisters, and we can attest to her words. I leave it to you to determine its veracity and whether it should be widely reported. I believe her fever has broken and the Maid will recover.

Yours in Christ,
The prioress, Philippa Jonys

My dear Lady Vale,

I fear the tides will soon turn against the priory as the visions of the Maid have become dangerous. I believe your idea of safeguarding your treasures and mine in the face of this uncertain future is timely. May we meet again?

Yours in Christ,
Mother Philippa

Vale House Manor, June 2023, Day 3

Giving papers at the C.C. has a very different feel than at any other conference I've attended. Although we've all written our work in advance, almost everyone has continued to edit—the conversations, ideas, and sights here all subtly work to recast our research. Everything *seems* casual—we're all tucked into chairs in the library, coffee or tea in hand—but the questions are detailed and pointed, thought out in a way that larger venues make impossible. Clearly this is why the volumes that the C.C. produces hold such valuable scholarship.

"Did Bocking deserve to hang with Elizabeth?" I ask the group rhetorically, as my opening. "Perhaps. He was, as I've outlined, not just an ordinary monk. Oxford educated, he was selected by Archbishop Warham to investigate the mysterious reports of a farmhand's vision. He was at that time the cellarer of the nearby Christ Church priory." I gesture outside as if I know where Bocking's monastery once stood, which I do not. I'm sure Westley does and would love to tell me. "Barton's book, as I will demonstrate today, has many references and allusions that are likely beyond the education of a local girl. I believe that many of the ideas at least originated with her spiritual advisor, if they were not authored by him."

After going over some of the geographic points I wanted to make, I turn to one page of Barton's book. "We can see here how much seems to be Bocking's own interpretation of what Elizabeth had said or where he glossed one or two of her words with an appropriate biblical citation, effectively making the book his own.

"It is no wonder that Elizabeth lost the support of nearly all the prominent Catholics toward the end of her life, including Bishop Fisher, although Bocking and a few other priests remained by her side at the end. The queen Catherine of Aragon refused to ever meet with her, clearly believing her a charlatan from the start and not a helper to her cause with Henry. The Catholic humanist Thomas More eventually spoke about her as if she were mentally ill and dreadfully led astray, though of course he would have the same fate as she—and his supposed backing of Barton would be one of the accusations levied against him in his conviction of treason. Finally, Cromwell's men continued discrediting rumors after her execution. Just as she was manipulated by men in life, so in death."

There is a round of appreciative nods, light applause, and a thumbs-up from Charles before hands are raised with questions. I call on Marla first. "Yes, Marla?"

"Thank you, Alison. Very illuminating. I have seen in my study of wills in this region that several local families were gifting items to the priory, and that this giving increased in number and in value when Elizabeth was there. Do you think there's a connection? Even if, as you say, the prioress was not a great fan, was this perhaps the reason she continued to support having her there?"

"Oh yes, certainly, Marla. It's clear that Barton greatly increased the visibility and wealth of the priory, although that also likely made it an easy target for its early dissolution. When Elizabeth's prophecies proved false—that is, Henry VIII married Anne Boleyn and did not, in fact, die—I am sure the prioress would have liked nothing better than to turn her out. But if, as your research will show, the money kept coming in, I can see why she wouldn't." I pause, thinking how much this information would enhance my book, and add, "I would love to see what you have found."

Marla says, "I would love to collaborate with you," as Roger's hand shoots up.

"Dear Alison," he nearly bellows, "have you found any ciphers or acrostics in the book, or another kind of puzzle or hidden message? They were so popular in those pamphlets."

"Gosh, Roger, I haven't even really looked for that yet—perhaps you can look through the images with me this afternoon? Maybe you can spot some?"

"I'd be delighted." He smiles broadly. "I have a follow-up question, if you don't mind."

"Sure, go ahead."

"Are any of the visions you have read about the manor house, or specifically about the grounds here? Do some of them seem genuinely prophetic to you about the future?" He leans forward, stroking his beard with his hand.

"No, nothing I read mentions the priory. But this is only part of the story. We know from a sermon at her condemnation that she had a second book that was never printed, so who knows what was in that. And, of course, other prophecies may have been heard but never written down." Looking disappointed, Roger leans over and whispers something to Westley.

I think this is a good ending note and hope that there are not any more questions, but of course, there is one more hand in the air. "Brian? Yes?"

"This is actually more of a comment than a question," he begins. Of course. How many men have I heard give that harmless-sounding qualifier before they eviscerate the basis of the talk or discredit some of its evidence? "I find it hard to believe that the prioress had nothing to do with the book and its publication. Once Elizabeth was in her charge, even with the power of Bocking and Fisher behind her, Philippa must have had significant input in what went on with her and what imprimatur they were giving the priory by association."

"You're saying I'm not giving Philippa enough credit here?" I've never understood the (usually male) impulse to flat-out disagree with a paper. Why not just say something like this privately later? Why bring it up in front of everyone just to show off?

"Right. I mean, Elizabeth could not read, but Philippa surely could. She was connected to the great families here and likely dealt directly with Bocking concerning the Holy Maid. I just think you should not be so confident that this is only about men manipulating a young woman. Women may have manipulated her, too." He leans back, clearly satisfied.

"Well," I counter, "we can also see Philippa as working with what she had. She may have been using Elizabeth for her own ends—bolstering the priory, filling its coffers. She may have just left the spiritual side of Elizabeth to Bocking and his ilk. After all, she did not have a noose around her neck in the end."

* * *

"TELL ME ABOUT the clock in the church tower," I say to Roger as we head into the dining room for lunch. "It looks very old. Does it still work?"

He shakes his head. "No, sadly. It doesn't. Who knows how long it's been broken? We have some village records from the nineteenth century that refer to the 'stopped clock' of the priory church, but no earlier records from the priory because of the dissolution and the manor because of—"

"—the fire," I finish. "What date is it given?"

"Ah," he says, "good question." Roger looks at me sidewise in his unnerving way, as if trying to read something in my eyes. "It's sixteenth century."

Marla interjects, "Your Elizabeth looked up at that clock, Alison, thinking about the *tick, tick, tick* of her impending doom perhaps."

"And hearing the bells marking the canonical hours of prayer," I say, liking that Marla thought of Elizabeth as mine.

"It is another one of the things we would like to restore here, should we ever get the funds. Lots of these clocks from that time were restored in the 1950s and '60s, but the Pitlock family was already down on its luck then and that is not where they decided to spend their money. But it is still so pretty to look at," Roger says.

Just before the lunch is served—small delicate sandwiches, the kind you imagine in a fancy afternoon tea, and a cold asparagus soup that is a welcome contrast to the rising heat of the day—Westley comes in and has a quick whispered conversation with Roger, leaning over his chair, his hand on his shoulder. Then he comes and sits down next to me. "What were you off doing?" I ask.

He shrugs and says, "Just running some errands. Roger said you are interested in the clock. I could have shown you the bell tower yesterday. I would really love to show it to you. We can go another day—tomorrow?—if you would like."

"Sure," I answer, automatically. "I'd like that." Wait, what? I want to take back the words almost as soon as they come out of my mouth. Would I like that? I think I might, but I don't want to. I open my mouth to qualify my answer, to add a "maybe," but he is already talking to Charles about soccer.

* * *

THE AFTERNOON IS set aside for information sharing. I pass along my images to Roger, who is looking for what may be hidden in the text, and Marla gives me stacks of copies of wills that she found in the local archives. Westley's paper is tomorrow, so he decides to sift through the wills with me as they may have some bearing on the local legends he is pursuing.

On the one hand, I can't deny that there remains the heat of something physical between us, so I enjoy this proximity. But on the other hand, I still so acutely remember the feeling of leaving Oxford that summer without so much as a shrug from Westley. Whatever I had imagined was between us meant something different to him. And then the next time I saw his name, it was in a scathingly critical review of my book. I scoot my chair a little farther away from him.

"What can the wills tell us?" I ask, hating to be in an area outside of my depth but desperate to glean what I can from Marla's expertise. I feel so lucky to have this week to see her work and get to know her.

Marla puts her hand on my arm. "I am so glad you asked, Alison. Most medieval and early-modern wills are formulaic and somewhat sparse—they say the name, place, and occupation of the will-makers, usually men, because the rules of coverture dictated their wives were 'covered' under their husbands, ordinarily, but some wealthy women and widows had their own, and then the few items of value—money, lands—that were to be distributed after their deaths. Occasionally, some lucky scholar will come across a gem like that in Shakespeare's will, where he famously left his wife, Ann, his 'second-best bed.' Remind me to email you some references that may be useful to your work." She removes her hand, but only after another encouraging smile that makes me feel that she sees my work as worthy of her help. She then taps her finger on the stack of copies I am holding. "Nearly all of the ones that I found are made in the same scratchy hand, indicating some local scribe whom everyone commissioned to do the work."

Westley takes the copies from my hands—did his fingers skim mine intentionally?—and reads the wills out loud to me, and I write down what is relevant. Marla is right that many of the bequests were to the priory. More than I would expect for such a small place.

"Here's one—Henry Wilson bequeathed three calves of a year old to the priory along with four pewter dishes," he reads. "Oh, here's another one—William Appleby gave a goose, a gander, and some bedding to the sisters." He flips through more pages, scanning down for a reference to St. Sepulchre's. "John Proudman gave them fifty pounds! Blimey, that's a lot of money. . . . Henry Tailor gives forty pounds to each of his daughters, but only when they get married, and five pounds to the priory. . . . Two silver spoons from Richard Baker . . ."

He pauses. "Oh, this is interesting, a chest of sundry items donated to the priory from Lady Agnes Vale! Well, well, I guess she wanted to make good in her own backyard. It doesn't say what the items were." He sits back. "That's the last of it."

"No second-best bed?" I joke. But Westley isn't looking at me; he's staring out the window, biting his bottom lip in thought, a habit I note he hasn't lost in the intervening years. He looks back down at the last will he is holding.

"Lady Agnes Vale," he says quietly. "I haven't read her first name before. She's of that era when all was lost to the fire. Literally all the family documents from that time are gone. This is a lucky find." He reads off the other items on the list. "Her handkerchiefs, some linen, gowns of various colors, a brass pot. These were all willed to her grandchildren, Alister and Margaret. It seems that the chest and its unknown contents is the most interesting item there. . . . And the date of this document is 1533. . . ." He trails off, but his eyes then brighten up and he says, "Oh!"

"Oh what?" I'm trying to keep up with whatever calculations he is running in his head, but the date has no special significance to me.

"This may be our last Lady Vale. I think the first postfire document we have is the ownership of the house in Margaret Pitlock's name." He opens up a file on his computer and shows me documents he has uploaded. "See here, Margaret Pitlock, née Vale, inherited the property and it became part of her husband's estate."

He turns back to the will he's holding. "Anyway, it's an interesting will. And look"—he hands me the copy—"it's in a different hand. She either wrote it herself or found another scribe who was not a professional."

Indeed, the hand is shakier, more hesitant. Someone who was clearly literate but perhaps out of practice. "Maybe she didn't want her business so widely known?"

"Yes. It would make sense after the Reformation, since they were

Catholic and had to keep to themselves while the country and its laws turned toward the Church of England, but this is early. I wonder if we can figure out Agnes's secrets."

* * *

JUST AS I start restacking the copies of the wills to return to Marla, Roger shouts triumphantly, "I believe I have found one!" He beckons us to his side. "I knew there should be something inside this book—they loved puzzles in that era. And look here," he says, pointing at a page. "It is an acrostic prayer, using the first letter of each line."

The lyric is supposedly one of Elizabeth's visions, perhaps invented or elaborated on by Bocking. I read it aloud:

"Venerate our Mother, seated
At the side of Jhesu, our meek other
Locking inside our heartchest the
Emeralds, rubies, and pearls of our devotion."

"See," Roger says excitedly as he points out the first letters of each line, which are capitalized and larger than the others. "Look at the initial letters here: V-A-L-E. Vale. This connects this family to the priory, or at least to Elizabeth."

"So interesting," I muse. "I wonder if they were somehow the patrons of Elizabeth's book? Helped pay for copies to be printed and distributed?"

"Possibly," Westley says, drawing the word out slowly, his brow furrowed. "The few records we have indicate they weren't a family that was very interested in art and culture, or no more than any other family of means would have been. This would have been a nice way to establish a link to the priory and to Elizabeth without being too showy about it."

"Perhaps Bocking rearranged or tweaked her vision a bit when he was writing it down so that the cipher worked. Lots of authors did that kind of thing," Roger says, as he expands the image on the screen so that the V-A-L-E is even more prominent.

"You know," muses Wes, "the few works the Vale family collected over the centuries were sold off, or of course destroyed in the fire, but a precious few are at a museum in Canterbury. If you would like, we can go see those before our evening's excursion. I know the collection well." He looks at me expectantly.

Of course he does. "Sure," I say somewhat reluctantly. I'm not sure at all. I tell myself that I will go for the research, certainly not for the company.

"Lovely idea," agrees Roger. "I'll join you." He slaps both hands on the table and stands up.

"I will join as well," Marla declares. She hadn't appeared to be listening to the exchange, seemingly lost in whatever she was reading on her computer screen, but I am pleased she will be coming and relieved I will not be alone with Westley for either the car ride or the museum visit. At least I think this feeling is relief. Not disappointment.

St. Sepulchre's Priory, December 1532

"It's onyx and gold," Lady Vale said, handing Philippa the necklace, as if she would not recognize its worth. The stones felt cool and heavy in her palm. "Can you hide it with the others?" she asked. "I will make a gift to the priory, of course."

This is how it worked when Agnes Vale came to meet with Philippa. Agnes would bring some treasure from the household, something she did not want her husband or her shrewish daughter-in-law to have, something that had been hers before her marriage and that had become the property of her husband when her father shook her betrothed's hand all those years ago, signaling the marriage Agnes had never wanted.

Each time, Philippa would take the item from Agnes and hide it, along with some of the gems she had received for an audience with Elizabeth. Then Lady Vale would make a real donation to the priory, something they could keep. Because the bargain they had made meant that someday Lady Vale would ask for her treasures back.

"Your husband and your daughter-in-law will not simply disappear, you understand," Philippa cautioned. "I can safeguard these for you, but when they are given back, they will again be his or hers. There will be papers in your household that outline the inheritances. There will be a will."

Agnes waved her hand as if to move a fly away from her face. "I have made my own will," she said, registering the shock on Philippa's face. "And I will take care of the other papers. Do not worry. John has barely a year left in him. He had passed forty-seven winters when we married. He has near seventy now. He is so infirm that the servants must change his bedsheets every morning." She had always been repulsed by him but was more so now that he had no control of his bladder, drooled when he ate the food the chambermaid had to cut into tiny pieces, and looked at her with watery, unseeing eyes.

"And the young Lady Vale?" Philippa pressed. She did not like how Agnes seemed to savor the impending death of her husband. Even after so many years, Philippa still was not sure what to make of the lady, whose money had paid for Elizabeth's book and whose company she both enjoyed and dreaded, mostly because enjoying the presence of such a woman was surely sinful. But she did have sympathy for Agnes. She knew how few choices women—especially married ones—were given, and to see her husband freely spend her family fortune must have been painful. Made worse, of course, by her son's choice of a relatively impoverished bride who coveted the family's societal position. No one felt secure these days, Philippa thought.

"Childbirth will certainly end her," Agnes said without sympathy. Philippa had seen the slight thing heavy with pregnancy at church, barely able to support her belly as she walked the pathway up the hill from the manor house. She did have the look of one whom the midwife might not be able to save should things go wrong, as they so often did.

"Mother prioress, you are the only person I trust to keep my treasures safe." Agnes spoke forcefully. "I hope it is not long until I come back to retrieve them, and you and the priory will be even more richly rewarded."

Lady Vale paused and looked down at her hands, smoothing her green damask dress. The prioress was glad to have only her linen smock and woolen habit, which gave an ease of movement that she saw the lady lacked.

Agnes leaned forward and spoke in almost a whisper. "I have another matter of which to speak with you."

"Oh?" Philippa braced herself for what was coming next, although the prospect of a secret was thrilling.

"The Holy Maid of Kent," said Agnes. "My cousin in London writes that the talk at the court is much about her these days. How she keeps insisting that Henry will die when he marries Anne Boleyn." Agnes looked up at Philippa, trying to read her face. If the prioress thought what went on here was confined to its walls, she was mistaken.

"*If* he marries her," corrected Philippa. "They are not married yet." Elizabeth was not at the priory very much these days; Father Bocking had her traveling so frequently. When she was there, the pilgrims came streaming in and begged to see her. There was no way St. Sepulchre's was going to be able to extract itself from that association.

"No, although some at court say she is already married. My cousin says the Boleyn woman is now the Marquess of Pembroke, and nothing will stop the marriage. Queen Catherine is in exile." Agnes took pride in being able to deliver so much news to the prioress. "You know I believe the Maid to be true," Agnes continued, looking closely at Philippa, "but I do not trust her confessor to protect her. She must silence herself. These words are too dangerous."

"I know you support our Holy Maid," the prioress said with a nod. "Your gift of patronage for the printing of her book was a great goodness. But some of these are not matters for us." She paused, considering her next words. "God will make sure that our defender and king, Henry, stays faithful to the Church."

Philippa worried, though, for her priory and the women it housed. She knew, too, that Elizabeth did not help their cause anymore, but her prophecies were too widespread and she too vocal to change their course.

"Be wary," Agnes cautioned. "Hide your own gems, too. When this fever for Luther has broken and the danger has passed, you can retrieve them. Make sure to tell some trusted few where they are hidden, should death come early for you or me. Let us think of ways to do this."

Philippa stood to usher Agnes out. "As the Gospel of Mark tells us," she said, "'But of that day or hour no man knoweth, neither the angels in heaven, nor the Son, but the Father.' We can only be sure that death will come."

Vale House Manor, June 2023, Day 3

I like museums almost as much as I like libraries. And I really, really love libraries. Especially manuscript rooms. The smell, the sound of quiet scribbling and pages turning, the feeling of shared purpose as a few scattered others and I study vellum and parchment from centuries past. The alchemy as a scribe's handwriting that seems completely illegible turns into something you can read with ease. It feels holy to me. It is a communion with the dead that feels far more effective than any séance ever could be.

Museums are sacred in a different way. They invite reflection. They, too, gesture to the dead speaking forward to the living. Or the living speaking back to the dead. But you can't touch the documents or paintings. You can't hold something that you knew someone else held. Nevertheless, I am happy to break up the day with some art.

The front passenger seat of Roger's ramshackle car is somehow locked in a forward position—"Must get this fixed someday," he mutters as we get in—so I am reluctantly squeezed in the back between Marla and Westley for what I am promised is a short ride. Despite my best attempts at ignoring it, I am acutely aware of the length of my leg touching Westley's.

I instead focus on conversation with Marla. "How did you end up in England?" I ask her.

"Oh, I followed a lover to graduate school," she says, laughing. I glance to the front seat but there is no reaction that I can tell from Roger. "And then, I realized my work was really here and not in Austria. I am ready to leave, though. It's never held my heart." At this, Roger's eyes find the rearview mirror, but only for a second.

"I almost did the same," says Westley. "Followed a lover, that is." I tense up at his words. Despite the years that have passed and the many loves he has no doubt had since then (I mean, I got married and divorced in that time), it still pains me to hear about any other lovers.

"Why didn't you?" asks Marla, oblivious to the thick, palpable tension I feel between me and Westley at the question. I find that I am holding my breath.

"She never asked me to come," he says, softly. I let my breath out slowly. That couldn't have been about me, right?

Roger forestalls any further conversation with a cheery "Here we are!" as he pulls the car into the lot next to the Beaney, Canterbury's art museum. "It's been a while since I've been here, but it's like seeing old friends. Where do you suggest we start, Westy?"

Westley doesn't seem at all put off, and enters the museum with authority, striding toward the galleries. "There's one painting you must see, Alison," he says. "It's a portrait of Lady Vale. We never knew her first name, but the period is right for it to be Agnes."

Roger and Westley walk at a clip in front and chat quietly, heads bowed together, with Marla and me a pace or two behind, trying to take in some of the works of art they are speeding past. There is an intimacy between them, bred, I suppose, by their proximity, with Westley from the village and Roger's connection to the manor. How well do they know each other? It seems to be better than I thought.

I'm glad for the separation between the four of us, enjoying the chance to have more time to talk to Marla without an audience.

"Your project is so interesting, Alison. What kind of interaction can you imagine between the people of the manor and the priory? Are these relationships personal or is it more ceremonial? What's your sense of that with Elizabeth?" she asks.

"Ah, well, I imagine the Vales went to church at least weekly, if not more. They would have seen the sisters there. And there could have been disputes or agreements just as there are between any neighbors. Perhaps some of the Vale women lived out their days at the priory? It's so hard to tell without the records."

Marla stops me in front of a Renaissance painting; a young man with delicate features and reddish hair looks out at his viewers. I glance ahead to see where Roger and Westley are, but they have turned a corner and are out of sight.

"I love this one," she says. "He looks like he has a secret to tell. Look how his hand is clasped tightly. He's holding on to something he doesn't want to relinquish." She follows my gaze down the hallway. "Don't worry about those men. Typical, that they race ahead to a destination and don't stop to see things along the way. It can make for sloppy scholarship, too. I like that you take your time with your research." I smile at her veiled criticism of Roger and Westley's work.

"Well, your work is an inspiration, Marla. You always see the details." We continue to take our time strolling, stopping each other to point out things we notice in the artwork, until we reach Westley and Roger at the portrait.

The painting exudes the wealth of its subject. Just sitting for a portrait was a costly endeavor, but the fine craftsmanship of this image suggests an artist of some renown who had traveled far to do the job, incurring an even greater expense than usual. ANNO 1533 is written in the corner. It's the year Henry VIII married Anne Boleyn. Did the woman in this portrait know what turmoil the country was about to face?

Pearls are delicately woven on silver thread through the woman's reddish-brown hair. Agnes's face (because I can only think of her as Agnes now) is turned to the side, but her eyes look directly at the viewer. She is not smiling, although there is intelligence around her eyes and some humor around the mouth. Looking at the lines in her face gives me the eerie impression of looking in a mirror, at a woman in middle age like me. Although by the time this portrait was made, Lady Vale likely had grown children and maybe even grandchildren.

Her gown encircles her neck tightly, accentuating its length but also giving the artist an opportunity to show his facility with painting fabric—every fold and every thread are lifelike. And the gems! The dress is dark velvet, almost black, and studded with pearls, absolutely covered in them. A necklace of gold and onyx (and more pearls), the size of a silver dollar, hangs in the middle of her chest.

She is holding an open book. I get as close as I can without triggering the museum's alarm to see what can be made out on the small image there. One page has a Latin phrase, but the words are so very tiny I cannot make them out. The other page features a painting of a woman, an unnamed saint with a halo. "Anyone have a magnifying glass?" I ask.

"Yes, actually," answers Roger, to my surprise. "These old eyes need it whenever I'm looking at manuscripts." He pulls a small glass out of his pocket and hands it to me.

"'*Quicumque dixerit . . .*,' I think . . . '*matri . . .*,' yes, and then '*Munus, quodcumque est ex me, tibi proderit*,'" I read.

Roger is nodding but Westley looks confused and says, a little sheepishly, "Can you translate that? Sorry, my Latin is crap." Ah, finally a gap in his knowledge.

"Sure. It means 'Whoever shall say to the mother, the gift that comes from me shall profit you.' It must be biblical, but it doesn't ring a bell. We can look it up later at the manor. I would guess this is a Book of Hours?" I ask Westley and Roger, who seem to be watching me looking at the painting rather than looking at the painting itself.

"Yes, seems to be," says Westley, his face almost touching mine to see through the magnifying glass. He has a woodsy, spicy smell. "That would make sense for a lady to have."

Books of Hours—small prayer books that contain calendars of saints' days and prayers specific for meditation and reflection—are one of the most common literary survivors of the era. Many wealthy women owned specially made ones that had saints specific to their names or birthdays or family connections.

"Neither the inscription nor whomever this saint could be is familiar to me," says Marla. "But there were quite a lot of them associated with the maternal. Talismans against death in childbirth or children dying young. It was a perilous life to be either a mother or a child."

"It's a female saint," I say, shaking off the feeling that the three are looking at me and not at the image of Lady Vale. "She's dressed in a nun's habit. But I can't make out anything more than that. It is all so minuscule."

Did I imagine it, or did Roger and Westley exchange a glance above my head?

* * *

"REMEMBER!" ROGER SHOUTS as I head toward the stairs after our return to the manor. "A quick and early dinner tonight because we have our surprise excursion!" His voice is strangely loud—after all, I am right in front of him. It's already four o'clock, so I have only about an hour to relax before the five o'clock cocktails.

Tomorrow we will hear the remaining papers, followed by more discussion time in the afternoon. Then we have two "free days" set aside for writing and following up on threads that have come up during our stay. Ideally, we all have complete drafts of our finished articles when we leave so that Roger can begin assembling the book from this year's C.C. And then I am off to London, where I have reserved some days at The British Library before returning home to New York.

I am about halfway up the staircase when Alex comes hurrying down. "Dr. Sage," he says, his voice breathy and fast, "that was a quick visit to Canterbury. How did you find the museum?"

"Was it quick?" I ask. "It felt like we spent a good deal of time there, although we only stayed in the one gallery. It was lovely. Some beautiful art." I take a step forward, but he doesn't move aside.

"I should have used the servants' stairs—I apologize. I thought you were all out for longer." He seems nervous. The servants' stairs? This butler's act he puts on is so odd, especially now that I know he is one of only two remaining employees in the manor house.

"Oh, I don't care. I didn't even know there were servants' stairs," I answer, and again make a motion as if to pass him.

He doesn't get the hint and continues to block my way. "Oh yes, these old houses often have another set of stairs and various ways of entering the hallways and rooms. Not seen nor heard, you know! So that we can easily and discreetly get to the bedrooms if needed." And with that, he finally steps aside, and I hastily go on to my room, entirely discomfited by the exchange.

The second I enter the room, I can tell that something is off. It's not only the vestiges of the dead-rat smell that hit me every time I walk in (and then, horrifyingly, I get used to it and forget about it). The bag holding my dirty clothes is closed, and I am absolutely sure I left it open. But more obvious is the appearance of the small desk where my papers and laptop are sitting in a neat pile.

I have many virtues, but neatness has never been among them. The desk here has already become a somewhat more restrained replica of my desk at home, covered in papers, propped-open books, and my laptop, perpetually open, at its center.

Now the laptop has been closed and moved to the side, the papers stacked next to it. I rifle through them and find nothing missing but notice that the Barton images have risen to the top of the pile when before I had the notes for my talk there. What could someone have been looking for? Was there a third member of the staff? A housekeeper, perhaps? The bed is notably still unmade, so that would have to be a terrible housekeeper.

I remember thinking I saw the curtain move that morning as well. Who is snooping in my room and why? I decide to text Jenny.

Hello! Reporting from the C.C. You were wrong, there is tweed. Also, warm beer and terrible coffee.

I pick at some peeling wallpaper as I wait for the three dots to turn into words.

Hi stranger! I'm dying to hear about it. You've been so quiet! I was worried.

Sorry, it's been so busy. Roger has not left room for much down time. And the cell phone reception is shit here. Barely works except a little bit in my room when I can connect to the equally unreliable Wi-Fi.

What's the manor house like? How's Calista?

A little Grey Gardens. Run down. They need an infusion of cash to update things. It was very grand once, though. Calista got Covid. Couldn't come ☹.

Oh really? She can't be too sick because she just emailed me yesterday about a collection she's editing.

She did? Weird. Roger made it sound like she was really sick . . .

So it's just you and Marla? Is she terrifying?

She's actually nice. I think we will be friends! But, on the not-nice side, I'm pretty sure the servant here is rifling through my things when I'm out of my room.

Ugh. Does the door lock?

Just the knob. And he has a key.

Do you think he's stolen anything?

I can't imagine I have anything worth stealing. I'm sure I'm just paranoid and he's just doing his job. How's New Haven?

Fine, although Rachel had a terrible case last night. A mugging and stabbing. She came home at about five in the morning, so I had kid duty all night long. Do you want the gory details, Meredith Grey?

Oh no! But yes please . . .

Patient died. The guy's girlfriend pulled the knife out and he bled out. The knife had been holding him together, but by the time Rachel was there, it was too late. She's been sleeping all day.

So sorry. Give her my love.

I will! And keep me posted on the C.C. Have to go chase a toddler.

* * *

"COME, COME, EVERYONE, let's move!" Roger downs the last of his wine and motions for us to finish up dinner, which tonight is fish and chips. I am happy about this one; I didn't plan on coming to England and not having my favorite of its cultural offerings. When he stands and begins to leave the room, everyone gets the hint and takes last swallows and sips. Roger's booming voice is a pied-piper clarion, and I, like the others, can't resist its call. "It's chilly tonight, a bit of a breeze, you may want to take a jumper. Let's go for our surprise evening excursion, hosted by our very own Westley Charney!"

Shit.

Now Roger and Westley are having an intense conversation, and I see, with some curiosity, that Marla is speaking quietly but firmly to Alex, who stands in the doorway to the library. What is everyone's business with Alex? He's the last person I want to speak to. I try to lean in to hear what is being said, but to no avail. Marla catches my eye, smiles her brilliant smile, and says one last indistinguishable word to Alex with her hand on his arm before she walks away.

I pull on my sweater and wait at the door for the rest and see Brian walking up to me. He leans in so closely I can smell the wine on his breath. "Ready for some spooky stuff?" he asks.

"Oh? Is this to be spooky?"

He nods. "Ghost tour. Westley knows all the good ones around here. Victorian ladies in white who lure children to their deaths, the man in old-timey clothes who you see dancing from afar but disappears when you are close, haunted houses, headless women. They have them all! Feel free to grab my hand if you get scared." He makes an exaggerated wink. Ugh. I forgot he can be overly friendly after a few drinks.

I take a step back. "Ah! Unlikely. I don't scare that easily. No vampires in the mix?"

I hear Westley's voice behind me. "You'd have to go farther north for that," he says. "You know, Whitby."

"Dracula's your only vampire then?"

"The only one I know." He smiles. "Come, though, I'll show you where it is on the map," he says, leading me to a large map of England hanging in the vestibule. "Sorry," he whispers as soon as our backs are to the gathering group, "didn't know how else to get you out of Brian's lascivious reach. He can be a bit of an arse, huh?" He raises his eyebrows, pantomiming grabbing with his hands, and I can't help but laugh.

"Thanks. He's mostly harmless unless there are some grad students around. Then he can be a nuisance. Always trying to impress them with the size of his enormous . . . ahem . . . publishing contracts."

Now it's Wes's turn to laugh. "That is not where I thought you were going with that."

"That was the point, Wes. It's called humor." We are both grinning as we exit the manor into the evening air.

* * *

For the next half an hour we stroll down the road toward the village in companionable conversation, the evening light still surprisingly bright. I find myself next to Marla and Roger, with Arjun and Brian not too far in front of us. Wes is leading the way, talking animatedly to Charles. I like watching him move his hands emphatically as he speaks, even though I can't hear the substance.

"So have either of you ever seen a ghost?" I ask Marla and Roger. It is as good a conversation starter as I have under the circumstances. Also, I want to steer clear of anything that treads on their working together or past Consortiums, now that I know they are having an affair. It's hard to think of anything else when you see them next to each other—it's suddenly so blindingly obvious, the way they communicate by small touch or whispers.

Marla shakes her head. She seems far too practical and levelheaded to believe in such a thing.

"Only the ghost of what the manor once was," Roger says somewhat bitterly. He cough-laughs and then goes on. "There don't seem to be any real ghosts of the manor house, but I have seen movement and lights in the church when there should not be anyone there. Sad sisters still angry at the dissolution, I suspect."

Marla gives a small smile. "Perhaps my university will fund a Chair of Ghost Studies in place of historians. They'll do anything to attract students, even if it means ruining academic standards and firing faculty. You should make sure you have a plan B, Alison, while you are still so young and a rising star."

"Not that young," I say with a laugh, and leave the compliment hanging that I am a rising star as I'm both thrilled and embarrassed Marla sees me that way. I feel very sorry for Marla and wonder if her smiles are masking sadness and anxiety about the future and what it holds. Universities are cutting out the humanities more and more. Why put money into history departments when computer science needs the newest equipment? Historians know that history repeats itself with astonishing regularity; soon no one will even be able to point that out because they won't know. Even though I study the scars of a country that tore itself apart at the whims of its rulers, and see that pattern repeat itself all over the world, I often feel like I am screaming into a void.

As I've become gloomier, Roger has regained his cheerfulness, and he points out landmarks as we walk, gossiping about who once lived in the houses lining the street. "Wild mint all along the path!" he shouts, as he pulls some up and chews. "Better than a breath mint!" His attachment to the place is genuine. I pick a few leaves and chew.

* * *

"WE'RE STARTING THE tour here," Wes says as we approach a house that might as well be the image that appears if you Google "haunted house." Fully run-down, windows partially boarded up, cobwebs everywhere, it clearly has not had an inhabitant in decades, if not centuries. He stops and turns toward the group. "This house is built on the grounds of an old monastery." He turns to me and says, "Actually, Alison, this was Edward Bocking's monastery. These were his monks and they refused to take the Oath of Succession—they were defiant to Henry VIII and Cromwell until the very end. And it was a bloody end. Seventeen of them were killed, each found guilty—starting with Edward Bocking, who was hanged with Elizabeth. The others died in various gruesome ways. Some were hanged, then drawn, then quartered. Several died of starvation in prison. Some were bound in chains and left for dead. By the time this monastery was dissolved, there was no living monk to mourn his brothers.

"And, as happened throughout England, the monastery was taken down brick by brick, and brick by brick a new home was constructed. And a family who had stayed loyal to Henry, who had proudly proclaimed their allegiance to his faith, were gifted the land.

"But immediately, things were not right here. In evenings, almost nightly, when the sun went down, they would hear what sounded like monks singing the evening prayer of vespers. And as they tried to sleep, they would be awoken by the sounds of matins, the prayers at dawn. Sometimes, even in broad daylight, their guests would swear they could hear the chanting of the prayers of terce at midmorning or nones in the afternoon.

"This family left these parts, and in 1870 a new home was built here for a new family. But the curse of taking church-given lands persisted. Again, the family reported the sounds of chanting and songs at regular hours throughout the night and on several days. It drove the eldest son to madness, and he was seen raging through the streets asking where the monks were hiding, saying he must stop their hideous mouths. He ended his days ranting in a cell in London at St. Mary Bethlehem, what you may know as the Bedlam asylum, asking for quiet, hands over his ears, begging the monks to stop their chanting.

"No other family has lived here since. But many villagers report hearing the monks in song. And if we stand still enough, as it is the hour of vespers, we may, too."

Wes puts his finger to his lips and looks out at the scholars. I shiver despite myself. The wind moving through the empty house with its broken windows and peeling paint does sound like a mournful chant. I think about how broken the country was during and after the Reformation, about assassination plots and priests hiding in holes, and seventeen dead men.

And Bocking, hanged. Did he use Elizabeth to his own ends? Did he deserve this fate?

* * *

I FIND MYSELF walking a little closer to Wes on the way to our final location near the priory ruins, after four different stops and their respective ghosts. The ghost tour is legitimately spooky, and I can fully understand how people's imaginations lead them to the supernatural with so many histories, violent ones especially, surrounding them.

Medieval manuscripts were written on vellum—animal skin stretched thin, dried out, and scraped down. This process was laborious and expensive, so sometimes a monk would decide an old text wasn't needed anymore and would scrape it off, so that the page could be used for something new. Every now and then, though, the old text is still visible, a specter. This is called a palimpsest, and it's what I think of when we reach the priory: there is something new on top, but—when held up to the right light—the old stories always bleed through.

"What did you think?" Wes asks as we lead the way back up the road toward the priory. Dusk has settled, and we walk quickly. "Are you ready for the scariest of the tales? It's up your alley. The Barton alley, that is." He runs a finger menacingly across his throat.

I find myself less annoyed that Wes is also researching Barton. His work on legends is more work on the community's legacy of the event than the event itself. It's even fun to have some work in common. "I'm ready. Bring me my headless nun, Wes," I say.

"That is officially the second time you have called me Wes tonight," he says, lowering his voice and leaning closer to me with a big grin. I can smell the mint on his breath.

Have I? But with his saying it, there is a recognition that he has already been Wes to me for a little while. The Wes I remember. "Yes, you've graduated from Westley to Wes." I shrug. "Be good and you can stay that way."

"I have no intention of being good," he says, his voice thick, glancing at me. I can feel that I am blushing, the warmth flooding to my face. I am saved from responding by Arjun, who jogs up next to us with a question for Wes about his last story.

When we arrive at the church, Wes begins his final tale. The sun is setting, and the church is illuminated from within, giving off its own ghostly glow in the mist.

"So, my friends, you have heard quite a bit about our Holy Maid of Kent from Alison already, and you will hear more from me tomorrow morning when I tell you the legend of the hidden jewels," he says to the group. "But tonight, I would like to tell you about the local story concerning Elizabeth, her hanging, her head, and her final lost prophecy."

Brian has somehow sidled up next to me, and Alex has suddenly joined us, appearing as if out of the mist. How can he be both so invisible and yet so long-limbed at the same time? Now that he is standing next to me, I am acutely aware of the Lurch-like physique swaying by my side.

"After Elizabeth was hanged for treason, supporters—we do not know who—went to retrieve her body along with those of the priests, so that they could be properly buried in consecrated ground. They did not want their erstwhile saint and her promoters to be placed in paupers' shared graves, as so many criminals were. However, they were stymied to find that Elizabeth's head had been cleanly removed from its body, preserved in tar, and placed on a spike on London Bridge to serve as warning for those who would speak against the king and cleave to the pope. She is the only woman in English history whose head was displayed in this way.

"There was no tolerance for papistry in Henry's new world order, and he *really* wanted to make sure that people saw Elizabeth as a heretic and a traitor in punishment for the visions she said she had regarding Henry and Anne Boleyn. Her supporters took the body, without its head, and had it buried at Greyfriars Church in London.

"As far as we know, they were unable to recover her head. When it was eventually taken down from the bridge, it seemed to disappear. Maybe thrown into the river? Maybe taken as a macabre souvenir? Who knows?

"The legends also say that she had one last prophecy that was so confusing, so dangerous, that the nuns made sure it never saw the light of day. Where did it go? Who heard it? Would it have saved her or made her death even more painful?

"Elizabeth wants her head back so that she can speak her final prophecy! She has searched throughout London but cannot find it there, so she has returned here to St. Sepulchre's, and walks the perimeter of the priory, past our manor windows, through the chapel, searching, ever searching. She is dressed in habit like a nun, but in her hand, she holds a veil with no head to cover.

"Some have seen her whole image in front of them, but most feel that they see her out of the corner of their eye. The villagers have long said if you meet her, she could take your head for her own. If you dare go to the church at night, you may encounter her. And anyone who dares can join me there now. Alex lit the candles so it should be an appropriate end to our ghost tour. And then we can retire to the library and have that drink I know you are all waiting for."

Wes finishes with the same flourish and bow he gave after each tale. I can't tell if the goose bumps on my arms are from the story or the chill in the air. I feel slightly dizzy.

* * *

THE OUTER DARKNESS contrasted with the flickering light within transforms the church entirely. If the hellmouth was frightening before, now it dances with a threatening glow; it is impossible to tell which are the flames on the wall and which are the reflections of the candles. The interplay of light and dark make it seem that the damned are truly burning, writhing, as the grinning beast swallows them one by one.

The candles animate the transi tomb, too. The alabaster glows on the top—Valentina truly on her way to heaven. But underneath, the shadows bleakly shroud the crevices and bones of the marble cadaver. The candles' flickering makes them look like they, too, are in hell, orange and glowing. The worm in the eye socket moves, dancing in the candlelight.

In truth, I feel a bit woozy, with the incense aroma of the candles and the steamy heat inside the church. I sit down in one of the pews to get my bearings, hearing the group talking and moving around me, then filing out. When I close my eyes, I see Elizabeth's disembodied head in my mind's eye, the skull of the transi tomb, not of marble but of flesh, skewered on a pike.

A firm hand on my shoulder makes me jump. "Are you okay?" Wes asks.

Once again, I feel that jolt move down from his fingers and through my whole body; I am electrified. I am afraid to speak so I just nod and stand, but wobble a bit, and Wes catches me and sits me back down.

"Sorry," I say, finding my voice. "How embarrassing. I guess I was a little more spooked than I knew after such masterful storytelling." I smile, hoping he will hear just the gentle sarcasm and not the desire that I am trying to beat back. I stand up again, more slowly, and feel steady this time. Looking around, I realize that we are the only two in the church.

"Sounds like you need a glass of something strong," he says in a low voice, looking into my eyes to assess if I am really all right. "That's the remedy around here for basically every ailment. Headache? Have a dram of this. Stomachache? A dram of that will do you. You broke your arm? Well, have you tried some whiskey?"

As we move toward the door, his arm guides me across my lower back. We are barely touching, although I feel it radiate through my entire body. "You know," he says, pausing in front of the hellmouth, "that painting was here almost as early as the priory itself. It probably goes back to the twelfth century."

He turns toward me as he speaks, his mouth so close, I can feel his breath hot on my face, still minty like mine. I lean in a millimeter closer, our lips almost touching. He stops talking and I just know he will kiss me. I close my eyes, waiting.

He doesn't.

I open my eyes. He has pulled back a little bit, looking unsure, with maybe even a hint of something uneasy in his eyes. What was I thinking?

"How are you feeling?" Wes asks, softly, still close enough that I can smell the mint. "Would you like to hear some more about the hellmouth before we leave?" We are next to the door now; two steps and we will be out in the cool night air.

This attraction feels almost masochistic, dangerous. Twenty years ago there was Wes, and it was hot but brief—held at bay by our age difference, by our geographies, by our places in our careers. And I met Pete so soon afterward. So, the prospect of being with Wes again feels less like freedom and more like transgression. But I want it. I want him. He is still talking, and to halt the chatter, I close the small gap between our lips and kiss him softly.

If I were religious, perhaps the hushed chill of this church would have stopped me, but I'm not. He answers my kiss, tentatively at first and then more insistently. I feel as if we are being watched, although we are assuredly alone here. It must be the eyes of the wall paintings, the stained glass, all around.

Before I can even process what is happening, he has pressed me against the wall, where I can feel him responding in other ways, too. This is a disaster. What am I doing? I should stop. We should stop. And I almost say so, but his lips move down to my neck and the frisson that sends through my body makes my teeth chatter so that speech is near impossible.

"I've been waiting twenty years to do that again," he breathes into my ear, his lips brushing it slightly. Sighing, I pull his hips tighter onto mine.

Chelsea, December 1532

Elizabeth was eager to meet with Sir Thomas More. Two years had passed since Cardinal Wolsey died in disgrace, heartbroken at the king's rejection, and Bocking realized the Maid needed a more powerful protector than Bishop Fisher. Elizabeth knew that More was very influential; the king had made him chancellor after Wolsey even though there was no doubt that More's loyalties lay with Rome. She had heard his name spoken with reverence and something a bit close to fear by Bocking and even Fisher.

"Holy Thomas has stopped many Lutheran books from coming here. Even that heretic Tyndale's English Bible," Bocking told her on the boat trip toward his home. He always spat when he was mad, and the English Bible made him especially so, drool forming in the creases of his lips. "The king listens to Thomas, even when they disagree. He is a rope binding Henry to Rome." He held up two fists as if he were pulling two ends of a tightrope.

Elizabeth nodded. She hoped that More would bind himself to her as well, a cable tethering her to strength and safety.

"If the chancellor can see how important and valuable you are, daughter, you will be well protected. Tell him all about your visions of the king and that goggle-eyed whore," he said as more spittle encircled his mouth.

She thought maybe she would have a vision there, in front of Sir Thomas, so that he could see how special she was. So that he, too, could become her advisor.

If she really thought about it, and she tried not to, she knew that the visions she called upon were not the same as that first sight of purgatory. These were more like pictures in her head, built from images she saw in the churches they visited or the books that Bocking read to her. And the one she had had about Henry and Anne had been vivid but different, as it was while she was feverish and sleeping. Although the stern prioress Philippa had tried to suggest that it was a dream, Elizabeth could see that Bocking and the others did not believe it so. Thus, she did not either.

Because they had traveled to Chelsea by boat, no crowds accompanied them. Beaufort House came into view as they turned a bend in the river. It was a grand home, if not a palace—three floors—just as big as the bishop's home had been. Men in Thomas More's livery helped them disembark and they walked up the gentle slope, through an orchard of apples and pears, toward the house.

A servant led Bocking and Elizabeth into a library such as she had never seen. There were more books there than Fisher, or Wolsey, or the king himself could have owned. Books on shelves, open on tables, stacked on a chair. The most astonishing sight of all, though, was a woman sitting at a table with a book open, writing. Elizabeth knew that women could read and write—certainly, she had seen the nuns do both—but this woman, wearing no religious habit, had pages of writing in front of her as if she had spent hours at the task. Seeing the visitors, she placed her book down and stood.

"Hello, Father Bocking, Sister Elizabeth." The woman bowed her head slightly, just one dark hair escaping from her tight velvet hood. "My father will be with you shortly. He is just finishing up with one of the king's messengers. I trust your journey was calm. I, too, live in Kent with my husband, but have come to see some of my father's books. I am translating an important treatise on our Lord's Prayer."

Elizabeth was too stunned to speak. A woman who could read and translate Latin? Whose father encouraged this? And she was not a nun? She was even more determined to show More what she could do, to convince this important man to be her champion as he had championed his own daughter.

To what heights could he lift her once he saw how exceptional she was? She imagined herself sitting at that table, a book in front of her, a man leaning over her shoulder—no, a woman, his daughter—pointing to something on the page.

"Welcome to the Great House," said a sonorous voice, popping Elizabeth's daydream like a soap bubble. They all turned to face Sir Thomas. He was dressed as if for court, the medallion of the chancellor around his neck as it once had hung around Wolsey's. "I see you have met my daughter, Lady Margaret Roper."

At this, Lady Margaret curtsied to her father and his guests, saying, "I bid your leave," and left the library, book in hand. Elizabeth's eyes followed her until she was fully out of sight. She wondered anew what her life would have been like had she been born to someone else, somewhere else. Would God still have chosen her to bear his messages?

"My child," Sir Thomas said, looking beyond Bocking and at her directly. This took her by surprise. Usually, these men spoke to her advisor, listening to her only when she was speaking in a vision. "I have been unexpectedly called to court so this visit must be short. Please tell me of your visions. What do you see? How do you know it is God who speaks to you and not a madness in your mind? What do you pray for?"

Elizabeth had become practiced at her words, at saying what she knew people wanted to hear. She raised her voice to the pitch that seemed to work best on these men, somewhere between a song and a shout. "I have seen purgatory and hell. God spoke to me and showed me these things. I saw that the Cobb boy would die, and he did. It was the gift of prophecy. And now I have seen Henry in hell with his concubine. The voice is true. It is God."

"Surely, you are not saying you saw our King Henry in hell? Our king who is divinely chosen to lead? You have misspoken, no? Or perhaps it was not really a vision, but a dream?" He looked directly in her eyes, speaking slowly. "It is all right, child, to say you have made a mistake. That you have misunderstood the cause of your distress."

"No," Bocking interrupted. "It is no dream, Sir Thomas. She is a real visionary. She is our St. Bridget, our St. Catherine—two visionaries whose gift from God made them advisors to the pope, whose books are read by every holy man in this country. Like them, this Holy Maid is speaking directly from God."

"The sainted Catherine and Bridget were singular. There are many women and men who claim they have visions from God, but they have been proven wrong or misled by the serpent Satan," More continued, still looking at Elizabeth and speaking directly to her. "How do you know what you feel is true?"

"Sir Thomas," Elizabeth answered, pulling threads of thought from the readings that Philippa had so often chosen for the nuns' meals and prayers, "many revelations are plain illusions of the Devil. These should be cast from one's mind and not given credence."

"Indeed," said More, bridging his fingers together, bidding Elizabeth to continue. The heavy gold chancellor's medallion caught the sunlight streaming through his window and made his face shimmer. Surrounded by his library, he seemed to Elizabeth the picture of wisdom.

"But they taste bitter," she explained, "and my visions taste sweet. They are from God. I have prayed with my confessor here and with the prioress at St. Sepulchre's before and after my trances. God is with me for those moments."

The chancellor nodded, but his look was pained. "Please, come walk with me, Father Bocking. Sister Elizabeth, you may sit and wait here." He gestured for Bocking to follow him into an adjacent room.

Sitting in the library, Elizabeth could just make out the muffled words that Sir Thomas was speaking to Bocking, although she suspected she was not supposed to hear them. "Father," More said, "I say to you here what I have said to the king from the beginning concerning this Maid of Kent. I am glad to hear she is virtuous and that she has dedicated herself to God. I believe that God is doing good works through her. But I refuse to support any visions that she may believe she has had concerning the matter of the king and his marriage, and I will not hear of them. Danger lies that way."

In response, Bocking's voice sounded chastened, in the tone he used with Fisher. "Sir Thomas, we know that you are all that is keeping Henry loyal to Rome. The Maid has seen his fate if he marries his concubine. You must support her. Let people know that she is true."

Thomas's voice rose. "The king has been trying to marry Anne Boleyn for five years. He is determined on this and will not be swayed. I fear this outcome is inevitable and Sister Elizabeth will only be putting your life and hers in peril by repeating her so-called visions. Henry will not stand for it, I assure you, and I will not be a party to it."

"You, who are known for bringing heretics to their deserved justice, are the last one I thought whose faith would fail." Bocking's voice was raised and wavering in a way that Elizabeth had not heard before. This was not the outcome he had anticipated.

"It has not. I have my faith firmly in place. I serve the king and I serve God, and if I can no longer serve both, I will choose to serve only God. I do not believe you and the Maid labor entirely in his service." A pause. Then more softly, "I do not believe I will be chancellor for much longer. I will not be able to protect you."

Vale House Manor, June 2023, Day 4

I grab my phone almost the minute my bedroom door clicks behind Wes as he sneaks back to his own room, kissing me until I had to literally push him out. I think I see Charles's door shutting at just about the same time but chalk it up to paranoia. There had been quite a lot of kissing last night, and also touching and giggling. It felt so good to feel desired, to feel like my body has a purpose other than marching listlessly through midlife, slowing down like a windup toy. I feel wound up. I feel adolescent. Giddy. It's three in the morning, but only late evening in New Haven.

Jenny!!

I tap into my phone. Please be awake.

Oh shit, I may have just made a colossal error in judgment. Are you up?

I am now. Actually, I've been up. Felix has a fever and it's taking forever to get him down. But your life sounds more interesting. Tell me!

The texts start ping-ponging as fast as we can write them.

Argh, I think I made a really big mistake.

Personal or professional?

Both?

Brian?

Ew!! No!! 😫 Way better. And worse.

Ok, spill. No judgement.

Westley Charney. Again.

WHAAAATTT?!

Yep.

OMG! He's still hot, I'll give you that. And still young! Go you! Has that been simmering for years? I had no idea he was even there. Isn't he an asshole now? Was it good? Will you do it again? How did it happen? I have so many questions!!

Yeah, he replaced Calista. And, yes, kind of an asshole. It was really very good. Yes, please, to doing it again, but I think it's a bad idea to repeat. Moment of weakness.

Did you just fool around or was it the whole enchilada? 🍆🍑

Just lots of kissing, etc. I feel like a teenager sneaking around behind my parents' backs! Everyone's rooms are on this floor. Charles is right next door!

Oh God, what if he heard us? I can't believe how stupid I've been.

Well, you still have what, four days to consummate this unholy alliance?

Haha, I think I'll nip this in the bud. But it was fun. But SO stupid of me!

Why? You're single. He's single. He's hot. You're hot.

So unprofessional.

When has that ever stopped anyone? Ask Brian for advice!

Point taken.

Still feel creeped out by the place? Or has Hot Westley kissed it away?

Ha. Something is off here. I can't figure out what. But yes, this makes it better.

Ok. To bed. Not expecting too much sleep tonight so have to get it where I can. Kind of like you getting it where you can with Westley.

* * *

My phone buzzes a 7:00 a.m. wake-up. Well, that was stupidly optimistic. I turn it off, wanting only to go back to sleep. Wes is going to present his work this morning. I don't think anyone noticed us together last night; when we finally came in from the church, only Arjun and Brian were in the library. Others must have gone to bed. Wes and I had tiptoed, whispering, into my room. Still, I can't shake the feeling that we were being watched.

Wes is still an ass, right? Too pedantic. Too cocky. My body feels different, though, or at least I feel different inside it. It is the first time since the divorce, or even long before the divorce, that I feel sexy. Take that, Miss Universe: middle-aged professors can be hot, too.

Giving up on sleep, I pull on my running clothes, figuring a quick jog will clear my mind. It is, to be fair, the first morning I haven't woken up with a slight hangover, but my mind is as muddy as if I had been on some kind of bender. Instead of the fuzziness of day-after-drinking, I am instead getting snippets of the prior evening as if in a slideshow. Wes's mouth at my ear. Hands on my body, sliding under my shirt and firm on my back. Hushed giggling as we enter my room. He had not forgotten how I liked to be kissed.

Heading up the path toward the church, I pick up my pace, thinking, surely, we had just been swept up in the moment of the ghost stories, the church by candlelight, the feeling of being outside the rest of the world while we are at the manor. Both time and place feel suspended. It is the first morning in years that I have not woken up feeling lonely, including the last years of my marriage.

As I jog the now-familiar route around the priory ruins, I see Roger and Alex entering the church. I wave, but they don't see me. Twenty minutes later, as I make my second loop, I see Roger walking back to the manor house alone.

I wonder: What else does he need to do at the church, other than unlock the door?

"Good morning, Roger!" I shout, running up alongside him. Is it my imagination, or does he look annoyed to see me?

His expression clears. "My dear Alison," he says, smiling.

"A morning visit to the church?"

"No, no. I was just taking my morning constitutional. The church was left open last night after the ghost tour." Odd. Maybe he and Alex are atoning for sins only they understand. He opens the door of the manor and holds it for me, bowing with a flourish of his hand.

"I trust you are enjoying yourself at our humble but mighty Consortium?" he asks as we enter.

"I am. Thank you again for having me," I say, as my eyes adjust from the brightness outside into the dimness of the manor house.

His brow furrows. "I am sorry Calista was ill, but it seems that you and Wes have been working together nicely on Barton." He meets my eye knowingly.

I feel myself reddening. Surely, this is an innocent comment, and I am misreading it. I manage to stammer, "Y-Yes, I miss Calista, too, but Wes's work is interesting." At this, I excuse myself to shower and race up the stairs to the safety of my room.

Hampton Court, January 1533

On the way to their second royal audience, Bocking had whispered, "I believe you have been summoned again to Hampton Court because the king is frightened by what you have seen. Your words are starting to sway him." She had frightened Henry? Good. Perhaps he would listen to her ever-urgent message.

Now when she came to London there were near two thousand souls waiting to see her as they walked through the streets, clamoring for her blessing; the king must know she could not be so easily dismissed.

Despite herself, Elizabeth was again impressed with the lavishness of the court. It had grown since her last visit, both the palace itself and the number of people running through it, all of them frantic. There were men dressed in the king's livery, and she counted the livery of at least fifteen other noble families. And there was a new livery: that of the Boleyn family, three black bull heads on white, a bloodred chevron running through it like a scar. This ferocious image steeled Elizabeth, strengthening her resolve to deliver her message directly to the king. His soul was imperiled!

Fisher was not with them this time; he had slowly started to back away from Elizabeth. Bocking called him "a coward, like Thomas More, unwilling to risk for his faith." More had been stripped of his chancellorship for refusing to support the king's break with Rome, but he thought his public silence on such things would protect him. Bocking argued he should be speaking out even more loudly.

So now instead of Fisher, she had quiet Brother Risby as her second companion. He was just a friar, not a bishop, but he must have had courage to come with them to the court.

A sallow-faced guard with a patchy beard led them down a different hallway than the last time. Clearly, they were not going to the chapel. They were brought to a small room, an antechamber, where instead of the king she was confronted by a man whom she had never seen, but whose name was spoken in a near whisper every time she heard it. "Sir Thomas Cromwell," the guard said with a bow before taking his leave.

Cromwell was Henry's most trusted advisor and a firm Lutheran. Elizabeth had been told that he was the one pouring poison in the king's ear, encouraging the break with Rome, dangling the whore as a prize for Henry's efforts. His eyes seemed too small for his face and his lips were so pale that they melted into his chin. His pointy nose reminded Elizabeth of a demon in the priory's hellmouth. He had broken men in the Tower, she had heard. He was the king's executioner, even if he did not wield the blade.

The roar of the crowd still in her ears, she knew she was loved, and he was hated. She curtsied but did not lower her eyes. "I have seen awful things for you," she said to Cromwell. Whether she had seen images of him in a vision didn't matter to her—he was such a terrible man, she was sure that dreadful things awaited him.

Cromwell, a follower of Luther, seemed unaffected by her bold prediction. He did not respond, made no gesture. "Luther is Lucifer," she added vehemently. This time he startled slightly and looked directly into Elizabeth's eyes, which she lowered despite herself.

"I should be more careful if I were you," Cromwell said, evenly, calmly, in a liquid voice. He opened a door opposite the one they had entered and announced, "Your Majesty, the so-called Maid of Kent and two of her misguided supporters are here for you."

Bocking growled disapproval, but Elizabeth assumed he dared not speak back to Cromwell in the presence of the king, whom they spied through the open doorway. He did not come to them, and Cromwell made no motion for them to enter the room.

With the door open between them, Elizabeth could see the king looking at her, his eyes narrowed. Henry had also grown in size since the last time she saw him, as if he and his palace were both gorging on the feasts around them. She noticed the slightest movement of Henry's hand, and Cromwell turned to her. "Tell His Majesty King Henry what you are now saying that you saw in one of your supposed visions."

"I witnessed you in grave danger, my king! If you marry that woman, you will both burn in hell. You must repent. She is a temptress sent from Satan! You must turn away from her and back to your good queen Catherine."

Henry's eyes widened and darted to the right, where some unseen person was standing. Was it her? Elizabeth wondered. The concubine? The thought enraged her.

She shouted, "If you marry her, you will both be dead within two months! I have seen it." She had not seen such a thing, but she was furious that Henry did not seem to believe her, that he would so blithely turn away from the pope, that her visions were being unheeded. She felt Bocking stiffen. He looked at her, alarmed.

Henry had turned a deep red. In fear? Anger? "Take her away," he whispered hoarsely, looking again to whomever was hiding. "She is a false prophet."

* * *

AGNES RETURNED TO the manor after another audience with the prioress at St. Sepulchre's. The artist she had commissioned to paint her portrait was to deliver the picture that afternoon—a picture featuring a necklace that was now in Philippa's safe hands.

If she was pleased with the portrait, she planned to commission more works. Her gift to the priory would be to repaint the rood screens. How she would love to paint over that horrid hellmouth, but the villagers and the sisters seemed to like it, and she did derive some pleasure imagining her husband, John, and daughter-in-law, Maude, among the condemned, burning for eternity, slowly and repeatedly ground between the teeth of the hellbeast.

Lord John Vale, landed gentry. His first wife had died in childbirth along with the baby. Agnes's father was a successful cloth merchant who met John when he bought some wool from the manor's tenant farmers. On her deathbed, Agnes's mother implored her husband to find a good match for their daughter. "Make her a proper lady," she said, and Agnes's father jumped at the chance for a match with John.

Her father provided a nice fat dowry and in exchange his daughter got a title. He never asked the nineteen-year-old Agnes how she felt about marrying forty-seven-year-old John. It's not that he had been unkind, exactly. He had just been . . . nothing. Boring. Disgusting. He mocked her interest in the news of the court, in the fashions of London, in poetry. He had hit her, once, when she bought a tapestry that he deemed too extravagant. And so, to keep herself from dying of boredom and away from his hands, Agnes had immersed herself in her faith. John could not very well complain when her reading was a prayer book or when she went to visit the sisters of the priory.

But now he was too infirm to notice what she bought. These days she spent her money as she wished. *Her* money. For that's how she thought of it, even if her husband believed it to be his. It was her family's wealth that propped up his position. He may have had the title to gift her—and he had never let her forget that she was simply a merchant's daughter—but she knew wealth and riches beyond what he had ever seen.

It was Agnes who had traveled across the sea and seen the courts of France, Italy, and Spain. It was she who could read and write as well as any clergy. To protect her wealth, she had purchased jewels and gowns, commissioned art, paid for edifying books to be printed. She knew that she was on the right side of the holy war that was waging in the king's court. She was not sure the Holy Maid was true, but she was certain that the lascivious king should not have abandoned the good Queen Catherine for that harlot.

When the portrait was delivered and hung, she gasped in pleasure. Her face was turned to the side, but her eyes looked out to the viewer and the small smile on her lips made her look as if she held a secret. Her pale skin contrasted with the high collar of her dress, its pearls looking so real, they could be plucked from the canvas. In the corner was written ANNO 1533. The painter said he always dated his paintings so that future children could look back on their beautiful matriarchs and patriarchs. Agnes liked the idea of her great-grandchildren studying her face, knowing what she had done for them, preserving their wealth, fighting for their faith.

Her wretched, swollen daughter-in-law, Maude, commented that Agnes looked full of grace, like the Virgin Mary herself, and she patted her belly as she always did when the Virgin or the baby Jesus was mentioned.

Agnes pretended not to hear her and instead opened the Book of Hours that she had recently commissioned from the Carmelite friars at Aylesford, who were known for their beautiful illuminations. She had asked them to include an image of the Holy Maid, the same one she had insisted be part of her portrait. It was far more beautiful and detailed in her hands than what the painter could replicate, but the symmetry of holding the object and seeing it again in her hands on the wall pleased her.

She decided she would ask the friars to color the black-and-white woodcut in her copy of Elizabeth's book of revelations, too. She wanted her copy to be special, to show her granddaughter someday that she had paid for such a holy book to find its way in the world.

She glanced at the belly of her son's widow. Yes, she thought, she was putting all the messages in place so when the time was right, her wealth would be returned. Her granddaughter (for she continued to be sure it was a girl) would be the one to figure it all out. She was certain.

Part Three

MATER

Vale House Manor, June 2023, Day 4

I arrive early to the library and compose a quick email to Calista. I've let it go far too long without checking in on her.

From: ASage@nyu.edu
To: calistacraig@saintandrews.edu
Subject: Checking in

Dear Calista,

How are you feeling? I am so very sad you did not make it to Vale House. It would have been so nice to have your company here and for there to be another scholar working on women (and under 60!). I hope that you are recovered and that we are able to see each other again soon. I also hope your children were occupied so that you could get some real rest—I know how that goes. Moms don't really get a chance to be sick.

Sending best wishes for a speedy recovery!
Alison

I have time to browse the books before the session begins. In a nice touch, Roger has displayed all the books of the participants on some lower shelves. My last book, *Do You See What I See?: Witness and the Woman Visionary,* looks as if the spine has not been broken (unlike Charles's and Marla's well-thumbed and marked-up books), so I suspect it was a last-minute Amazon purchase made once I accepted the invitation to the C.C.

If other parts of the manor feature peeling paint and loose floorboards, the library and its treasures seem to have gotten all of the upkeep. Roger says it was rebuilt in the late sixteenth century, while the rest of the manor is either earlier or much later, so he thinks the fire started here. The room still boasts a great fireplace.

As much time as we have spent in the library, I haven't really been able to parse its books. It must contain treasures—some volumes look like they have been at the house for centuries. I'm hoping to identify the biblical quotation in the Vale portrait, and quickly find the first thing I need, a biblical concordance. I scan the index for the word "mother," since the passage in the painting reads, "Whoever shall say to the mother, the gift that comes from me shall profit you."

There are a lot of entries for "mother," but I take a guess that the passage is from the New Testament, given that so many of the concerns of the Reformation involved interpretations of those books. I find the full passage in the Gospel of Matthew; it's an admonishment from Christ to those who were not honoring their fathers or mothers. But, curiously, the quote includes the word "father":

"Honor thy father and mother: He that shall curse father or mother, let him die the death. But you say: Whosoever shall say to father or mother, the gift whatsoever proceedeth from me shall profit thee. And he shall not honor his father or his mother: and you have made void the commandment of God for your tradition." Why would the painter choose only the middle of these passages?

Having located the citation, I feel no more enlightened. I sit and ponder, listening to the *tick-tick-tick* of the grandfather clock. I have about half an hour before the other participants start to wander in and take their places. Why would Lady Vale have a warning painted into her portrait about not honoring the mother? Why leave out the father? Is she talking about Mary? Is it a message about herself? And this talk of "gifts" and "profit"—does she mean something tangible, like her wealth? Or a spiritual profit?

I would like to know more about this Lady Vale. It's not taking me too far afield from my work on Barton; after all, that acrostic in the book certainly indicates a close connection between the family here and the activities of the priory.

I pull down another book: *The Correspondence of Sir Thomas More.* King Henry VIII was incensed when More refused to attend Anne Boleyn's coronation, but that was not enough to imprison and execute him. Instead, Thomas Cromwell convicted More—falsely, surely—for taking bribes. Ultimately, Thomas More's death was entangled with Elizabeth Barton's.

I find what I am looking for: a long letter from More to Cromwell, defending himself against Cromwell's accusations, chief among them that he had supported Elizabeth Barton and her visions. He wrote that he had found her godly when he met her but had told her "any revelation of the king's matters I would not hear of." He goes on to praise Cromwell for unmasking Barton's deceit, writing that he had done a good deed in "bringing forth to light such detestable hypocrisy."

I read these words from one important Tudor-era Thomas to another, filled with the familiar academic sorrow for a woman in the middle, manipulated by both sides to their ends. I flip through some other books but don't see any that would be useful for my research. As Arjun noted, most seem to be Victorian purchases intended to make the library seem full and fancy. A shame.

Marla and Roger come in together. They're conversing quietly, affectionately leaning toward each other, but stop when they see me. "Hello!" I say cheerfully, trying not to make eye contact since I am compelled to keep up the charade that I don't know they are intimate. I also feel more complicit after my night with Wes and am somewhat chagrined that Roger may know about it. The manor is starting to resemble a freshman dormitory.

"Ah! Someone is finally using the library for its purpose," says Roger, walking over to see what I have found. "Any treasures? There is so much uncatalogued here. It is my retirement project, but I haven't begun."

"Not yet, at least not for me." I shrug. "There may be things for those working on post-Reformation materials, but it seems there is little from the sixteenth century."

Marla nods. "Fire," she says curtly, before sitting down. "You'd have to go to the village archives for anything else. And there is not much there other than the wills and some tax documents."

"Fire," agrees Roger. "Basically, everything starts over with the Pitlock ownership. Not great for you, since you want the last Vale—he seems to be our likely patron, the one who was interested in the priory and Barton."

Or *she* was our likely patron. After seeing the portrait, I can't help but think that it was Lady Vale who was connected to the priory. How many accomplishments of women have been wrongly attributed to their husbands and sons in the annals of history?

Roger is still talking. "Think of what we've lost over the millennia because of the unfortunate confluence of paper and flame."

"Are we talking about Alexandria?" says Charles, as he walks into the room, chewing the remnants of some unseen pastry. "I've never known a scholar who does not dream of what would have been if the fire had not destroyed it. Possibly two hundred thousand treasures of the ancient world." He sits down in his usual place near the window.

Roger laughs. "Yes, that one will always smart. But we were talking on a smaller scale. Closer to home. Think, we almost lost *Beowulf* in the 1730s! What other masterpieces never made it into our hands?"

"But isn't that our job as scholars," I ask, "to find what is lost or at least make a conjecture? Remember the past so that the dead can speak again?"

The others nod but Roger says, "As long as they are speaking on paper. I think we have had enough ghost stories."

* * *

WHEN EVERYONE HAS arrived, I turn my attention to Wes, who is finally going to give his full paper. Although Wes is the only other one working on Barton, Brian's paper on the sexual proclivities of Henry VIII was tangentially related. He had a nice bit on Bishop Fisher's sermons against sex and how drastically it weakened a man, so I can see how the bishop's championing of Barton's visions fit into his worldview about Henry's sins.

Marla's paper on wills was also helpful. I have a better idea of how large the priory loomed in the villagers' lives, since so many of them directed their treasures to go there after death, ideally shortening their time in purgatory and speeding their passage to heaven. Of course, once the priory was dissolved, it didn't matter anymore. I wonder what it had been like for the sisters at St. Sepulchre's, to see the villagers slowly turn against them, cheering when their lands were taken away and they were turned out, nuns no more.

Wes has dressed up for the occasion. Khakis instead of jeans, a white button-down with the sleeves casually rolled up, the first two buttons undone. He's also replaced his sneakers with brogues. Handsome. I could unbutton more of that shirt. Maybe I should have last night. . . . *Fuck, concentrate.* I look around to make sure no one has noticed how red I must suddenly be, then turn my attention to getting my laptop ready for note-taking.

He clears his throat and glances up, looking directly at me with a lopsided grin I have reacquainted myself with in the last few hours. I pretend not to notice but I can't help smiling. "I would like to talk in more detail about the legend around here concerning the aftermath of Elizabeth Barton's execution. Let me set the scene," he says. He finally turns to look at the others, standing up. I love that he is a bit of a showman. Wait, what? No, I don't. It's exactly what I *don't* like about many scholars, and certainly what I don't like about him. They distract from the work. What is it about Wes that always has me so turned around?

"The nuns at the priory had word that Elizabeth was sentenced to death, which would have put many things in motion. They, of course, knew something was coming. Archbishop Cranmer had dissolved Henry's marriage to Catherine of Aragon when it was clear the pope would never capitulate. The pope's excommunication of the king and archbishop did not sway them in their actions.

"Our prioress, Philippa Jonys, would first and foremost want to protect the other sisters from any taint of association with the Holy Maid of Kent, but this battle was larger than St. Sepulchre's. Cromwell was in a fury. He was talking about dissolving every monastery and nunnery and turning that land and its profitability over to the crown. First to go would be those whose inhabitants had refused to acknowledge Henry VIII as leader of the newly formed Church of England and to formally break with the pope."

He pauses to let this sink in. "The story goes that Philippa and one of the Vales—probably Lord John Vale—had been in contact at some point before all hell broke loose, and that they both had reasons for wanting to hide some treasures.

"For Philippa, she wanted to secure the future of the priory, because of course everyone thought this whim of Henry's was momentary and that he would come to his senses and return to the Catholic fold. Or, at worst, that when Mary ascended to the throne the country would return to the pope—as it did when she became queen, as we know, but for such a very short time."

He stops and raises his arms theatrically.

"I believe that Lord Vale decided to help Philippa hide the gems and other treasures the prioress had received from hopeful pilgrims wanting an audience with the potential saint, the Holy Maid of Kent. The legends also speak of more prophecies, dangerous ones, that fell into the Vale hands. Were they hidden, too?

"Lord Vale may have hidden Philippa's treasures on this very property, in fact, although I think the family has looked many times over the centuries to no avail. Was he saving them for the return of the priory? If so, he died before he saw that happen, as indeed it never did."

Okay, okay—I admit that Wes is a good storyteller; he has all of us rapt.

"Generations of the Vale family insisted that their wealth was depleted by the Reformation. Had the Vales hidden their own treasures as well? And if so, for whom? Their grandchildren? Only Margaret Vale returned here after marrying into the Pitlock family, from whom Janine, our host's lovely wife, descends." He gestures at Roger.

I glance over at Marla, whom I expect to see looking a bit grim at the mention of Janine, but she has her pleasant smile on her face. She catches my eye and winks.

"Margaret restored the manor to its former glory, fixing what had been destroyed in the fire. Apparently if there was any treasure for her to find, it was forever lost. But the rumor here in the village is that one of the Vales, or Philippa, or perhaps both together, left a map. Please, this week as you work—especially you, Alison and Marla"—he points at us with a ringmaster's flourish—"since your documents have so much bearing on this place—please let me know if you come across a map." He smiles. "And make all of us rich!"

All of the heads in the room swivel toward me. Even Alex, who had slipped into the room for Wes's talk, is staring in my direction. Surely, they don't really think I hold the key to any of this fabled money?

"How rich are we talking about?" Brian jokes. Everyone laughs along, although Roger and Wes share a look of some concern that I can't quite make out.

"Well," says Wes, "certainly the gems and metals themselves would be worth rather a lot—diamonds, rubies, sapphires, emeralds, gold. These were all used in aristocratic Tudor jewelry. But the historical significance would increase their value. More than a million pounds, for sure."

"Hear, hear," says Roger, "I will toast to that. In fact, I think Alex is here to tell us it's time for lunch so we all can continue to discuss this marvelous bit of legend our folklorist has brought to us. I would love to hear any ideas that Alison has come up with as to possible hiding places."

I smile, but it is a fake smile. This seems a ludicrous and pointless endeavor.

"How marvelous," says Charles. "Tell us where to look, Alison." His eyes twinkle but there is a bit of an edge to his voice. I feel put on the spot.

I shrug. I think I can at least try to tie together the threads of Agnes Vale, Philippa Jonys, and Elizabeth Barton. For some reason, I am sure that it's Agnes, and not Lord Vale, who was conspiring with Philippa. Knitting a story of the past is far more interesting than searching for a treasure that surely doesn't exist.

The group files out of the library and heads to the dining room for lunch. Before following, I quickly pull up my email and am glad to see one from Calista, but I read it in total confusion.

From: calistacraig@saintandrews.edu
To: ASage@nyu.edu
Subject: RE: Checking in

Dear Alison,

I am sorry, I am not exactly clear what you are talking about. I am fine other than a little put out by the whole situation. You made your decision, although I wish you had spoken to me about it. It took a lot of arranging my schedule and my children's to make time for the Consortium, as I'm sure you understand, and then to have it pulled out from under me was a bit of a shock. I'm frankly surprised you think it's ok to email me as if everything is normal.
Calista

Shame and guilt wash over me and settle in my stomach, even though I know I have nothing to do with whatever Calista is referencing.

Just as I am about to type a response, there is a firm hand on my shoulder; it slides down my arm slowly. "It's very hard to get you alone here." Wes. I close the laptop quickly, intuitively not wanting him to see Calista's email. He leans over from behind me and kisses my neck, his hand still on my forearm. Despite myself, I shiver, my eyes closing almost involuntarily.

A small moan escapes from my mouth. "*Mmmm.*" What is wrong with me? "We are wanted at lunch," I manage.

"So we are," he murmurs, kissing my neck again.

"Let's not give people a reason to gossip," I say, turning my body slightly away but slowly, savoring the feeling of his hand sliding off of me.

"Alex is still setting up. We have some time. What did you think of my paper?" he asks, pulling out the chair next to me and sitting in it backward, his arms folded and resting on its back, legs straddling it. He rests his chin on his hands. I try to focus on the question and not the thought of him in my bed. Or that weird email from Calista. Everything feels very entangled. He's so cocky, so frustrating. But I want to kiss him again. And the old rhythm of our collaboration is coming back to me—how much I enjoyed sharing ideas with him and hearing his. That summer a million years ago helped me get my first book together, shaped ideas that would become the foundation of my career. Wes was part of that.

"Your paper was interesting," I say. "Surely, there are many comparable legends like it from other wealthy families. What's more exciting than lost treasures, haunted priories, secret maps? I think I saw that movie once."

He laughs. "Yes, it's all a bit far-fetched, but there are some clues that maybe it's not entirely rubbish. Although I'm not sure what the treasure actually could be. When I was a graduate student, my advisor had spent a lifetime working on a similar puzzle and when it was finally solved—which it was—the treasure was a family Bible. Very nice for the family, sure, with dates of births and marriages neatly listed, but not too exciting for someone who was hoping to find a cache of diamonds." As Wes stands up, he leans over and kisses me deeply. Shit. I am really enjoying this, and I do not have time for this distraction. Also, he is still young and lives in England and what am I even doing? "Shall we go in for lunch now?" he whispers, teeth on my earlobe, hot breath on my ear. "Or skip it and spend the afternoon in bed?"

"I think our absence would be noted since we make up more than a quarter of this household."

"No, no, less than that if you count Alex and Mrs. Bunch," he says, smiling. "We can definitely get away with it."

"I haven't met the elusive cook yet."

"I'll take you in to meet her later. She always has some pastries or other treats tucked away. Now, leave that computer and come eat. You need some sustenance after that workout last night. And energy for tonight."

I will my cheeks not to blush, but to no avail. I am not sure there will be the kind of activity Wes seems to be hoping for tonight, but instead of protesting I say, "Okay, you win. Let's go eat." I vow to write back to Calista later and get to the bottom of this misunderstanding.

St. Sepulchre's Priory, April 1533

The prioress led Bishop Fisher into the reception room in her quarters where the three of them could have a private audience. She knew Father Bocking was on his way, too, but she wanted Elizabeth to hear what the bishop had to say before Bocking arrived.

"This madness has to stop," Fisher said as soon as they were seated. "Your visions are no longer true or useful to our purpose, Elizabeth. You have put your life at risk and the lives of all of us who have supported you. You must retract your vision about the king and his new queen. I am as angry as you are at the break with Rome, but speaking this vision is not in aid of our cause."

"I have all of the support I need," Elizabeth countered. To Philippa, she looked wild-eyed, as if she held only a tenuous grasp of reason.

"You have *no* support!" raged Fisher, his voice rising into a shout. "Wolsey is dead. Thomas More has fallen deeply out of favor with the king. Thomas Cranmer is now the Archbishop of Canterbury, and he will do whatever Cromwell tells him. The king has divorced Catherine and has married Anne Boleyn. People are being hanged. People are being burned. And you will be next. I may be as well for refusing to accept this new religious order. I will burn for God, girl, but I will not burn for you."

"I am not a girl. I am the Holy Maid. And Father Bocking has not abandoned me," whispered Elizabeth. "God has not abandoned me. You will burn in hell as surely as will the king. I have seen it! I have seen you all burning while I am sitting at the right hand of Jesus."

Fisher moved to speak again, his angular face sweaty with rage, but Philippa interrupted. "Child," she said softly, putting her hand firmly on Elizabeth's arm, "the bishop is saying that the Devil has led you astray. That is what he does. He tries to convince you that the visions you are having are sent from God, but they are sent from the demon himself.

You would not be the first to be led so far afield. Repent, admit your error, and you can live your life here at the priory in prayer and peace." She said the last part through clenched teeth, because the thought of Elizabeth remaining among the sisters was not a peaceful one. But it was better than seeing the girl executed.

"*You* are the ones misled by the Devil," said Elizabeth, pointing at both of them, just as Father Bocking was led into the room by a novice. "Satan is at work here."

"I agree," said Bocking from the doorway, taking in the scene, the red-faced Fisher, standing now, and Philippa's tight-lipped restraint. He stood next to Elizabeth and put his hand on her shoulder, pulling her out of Philippa's grasp. "You have abandoned the Holy Maid in her hour of need just as Jesus was abandoned by the apostles in his. You are failing the tests that God has sent us." With that, he led Elizabeth out of the room.

Fisher and the prioress regarded each other with alarm. "You must convince her to recant," the bishop warned. "She is implicating all of us. Cromwell's men are adept at spreading poison. Everywhere I go there are whispers about her, that she is having sexual relations with the priests who support her, that she speaks out of madness."

"There is no fornicating here," Philippa replied, aghast.

"Of course not," Fisher spat, "but the gossip does its work well."

There had always been rumors about Elizabeth, always detractors. As much as people wanted the visionary to be in direct contact with God, they also wanted her to be dismissed as a fraud. As the mood in England was turning more firmly toward Luther, it turned more directly against anything that smacked of superstition or papistry. And Elizabeth represented both.

Fisher raised his voice one last time, a single bony finger pointed high in the air. "I wash my hands of her. She has gone too far. I will not hang for a stubborn girl." He stormed out before Philippa could respond.

* * *

Not long after the bishop's visit, the news reached the priory that Cromwell had increased his arrests. Those who opposed the king were tortured. They were hanging. They were losing their heads. They were dying the villains' deaths that Elizabeth said she had foreseen for Henry and his bride.

One evening after more troubling news from London, the prioress went to Elizabeth's cell to find the girl kneeling before her small altar, which was bare but for a small painting of the Virgin Mary with her eyes lifted and hands in prayer. The Maid's habit was disheveled, her hair falling out of her veil. Philippa sat on the cot. "Elizabeth," she said softly, as if approaching a frightened animal, "I believe the king's men will come for you soon. Make sure that you are confessed. When you are shriven and ready to go to God, your soul will be at peace, no matter what may come. You must be brave."

Elizabeth did not turn her head to look at the prioress, but she moved her still-defiant and wild eyes toward Philippa. For the first time, there was a trace of uncertainty and fear there. She said nothing, though, and bowed her head more deeply in prayer. Her hands were clasped so tightly that her fingertips were white with exertion.

Not long after the sisters had gone to sleep that night, Sister Maria came running into the prioress's quarters, rousing Philippa from her restless slumber.

"Mater," the nun said, breathless, "the Holy Maid. She is having a vision. It is new. She is raving in a way I have never seen before. She is hot as if a fire burns within, although her skin remains pale." Maria seemed herself febrile, panting, both terrified and excited.

"Get me a quill and some parchment," said Philippa. "Perhaps she will recant. It may save her."

The sister ran to the prioress's office, returning with a quill and ink but no parchment. Instead, she offered a book. "This is her book of visions," Maria said. "There are empty pages in the back."

Other than the few letters the prioress had to compose in her position, she seldom wrote. Her hand was unpracticed for speed. She had once been the cellarer of the priory and frequently wrote lists: food they had, items and alms received by the nuns. Philippa could feel the memory of it in her fingers, but still her hand ached as she held the quill. To write down a vision as it happened . . . she hoped she could do it. She followed the nun through the cloister to Elizabeth's cell, struck by the feeling of cold air on her head, which was just wrapped in a light cloth—she was so rarely without her veil.

There were two visions, and they were indeed new. Hand shaking, Philippa wrote them down as quickly as she could, but fortunately the Maid repeated them three, four, five times. Exactly the same each time. Every time Elizabeth gasped, Philippa started a new line.

Maria was right—these visions were unlike any of the others that Philippa had witnessed.

The first was as if Elizabeth had seen and heard the plans that she and Agnes had been putting in place; it was part of their map, their secrets laid bare, a cipher inside her words.

The second vision was extraordinary. Philippa did not know what it meant exactly, but she knew enough that it meant danger if it were to be repeated.

When the Maid awoke, bathed in sweat despite the cold of the February air, she had no recollection of her words, nor could she explain them.

Later that morning, back in her chamber, Philippa regarded the book in the morning light. It looked sinister, but the message within it carried some hope. The Maid remained asleep. The nuns were at their morning duties. Whom should she summon? Bocking? No. He had done enough damage to the priory. Philippa put her head in her hands and thought before beckoning one of the nuns.

"Please, Sister Agatha, summon a messenger. I must get a notice to Lady Vale."

Vale House Manor, June 2023, Day 4

After lunch, Wes suggests I come with him to meet Mrs. Bunch and see the kitchen. "And then maybe we can skip the afternoon writing session and take a nap?" he asks, hopefully.

"I think I have too much work to do for that."

He stops and takes me by the shoulders. "We wouldn't actually nap, Alison. . . . I want to spend as much time with you while you're here, preferably in bed, as I can."

"Yes, Wes. I understood your proposition. Look, last night was a lot of fun, but I'd like to keep things professional. I think we are relying on nostalgia here." Are we? "A lot has changed since we saw each other last." I sound way more convincing than I feel. I hope he isn't convinced.

"It seems to me," he says, almost in a whisper, "that this is kismet. You, here with me. Single again. Working together again. Let's not have it slip through our fingers."

"Let's just take things slow here, okay?" I say. "Right now, I am focused on the work."

"Uh-huh," he says dubiously. "Okay. I can do professional. Come then, the kitchen is this way." He takes my hand and leads me through the dining room, to a small butler's pantry; then, through another door, the kitchen materializes. It feels like a step back in time. Like the library, this is clearly a room that's been integral to the home and the families who have lived there.

"The kitchen is the oldest surviving part of the manor house," Wes explains, moving his hair out of his eyes in a way I've always found especially sexy, "dating back to the thirteenth century when the house was part of the priory."

As Wes talks about the house, I am taking in the kitchen. Although full of all the conveniences of the modern age (a fridge, a gas stove, a dishwasher—all looking like they are ready to be replaced), the room also boasts a giant stone hearth that, while now only decorative, had clearly been vital to the kitchen for many centuries. "Oh! It's charming," I say, and I mean it. It is the most inviting space I have been in since my arrival at the manor home. The clean white walls and open windows add a glow to the whole space, and the smells of something delicious—bread?—waft from the oven. A small wooden door, arched like a tiny gothic medieval church window, opens onto a pathway that leads to the priory grounds.

A plump, gray-haired woman with an apron, as if coming directly from central casting for a British housekeeper, enters from an adjoining room—the pantry, I suppose. She smiles broadly when she sees Wes and opens her arms for an embrace. "Westy!" she says. "You've barely come to see me all week! I was starting to feel neglected. I've even been holding on to some of your favorite biscuits in anticipation, although they have a tendency to disappear when I am not around." She points to a cookie jar on the counter, laughing. "Alex likes them, too."

"I'm so sorry, Mrs. Bunch," Wes says, "we really have been very busy. Roger packs this week tightly, as you know. I've brought a newcomer, Alison, to meet you. I mean, I guess I'm a newcomer to the Consortium, too, if not the house."

Obviously Wes is a local, but surely all of the people from the village do not know the house and its people so well?

"Mrs. Bunch," I say, extending my hand, "thank you for making this week so delicious. I doubt I'll fit into my pants by the time I leave."

"So pleased to meet you, Alison," Mrs. Bunch says. "It's about time Roger invited some more women other than that skinny Marla. She eats like a bird. You look like you are someone who enjoys her food."

I consider whether this is a compliment and decide to take it as such. "I do. And yours is exquisite."

"Come, come, have a biscuit and some tea while I get this bread out of the oven." She gestures to the small table by a window with a familiar view; my room must be right above. Mrs. Bunch brings over a tray with the teapot and cups and a few brown cookies. "A pretty view, although it's been a while since the gardener has clipped enough for me to see it."

"Can't Alex do it?" I ask.

"Oh, that lad is so blundering, he'd cut off his own hand. I can't tell you how many dishes he's broken. Anyway, Roger has him doing all sorts of extra tasks around here. I can barely get him to serve the meals."

I take a bite of the cookie. It is spicy and sweet and altogether delicious.

Mrs. Bunch smiles at Wes. "You've always loved these biscuits, Westy. I made a batch the minute Roger told me you would be joining the group. Congratulations, by the way, I know you've wanted to be included for a while." She rumples his hair like he's a child, but Wes doesn't seem to mind.

"Thanks." He grins. "I was lucky this year." My mind flashes to the email from Calista. What did she mean when she said she was surprised that I would even write to her? Was Calista perhaps feverish with Covid?

I stand up. "Thank you so much for the cookie, Mrs. Bunch. Wes, I should get back to the library. The afternoon session is about to start, and I have an email I would like to send beforehand."

"I'll see you there," Wes says, reaching for a third cookie. "Just want to finish this tea and have a quick catch-up."

* * *

I AM NOT, as I hoped, the first to arrive in the library. Marla and Charles are already there, laptops open, typing away. Roger is there, too, speaking quietly to Alex, who makes a hasty exit as I walk in. The days seem to be going by so quickly, and now that the presenting is done we are meant to share research and collaborate. So far, though, I've found the sharing and collaborating a bit guarded, protective. It seems all are giving half information, keeping the real stuff to themselves.

"Alison," Roger says, waving me over to his seat, "come here and let's look at the Barton book together. I feel like we are missing something."

I am going to have to find a more private moment to write Calista. I come and stand behind him, opening the PDF of the book on my laptop.

"Flip to the end," he says. "Look here. The last page is missing. There should be a woodcut or some other image of Elizabeth. That's usually how these books concluded, and the page is cut out."

I nod. "Yes, I know. The book had at least two pages that had rotted away. I thought maybe we were missing something. But a lot of these books recycled images from others. It could have been any female saint or even a standard image of the Virgin Mary. I think we can only guess what was there."

Roger flips back to the acrostic that he discovered yesterday. "And I think we need to take another look at this," he says. Wes has now joined us and stands behind Roger's chair next to me, looking over. I try to concentrate on what Roger is saying as Wes's hand gently, secretly touches mine. Neither one of us moves our hands away.

"'Venerate our Mother, seated / At the side of Jhesu, our meek other / Locking inside our heartchest the / Emeralds, rubies, and pearls of our devotion,'" Roger reads. "I wonder if this is some kind of clue as to Wes's jewels?" Wes stops stroking my hand and leans farther over the chair. Charles and Marla walk over to see what we have found, and I quickly move my own hand into my pocket.

"'Chest,' of course, has two meanings, on our bodies but also a real thing that locks away valuables. These gems of devotion may be more than metaphorical?" Roger asks.

"There was that chest willed in Lady Vale's document," adds Marla.

I ask, "Maybe they hid it somewhere in the manor having to do with the Virgin Mary? Anything here that is devoted to her?"

Roger shakes his head. "Not that I know of. Or if there was, it is long gone. There's the rood screen of Mary in the church, but that is hardly big enough to hide a chest of jewels. It's only a few inches thick. Although worth investigating, I think . . ." He looks up at Wes for a moment, raising his eyebrows as their eyes meet. "Let's keep thinking about it," Roger says. "We may solve this mystery yet."

"Like most of the folklore here," Wes says, "there's probably not much of a mystery to solve. It's a story that has been told and retold. Embellished. The kernel of truth lost to us in time."

Roger nods. "You're likely right, Westy. But wouldn't it be fun if it wasn't?"

The Tower, London, November 1533

Elizabeth was freezing. Although she was underground, it felt like a cold wind was always blowing unabated. The men who had brought her by boat to the Tower had little care that her linen shift had gotten wet and stuck to her body as it became stiffened with ice. How often had she wished to be rid of the heavy nun's habit? Now she would have given anything to be wrapped in its warmth.

The manacles they had placed on her wrists at her arrest had worn away much of the skin there, and they bled and burned by the time the barge passed under London Bridge with its grisly audience of severed heads watching her go by with their empty eye sockets. She closed her own eyes to the image but could still hear the birds gnawing away at the feast lined up on the spikes, shrieking with pleasure.

The guards had timed her arrival with the low tide so that she could be brought through Traitors' Gate, a lattice of metal bars rising above the murky green water of the Thames. As the gate shut behind her once the barge came through, Elizabeth did not turn to see them secure the lock, but her ears again betrayed her so that she could feel that metal scrape upon metal and seal her in. She had hoped they would release her from the chains, but they had not, and the heavy manacles continued to chafe what little unbroken skin she had left. At least her wrists were numbing in the cold.

"Where's the bishop?" she had asked the men when they came for her at the priory, men who brutally pushed aside the nuns who had tried to stop them from entering. "He will vouch for me!" But they only laughed and told her no one would speak for her, and those who did were also criminals. It was only when she realized that the men were in Cromwell's livery and not the king's that she felt truly afraid.

She looked each of Cromwell's men in the eye and told them that she had seen them in hell in a vision, even though she had not. It was her only weapon left. At least one of them looked to the ground and paled at her words. He rubbed his callused hands together as if he were the one who was chilled. That man led the way as they went down the stone stairs, around and around into the depths of the earth. She tripped twice, falling to the ground and smashing her knees, her bound arms useless to break the fall. And then she was put alone in a bare cell, a frayed pallet on the ground. A bucket for her toileting. The room smelled of rotten meat and human waste.

With little food other than stale bread and only water to drink, and nothing more than a thin blanket to keep her warm against the howling wind, Elizabeth lost track of time. The water in her cup froze to ice. The mice and rats had no care of her; they ran around the cell as if she were not there and nipped at her scabbed skin when she tried to sleep. Sleep did not come easily.

Bocking had told her that God would always come to her aid. He had not yet done so. She tried to kneel to pray but her knees would not support her body and she instead lay, baby-like, asking God for his intervention.

Men came in and out, throwing some stale food near her to scavenge before the rats did. They never cleaned her bucket. Never took it. After some number of days—was it three? four?—Thomas Cromwell appeared. With him was a tall, beardless man Elizabeth had never seen. They both wrinkled their noses at the smell of the place, and Cromwell held a cloth over his mouth and nose to block out the fetid odor that she no longer detected. The stranger was dressed as an archbishop, a heavy crucifix adorned in gemstones hanging from his neck. The name came to her: *Cranmer.* The Archbishop of Canterbury. "Cromwell's puppet," she had heard Bocking say.

Elizabeth knew the man was a heretic, retaining the garments and titles of the true faith but not the holiness of his predecessors. "You are a false emissary of God," she said weakly. "You will burn alongside your king and his harlot."

Cromwell laughed. "Enough of an examination, Archbishop? You can see that her visions are false. She is a charlatan and a liar and has had sexual congress with her confessor."

Elizabeth's eyes grew wide at his words. "You lie," she whispered. "You are already marked for hell, Cromwell."

Cranmer looked closely at Elizabeth. "Who tells you to say these things? Who has guided your voice in its deceit?"

Elizabeth was resolute. "God tells me the truth and I speak it. My prophecies are true. I am a true visionary and prophet, and I say that you"—she lifted her hands toward him, chained together as they were—"and this man"—she spat at Cromwell—"with your so-called king and his whore will go to hell. Henry will die a villain's death within a year. I have seen it."

She said it because Bocking wanted her to. Because he told her she was the last help for the king. Because without her the country would crumble.

Bocking had so eagerly written down her words. Where was he now?

She was like Christ now. Abandoned by those she loved before her final trial.

Cranmer nodded at Cromwell. "I have seen enough. She is a false prophet. You may extract the confession you need."

"Very well," Cromwell said. "Send in my men as you leave." He turned to Elizabeth and pointed at a hook on the ceiling. He spoke slowly, deliberately. "They will unchain you and then manacle your wrists again—this time behind your back. And the chain between your manacles will hang there on that hook and your feet will dangle below. First, your shoulders will come away from your body. I have heard that pain is terrible. Your wrists, too, will have no skin remaining. They will be flayed by the chains. Your arms will ache, your head will have no place to rest. You will beg to have your feet again on the ground."

He paused and turned back to her. "This is your final chance to confess of your own volition."

She spat again at his feet.

Vale House Manor, June 2023, Day 4

When I realize that everyone else is occupied by their work, I finally take a second to write my reply.

From: ASage@nyu.edu
To: calistacraig@saintandrews.edu
Subject: RE: RE: Checking in

Dear Calista,

I am so sorry, but I think there is some confusion here. I was expecting you to be at the manor when I arrived a few days ago and was then told by your replacement (Westley Charney) that you had Covid and that Roger had asked him to come when you could not. Is this not how it happened? I'm sorry, I am very confused by the tone and substance of your last email. If I have done something to offend you, please let me know so that I can make it right.
Alison

I assume and hope it's all just been some giant misunderstanding that will be cleared up quickly. I turn back to my computer and continue to type up my notes on the priory, as well as some of my suspicions about Agnes Vale and the role she may have played in Elizabeth's book. I put my headphones on, listening to Mozart's *Don Giovanni,* and am so absorbed in my writing that by the time I stop to stretch and look around the room, I realize that only Charles and I remain quietly working in the library. When I raise my head from my work, I find Charles looking at me closely.

"Where did everyone go?" I ask.

"Roger and Marla went back to the village archives to see what else they could find there or if there were any local records they had missed," Charles answers. "Arjun and Brian went on a bike ride." I am pretty sure that is code for a drink at the King's Head. "I am not sure where Wes is," he adds slowly, looking closely at me, "if that's whom you seek."

"Nope," I say. Shit. Am I paranoid or does everyone seem to have an idea what happened with us? "Just curious. Did I hear your door shut late last night, Charles?" Two can play this game. If he's going to probe me about Wes, I can try to figure out where he was going at one in the morning.

He looks like a deer in headlights. I'm not sure what he was doing, but he definitely did not want me to know about it. "I-I have no idea what you're talking about," he stammers.

I consider us even and walk over to the section of the library where I've seen most of the reference books. "What are you looking for? Does it lead to our buried treasure?" Charles asks, somewhat earnestly, although I can only imagine he is joking or just all too happy to change the subject from nighttime wanderings.

"The rood screen in the church has some of the usual suspects of women saints, but there is one I have never seen. She has a halo with jewels and is holding a book; the inscription says they were only able to bury her skull."

"Hmmm . . . doesn't ring a bell for me, either. Are you looking up decapitated saints?" Charles joins me to search the shelves.

"There are a few saints who fit the bill, but most are obscure. St. Afra? St. Eurosia? I guess the best bets are St. Cecilia or St. Winifred."

"There's a book of saints here somewhere, I saw it this morning. . . . Ah, here it is." Charles pulls the book down and starts flipping through it. "Let's see, here's St. Cecilia . . . Roman noblewoman . . . wouldn't consummate marriage unless her husband converted." He looks up. "That's one way to put the brakes on your wedding night." He continues to read aloud as he moves his forefinger along the page. "Converted him (well, obviously) and several others until she was beheaded by Marcus Aurelius for her efforts. Her head miraculously preached for three days."

"Right, and I know she does show up on rood screens around England—she's one of the more popular medieval saints—but I think she's usually holding a crown," I say. "And I've never seen that Latin inscription in relationship to Cecilia, but that could have been a fancy of the painter. So, she's a possibility. Look up Winifred."

Charles flips through the pages again until he finds the right passage. "Daughter of a Welsh nobleman—well, that's a little closer to home—oh, yes, this is a good one. I know it." He looks up at me over his reading glasses. "She was supposed to marry a prince but chose to be celibate, so he cut off her head."

"Gruesome," I say. But typical, I think, that a man would rather kill a woman than be shunned by her. "It's no wonder these saints' lives were so popular. Sex and violence! Sells in the Middle Ages. Sells today. Winifred should have gone the Cecilia route and made the prince convert instead."

From the corner of my eye, I see Wes enter the library. Even though my body is angled toward Charles, I am fully aware of every motion of Wes's body as he walks toward us.

"It doesn't stop there," says Charles. "Winifred's head rolled down a hill and where it landed a spring came up with healing waters. Then her uncle was somehow able to restore her head to its body, no doubt with the help of the same healing waters, and she became abbess of the church next to the spring, which they turned into a well and which still attracts pilgrims." He puts the book down. "Could she be your girl?"

"What are you talking about?" Wes says. "Headless women? Magic springs?"

"Not your research on more neighborhood ghosts," Charles says to Wes. "This is for Alison."

"How did you know I was working on other rumored ghosts around here?" says Wes, raising an eyebrow in surprise.

"Oh, I . . . I am sure you mentioned something about that," stutters Charles. "Anyway, we are discussing St. Winifred. Alison is trying to figure out who the saint with the skull could be in the church." Wes continues to look at Charles a little strangely but turns his focus to me.

"I don't think it is her, either, since she was ultimately buried *with* her head," I say. "But thank you for the assist, Charles. There is no image of a well or water in the rood screen. Just gems and that strange inscription of only burying the skull. I like to think of Elizabeth sitting in that priory church and contemplating those saints."

As I say this, a thought hits me like a thunderbolt. "Could that image be of Elizabeth herself? What years are those rood screens?" I can't believe it hadn't been my first thought. I was so fixated on the idea of a saint that I had overlooked the most obvious. Although it was not unusual to venerate local holy people as if they were canonized saints, it would have been exceedingly defiant of the painter to depict a convicted traitor and heretic in such a way in the wake of the Reformation. Who would have dared such an image?

Wes is now next to me. "The screen paintings would predate Elizabeth, usually, but it could have been repainted. Maybe we should go back and look more closely. Don't I also owe you a tour of the bell tower?"

I avoid looking directly at Charles, whom I can see has a smirk on his face. "Yes," I say firmly, standing up, "let's go see."

* * *

"WHAT WAS THAT between you and Charles?" I ask Wes as we leave the manor. "About your research?"

"I am not altogether sure," says Wes, "but my notes on ghosts were left in the library last night and I couldn't find them this morning. I thought maybe Alex or Mrs. Bunch had taken them for rubbish and tossed them. Now I wonder if Charles had picked them up for some reason."

I am about to answer when we bump into Alex. Or, rather, he seems to be blocking our way. "Hello, Dr. Sage, Westy," he says, nodding at both of us. "Where are you off to on this fine day? A stroll through the garden?"

"Back to the church," I say, forcing joviality. "I haven't seen the bell tower yet."

"You two enjoyed the church quite a bit last night, no?" Alex says with something between a sneer and a grin.

I feel the heat roar up into my cheeks. "Excuse me?" I practically spit out.

"You were quite a bit later than the rest of the party after the ghost tour," Alex says. I can't even look at him, unsure of what he knows or suspects.

"Ah, yes," says Wes. "Alison was interested in seeing the hellmouth by candlelight."

"Yes, it's something, isn't it?" says Alex. "All those sinners burning to their deaths. The liars, the heretics . . . the fornicators." Now I am sure he is looking pointedly at me.

"Yes, those medieval people sure had wild imaginations and stringent ideas of sinning," I say, nudging the back of Wes's foot with my own. "Well, we'd better get moving, I don't want to miss that afternoon light."

"Of course," says Alex, stepping aside. "Let me know, Westy, if you find anything of interest."

As soon as we are out of earshot, I turn to Wes. "What the hell was that?! He's so creepy."

"Oh, he's harmless," says Wes. "I've known him all his life, a village boy. He's an awkward lad, but good-hearted. His family has long worked for the Pitlocks. I'm sure he doesn't understand what we all see in these old ruins and papers."

"He doesn't seem harmless to me. I think he may have been nosing around in my room," I fume. "And he certainly seemed to have an idea about what's going on with us."

Wes turns to face me, grabbing my hand so that there are only a few inches between us. "Then he knows more than me, Alison," he says, a catch in his voice. "What is going on with us?"

I hold my breath for a moment, not sure what to say. Finally, I eke out a "We had a fun night. A nice reminder of the past. Let's not make it more than it is, Wes." Holding his hand feels so natural, so normal. I want to pull him in and draw him closer but don't.

"Is that what you want?" he says, looking down. "One moment you are in my arms, the next you are kicking me out of your room. I feel a charge between us, and yet you tell me you want to keep things professional. I used to be able to read your signals, and I can't anymore." I resist the urge to reach my hand to the lock of hair that has fallen in front of his long-lashed eyes. Those blue, blue eyes that are now looking up at me and trying to catch mine, but I focus instead on the top of his unbuttoned collar.

I am more aware of my own body than I have been in months, years, as if it has been shaken awake. Every sense feels heightened: the sound of bees buzzing nearby, the whoosh of the wind through the wildflowers around us and their heady scent. I feel every centimeter of my palm in his hand.

"I don't know, Wes. I mean, this *can't* be anything real. We have such different lives now, and you live here." I gesture around us. "I live in

New York, where I am happily tied to two children and also have an ex-husband floating about."

"Can you tell me you haven't wanted this . . . haven't you thought about it ever since we were together?" he asks. "Because I have."

I shake my head and let go of his hand. "I did. But you just let me leave. You didn't ask me to stay. You didn't even walk me to the train station. You didn't email or call or anything when I was back in New York. The next I heard from you was the review in *Historical English Studies* where you said my book had, and I quote, 'interesting points hidden amidst remarkably inelegant writing.' Remember that?" I'm suddenly angry now, the past boiling up when I have been trying to turn down its heat the past few days. I pull my hand out of his.

Wes looks stricken, as if I had slapped him across the face. "*You* were the one who left. You didn't even pretend to look for a way to stay. From the day you arrived here, you talked about the dream job waiting for you at the other end. You told me over and over again that our work was the most important thing about our collaboration. Our *work*. Not whatever was going on between us." It's my turn to be shocked. I can't believe what I am hearing. "I didn't come to the station because I couldn't bear to watch you leave, Alison. I wrote that review because I was so furious with you and it was one way to get back at you. And when I was invited to be here and knew that I would see you, I almost didn't come. But I did. I thought twenty years, surely, whatever was between us was long dead. And then you arrived, and it was as if those years never happened. I knew immediately I wanted to pick up where we had left off. That I had made a terrible mistake letting you go." I realize I have been holding my breath the whole time he has been talking. His story of that summer, my departure, is so entirely different from my experience of it. Were we living in two separate realities? I am standing here, stupefied.

He looks around to make sure we're alone and, satisfied, runs his fingers through my hair, pulling me toward him at the same time. He kisses my forehead, and then my nose, and then my lips, softly. "I object to you saying this can't be anything real. It was and it is."

The Tower, London, November 1533

"Let me know when you are finished with her," Cromwell said, leaving the room as the guards readied the torment. The guard, a short man with only one eye, the other scarred-over flesh in its place, grunted his agreement. Elizabeth felt unmoored without Bocking by her side, without the convent walls holding her safely within. Where was God's light now? She closed her eyes and prayed that he would come and save her. She had done so much for him, had done it all in his name, why wasn't he here?

Elizabeth whimpered as the other guard, broad-shouldered and muscular like the farmhands she once knew, took her raw and bloody wrists—they looked like uncooked meat—and undid the manacles, securing them anew behind her back. His callused hands were rough on hers, hers that had been allowed to soften the last few years. She prayed aloud, "Dear Jesus, this is your holy and sainted daughter Elizabeth, the Holy Maid of Kent. Please deliver me from this evil!"

She summoned the voice she used when she was shouting her prophecies in town squares, the voice she had seen bring people to their knees in prayer, hopeful that it would give these torturers pause, but Cromwell's men were unmoved. They pushed her to step up onto a wooden box, and she cried as they pulled her arms up and placed the link between her cuffs onto the hook.

"Listen, woman," said one of the guards, gruffly. "We are going to hoist you up. Your sinews will burst. Your bones will break."

"God will save me," Elizabeth said, but she was not as sure as she had been, now that she could feel her arms pulled behind her by the men. Already her arms were stretched beyond what they could bear.

The guard did not respond, and instead kicked the box out from under Elizabeth's feet. As she dropped, she felt a wrenching pain in her shoulders. She heard the snap of her bones and muscle. She tried to scream but could make no sound because she had no breath. She could feel her shoulders up next to her ears, where they did not belong.

Just before it mercifully went black, her mind flashed to the mangled bodies writhing in the hellmouth.

She was next aware only of the searing pain in her neck, her shoulders, her arms, her back. White-hot misery, as if the muscles and bones inside her body were on fire and burning her from the inside out. She could not tell where the pain began and where it ended. Elizabeth opened her eyes with effort to see Cromwell sitting at a table that he somehow had spirited into the cell. On the table was a paper and quill. Slowly, she realized that she was lying on the floor, her wrists unfettered but her arms lying useless beside her. She could not move them for the agony.

"Speak your confession," Cromwell said, dipping his quill into ink. "Or the rack will be next. It will do to the rest of the body what has now been done to your arms."

Elizabeth tried to speak but could only moan in response.

Cromwell looked up from his paper. "Bocking has confessed," he said. "Merely the promise of the rack was enough. He said your words were false. He said that he used your words for the papal cause and because he hated the Lutherans."

Again, something inside Elizabeth snapped, but this time it was not her body. The realizations hit her one after the other, a drumbeat.

Bocking had known.

He had known she was not always sure what she had seen.

He encouraged her embellishment.

He knew she would end up here, broken in body and spirit.

He had known.

Cromwell studied her carefully. "Did Edward Bocking tell you to feign these trances?" he asked.

Elizabeth sobbed and nodded. "Yes."

"Did Edward Bocking tell you what to say to the people who gave you audience?"

"Yes."

"And all of your visions have been false?"

Even in her agony, Elizabeth paused. Cromwell sat with the quill poised, ready to record her words. The pain was searing into her head now, working its way up through her neck over the back of her skull. Her shoulders throbbed as if her body itself was begging her compliance. But she could still see and feel that warm light from her vision at the Cobb farm, the looks of the nuns when she recovered from her trance at St. Sepulchre's, hear the voice that spoke to her. She shook her head. "No. Some of them were true. I was chosen by God."

Cromwell put the pen down and said, so quietly that she could barely hear him over the throbbing in her ears, "Elizabeth, I will promise you a swift execution for your true confession. If you are defiant, you will suffer a painful death." He nodded to the one-eyed guard, who reached down and pulled one of her arms. Cromwell said, "I will ask again. Have all your visions been false?"

The pain was unbearable, as if her arm were being ripped from her body. She cried, "Yes!" as she again gave in to a merciful blackness.

Cromwell gathered his papers and addressed the guards. "Now we can question Bocking."

Vale House Manor, June 2023, Day 4

The church is empty, as usual. In this light, flames of the hellmouth, while still frightening, are less animated; the transi-tomb cadaver remains at rest. Being in here makes me again think of Elizabeth in a new way. Not just as a historical character but as a person who stood in this very spot and saw many of these same sights. She was surrounded by reminders of death; was it still a surprise when it finally came for her so violently?

Wes comes up behind me and puts his arms around me, chin nestled on my shoulder next to my neck. It feels overly familiar and lovely all at once and I don't want him to stop. "We don't have to look at the rood screen, you know," he says, suggestively. "We have nowhere to be until dinner."

I swat him off. "Actually, I do want to look at it. This is really what I'm here for, Wes. I need some time to process what you said, I'm still taking it in. Hell, I'm still recovering from my divorce. I don't know the answer to your question about what exactly is going on between us, but I do know there is no easy way it can continue. Let's enjoy ourselves while we are here—but also can you let me get some work done?"

He puts his hands up in surrender. "Okay, okay. You win. Let's look at the rood screen together and then head up the bell tower."

The rood-screen panels only come up to my waist, so I must crouch down to really examine the saint painted there: her eyes looking upward rather than modestly downcast, jewels around her head, a book, an arm outstretched. I put on my reading glasses for a better look, but there is nothing identifying her, no words or images.

"I guess this *could* be Elizabeth," I say. "Although the inscription is strange. *Cumque issent ut sepelirent eam non invenerunt nisi calvariam* means 'And when they went to bury her, they found nothing but the skull.' But of course, in Elizabeth's case, the skull was the one thing they *didn't* have."

Wes looks thoughtful and crouches down next to me. "Unless, of course, there were two burials. When she was buried at Greyfriars they buried her body without her head, but perhaps her skull was buried somewhere else. Think of it a bit like the translation of saints' relics."

I consider this. When a dead person was declared a saint, the body was frequently exhumed, with the body parts separated and sent to different churches and places to spread around the relics (and the power they supposedly contained). St. Catherine of Siena's head, for example, is still on display in a glass reliquary in Siena, and her finger is in another church. In Padua, once, I waited in line with all the other pilgrims to see St. Anthony's tongue. In Bruges, there's a supposed vial of Jesus's blood. European churches at the time of the Reformation were populated by fragments of bodies: bones, hair, fingernails. Any Catholic church, even today, has relics in its altar. It would not have been unusual for Elizabeth's head to deliberately rest somewhere other than with her body, especially if she had supporters who thought her a saint, a Catholic martyr after her execution.

"Does the paint on this panel look more recent to you than on the other ones?" I ask. It is so hard to tell. Even if it had been painted a century later than the earlier panels, nothing on the rood screen was more recent than 1600, I would wager.

"It does," says Wes slowly. "It's much clearer than the others. Look how faded the blue is in Mary's veil, or the red in Barbara's cloak. But the jewels in this saint's crown are still quite vibrant. Also, the writing has flaked off almost everywhere else, but it's still dark here." He stands up from his crouch. "It looks like the writing is finally flaking off over the hellmouth, though. I hope they get the funds to restore it."

I glance up at the inscription over the hellmouth. I can see what he means; some of the words are losing their sharpness. It is very hard to read in this dim light, but that could also be my middle-aged eyes. *Sigh.* At least I live in the age of reading glasses and portable flashlights. The prioress Philippa and Lady Agnes Vale would have had no such crutches should they have made it to middle age. Elizabeth certainly hadn't.

"Well, I think Elizabeth has risen to the top of my list of suspects for rood-screen immortality," I say, standing up and stretching my legs. "Oh!" I startle, as my hair is blown in front of my face. "Where is that breeze coming from? Did we leave the door open?"

"No," says Wes, pointing at the wall behind me, "that would be the leper's squint. If the wind is just right, it can really howl in here."

I turn and, for the first time, see the little peephole from the interior of the church. It isn't as visible from this side, constructed as it was for looking in rather than out. There's a small shaft of light coming through it.

"Do you think . . . last night . . . Alex . . . the squint?" I ask, grossed out at the thought.

"No, no, that would be altogether too heinous. Although you never know what someone's kink is," he says with a laugh. "We gave him a good show if so!"

I don't think it is funny but shake it off for now. "Well, let's go see the bell tower."

* * *

As we walk through the church, I notice a few brass slabs inlaid in the floors. They have images of long-dead men and women that I know represent important members of the village, the manor, and of course the priory. Most have inscriptions so worn down as to be unreadable.

The stairs to the bell tower are behind a small door across from the church entrance. Right in front of it, there is a brass slab that depicts a woman—a nun. Her hands are folded in prayer, palms touching, fingers pointing straight toward heaven. The words engraved in the brass memorialize whoever is buried there, but they are faint. I can make out bits: the first line reads . . . AT . . . PACE. The second: . . . ER . . . A . . . NYS. The third: PR . . . SEP . . . Then, more clearly: HAVE MERCY THIS XIII DAY OF NOVEMBRE 1536.

"Any idea who this is?" I ask. "I guess the first line is *requiescat in pace,* 'rest in peace,' but the remainder seems impossible to make out without more clues."

"I think this is a prioress," says Wes, standing close behind me. "One of the last ones, because there aren't any later tombs of nuns in here. Centuries of feet, and some deliberate erasure after the Reformation, have worn the words down too much to know more, I'm afraid. But the third line looks like it could be 'prioress of St. Sepulchre's.' The death date would be basically simultaneous with the dissolution of the priory, but she still may have had some patrons around here who thought it was important that she get properly memorialized."

"Vale?" I ask. "If we had a crayon or a pencil we could do a rubbing of it on paper. That might make it clearer." I have a thought in the corner of my head, just out of reach. I will take it out to examine later when I am not so distracted by Wes.

Wes opens the door to the tower, with a warning. "The staircase is extremely narrow and steep," he says. "Be careful—one wrong step and you'd be at the bottom with a broken neck. I think you should go first, so if you fall, I can catch you. I have a bit more experience with these."

I look up the staircase. It is indeed the tightest spiral staircase I have ever seen, with uneven stone stairs turning around and around as they wind upward toward the bell and the clock. I am reassured by the gentle push of Wes's hand on my back as we ascend. "How many steps *are* there?" I pant, as we wind on upward, thinking my running is obviously not enough to keep me in shape.

"One hundred twenty," answers Wes. "I used to count them obsessively as a kid, running up and down, to my parents' chagrin." The last ten or so steps of the tower turn into wood ("Stone mason must have quit," jokes Wes), and as we reach the top stair, I trip and nearly fall. "Meant to warn you," says Wes. "They're all a bit uneven, but the carpenter was drunk with that last one."

I kick the step and hear its hollow thud. "I guess when Roger finally gets the funds for restoration, he may want to take care of it. Seems like a liability."

"Spoken like an American," Wes says. At the top of the bell tower, we arrive at a very small room surrounding the now-empty space where pullies and bells once hung. There are small windows that look out onto the expanse of the priory on one side and the manor house on the other.

"No bell?" I pant as Wes comes up the stairs behind me. "Can we still call it a bell tower?"

"No bell," he confirms. "It's been missing for decades. My grandmum remembers it ringing, but not my mum. I suspect it was melted down for artillery during the war—a few bells met that fate. Without the funds to replace it, the church has sat silent. There's not really a congregation here. It's more of a place of interest for the villagers. There's a wedding occasionally, which is why Roger's wife wants to rent out the manor house more. Make it a package deal."

He leans against the wall. I can't help but notice how handsome he is in his nicer clothes, sunglasses on top of his head pushing that dark hair out of his eyes, just the right amount of stubble, a grin on his face that I can only classify as wicked.

"What?" I ask, smiling, too. "Why are you looking at me like that?"

"Like what?" he says, walking toward me until I am the one with my back to the wall. He never breaks eye contact. God, I want him.

"Like that," I whisper as he stares intently at me. He has pinned me to the wall, an arm on either side. I like the feeling of being trapped.

"Oh, like this." He leans down and kisses me. "Because I wanted to kiss you in the bell tower. And now I have." He kisses me again, leaning his full weight against me. I give in to the feeling of his warm body and the cool stone.

St. Sepulchre's Priory, February 1534

Philippa paced back and forth, waiting for Lady Vale to arrive now that the snow had stopped falling. What was taking her so long? They had been clear that the minute the Holy Maid was taken into the Crown's custody, as they knew she would be, the lady would come quickly to take the gems and start to enact the plan for hiding them. They were no longer safe in the priory. Henry's complete break with Rome meant danger for those who remained loyal to the pope. Cromwell's men could come to the priory at any moment and take all that was there. Both women wanted to ensure a future for their faith in this country, once the king came to his senses or a righteous and godly monarch was again on the throne. And for that, they would need money.

She called in one of the nuns. "Sister Cecily," she pressed, "are you sure the lady has not yet come to the priory?"

The nun, who had come to them as a slight young novice and now, broad-shouldered, towered above the others, had to bend her head to look in on the prioress's doorway. "She has not, Mater, but I have seen both the doctor and the midwife enter their doors, so there is something amiss there."

Philippa had never once walked to the manor house; once a Benedictine nun crossed the threshold into her convent, took her vows, and married herself to Christ, she remained in that place until her death, shut out from the rest of the world. But time was too short, and the rules of her enclosure no longer applied in this crisis.

Although Philippa's feet had not taken her past the priory walls in more than forty years, now she walked to the manor house with a deliberate gait, as if it were routine. She knew that this transgression was permitted for some prioresses in other orders, but even so she prayed silently to God to forgive her. As she walked, the ice clung to the base of her habit, peeping out from underneath the blanket she had wrapped herself in to ward off the cold. Her feet sank into the sizable cushion of snow that covered the ground. It was, thank Jesus, Lady Vale who answered the door.

"My lady prioress," Agnes said loudly, clearly for the ears of those behind her, surprise and relief both apparent in her eyes. "Have you come to pray in our hour of need?"

"Yes," Philippa said, "my sisters had seen the doctor arriving here and then the midwife. I thought perhaps the priest would not be able to come in the snow. Is it Maude's time?"

"Both Maude's and John's," Agnes said as she stepped aside to let Philippa in, out of the howling wind. "It is as if her cries of labor are sending him to his death. Maude's travail is not going well. The baby does not want to come out, and she is tired. John is breathing his last, I am sure. We are, as you surmised, still waiting for the priest to arrive so that he can administer his final unction, but perhaps you can pray over John now? And then you can pray for Maude." She lowered her voice. "I wanted to send you word, but there has been no time. I have not forgotten what needs to be done. But now I am focused on the life of my granddaughter. Also, John has redone his will. He wants this manor to go to his nephew and not the grandchildren; I do not think he even understands that Maude is his daughter-in-law. I am not sure what to do."

Philippa nodded. "We will think on it. It is not the most pressing problem today." Even though the mood in the manor house was grim, the prioress could not help but notice the comforts of this place, the tapestries, the warm fire. Despite her sadness, Agnes had made this a home.

She followed the lady up the wooden stairs to her husband's chamber. John lay on the bed, eyes unseeing, the doctor draining blood from his arm into a waiting basin. He looked up when Agnes and Philippa entered. "The letting is not helping. He has but an hour. Is the priest here?"

Agnes shook her head. "I believe he will not make it in this weather. I have the prioress here to pray for him. She cannot administer the sacrament, but surely she can help send his soul to heaven." They heard screams coming from the next room. The doctor looked doubtful but stepped aside so that Philippa could pray. Just as she bowed her head, John took his final breath, a rattling gasp that ended in stillness.

As soon as the prioress finished saying a blessing over John's lifeless body, the doctor departed, no longer needed as the midwife would see to the birthing. The door had barely shut behind him when Agnes and Philippa heard the baby's cry down the hall. They raced to Maude's room.

"It's a healthy boy, Lady," said the midwife, handing her the child.

Agnes took the baby, stunned. "A boy?"

Maude smiled weakly from her bed. "John," she breathed.

"Not John, you fool," snapped Agnes. "John has just left this world. Give this child his own name. What is the name of your father?"

"Alister," said Maude.

"Yes, fine, Alister." Agnes looked down at the baby. Even though she had so hoped for a granddaughter, she could feel the stirrings of love like when she had held her own son in her arms. Without a father for the child, she would be able to teach him what it really meant to be a man.

Maude groaned again in pain. Agnes looked up; she had expected Maude to die in childbirth. She was surprised the girl was still moving, much less moaning. Agnes said, "The afterbirth?"

The midwife felt her abdomen. "There is another child," she answered. "Twins."

Philippa had been standing, frozen in the doorway, overwhelmed by so much pain at this juncture of life and death. Now she prayed, fiercely, for the life of the children and for the life of the mother. She knew Agnes had no love for Maude, but the prioress could not hope for her death.

The second baby came quickly. She was smaller and silent. Blue. Philippa closed her eyes and prayed more fervently. *Please, Lord,* she thought, *please give your breath of life to this child.*

The midwife was vigorously rubbing the girl, holding her upside down, sweeping her finger through the child's mouth, clapping her on the back. And then the infant breathed in, and she screamed.

"Valentina," said Agnes. "She should be Valentina after her great-great-grandmother."

Maude shook her head. “Margaret.”

“It is fitting,” agreed Philippa, “the patron saint of childbirth.”

Agnes was so happy to see her granddaughter breathe, she merely nodded assent. “Margaret,” she repeated. She looked up as the midwife put the second baby in her arms. Maude was already asleep.

Vale House Manor, June 2023, Day 4

When I go into the library for our predinner cocktails, I see Mrs. Bunch setting out the appetizers: a selection of cheeses, a thinly sliced baguette, some sort of jam. My mouth waters just looking at the bounty.

"You spoil us, Mrs. Bunch. I won't want to leave. Does Alex have a night off?" I ask as I pour myself a glass of white wine, fingers crossed that the servant is indeed far away for the evening.

"No, I had to send him to town for a few errands—we were low on sugar—and then I told him to organize the pantry and sharpen the knives." She laughs. "You and Wes are always welcome after hours," she says with a smile, then winks in a kind of exaggerated way. Does everyone suspect that something is going on between us?

As Mrs. Bunch exits through the door toward the kitchen, the rest of the group is filing into the library. Charles breaks into a little jog. "Mrs. Bunch! May I have a word?" He disappears behind the door with her and reappears shortly afterward looking pleased with himself. I marvel again at the familiarity so many of the others seem to have with this place and the people here.

I am about to ask Charles what he seems so happy about, but Roger grabs my arm and says excitedly, "Marla may have found something of use in the archives! Some tax documents related to the Vale family. She's bringing them to the drinks. She just wanted to change before dinner."

"That's so exciting, Roger," I say. "I can't wait to hear about it." I cross my fingers that it will help with my research as well.

"I think it makes us understand things a bit better. But it's Marla's document, I'll let her tell you about it."

As if summoned by the sound of her name, Marla walks in, holding a few papers. She reaches for the glass of wine that Roger offers. "Thank you, Roger." She takes a sip. "Mmm. That's a nice merlot. You've really been breaking into the cellar this week." She then turns to me. "Has Roger filled you in on the document?"

"A little bit. He said you found a tax document that may give us more insight into the Vales and the priory?"

Marla beckons me over to the settee, patting the space beside her. "Here, Alison," she says. I am thrilled to be chosen to sit next to her while Roger and Wes have to lean over our backs to see closely. As she speaks, she turns her attention entirely to me. "My project seems to have shifted a bit during this week, which is often how it happens. I decided to investigate the documents related to the manor and the priory rather than more general items in the archive. It occurred to me that we should consult the *Valor Ecclesiasticus,* the valuation of Church lands that Henry VIII ordered done in 1535 as part of his reclaiming of them."

"Oh, yeah, the king's books," I say. "There should be an entry for St. Sepulchre's."

"There is. It tells us that the land was taxed and how it was distributed—not just St. Sepulchre's but all the monasteries and nunneries around here. St. Sepulchre's was valued at thirty-eight pounds' rent per year, with some of that being paid to the manor house."

"That's about twenty thousand dollars in today's money," says Brian, who has been listening while pouring himself a glass of wine. We look over at him, somewhat astonished.

"I'm always calculating the costs of maintaining falcons." He shrugs. "I know the conversions pretty well." He raises his wineglass to the small group and then walks back over to the game table, where Arjun waits for him at the chessboard. I can tell they are both listening in, though, as the game doesn't start and I can see that neither is speaking as they lean slightly in our direction.

"But that doesn't tell us anything we don't already know, right?" I ask. "We knew the priory would have been reclaimed and redistributed, likely to the local people here who showed some loyalty to the king. At least publicly."

"Yes," Marla says, "but in addition to that giant survey that Henry did, many local shires kept more informal information about lands and who lived there. Sometimes they were compiled by the local tax collector, so he knew what to expect at each house." Marla places a document in my hands. "This is one such record for the area written in 1536. In it, the manor is listed as under the ownership of Alister and Margaret Vale, under the stewardship of their grandmother Agnes. Her husband, John Vale, and daughter-in-law, Maude Vale, are noted in the document to be recently deceased. I suppose her son must have already been dead to not be the owner of the manor after the death of her husband."

"Amazing that before this week we did not know Agnes's name and now we have had it twice," remarks Wes. He pulls a chair up opposite Marla and me, stretching out his long legs. "So now we know how it all eventually ends up going to Margaret Vale Pitlock and her husband. I wish it told us more about the priory, though."

"Well, it does a bit," Marla muses, pulling out another document. "The earlier taxes we have for them are about seven years prior. In that earlier survey, the land was much smaller, and it was all owned by John Vale, with his son, John Vale Jr., listed as heir. Obviously, both he and his son died in the meantime, but more important, the footprint of the manor and its land expands considerably. They received the priory land at the Reformation—that would have been an unusual gift for a Catholic family, so they must have really been keeping their faith secret."

"Do we have records of Agnes's death?" I ask.

"They're not here," Roger answers. "At least I've never come across them. And so far, nothing in the archives. If she were buried *inside* the church, you may be able to find an inscription, but I can't think of any in there that are the right gender and time."

"But she had survived childbirth," I say, "so her chances of living to an oldish age were pretty good. Let's say she lived to be seventy, which is not out of the realm of possibility once she's made it past the childbearing years—"

"Right," Wes interrupts, "then she would have lived into the 1560s. She would have seen Bloody Mary Tudor come and go and the country's grasp of Catholicism dissolve into Elizabeth's hands. Even more reason to protect her fortune."

Marla places the documents in my lap and looks at Wes. "Sorry, Wes, not the treasure map you were hoping for." I can't help but notice the meaningful way she says it, and the glance that seems to pass between them.

* * *

AFTER DINNER (PHEASANT with the most fantastic mushroom sauce; Mrs. Bunch is a treasure), the group goes once more to the library. Brian has a slideshow he wants to present about some of the hawking documents and images he has found.

Shoot me now, please.

I tell everyone I have a few more things to work on and excuse myself early, avoiding eye contact with Wes, who is clearly trying to figure out where I am going, why, and whether he can join me. But without a ready-made excuse at hand, he's trapped looking at images of peregrines and merlins.

I need to send some emails, and I hope that Calista has emailed me back with an explanation about what is going on. Additionally, as invigorating as the week has been, I need some time alone. There's a reason I chose a profession that involves many hours working in a silent archive.

As soon as I get to my room, I again have the feeling that someone has been there while I was out. The bag is where I left it this time, my papers appropriately untidy, but one of the books I have been consulting—which I am sure I left open because I wanted to double-check something after dinner—is closed. A paper with various notes I wrote about the mysteries surrounding this place is now on top, when I'm certain it had been inserted into a book beforehand. I review it again:

> Agnes Vale / Lady of the manor when Barton was at the priory. Was she the patron of the book? Did she pay for Barton on the rood screen?
>
> Why the reference to Mater in Agnes's portrait—is it a clue?
>
> Mater? Mary?—There is an image of Virgin Mary on the rood screen adjacent to Barton. Can something be hidden in there?
>
> Memento Mori—the hellmouth, the skull, the transi tomb.
>
> Are we missing a prophecy? An image? What's in the back of the book?

I go into the bathroom to see about my toiletries. They seem unmoved. Rifling through my makeup bag, one of the nagging threads that has been hanging in my brain finds its connection. I glance at the clock—the emails will have to wait.

I slip out of the room and peek into the library to see if I can get Wes's attention. No such luck. He seems genuinely interested in what Brian has to say, a hand raised in question. I turn and bump headlong into Charles.

"Oh, Alison . . . hello. I thought everyone would be in the lecture," he says, seeming flustered.

"Hi, Charles, yeah, I skipped to do a few things I still needed to do. You?"

"Oh, I'm heading in now. Just got caught up on an errand. I'll give your regrets to Brian, although this is not really the kind of place where you should skip a talk." He gives me an admonishing look and slips through the door before I can protest or explain.

"Dr. Sage." I hear Alex's oily voice behind me. "Were you entering the room to hear the lecture? I suspect you find hawking boring." Is he scoffing at me? He is.

"Um, no. I just thought of something I would like to see at the church. Is it still open? And could you possibly find a piece of white paper I could have?" I figure I might as well go for it—and now, while everyone is busy, is as good a time as any. At least I will be alone.

"It's open," Alex says, walking over to a small table in the entryway and pulling out the drawer, revealing a stack of paper and some pens. "We haven't locked it all week. We keep writing material in here, and you are welcome to them. Would you like company on the walk? It can be a little tricky in the dark. And it gets very, very dark."

"I'm fine," I say hurriedly, thinking there could be nothing worse than having to make conversation with Alex. I take a piece of paper out of the drawer. "I have the flashlight on my phone."

"Here," Alex says, opening another drawer, "take a torch as well."

"Thanks." I take hold of the industrial flashlight he hands me and head out before he insists on joining. Something Alex said is nagging at me. What is it? I feel the way I sometimes do in the archives, looking through manuscripts. I know that these pieces all connect and that they are somehow important but haven't quite figured out how or why the puzzle fits yet.

I am not asking the right questions.

It's light so late here; I realize as I walk out that I don't need the flashlight at all. It must be almost 9:00 P.M. and the sun has not yet set. The church's hush surrounds me as I enter and fumble for the lights, even though I see well enough in the waning daylight. It is the first time

I have been in here entirely alone—no Wes, no Roger. And it does not feel peaceful. An air of menacing unease pervades the space. I reflect on all the lives that were lost on the battlefield of religion. Protestants killing Catholics. Catholics killing Protestants.

These are not restful souls.

As I close the door behind me, I realize what Alex said that bothered me: that the church hadn't been locked all week. So what was Roger doing here every morning?

I carry the white paper over to the grave in front of the bell-tower door, the brass image of the nun at prayer, and lay it over the inscription, pressing hard so that the words can be felt through them. Then, carefully, I take out the eyebrow pencil that Miss Canada gave me what seems like years ago in the women's bathroom in Atlantic City and slowly shade the letters through the paper. A rubbing. The words come through the centuries to me:

REQUIESCAT IN PACE

MATER PHILIPPA JONYS

PRIORESS OF SAINT SEPULCHRE'S

HAVE MERCY THIS XIII DAY OF NOVEMBRE 1536.

I had been right about the first line, and Wes was correct about the third, but the elusive and crucial middle line now appears. This is Philippa's grave! The last prioress of St. Sepulchre's and the one who had been in charge while Elizabeth Barton was here, buried right before me under the church's floor. I sit, triumphant, back on my heels.

But there's another thread flapping in my brain . . . what is the connection I am trying to make?

It is the first time I have really seen the church with its lights on, and I look to see what may be different. The rood screens seem to glow brighter, especially the gems on the saint who may be Elizabeth.

Could the rood screen hold a map of some kind? Or this supposed treasure itself? I appreciate the zeal with which Wes follows his local legends, but I highly doubt we will uncover anything of material value. Historic value? Maybe. How much history has been discovered by following clues to an unexpected conclusion? I follow the saint's eyes up to the heavens, hoping for some kind of sign in the arched ceiling.

Nothing. I knock around the screen's edges to see if there is anything hollow, any space where something could be hidden. It sounds solid.

I turn to the hellmouth, that image of terror that has greeted each churchgoer for so many centuries, reminding them of their death. In the harsh electric light, it seems stripped of its horror, its colors too faded. The biblical inscription shines above, *DE DIE AUTEM ILLA ET HORA NEMO SCIT, NEQUE ANGELI CAELORUM, NISI SOLUS PATER*: "But of that day and hour no one knows, not the angels in heaven, no one but the Father alone." In this light, the flaking letters are more obvious, the need for restoration more dire. I can see that the "P" on "Pater" is almost entirely worn off.

Was there more writing underneath? An earlier version of the inscription perhaps that was painted over when it started to fade? I walk over to the wall and look up, shining the bright flashlight directly on the words. Yes, there is distinctly another letter under the "P." My angle isn't good, so I walk over to the side and take a picture with my phone. I have found some secrets in manuscripts before as the palimpsest of an earlier text gets revealed, aided by blowing a photo up on my computer. Perhaps this will work the same way.

I contemplate the church and all its secrets as I walk outside, the paper with my brass rubbing in hand. It is now, as warned, really, really dark. And just then, the flashlight stops working. I turn it off and back on, knocking it against my hand.

Nothing. *Shit.*

The meager light on my phone will have to do. It basically only lights about six inches in front of my feet, so I keep my head down to make sure I don't trip and break my neck on the way back. It is only a ten-minute walk, but in the dark like this, it feels much longer. I hear something in the hedge next to me—a person? An animal? I pick up my pace, relieved when I crest the hill and see the lights of the manor below, silhouettes of bats swooping in the windows' glow.

I tiptoe past the library in case anyone remains there, postlecture. The sound of billiard balls crashing comes from down the hall, with Arjun's loud laughter. Only when I am back in my room do I realize that I forgot to turn off the lights in the church. I can see it illuminated just out of the corner of my window. I notice Alex walking toward the church himself, a bright flashlight in his hand.

* * *

UPSTAIRS IN MY room, there is still no response from Calista, so I instead catch up on other tasks. A pang blossoms inside me as I write emails to the twins at camp. I am always so happy to see them go off for a few weeks, and then merely days in, I feel the physical ache of their absence. I also hate myself for it, but I write Pete to remind him that it's his mother's birthday, as I know he won't have remembered.

Things like this have always been my job—the birthday cards, the presents—and the habit does not die easily. But I love my mother-in-law and know how hurt she will be if Pete forgets. My ex-mother-in-law. Something else I had not realized about divorce was how many people I would lose, not just Pete. Couples we had spent countless vacations and dinners with but who had been Pete's friends first and foremost, his cousins, college roommates and their spouses. Even though they all promised it would make no difference—*poof*—like a magic trick they were gone from my life. An ache every time I see Pete in one of their Facebook photos—a dinner, a weekend away—a painful reminder that he has won them in the custody battle that I didn't realize we were having.

Something about being with Wes again has put back in place a part of me that was knocked loose by the divorce, a part that I also didn't realize I would lose. It's a reminder of who I was before Pete. This time I know that whatever's going on between us is temporary, just the span of the Consortium. There are only three days left of the C.C., and I *am* having fun with him. Perhaps I shouldn't be too hasty to shut it down. And why can't I just have a conference fling? I've seen men do it my whole career.

It is amidst these thoughts that I hear a tentative knock on the door. My watch reads 10:00 P.M. I am unfortunately dressed in vastly unflattering sweatpants and a T-shirt, the only pajamas I packed, not anticipating a love affair of any kind. Still, I open the door a crack, half fearing that I will see Alex standing there with some fun fact about the manor, but no, it is Wes. Still in his nicer clothes from this morning's talk, looking handsome, unshaven, a bit concerned.

"Am I invited in or was your skipping of the evening lecture a 'fuck-you' to me as well as the age-old sport of hawking?" he asks in a low voice.

I grab his hand and pull him inside before anyone can hear or see him there; although I think I see Arjun's door ajar, the coast is clear. "It's not a fuck-you," I tell him once my door is shut. "I just had some emails I needed to write. My children." I wish Calista had written me back. "I have something to show you," I tell him.

"Does it involve you getting naked? Because I am all in for whatever you must show me then," he says, with that same familiar grin.

"No," I say, unable to suppress a smile as I hand him the rubbing, "but it did involve me going to the church instead of hearing about the falconry."

"Hawking," he corrects.

"No difference to me." I shrug, and as he opens his mouth to tell me, I put my finger over his lips. "Trust me," I add, "I really, really don't care. I can die very happily without knowing the difference between hawking and falconry." He kisses my finger, and then takes my hand and kisses my palm, softly pressing his tongue against it, and then pulls me next to him on the bed and kisses my lips.

"Mmmm . . . ," I sigh, sinking into him. "Have you even looked at the paper I just handed you?"

He pulls back slightly and reads it, one hand rubbing my thigh. "Oh, wow! Wherever did you find a crayon?"

"My secret," I answer.

"Well, good show. It was Philippa's grave, then. I think you're right that the Vales must have paid for it—I suspect Agnes after the document Marla showed us tonight. It seems that by 1536, the year on the grave, John was already dead, and the twins were just babies. The dissolution must have killed Philippa—her death was almost at the exact same time."

I think about Philippa, having always found the nuns I study as somehow like me (at least some of them—the ones who chose that life, not the ones who were dropped off by their parents because they were not marriage material or because the parents had made some spiritual promise to the Church to offer one of their own for the cloistered life). There were nuns who opted for the convent because it meant a life of contemplation and study, a life dedicated to something greater than what most women had before them—marriage, children, and the dangers of childbirth. They were readers and thinkers. And to rise to prioress, Philippa would have had to have been tough, smart, ambitious, respected. All the things that I hope I am.

And then to have it simply taken away.

As I have often before, I reflect on the thousands upon thousands of priests, monks, friars, and nuns who were unceremoniously stripped of their titles, homes, and beliefs during the dissolution of the monasteries. For a woman like Philippa to be told that the life she had built was no longer valid, that the sisters she had governed were just regular women again, that the Church she had been devoted to was a false one . . . could it kill a woman? I suppose it could. It's like the situation suddenly facing Marla—an unwanted retirement, her identity as a professor snatched away without her consent.

Wes has returned the paper to my desk while I was momentarily lost in contemplation. He stands in front of me and then pushes me back on the bed, lightly holding me down. "You'll have to make me stop talking if you don't want to know more about the history of hawking," he says, between kisses on my neck, a hand up my oversized T-shirt. "It begins with *The Book of Saint Albans*. . . ."

"Shut up, Wes," I say, deciding to give in to the deliciousness of the moment, kissing him deeply.

Paul's Cross, London, November 1533

Anne Boleyn's chosen preacher, John Capon, was reading his sermon for the second time. The first time, the speech had been at Canterbury. It was important that this was done near Elizabeth's home grounds so that anyone who had dared seek out her counsel or gone to St. Sepulchre's on pilgrimage would know what a charlatan she was, what a liar, what a whore.

This second sermon, though, in London, was at the behest of Cromwell. It had a much larger audience.

Capon was only an abbot, but he was sure that after this sermon condemning these frauds, he would be made a bishop. He had the favor of the queen, after all. She had been most grateful for the work he had done in helping secure the king's divorce. If he could fully turn the tide of popular opinion against Elizabeth Barton and her ilk, well, then the bishopric he desired would be almost assured. The queen would see to it as reward.

The Mad Maid, looking every inch worthy of that moniker, was behind Capon, where everyone could see her, in a torn and dirty shift that barely came to her knees. She seemed unable to lift her head, and she swayed back and forth on unstable legs, her arms hanging unnaturally and useless at her sides. Next to her was her equally broken confessor, the architect of it all, Edward Bocking, hands tied behind his back. A few of the other misled monks who had traveled with them were lined up by his side. The Maid no longer wore her habit, but the monks were still in theirs, although the garments were tattered. Let people see who these papists really were: liars.

Capon was used to delivering his sermons inside churches, but the choice of Paul's Cross was an inspired one. This place was the real lectern of the city. It was where preachers of all sorts made their sermons, where official court announcements were made, where people were always gathered, ready to hear what was next. This was the people's church, and as they had left the pope behind and moved toward King Henry as supreme head of the Church, the new Church of England, this was going to be where the hearts and minds of the people would be converted to the one true religion.

Capon stood at the pulpit where people could see him as well as the traitors behind him. He was going to be sure they heard him.

"This woman"—he pointed at Barton—"this woman has confessed that she was ill, and in her illness, believed she had seen God. She spoke words that she did not herself remember. She has confessed this! It was the work of a fever, not the work of our Lord."

The crowd started to boo. They had believed the Holy Maid! She had lied to them!

"And her confessor, Bocking." He pointed to the man beside Elizabeth. "He knew she was false. He encouraged her in her feigning and her treachery. He spoke to her of heresies, and of the king's marriage, and of the parliament, and of diverse matters that she could not understand, and she claimed to have visions thereof. My people, she was feigning them. I remind you all—she has confessed. He is the one who told her what to say and when!"

Bocking and Elizabeth were both looking down at the ground. They had no more fight in them in either flesh or spirit. They had been abandoned by Fisher. Fisher! Who had been with them since the beginning. Now they had only God.

"There are too many lies in her book to recount. These are false seducers of the people. Let me remind you," Capon continued, as if the people needed reminding, "this so-called Holy Maid claimed she had a vision that if our blessed King Henry married his queen Anne Boleyn, then he would die within a month. She said he would die a villain's death."

He paused again for effect, letting everyone calculate in their minds how very wrong this prediction had been. He continued, "And this lie was widely sown throughout the land. She said it every moment she could. Bocking gathered large crowds to hear it. She said it to the king himself." He turned accusingly to Elizabeth and Bocking, willing them to make eye contact with him. He knew he commanded this stage. They kept their eyes downcast.

"And the king delayed his marriage to the good queen because of this false revelation until he was sure that God had called him to it. And when a month had passed, and the queen and king lived on in good health and a sanctioned marriage, well then, this Elizabeth and this Bocking had a new prophecy."

He smirked. Even if they knew what was coming next, they were pushing forward, silently, all ears turned toward Capon and his pulpit. "The new prophecy was that he was no longer the king after that month when he still lived."

Capon laughed. "It seems to me that our king is still king, is he not? He is a good king, is he not? He was and still is the divinely anointed king, especially as he has rejected the pope and all the superstitions of papistry."

The crowd was nodding now. They were with him. They wanted to see Elizabeth and Bocking and their duplicities burn. "Her book of falsities was sent around this country. It should be burned. It is a book of lies. A book of falsehoods. She did not have visions from God."

He knew that the next was his best line. The one that would get the most reaction. In Canterbury some of the women actually swooned, so he paused for a long moment. He waited until all eyes were on his pulpit, flitting nervously behind him to the nun and her men. "Her visions were of the Devil. This is the work of the demon before you."

Now he had them. The rest was just filling in the horrid details. "The Maid hath confessed that she would leave her cell at the priory when the other sisters were asleep to commune with the Devil."

Gasps from the crowd.

He smiled, despite himself. "She has written in this book that if you are a sinner and not shriven, not confessed, but see and touch her—the Holy Maid herself—then you shall go to heaven. She is not Jesus. This is heresy!"

He wanted to make sure he hit all the points here.

She was a liar.

She was demonic.

She was a heretic.

There should be no doubt as to why the woman should hang and her book burn. "She looks penitent before you," he concluded. And she did: she was emaciated and drawn, her eyes never lifting above the ground.

A mere shadow of the meek girl she once was on the Cobb farm. "She is not penitent. She hath confessed but not repented. She will burn by God's law, for certain, but she should also be convicted by man's. She hath led you astray. She hath spoken against our good king and queen. I pray for her soul."

Vale House Manor, June 2023, Days 4–5

I put aside any reluctance about falling back into sex with Wes. I don't feel reckless, exactly, but rather almost clearheaded about it, knowing that it is what I need right now. Who will get hurt this time? No one. I'll make sure that he understands what this is. No ambiguities.

I do not ask Wes to leave in the middle of the night. I lie with my head on his chest, listening to him breathe, to his heartbeat, smelling him—a mixture of leather and sweat that I associate more with an archive than with sex. He strokes my hair, runs his hand over my bare back.

"You know . . . ," I start, thinking out loud. Despite the activities of the last half hour, I still have much of my mind in my work (which was one of the core problems with Pete; I could never be fully present because the contents of my own brain were already so crowded). "In the sermon denouncing Elizabeth, Capon says there was a second book of visions that Bocking had recorded. Not one that was printed, but one that was full of her accusations against Anne and Henry and a myriad of other crazy stuff she did. There are probably a ton of revelations and prophecies that we don't even know about."

Wes props himself up on his elbow, facing me. I should be self-conscious about my hair, my nakedness, my body with its folds and scars, but instead I feel liberated, dispassionate about those concerns. They slip away, at least here in the confines of my bedroom.

"We have his sermon?"

"Oh, yes, it circulated in a pamphlet that of course *did* survive. Henry VIII wanted there to be no doubt why she had to be executed. It was a warning to others who may oppose the king, his marriage, or the newly formed Church of England."

"No copies of the second book?" he asks, hopefully. "Another prophecy might tell us where the treasure is hidden. Or that we should buy stock in some company that will be very lucrative in the next five years." Wes rolls onto his back as he ponders this, his hands behind his head, deliciously naked atop the covers.

"Haha." I push him gently. "I wish her revelations were so useful. Copies? Nope. None. I mean, there were probably only a very few, maybe just one, and definitely handwritten," I say. "If the Crown made some seven hundred copies of her printed book disappear, they certainly could have done it with one handwritten manuscript. We know what Capon says was written there, but of course his whole sermon is a takedown, a smear job."

He faces me and traces my bare body from my shoulder down to my hip with his finger. Coupled with the breeze wafting in from the window, his touch leaves a trail of goose bumps.

"You're really great at postcoital pillow talk," he teases. "You may have me ready for another go in no time at all." I don't admit that I find talking with him about all of this erotic. Who was it that said the brain is the biggest sex organ?

"This is the risk of sleeping with me," I say. "This is how my mind works. That was amazing twenty minutes ago, but you've left me to my own devices too long."

"Let me remedy that," Wes says, rolling over and straddling me, his hair falling into his face, so that I have to reach up and move it to see his eyes, desperate to touch him. "There's plenty of time for Barton talk in the morning. I have other research to do tonight."

"Okay, okay," I relent. "You drive a hard bargain."

He smiles. "A hard bargain? Is that what you Americans call it?"

"Come here," I say with a laugh as I pull him down to kiss me.

* * *

When I get down to the dining room the next morning, waiting an appropriate amount of time after Wes has left and descended on his own, I find the occupants in a state of confusion. Mrs. Bunch has brought out the pastry items on a tray, but there is no coffee or tea or any of the condiments that usually accompany breakfast. Arjun and Charles are already there, and as they approach me Arjun says in a low voice, "Apparently Alex didn't show up this morning for work. Mrs. Bunch doesn't want to tell Roger because she doesn't want Alex to get in trouble, but now he's over an hour late. Wes went to see if he's in his room. If he's not, I guess we must let Roger know." Arjun seems delighted by the whiff of scandal surrounding a wayward servant.

"Where is Alex's room?" I ask. It never occurred to me that he slept somewhere in the manor.

"There are servants' quarters on the top floor. Just a few rooms. Part of the way Roger can afford any help at all is that the staff lives here rent-free. Although I think the cook lives somewhere in the village." Charles is speaking to me, but his eyes keep moving between the door and Mrs. Bunch, fully taking in the intrigue of the morning.

Arjun chimes in. "My money is on oversleeping. He hasn't had much of a break this week. There has been lots of activity here, and later than usual." He looks meaningfully at Charles, who gives a somewhat guilty smile back in agreement. Is this about me and Wes again? God, these people need some entertainment other than my sex life.

Just then Roger, Marla, and Wes enter the room. Wes shakes his head in a silent "no" to Charles. Roger crosses directly to Mrs. Bunch, and they quietly confer. He then turns to the group, which by now is mostly complete except for Brian (who is often late for breakfast).

Roger clears his throat. "My friends, it appears that Alex is missing. His bed was not slept in last night and he has not shown up for work this morning." He shifts uncomfortably. "I'm so sorry to throw a wrench into our time here like this, but I think we need to find out where he is before we can move on with our day. Does anyone have any information? I last saw Alex as he was clearing the plates following Brian's lecture. That must have been around nine forty-five because I was in bed around ten o'clock." His eyes find Marla's, and she gives the slightest nod of agreement. "Did anyone see him afterward? Or hear anything? I'm afraid I am a very heavy sleeper so cannot account for anything between ten and about an hour ago."

Marla then speaks. "And some of the notes I had left here have disappeared. Westley's, as well. I can't imagine what Alex would want with them, but something is amiss."

Mrs. Bunch arrives with tea and coffee, saying, "You might as well have some of this while you think on it." Clearly she is the most distressed of all of us, and she hovers around the pastries, rearranging them, obviously listening in on the conversation around her. "Someone was in the kitchen last night, because there are dishes in the sink. Alex normally would have cleaned up while I was making breakfast. Westy?"

Wes shakes his head. "Not me."

Charles sighs and reluctantly says, "I was up doing some work in the library. I couldn't sleep." He shoots a somewhat guilty look toward the group. "Perhaps I inadvertently moved some of the notes." He shifts uncomfortably. "And I did steal down to the kitchen for a snack." *Stealing people's research is more like it,* I think, but no one says aloud what I am sure we all are thinking.

I pour a cup of coffee and sit down at the table and save Charles by turning the group's focus back to the missing servant. He owes me one. "Could Alex have had a night out with friends or visited his mother or something?" I ask tentatively. "Is it so unusual that he is not here?"

Roger clears his throat, searching for words. "Well, um, it is very unlike Alex when we have a group here. He is needed for so many different things, and the fact that he had not returned to his bed at all is very concerning. I have tasked him with some, er, let's say *delicate* work this week and I am worried that it may have gone awry."

Now I am thoroughly confused, and I can see by the faces of Charles and Arjun that I am not alone. What time did I see Alex go turn the lights off at the church? It was just before Wes joined me, so maybe right around ten. I say to Roger, "I saw him last night probably just after you did. He was headed to the church. I saw him from my window."

"The church?"

"Yes, it was probably my fault. I went during the lecture to verify something." Thank God Brian isn't here to learn why I skipped his talk. "I accidentally left the light on. I suspect he went to turn it off?"

Roger heads immediately to the door. "Westy," he calls, "join me?"

Wes takes my hand and pulls me toward the door as well. "Yes, we will both come and help you look." I gently remove my hand from his and follow.

Something in their alarm has filled me with anxiety, and the priory church looms before us in a menacing way as we make our approach.

At first glance, nothing seems amiss in the church. The lights are off, so Alex achieved that objective if that was his purpose. Wes at least seems relaxed.

"Aren't you worried about Alex?" I ask.

"Not really. He probably went for a pint at the King's Head and ended up in some village girl's bed." He grins. "I also speak from experience there."

"I'm sure you do."

We hear Roger shouting from up ahead. "Oh God! Oh God! The rood screen!"

We run to him and gasp in unison. The image of the Virgin Mary has been pried away from the screen. Unlike the Reformation-era scratching out of St. Thomas Becket's face, this defacer has cut out the screen carefully, as if with a saw. The pieces lay about on the floor with splinters of wood everywhere.

"I think someone was trying to see if anything was hidden here," I say. After all, I recently had the same thought. "We talked about the possibility of Mary being the 'mother' in that Book of Hours. Obviously, we were wrong." It's clear that the wood was not hollow, that the early medieval artifact was ruined for the promise of a treasure that likely doesn't exist.

Roger is sitting with his head in his hands. "At least the image is intact," he says softly. "This was done with some care for the picture. But this is a horrific act of vandalism. Who would do such a thing?"

Alex—that's no doubt what we're all thinking. But there is no sign of him in the church.

"Let's take the back exit," says Wes. "It's the way Alex would have walked here from the kitchens when Alison saw him. Maybe we can find a clue."

* * *

We find the back door—the one that would have connected the priory with the manor grounds—not only unlocked but ajar. For centuries the servants of the manor would have passed through it in order to go to weekly mass; the noblemen and women who occupied the manor would have entered through the front door, the one that showed their position and importance as they walked down the aisle to their reserved spaces in the front pews.

We aren't far down the path when I see sneakers sticking out from the hedges. I immediately recognize the Adidas sneakers that Alex has been wearing all week, shoes that stick out in their bright whiteness, accentuated by pants that are always a little too short.

As we get closer, more of Alex's body comes into view: he's collapsed on his side, half-concealed by the bushes under which he is crumpled. Wes puts his arm out to stop me from walking farther. Something in the way the feet are angled—the manner in which they splay outward—keeps us from running up or calling Alex's name.

Roger walks ahead, around the bend of the path, and chokes on a scream. He beckons for me and Wes to follow.

I hold back. I don't want to see, even though I know that it's Alex and by the odd, frozen angle of his body, he may be dead. It seems like a violation of his privacy to get any closer.

Although I can see his arm now, also splayed. He is holding a small saw.

Wes makes a sound that's almost primal, somewhere between a shout and a gag. The two men are frozen. Someone needs to move, to do something.

I slowly approach.

Indeed, Alex is dead.

No trying to revive him or calling an ambulance. His head is smashed in, unrecognizable, nearly severed from his body.

A word comes to my mind: "pulp."

I close my eyes against the sight, and immediately I see the maggots in the rat, then the grinning cadaver of the transi tomb.

Roger turns to vomit. When the dirt and iron smell of Alex's blood reaches my nose, I feel like I will be sick as well.

Breathe. Calm. I reach out and grab Wes's hand, and he pulls me into his body. I inhale his smell deeply, hoping to clear my nose of the foul stench of death. I lean heavily on him, allowing him to hold me up.

"Stay here with Roger," Wes says into my hair. He's the only one maintaining any composure. He pulls back and holds my shoulders, makes sure I can see his eyes. "Look at me. You're okay. I'm going back to the manor to call the police. I'll be back as soon as I can." I want him to stay, but before I can speak he is already running down the path, away from us.

I move Roger over to a mossy stone bench, away from the body.

"Come sit here," I say, slowly, pointing to the seat, as if he might not understand English. My legs are shaking and if I don't sit down right away, I can't guarantee that I will keep standing.

I put my head in my hands and take some deep breaths, waiting for the nausea to pass. I can feel Roger nearly hyperventilating next to me.

"This is my fault. This is my fault," Roger wails. From the bench we can see only Alex's Adidas-clad feet, not the bloody, stringy mess that had once been his head.

I place my hand on Roger's shoulder. "*Shhh* . . . It's not your fault. Let's just sit here and wait for the police." Who could have done such a thing? What awful stuff was Alex mixed up in? I start to feel guilty about all the terrible things I had thought about Alex. No matter how creepy, no one deserves this.

Roger has calmed down a bit. "I have to let Janine know," he says. "She is close to Alex's mother. Oh God, she will be devastated. She was so proud with him working here." He again starts to breathe rapidly, pulling on his beard.

To my great relief, I see Wes running back up the pathway. He sits next to us and takes my hand. "I've called the police. They are on their way. They said not to touch the bo—er, Alex. To just leave everything as it was." He gives my hand a squeeze and then leans over me to speak to Roger. "Do you want me to call Aunt Janine, Roger?"

Aunt Janine?

Roger looks at Wes and shakes his head, pulling on his beard some more. "No, I should do it. Can you take me back to the house, Westy? To make the call?"

Wes nods.

"Alison, you should stay here until the police arrive." I nod, not at all happy with the task I have been assigned, but I see no way to object. Wes stands and pulls Roger to his feet, putting his arm around him and supporting the suddenly enfeebled man. Roger's large frame seems to have shrunk two sizes, and Wes looks the bigger one as they walk back toward the manor.

Tyburn Gallows, April 1534

"You're going to hang today," the prison guard said, leering at Elizabeth. Her shift was so dirty and ripped that she had long ago given up modesty, and she no longer flushed with shame that these men saw her breasts. She was too tired, too pained to care. She simply closed her eyes and saw this one chewed in the hellmouth, a bloody pulp. He would get his punishment in the next life, if not in this one.

"Treason," the guard said, his smile revealing broken, blackened teeth. "That will bring a big crowd."

He bent down and unlocked her leg. It had been chained to the wall for . . . days? Weeks? Time had no meaning in this place without windows or air.

She turned her face to the guard and croaked out the only weapon she had left. "I see you in hell. You are in the teeth of Satan's beast." But the words were merely a hoarse whisper, and the guard showed no fear. Instead, he laughed his hot breath in her face.

"Everyone knows you're a false prophet. You've confessed. And others have confessed that they helped you deceive the people. I am not afraid of your lying words."

"They lie. I've had no trial."

"No trial needed for traitors! Let your pope save you now." He yanked Elizabeth by one of her useless arms, and her legs somehow managed to follow him out of the cellar and through the crowds of prisoners that populated the upper levels of Newgate: men, women, even children. Their waste had been trickling down to the cellar where she had been kept with the other prisoners sentenced to death. Even the fetid air of the upper floor was fresh compared to what she had been forced to breathe. She knew she was supposed to be afraid, but she was just too tired, too broken for fear. Death would be release.

The guard shoved her out into a courtyard, where she cried in relief at seeing the sky and gulping the air. Her relief initially doubled when she saw Bocking among the others on the cart. They would not dare execute a priest. Would they? Perhaps they were not being led to their death.

"We are going to Tyburn Tree, sister," Bocking said flatly, destroying her brief moment of hope, as she was shoved into the cart next to him. "Please pray for our souls."

Tyburn Tree. The gallows. She knew of this terrible place, where as many as fifteen people at once could hang for their crimes. Today they would be six—Elizabeth and five of her supporters.

"You surely are," the cart driver called back, causing laughter among the guards sitting with the condemned. "The good tickets sold out early and most businesses shut down because everyone wants to watch today. You're important, Mad Maid." For the first time in a long while, Elizabeth wished she was just a farmhand again.

The crowds were already waiting for them as they passed beyond the walls of Newgate. Jeering, throwing food and feces at them, the people were shouting:

"Traitor!"

"False prophet!"

"Liar!"

Elizabeth closed her eyes to the noise; she tried to summon the warm light of God inside her. She could not.

* * *

THE ROUTE FROM Newgate Prison to the gallows was only three miles, but it took almost four hours. The crowds slowed the procession as people taunted them, telling them they would soon be dancing the Tyburn jig for all to see.

The crowd's chatter was excited as the wooden cart made its way to the center of Marylebone parish and stopped under the Tree. The people gathered there delighted in the recounting of her many sins—she told the king to his face that his wife was a whore! She seduced priests and had sex with them and with sisters at the convent! She feigned all her revelations! Also, she had admitted her crime, they said knowingly to one another. Although people knew how Cromwell extracted his confessions—and they could clearly see the way her arms hung, useless, by her body—the confession was still proof of her deceit.

In addition to Elizabeth and Bocking, there were four other men: one priest, one monk, and two friars. Those heretics all refused to take the Oath of Succession and stood by the Holy Maid's visions.

The executioner shouted the name of each criminal and their crime, stripping them of any titles they held in life, defrocking the priests as he did so.

"John Dering, once Benedictine monk of Christ Church, Canterbury. Sentenced to death for the crime of treason to the Crown."

The crowd shouted and booed.

"Henry Gold, once parson of St. Mary Aldermanbury, London. Sentenced to death for the crime of treason to the Crown."

"*Boo!*"

"Hugh Rich, once Franciscan friar of Richmond. Sentenced to death for the crime of treason to the Crown."

"*Traitor!*"

"Richard Risby, once Franciscan friar of Greyfriars, Canterbury. Sentenced to death for the crime of treason to the Crown."

"*Papist!*"

The executioner paused. He waited until the crowd had settled into a silence. The guards had given the ropes to the men, who passed them along until they were atop the Tree, which, of course, was not a tree at all but a carefully constructed triangular gallows designed to hang at least a dozen men at the same time. The ropes were then tied tightly to its beams by waiting workers. The other ends of the ropes were around their necks. The men and Elizabeth clutched the sides of the cart as if they could will the horses to stay still, to keep it below their feet. Once they were prodded to move the cart, the tethers on the condemned would keep them there, hanging. This was what the people had come to see—the hangman needed to make sure they heard and saw it. First Bocking and then Elizabeth. Cromwell's men had been clear—work the crowd up, make sure they lusted for her blood, then give it to them.

"And here we have this so-called Holy Maid. Elizabeth is known to have fornicated with priests and nuns and communed with the Devil." He pointed to Elizabeth, and the jeers were so loud they threatened to drown him out. He shouted the rest. "And here is the man who helped spin and sell her lies. They will shortly die for their crimes of stealing money from pilgrims and for the crime of treason." Now he was yelling over the crowd. "The unforgivable crime of faking revelations wherein they desired the death of the king and the queen."

"*Heretic!*"

"*Liar!*"

"*False prophet!*"

"Edward Bocking, once Benedictine monk of Christ Church, Canterbury. Sentenced to death for the crime of treason to the Crown."

"*Hang them!*"

"Elizabeth Barton, once a nun of St. Sepulchre's Priory, Kent. Sentenced to death for the crime of treason to the Crown."

Elizabeth was at first unafraid at the Tree. Even through her exhausted, muddled mind, the searing pain in her shoulders and head, she believed that God would save her. When they first placed the chafing rope around her neck, she welcomed it.

Death would not yet come for her like it had for others. It may at last be her hour, but her bridegroom was waiting for her in heaven.

There were already corpses swinging and awaiting company, hanged earlier that day. Birds voraciously picking at the flesh despite the roar of the crowd.

The people gathered there were shouting and cheering for this ceremony of death. Her eyes fixed on a family up front, a small child on the shoulders of a man. A day out. To watch them hang.

She moved her gaze, for her head would no longer move as she willed it, to the hangmen who climbed onto the cart, making sure the nooses around their necks were secure. There were six of them waiting to die, but the crowd was there only for her.

"The Mad Maid of Kent! Did you foresee this?"

"Do the Tyburn jig for us, Holy Maid!" the man with the child spat out, laughing. The child clapped.

"What good are your prophecies now?" shouted another spectator.

And the chorus: "*Liar! False prophet!*"

Was she? Elizabeth no longer knew, with her weakened body and confused thoughts, what was real and what was not, what had been true and what was false. She closed her eyes tightly and tried to remember the voice of God. She had heard it once. She knew she had. But here, there was only the sound of the people demanding her death.

The horses took some steps ahead, frightened by the noise, and she felt the noose tighten. Through the fog in her head, she heard the cart driver shout to stop. It was not yet time.

She swallowed the bile that rose in her throat. It tasted like fear.

Then the executioner nodded to the cart driver, who whipped the horses to move. They followed their command, and as the horses galloped away, taking the cart with them, the six bodies stayed tethered firmly to the Tree.

As she felt her toes leave the cart, she was immediately desperate for breath, her body in its jerky dance under the Tyburn Tree. She tried to will her arms to pull the rope away, but they continued to hang useless at her side.

Some fell heavy, their necks breaking almost instantly.

The rest convulsed, kicked, clawed at their necks. Their feet were mere inches from the ground, taunting them.

But she was as light as air. No quick death for her. She felt her bowels give way, her legs running as if they could escape her body.

She was gripped with terror, until the very last moment when it all went black.

Vale House Manor, June 2023, Day 5

The first two officers arrive and immediately set up outside the church, next to the path, putting tape around the area where Alex's body lies. I don't know if it's their uniforms or my shock, but they are indistinguishable from each other. Police doppelgängers, young, cherubic men. One of them radios information in a murmur that I can't quite hear.

"Can I go back to the manor now?" I ask, as one comes walking toward me. How old is he? Eighteen? I do not feel like I am in capable hands. I really want to get out of this place as quickly as I can.

He looks at me closely. "If you don't mind waiting here for the DCs, we'd prefer that. I would like you to give him your statement here, before . . . heading back." *Before speaking to the others,* I think. He wants me to remain isolated. I've binged enough police procedurals to know how this goes down.

"DCs?"

"Detective constables. They'll also send a DS and a DI." I don't even bother to ask. "We've called them in. A doctor, too, to certify the death."

Any idiot could certify this death. I'm annoyed that I'm being stopped; all I want is to be out of this place. I realize I am shivering even though it's warm.

"How many are back at the house? We will need to interview all of them." I do not understand why I am suddenly the one giving out all this information. Wes and Roger are at the manor, likely conveying the awful news to the group, to Mrs. Bunch, and to whomever had the hard task of calling Alex's mother. My heart aches for a mother hearing that her son is dead.

And Janine. Aunt Janine. Wes and Roger are *family*? Am I the only one who didn't know what seems to be a salient piece of information?

"There are seven back at the house," I say quietly. "I can't imagine any of them are capable of murder." I calculate how quickly I can get to

London after the police are done with me. How quickly I can be on a plane going home.

"Who said anything about murder?" the policeman asks coyly, looking at me suspiciously.

"Um, his head is bashed in? I don't think you trip and fall and have your head bashed in?"

He nods. "Yes, I suppose you're right. I've seen a few accidental deaths in my day. And this doesn't look right." What idiocy am I dealing with here? Just when he almost opens his mouth to speak again, we hear several sirens coming up the main road. I guess three or four cars. Some are headed toward the church and others to the manor.

The officer's phone rings, and he turns away from me as he speaks into it. "Yes, DI Monroe, I have one of the people who found the body here." He pauses. "Yes. On the path leading from the back of the church."

Moments after he hangs up, an older woman—maybe in her sixties—with dark-gray hair coiled tightly in a bun walks up the path alongside a red-haired middle-aged man with a trim goatee. Neither is in uniform. She is wearing gray slacks and a long-sleeved white T-shirt; he is dressed in khakis and a button-down. Both have badges displayed on lanyards around their necks.

The woman is the first to speak. She nods to the policeman, then extends her hand to me. "Hello, I'm DI Monroe and this is DS White."

"Alison Sage."

She turns to her partner. "Let's take this witness statement here and then we can interview the others in the house." As she speaks, four people in hazmat suits approach, and Monroe moves her chin in the direction of the body. A photographer is with them, lugging equipment. I avert my eyes, imagining the grim life of a photographer who focuses on death day after day. DI Monroe sits down next to me on the bench. I can tell she is practiced at this; her very presence is reassuring. "So, you were the first to find the body?" she asks.

I see that White is recording my words, both with a small tape recorder and by taking notes in a spiral-bound notepad. How many murders has Monroe investigated? How many corpses has she had to process in her days as a policewoman?

"Um, yes and no," I start, willing Wes to return to the church path. "I came with two others. There were three of us. One was Alex's"—I nod in the direction of the body—"boss, I guess. He's part of the family that owns the manor. I think they went to let his mother know."

And then, to my great surprise, I start to weep.

* * *

I SPEAK TO Monroe for at least an hour. She seems particularly interested in the fact that I was, as far as they could tell, the last one in the church and to see Alex before he was found this morning.

"You did not know the deceased very well?"

"No, no, not at all really. I arrived just four days ago. It was the first time I had met him and only the second time I had met Roger, his employer. I've never been here before, but a lot of the others have."

"And the others here? Who did you know?"

"Um, I guess I knew everyone a little bit. Nobody well except maybe Charles, but even then, only professionally. I knew Westley beforehand, too, but hadn't seen him in years."

"And this is some kind of reunion? Reenactment? What exactly is taking place here?"

I almost laugh. Someone else thinking this was some sort of Renaissance fair.

"No, neither. It's a consortium, a week where we share research and talk about our work. It's meant as a way to collaborate and be productive."

"Uh-huh." Monroe looks doubtful. "And your research is what, exactly?"

I try to explain my work the best I can in layman's terms, and why the priory and the church were interesting to me, noting that it also touches on what Wes and Roger and Marla are working on. I explain the others' work in a few sentences. No need to go through their résumés. I assume they, like me, are eager to pack their bags and get out of here. When will they remove the body?

White looks at Monroe. "Time to walk to the manor?" he asks.

"Come," says Monroe, taking me by the elbow. "Let's go back to the manor house. There are officers setting up a queue for the rest of the interviews. Thank you for the lay of the land. We will talk more later. And Alison—"

"Yes?"

"Let me know directly if there is anything you think I should know or if something seems out of character with the other scholars here."

* * *

Monroe and White meet with each of the participants, plus Mrs. Bunch, recording our interviews and preventing us from talking to one another (the place is suddenly crawling with officers, both in and out of uniform) until they are completed. While the interviews with Brian, Arjun, Marla, and me go relatively quickly, the ones with Roger, Wes, and Mrs. Bunch are endless. Charles's, too, seems extra long. The morning collapses into what could have been seconds or hours, starting with the discovery of Alex's body and culminating now when we all, postinterviews, are gathered in the library.

A murder!

Here.

While we slept.

We can't wrap our heads around it.

Looking at each person around me, I ask myself, *Would they want to kill Alex? And why?* Answers elude me. Certainly no one here seems capable of a premeditated murder, and if it had been planned, it seems sloppy to me, leaving Alex out in the path for anyone to find. I can only believe the responsible party is not here, that it's someone outside the manor house. Alex must have been mixed up in something bad and gotten in over his head.

I join Brian and Arjun at the game table, where they ask me to describe in detail what I saw this morning when we went to the church and found Alex's body. I describe it in spare detail, unwilling to conjure the image of Alex's head back to my mind.

"They can't keep us here, right?" Brian muses nervously. Alarmingly, Monroe has collected our passports "for the moment."

"Can we talk about Charles?" Arjun says in a low voice. "Looking at our notes while we slept? Can we get the police to investigate him while they're at it?" His attempt at a joke.

"His last book was a disaster," says Brian, in an even quieter tone. "But I am surprised he would sink so low. Some people truly aren't what they seem." I look to see if Charles can hear us, but he is far separated from the group, looking at the bookshelves, alone.

Just then, Mrs. Bunch, finally released from her interview, enters the library with a simple lunch. "The police have momentarily taken over the dining room for interviews," she explains, "so I think you'll eat in here. I've just brought some sandwiches and crisps."

White keeps close watch on all of us while we eat. Once I'm finished, I ask if I am allowed to return to my room. White nods. "Of course. We know where to find you. You should know that we've done a quick once-over of all the rooms, so some things may be out of order."

My room was so often out of order this week, I'm not sure I'd notice. Still, I don't like the idea of someone pawing through my underwear or my research. Not sure which is more personal.

Wes is sitting on the settee with Roger and Marla, all three with heads very close together. I suppose Roger and Wes feel especially connected to Alex, knowing him as they did. Marla has her hand protectively on Roger's knee, rubbing it gently. She smiles as I approach.

"Are you okay, Alison dear?" she asks softly. Her eyes look red-rimmed, like Roger's. "It sounds like you had quite a shock this morning." She squeezes Roger's knee. "You all did."

I nod limply. "Yes. I'm headed upstairs now. I'm hoping to change my ticket so that I can leave tomorrow."

Roger looks up, startled. "But our work here is not done."

"I don't think I have any work left in me now, Roger. I'm sure you understand." He must really be in shock to think the C.C. can somehow continue after this. I turn to head upstairs, and although I can't hear the substance of the mumbled conversation between Roger, Marla, and Wes, I feel that I am its topic.

* * *

I LIE DOWN on my bed and close my eyes. *Please make this be a horrible dream. A nightmare.* An awful nightmare and I will wake up and Wes will be here in my bed and Alex will be creeping around outside. I feel strangely numb, as if I had watched it all in a movie or read it in a book, not that I had seen that body for real. I open my eyes. I need to do something concrete. Move. I sit up and, fighting a new wave of nausea, decide to look for flights.

I get out my laptop and pull up my reservation, looking for ways out tomorrow. The sooner the better. Home. Where there are no dead bodies. No brains smashed open. Nothing going on that I can't quite put my finger on. As I look through the possibilities to New York, my email pings. Calista. Shit. Not now.

From: calistacraig@saintandrews.edu
To: ASage@nyu.edu
Subject: RE: RE: RE: Checking in

Alison,

I have been thinking about what to say to you. This is what I know: I was prepared to come to the Consortium. About a week—maybe ten days—prior, I received an email from Roger saying you (yes, *you*) had requested that Westley Charney be invited as his work would be most relevant to your project. As the week was limited to six guests because of lodging space and funding, and because in addition to you, I was the last in, Roger hoped I understood why my invitation was being rescinded. I did not understand. You may not have specifically requested that it be my spot that was taken, but that was the result of your request to have Westley attend. You were the darling of the Consortium this time given the major discovery on Barton, so Roger felt that he had to concede to your wishes here.

Is that clear enough?
Calista

My head is swimming. I want to run downstairs and confront Roger and Wes immediately, but now is clearly not the time. I can't possibly respond to Calista unless I know exactly what happened. There must have been a miscommunication—right?

A knock on the door. "Yes?" I say wearily, not moving from the bed.

"Dr. Sage?" It's DI Monroe. "I have some follow-up questions. I am coming in, okay?" The door opens and Monroe enters with the silent White. I sit up and motion to the empty chair by the desk.

"Be my guest," I say. "I'm just here trying to find flights home tomorrow. I think this puts a firm end to the Consortium."

"I'm afraid I can't let you leave that soon," says Monroe. She looks closely at me, judging my reaction. She sits down on the chair while White stands quietly behind her, an intimidating shadow.

"Excuse me? Can you just detain me like that? I saw something horrible and gruesome this morning and an awful thing has happened here. And now I am good and done with this place and I want to go home to my own bed, and my children, and my own country." I can feel the tears hot on my face. I am frustrated. And exhausted.

"I am sorry," Monroe says as if speaking to a petulant child. "But you must understand. This is a murder investigation. CCTV footage shows no one else entering the private road that leads to the priory and the manor other than those of you who are already here. One of you could be our killer. I can't just let you get on a plane to America. I can't even let you leave the property until we have properly done an investigation and vetted everyone." She leans forward a bit toward me.

"We are going to leave an officer here. You will be quite safe and protected. No one and everyone is a suspect right now. But I do have some more questions for you. Maybe we can uncover this all sooner rather than later."

Wait, is she suggesting *I* am a suspect? "I have nothing to do with any of this," I say. "It's just some horrible coincidence that this happened while we are all here. It must be someone else, not one of the scholars here." I run through them all in my head. Not one can I see as a killer. "Are you sure Alex doesn't have some unsavory friends? He was always skulking about. There was something off about him."

There. I said it. Maybe he creeped out the wrong person. Monroe nods and makes encouraging noises of agreement, noting something in her book. "Can you be specific about the so-called skulking?" she asks.

"I am pretty sure he came into my room at least once when I wasn't here. He was just always around or standing in my way. He often seemed to be listening in on conversations or having side meetings with the other participants. He made suggestive comments about me and another scholar." Shit. I didn't mean to say that last part. But then again, I have nothing to hide here.

"Dr. Charney?" asks Monroe. I nod. How did she know? She answers my unspoken question. "Yes, your names have come up together a few times in these interviews. You were having sexual relations?"

Another wave of nausea, this time at the thought of being the subject of the Consortium gossip. I nod tightly.

"And do you believe Alex could have been jealous about this?" she asks, pen poised above her notebook.

"Um, no, I don't think that was it." God, I hope not. "He just made comments about fornicators and kind of suggested he had seen us together or knew we had been. We were being discreet."

Monroe looks up from her pad. "Nearly all the participants have mentioned it, including Dr. Charney himself. You were apparently not as discreet as you thought you were."

I look down at my feet, mortified. Nod again. "Okay." Facing everyone after this will be humiliating.

"Why were you at the church last night when everyone else was in the library? I understand your colleague Charles Madingley was perhaps snooping to find out details of others' research. Were you helping him? I understand you are his protégée?" She looks at me pointedly.

"No!" I say firmly, alarmed that anyone would think that of me. "I mean, yes, he mentored me many years ago, but I do not steal research. I had no idea that Charles was doing anything like that until this morning."

"Would he kill for it?" She asks this casually, and I can't tell if she's serious or not.

"No. No. Absolutely not," I say, certain that I am right. Charles can be vain and maybe worried about his own obsolescence, but he's not a murderer.

Monroe leans forward but does not look as convinced as I think she should be. "Well then, tell me more about your own research, Alison. And why you were at the church."

I explain everything, starting with Barton and ending with the brass rubbing, which I show to Monroe.

"I see," she says. "May I take this?" She is already tucking it into her notebook, not waiting for my answer.

"Please," I answer. I have a photo of it now, anyway.

It's near dinnertime when Monroe finally leaves. She tells me she will be back in the morning and that the group is to remain on the manor-house and priory grounds. A police car will be stationed at the road to the village.

Vale House Manor, May 1534

The messenger, Geoffrey, arrived late at night. The weather was rather hot for May, and the ride was a long one. It had taken his palfrey the better part of two days to come from London, without the rest in the middle the horse badly needed, so the last ten miles were very slow. He knew Lady Vale would be distressed at the news he was bringing, though, and that a stable and hay waited for Lancelot upon their arrival. Geoffrey handed him off to the stablehand and, despite the late hour, knocked on the door of Vale House Manor.

Agnes perhaps should have been more careful, should have told him to come back the next morning—she did not know whether her servants were entirely loyal to her. But, instead, she ordered a fire in the library, deciding that, as the sole mistress of the household, she would do what she needed to do. She knew at least one of her servants had been distressed at John's death. But Geoffrey had been a loyal messenger from the start. She would just have to hope the others were as well.

"Lady Vale," said Geoffrey, taking his hat off as she led him to the library. "I witnessed the execution as you demanded. She is certainly dead, as is Bocking."

Agnes closed her eyes. She knew it was going to happen, but part of her had hoped that God—or one of his emissaries—would intervene on the Holy Maid's behalf. She was never fully convinced of all the girl's visions, but she had witnessed some of the trances, and they had seemed real to her. She also heard some of the rumors about what had supposedly taken place at the priory—the fornicating, the cavorting with the Devil—and she knew with certainty that no such filth could stand under Philippa's firm rule. If those were lies, certainly the accusation of feigning visions could also be one.

"My lady, there is more," Geoffrey said, accepting the ale that the maid brought, drinking deeply while he waited for the girl to leave the room. "They removed her head," he said in a low voice. "All of their heads. I watched that evening as they lowered the bodies and they sawed off their heads with butcher knives, not even an executioner's blade." He shuddered, then wiped his mouth with the back of his hand before setting down the empty tankard. "They have dipped the heads in tar and placed them on pikes at Drawbridge Gate, London Bridge."

He paused, thinking perhaps Lady Vale would swoon at such a thought. But she fixed him with a steady gaze. "There are near twenty-five heads right now," he continued. "It is not hard to tell which is the Maid's. She is the only woman I know who has ever been there. The other heads—you can't tell who they are. They will be there at least a month, if not more."

"And the body?" Agnes asked.

"I have, as you asked, paid to have it buried at Greyfriars. It will be consecrated ground." He hesitated. "Do you want me to retrieve the head?"

"Can you?" Agnes shifted forward. She had not considered that the head would be separate from the body, nor upon learning this fact that the head could somehow be salvaged.

"I have heard that you can, er, pay the master of the heads and he will allow it to be removed at night, secretly. It will have to stay a little while, as I said, at least a month. It is a warning to other traitors, but then I believe I could."

Agnes stood and walked over to a small chest in the library that she kept on the shelves alongside some of her books. She had the key around her neck, and she removed it to open the box. "How much for your trouble?" she asked. "And to convince the master of the heads?"

Vale House Manor, June 2023, Day 5

At least two cars are parked outside, and another one blocks the road that leads out of the grounds and to the village. One policeman stands—well, *sits*—watch just inside the manor door. Roger appears depleted but calm when I return to the library. I feel I shouldn't yet confront him about the email from Calista. But I can confront Wes.

I pour myself a giant glass of red wine. Wes is sitting; he still looks shell-shocked, as do the others. There is very little conversation, with everyone on their phones, presumably updating loved ones. It occurs to me that I really should text Jenny and probably Pete.

"Wes, can we talk?" I resist the urge to put my hand on his shoulder, to touch him. Partly because I do not want to do that in front of everyone else—even if apparently everyone knows that something is going on between us—but also because I am so angry at him, for whatever part he played in the Calista switch, because he did not disclose his real relationship (family!) with Roger, because even though I want to go home so badly I also feel a kernel of reluctance to leave him again.

He looks up and nods.

"Privately?"

He stands up and gestures for me to lead the way. I am not sure where to go. We head into the dining room, but the police have taken over the table there.

"The billiards room?" he says, pointing down the hall. I follow him there. I recall that just two days ago he was bouncing out of his shoes; now he is slow, quiet. Were he and Alex close? Although Wes is older, they grew up in the same village.

The walls of the billiards room have the same dark wood panels as the library and dining room, but this room is smaller, and dominated by a red-felted pool table. Cue sticks hang on the wall; balls rest in triangular formation, waiting for a game on the table. There is just one small window looking out onto the back of the house, and it's completely covered by a vine in the overgrown garden.

I shut the door behind us and motion for Wes to join me on the narrow wooden bench built in along the wall.

He looks at me expectantly.

"What is your relationship to Roger?" This seems an easier one to start with.

"Family friend."

"Well, you called his wife 'Aunt Janine,' so I'm a little confused. I thought you knew him professionally, and you've never said different, but I can see by your familiarity with this place, with Mrs. Bunch, the fact that he calls you 'Westy,' that it's more than a professional relationship." I am trying to remain measured, to breathe myself calm, but I can hear the anger rising in my voice, a little shake of rage beneath it.

"Not really an aunt," he says, running his fingers through his thick hair. "She's a longtime friend of my mum's. Not best friends, exactly, but very close, part of a tight group of women. I call them all 'aunt,' not sure why. I reckon because my mum wanted formality with most people, a title and their surname, and first names felt too informal for her, so she made them all aunts."

He pauses, waiting to see if I will respond before continuing. "So, anyway, yeah, I've known Aunt Janine my whole life, and I guess I've known Alex all of his. His mom worked here for years. Helena Goode. I was sixteen when Alex was born, though, so I didn't have a whole lot of interest in him, but I came to the manor house a lot with Aunt Janine, for a week or whatever, and Mrs. Goode and Alex were around. Sometimes Mum and I would come stay here with them, like a holiday."

He looks at me and keeps talking as if he is relieved someone has finally opened the floodgates, allowing him to explain.

"I didn't really like the kid that much, but Mrs. Goode was nice. And Aunt Janine had known her since she was a child. . . . I think her parents also worked here in some capacity when the manor had more staff. Aunt Janine and Mrs. Goode are sort of friends, as much as you can be friends with someone who works for your family. And I loved being here with Aunt Janine. She married Roger about thirty years ago but stayed close to my mum. We spent a lot of time here."

He's rambling, but I decide to let him. "And then when I studied for my doctorate and realized that Aunt Janine's husband, whom I just knew as Roger—didn't know what he did, or anything, really—well, I learned that Roger was actually kind of a big shot, and he helped me at Oxford a lot. He helped me get my job. And since now I was back around here, we saw each other more. We are more than colleagues but less than friends."

He takes a shaky breath. I think he may start to cry. I intended to keep a furious separation between us, but now sympathy is replacing the anger. I put my arm around him and it feels good to touch him. Even now I register how natural it feels, how right. "I am so sorry about Alex and for your Aunt Janine. And especially for Mrs. Goode."

"It's just all such a mess," says Wes. He takes my hand. "Are you ready to go back and join the group? Our absence will be noticed."

I shake my head. "There's something else I need to understand, Wes. About Calista."

A look of apprehension crosses his face. "Yes?"

"I wrote her to see how she was. You know, Covid." I'm not going to make this easy for him.

"I see."

"And she wrote back and said that she was not ill, that her invitation had been rescinded. That she was told by Roger that I had requested you in her place. Me! Can you explain?"

He won't meet my gaze. "I can't, really. I didn't know that's what Roger told her. He told me to start working on the Barton legend after he heard your paper at ManSock, to see if there was really something there. I think we both had thought it was just a bunch of nonsense, but somehow your finding the book made it more real. Honestly, he wasn't going to even have a Consortium this year, but after ManSock decided he needed to bring you to the manor, so he threw it together last minute.

"At first I didn't find much, so he wasn't going to include me, but then I started to see there were different snippets of this legend. When I told him maybe there was something there, he said he would find a way to get me in the conference. I thought it was a lucky break that Calista was ill, honestly, but I started to suspect that maybe that wasn't the case." He's looking down at his feet, moving a toe back and forth across a scratch in the wood.

He stops and looks directly at me now, grasping both of my hands. "Alison, I am being totally honest with you. I know that Roger believes the treasure of the priory is hidden somewhere here. He thinks it will save this place. The money. He may have gone about it in entirely the wrong way, but I don't think his intentions are bad. He wants us to crack this puzzle. I don't think he ever imagined that something so awful could have happened."

"What *did* happen? Who could have done this? What does this have to do with a stupid treasure hunt?"

He puts his head down in his hands, elbows resting on his knees. "Roger is convinced some Reformation fortune is hidden in the church. He doesn't know where but hoped we could figure it out. I told him you thought the unnamed saint in the rood screen was Elizabeth, but that's the only connection to Barton we've found there. And Roger was there when you speculated that the 'mother' mentioned in the Beaney portrait may have been Mary. So maybe . . ." He trails off and doesn't finish his sentence.

"Maybe?" I prod.

"Maybe he had Alex break open the rood screen to see what was there behind Mary? Or, maybe Alex decided to look on his own? It sure didn't seem that Roger knew about it."

"And then Roger killed him for it?" I think of Roger's face when we discovered Alex. He was horrified, shocked, sick. I can't imagine he's that good an actor.

"Seems unlikely, I know," says Wes. He shakes his head. "I just don't know who could have murdered him."

"Maybe someone else is trying to find the treasure? And thought Alex was about to get it?"

Could it have been you, Wes? I dismiss that thought almost immediately. Wes was with me all night. Why would I even think he was capable of that?

Can it have been Roger after all? Did he follow Alex and then, when there was no treasure in the rood screen, murder him on the way back to the manor?

It's all so muddled.

My resolve to go back home to Brooklyn is strengthened. I stand up, but Wes pulls me back to him.

"Can we just put it all aside for a moment? Be together while we can?" he pleads, pulling me close and kissing me. I lean against him, returning his kiss, and allow myself to feel supported. Maybe this does not need to end when I return to New York.

Vale House Manor, July 1534

When Maude died, mere days after the birth of the twins, Agnes had to send a girl into the village to find a satisfactory nursemaid. Wet nurses were not hard to find; often only either the baby or the mother survived. Sure enough, the girl came back with a wench whose own baby had died at birth just a day after Maude's labor. She turned out to be very suitable, a thick peasant girl who doted on the twins. Better than Maude would have been, surely.

Lady Vale left the twins with that wet nurse and the servants while she went to the priory. It was bleak over at St. Sepulchre's these days. A few of the sisters had already left the order and gone back home to live with parents or siblings. They did not want to see how it all ended. Agnes had heard that some of the religious houses were setting up escape plans in Flanders, Portugal, or Spain. Ways to start anew abroad. She could not imagine Philippa or any of her nuns doing so. She could not even imagine them leaving Kent.

"It is Lady Vale," Agnes called as she entered the gates. Gone were the days when a novice would greet her and seek Philippa out while she waited. Now Philippa walked out alone to meet her and beckoned for Agnes to follow to her lodgings, which now matched the rest of the priory in austerity rather than serving as a contrast, as it once did. At least she still had her books.

The prioress was looking thin. The good years of Elizabeth's residency had kept all the nuns healthy and ruddy, but now that so much rent had to be paid to the Crown and even to Agnes herself (although Agnes funneled that back to the priory by way of donation), everything about their lives was leaner. Philippa had moved her gems to the manor house—John and Maude were gone, and so it was a safe place for the moment. They both knew they had to hide them again, though, somewhere safer than the manor. Exposed Catholics were subject to raids or even having their titles and property abruptly taken away.

Agnes placed the treasure she had brought, wrapped in fine cloth, on the table in front of Philippa. "Mater," she said, "I have brought you the saint. My men in London were able to bribe the"—she shuddered to even think about it—"master of the heads." Agnes slowly unwound the cloth to reveal the relic. It was unlike any skull she had ever seen. The tar had preserved it, with flesh and hair—blackened and hardened—still stuck to the bone. The eye sockets were mercifully empty.

Philippa swallowed her horror at seeing Elizabeth almost as she had known her in life, now disembodied and sitting before her in death. She still had her doubts about how much of the girl's revelations had been real, but no one deserved the death she had had. She said a quick blessing over the head, thinking, too, of the men who had died with Elizabeth, whose skulls would eventually end up in the river or thrown away.

This relic was important, though. If the priory was to eventually rebuild, it needed not only money but a reason for pilgrims to come. Philippa thought maybe Elizabeth would be a new Thomas Becket, a saint who had opposed a king, who had died for that opposition and adherence to her faith. It may not have been what happened, exactly, but it was the story that she could tell.

"I know where to hide this and our gems," said Philippa. "I have been thinking about it and praying, too, and Elizabeth herself aided me in answering this prayer. First, I have something else for your safekeeping." She handed two books to Agnes, one printed and the other in Bocking's familiar hand. "One is your copy of Elizabeth's book," Philippa said, "but I have written some more on the last pages. The other was Bocking's—more things he had written of Elizabeth's, mostly concerning the king. I believe it should be destroyed. But I leave that to you."

Agnes looked at the books in her hands and flipped through their pages. She did not need to ask why they needed to be hidden. "And the hiding places?"

Philippa nodded grimly. "I have a plan."

Part Four

MEMENTO MORI

Vale House Manor, June 2023, Day 5

The mood at dinner tonight is somber. The police temporarily vacated the dining room so that we could eat, but the sideboard has reminders that they are there—binders, legal pads. No one quite knows what to say, or whether conversation is even really permitted. Charles's earlier admission has made even talk about our work more guarded than usual. Roger, who has been the master of ceremonies for so many days, is clearly deflated, as if someone has let the air out of his bombast.

Arjun finally addresses the group. "So, I spoke to my daughter, Priyanka—you may remember that she's a police officer. She explained the process to me. I think we may be kept here another day or so until they can be sure they have all the information they need from us."

Shit. I just want to go home. I can't stop thinking about the splay of Alex's feet, the pulp of his head.

". . . so this is the 'major crime squad,'" Arjun is saying. "I am not sure we've met everyone, but Priyanka said it would have several detective constables, a detective sergeant, and a detective inspector."

"What's the difference?" Brian asks.

"Hierarchy," says Arjun. "The DI is in charge. I think that's all you need to know."

"Monroe," I say.

Everyone nods.

"Also, Priyanka said the body will likely be removed tonight. That may be the van we saw headed toward the church a bit earlier. They'll take it to the morgue for an autopsy."

"An autopsy?" asks Brian. "Isn't it obvious how he died? You all said someone whacked him in the head. Don't need a detective to tell you that."

Roger winces a bit at the word "whacked." Marla puts her hand on his arm and gives it a slight squeeze.

"I guess he could have died another way—poisoning first or something. You never know." Arjun shrugs, then notices Roger's demeanor. "Roger," he says, "we are all thinking of you and Janine. I know you've known Alex since he was a boy. It's a horror. I am so sorry."

Roger nods. "He was a good lad," he says. "He didn't deserve this."

Wes holds my hand under the table and I let him.

* * *

FINALLY, A CONVERSATION has taken hold at the other end of the table between Brian, Charles, and Arjun about traffic and trains and planes and how and when we will be able to leave. I decide I need to talk to Roger, after the revelations from Wes.

"Roger," I say. Wes shoots me a sideways warning look, but I continue. "What will happen now to the work we have done this week? I am so sorry it has ended in such an awful way. Do you think Alex was somehow influenced by the direction of the research that Wes and I have been doing?"

Marla has been listening to the others talk, but she turns her full attention to me as Roger answers. "I suppose we are half-done," he says. "I hope you can all conclude your articles on your own and we can get the volume completed. We could dedicate it to Alex. As for whether he was influenced by the research . . ." He pauses. "I thought maybe we were closer to solving the puzzle when you realized our unknown saint on the rood screen was probably Elizabeth and that the panel of the Virgin Mary, the Mother, may be a hiding place. I don't know why it had never occurred to me before. Alex told me he was going to turn the light off in the church—and I told him to take a closer look at the panel, just see if there was something we had missed."

He turns to Marla. "Right? You were there. I never suggested he should break the rood screen."

Marla nods.

"But I guess he took matters into his own hands? I didn't think that he would want the money for himself. I believed that we all wanted to save this place."

"That may account for the destroyed rood screen, but it doesn't explain who murdered him," I say.

"No. It doesn't. I know they said the CCTV didn't show anyone coming here, but I think it must be someone from outside. Some sort of horrible coincidence. Maybe Alex had gotten into some trouble in the village. I have suggested as much to the police, and they are looking into it. . . ." He trails off, pinching the bridge of his nose with a sigh.

"In any event, I think the search for the treasure was always a fool's errand—that money likely disappeared centuries ago into the pocket of one of Cromwell's men. Perhaps it is time to say goodbye to this place and its history. I thought I was doing right by it, saving it the way it was meant to be saved, preserving its past. But some pasts should stay there. Janine and I have talked about retirement in the States, and perhaps it's time."

I notice Marla stiffen slightly at the mention of Janine, but she begins talking quietly to Wes, betraying little to anyone who isn't watching closely.

Roger pats my arm and leans in toward me, saying softly, "Wes told me you found out about my little subterfuge with Calista. I am sorry. I let my fancy and whims get ahead of me. And look where we've ended up as a result."

* * *

As Mrs. Bunch clears after dinner, one of the policemen on duty comes into the room to address all of us. Tall, broad, and ruddy, he seems annoyed at his job babysitting a bunch of academics.

"I know you have been asking about how long you need to stay on the premises," he says in a bored voice. "I have an update from DI Monroe." He consults his phone, then reads a message aloud. "'Please let the group know that we are working as fast as we can to process the evidence and should be allowing some of the participants to leave as early as tomorrow.'" There is a collective sigh in the room, and the mood lifts slightly. I hope I am in that group of "some."

Roger and Marla leave soon after; clearly they have decided to abandon what little discretion they had. I am now feeling slightly better about the whole Calista thing even though it was a clear misjudgment on Roger's part. It may have been idiotic and unprofessional, but it wasn't intentionally malicious. On the other hand, it recasts my invitation to the C.C. in an entirely different light. I wasn't invited because I was a "rising star" or had made an impressive keynote debut at ManSock; I was invited because Roger thought I could be the key to this futile—and now fatal—treasure hunt. The pride I felt swell inside me at that invitation, which had buoyed me up these last few days, deflated and sagged.

Everyone else appears at a bit of a loss as to what to do now that Roger has left, so Charles speaks, assuming the director role. "I think we should make it an early night tonight. Contact our loved ones and let them know what is going on here and get some rest after such an eventful day. Hopefully, tomorrow they will have figured out what happened, and we can go to our homes. In any event, I'm headed up to call Dicky."

Everyone seems comforted to have marching orders, me included. I smile gratefully at Charles. "Good night, all," I say. "See you tomorrow."

Wes has already left. I realize I am disappointed at that. Another deflation. But my heart lifts when I find that he is waiting for me at the bottom of the stairs. "I have a bottle of wine, a corkscrew, and two glasses," he says, holding up his offerings. "Let's go to your room."

I nod, looking around to make sure we aren't seen. Despite what people know, I have no desire to rub it in their faces. I smile and wordlessly grab the bottle with one hand and take his now-empty hand with my other, pulling him up the stairs.

Once in my room, Wes walks over to my desk and takes his sweet time opening the wine as he speaks. "I don't think Roger's right about the gems being lost or sold over the centuries," he says. "If they were, that would have somehow come down in one of the stories, some of the folklore. The stories here are so consistent that the priory had a treasure, and it has been hidden. After this week, I am also sure that Lady Vale had something to do with it. Let's try to figure this out together."

I can't help but feel annoyed by his suggestion. "Wes, isn't it time to drop this? There is no treasure. The book holds no secrets." I take a deep breath to keep from crying. "I'm sorry to disappoint everyone here. I came because I thought Roger wanted to hear more about my discovery, about my work. Not because I could help with this crusade. I'm not a detective. And now we have fucking real detectives here because Alex is dead. Dead, Wes!" My voice is rising and I can feel myself giving in to the anger that is boiling up inside me. Anger at seeing Alex's body. Anger that I am still here. Anger that despite it all, I still want to be with Wes tonight.

Wes walks over and puts a glass in my hand and then places his palm, softly, on my cheek. He kisses me. "Alison," he says, "you are here because you are brilliant. The treasure hunt is just a lark. It always has been. Roger himself said that what happened to Alex is not connected to it. Let's just relax, have some wine, work through this problem. It's something to do whilst we wait for the police to be done. And if it *does* in some way connect to Alex's death, then we can help them figure it out." He kisses me again. "Please?" he says, his eyes staring directly into mine. "It will help me keep my mind off of this horrible day."

I soften to the idea of talking about the treasure.

Examine evidence. Come up with a thesis. This is my training; these are my skills.

Vale House Manor, July 1535

When the terrible news reached them, Philippa was at Lady Vale's, having supper. After that first reluctant visit to the manor house, she found herself there more frequently. It had been a year since Elizabeth's death and although she had been unpopular at the convent, the event had shattered the community.

Philippa was not needed much at the priory with so few sisters. Cromwell's men had come and taken most of the books from their library—certainly all of Elizabeth's, but many others as well. They were papist, she was told. Superstitious. False. Lady Vale had to surrender some books, too, though not many; if she crossed out offending words or scratched out certain images, she was permitted to keep them.

Philippa could not believe what they had done to the images of the saints in the church. Their faces were no more. But the heretics did not dare touch the image of the Virgin Mary, and even now the painter Agnes had commissioned was working on the new panel, part of their shared message to the future.

Lady Vale's servant, Lettice, came in, eyeing Philippa with suspicion, as she always did—it had taken the prioress some getting used to after years of commanding respect to be an object of such derision. "My lady," Lettice said to Agnes with a curtsy, "there is a messenger here with news from London."

Agnes nodded and Lettice went to fetch the guest. It was Geoffrey, who merely a year prior had come with the news about Elizabeth. His appearance always gave Agnes a chill. News from London. It was never good.

As soon as they were alone, Geoffrey spoke. "Thomas More is dead."

Each word added a weight to her heart. More had been the most visible and prominent holdout, refusing to sign King Henry's Oath of

Succession, which, among other things, firmly severed England from the pope.

"Hanged?" asked Agnes.

"No, Lady Vale, beheaded."

She sighed. More merciful. But another head separated from its body, presumably placed on a spike on the bridge along with all the others. Geoffrey turned to Philippa. "Mater prioress," he said, "they are talking about 'dissolving' the monasteries. They will not exist anymore at all. I hope you have a place to go after they do."

Philippa made brief eye contact with Agnes. "I have some ideas. Thank you for your concerns. I will pray for your soul. And for the soul of Sir Thomas More."

When Geoffrey was gone, Agnes turned to Philippa. "Our treasures are well hidden. I think when the priory is no longer, I should leave this place for a while. Go to London with the twins, let Cromwell and his men think we have nothing for them here. One day we will come back. I will be sure to let Alister and Margaret know how they can uncover our goods when the country is restored to its rightful place in heaven."

Philippa nodded. "And the papers that Lord Vale wrote about this place? His property?"

Agnes said curtly, "Do not worry about these things."

Philippa had learned not to underestimate Agnes's will or strength. "Let us enjoy our time here together while we have it, Lady Vale."

Vale House Manor, June 2023, Days 5–6

"Let's see what we have here so far," I say. "What are the clues?" I am sitting cross-legged on the bed, my papers spread out before us and my laptop open. I've changed into my pj's: sweatpants and a T-shirt. I'm grateful for the wine, although I wrinkle my nose as I take a sip. "Not one of the best bottles," I remark.

Wes shrugs. "Beggars can't be choosers. I had to take what was in the kitchen, not the wine cellar. Sorry! Next time I'll nick a Bordeaux." I note that his glass is full, so I guess he truly finds it undrinkable. I drink anyway, knowing I will never relax from the day's events without its dulling effect. Then more softly, "I wanted to do something nice for you after such an awful day. I've been so happy here with you, and now it's just a mess."

"The wine will do." I smile and take another sip to prove it. "And the gesture is truly appreciated." It's nice to be taken care of.

"So . . . Elizabeth's book," says Wes.

"The book," I repeat. "That gives us the acrostic." I open a file on my computer and show it to Wes, reading aloud. "'Venerate our Mother, seated / At the side of Jhesu, our meek other / Locking inside our heart-chest the / Emeralds, rubies, and pearls of our devotion.'"

"So, one," Wes says, ticking items off on his fingers. "We know by the acrostic that the Vales were connected to the priory in a significant way. That they probably paid for Elizabeth's book to be printed. Two: there is something here about venerating the Mother, which we assume is Mary. And three: the reference to jewels is here, that they are locked inside a chest."

"Well, these are metaphorical jewels, right? Jewels of our devotion? It could be that the language of treasure is just so prevalent in these texts that people took that the wrong way and a legend was born."

"Maybe," says Wes doubtfully. "What's next? The painting of Lady Vale?"

"Sure, okay." I pull up the image of the painting that the museum has on its website. "The quotation in the Book of Hours that Agnes Vale holds in the portrait, 'Whoever shall say to the mother, the gift that comes from me shall profit you.' Again, gifts from the mother, for the mother." I enlarge the image of the saint in the book Lady Vale is holding. "And I guess this could be Elizabeth. It's a woman dressed as a Benedictine nun. It at least points to the priory again."

Wes is quiet for a moment, looking at the image. "Elizabeth would have been alive when this painting was commissioned, so it makes sense she wouldn't have her jeweled nimbus yet—the halo would only be conferred in heaven when she was declared a saint. That's different from the image of her on the rood screen, which was surely painted after her death."

"Yes. So potentially we have two images of Elizabeth. One that speaks about giving profit to the mother. One that shows jewels. I don't think either tells us where anything is hidden, but they tell us what could be hidden if we think literally. And I don't think the image of Mary is relevant, especially now that it's been cut open. It's the image of Elizabeth we need to look at."

I pull up a picture I had taken of the rood screen, the unnamed saint in Benedictine habit, jewels around her head. "See," I say as I enlarge the halo, "these gems are so unusual. I've never seen them depicted in a nimbus like this before. I think the image shows that *they* are the treasure—rubies, pearls."

"The treasure that came to the priory because of Elizabeth?" Wes asks.

"Maybe . . . ," I say, doubtful that this exercise will yield any results, "or that Elizabeth is the treasure and this is a futile hunt."

Wes refills my empty wineglass, then studies the image, his hand absentmindedly rubbing my back. "What about her arm," he asks, ignoring my skepticism, "outstretched like that? That's also an anomaly. Could it be pointing to something?"

"I think it points to the wall, which has the hellmouth on it," I say. "Could that be indicating the hiding spot somehow?" I suddenly remember what I saw at the church the night before in the inscription above the painting. "Wait, Wes, I totally forgot to show you something. I got so caught up last night in . . . well, in you . . . and then obviously what happened today." I flip through the photos on my phone until I come to the fading transcription, the letter "P" that is flaking off bit by bit on the word "Pater." I magnify the image as much as possible, Wes looking beside me. "Look!" I almost shout. "The 'P' is nearly gone, but you can see an 'M' underneath. This word wasn't 'Pater,' it's 'Mater.' 'Mother.'" I am almost shaking now that the years have revealed their secret.

"So, the hellmouth is a memento mori for the mother . . . ," Wes says, his excitement matching mine. "The matriarch in the transi tomb! Could the mother be Valentina?"

"Could you hide a treasure in a tomb? That lid must weigh a ton." I hold my glass out for a refill, the rancid taste in the wine less apparent as I drink more.

"You could hide one in there, absolutely. I think you could move it with a crowbar. And the tomb could be the 'chest' mentioned in the acrostic." He offers the bottle. "Here, you probably need more wine than I do after today."

Even as he says it, my mind flashes to Alex's head, bashed in. I'm having trouble putting all my thoughts together. A crowbar would have made an excellent murder weapon. Had someone already figured out the tomb as a site of interest? Were they on their way to the church with that tool when they encountered Alex?

Roger.

He would have been incensed that the rood screen had been desecrated. Could he and Alex have had some sort of altercation? Maybe Roger *is* that good an actor. After all, he had no problem lying about Calista this whole time.

"I think we should talk to the police," I say. "I can't help but feel this is connected to Alex's death, although I'm not sure how." I drain my glass again.

"I don't know," says Wes. He fills my wineglass again; the bottle is nearly empty. I fear it's mostly been me—Wes seems to hardly have had any wine at all even though he clinks my glass with his. "I think we should drink this terrible wine, sleep on it, and tell the police in the morning when Monroe is back. There's only one detective here and the others are just the guys sitting outside in their cars, wondering why they drew the short straw to watch a bunch of nerdy scholars."

I take another big sip of the wine, not caring at all about its quality anymore. "Maybe you're right." The heaviness of Alex's death outweighs the thrill of potentially solving a mystery. And the question of who murdered him hangs over just about everything. I feel my will to argue slip away into the comfort of being with Wes and the fatigue of the day. "It just seems to me that there is someone out there—maybe *here*—who wants that treasure so badly that they would kill for it." I yawn.

"I don't disagree," Wes says, as he pours the dregs of the bottle into my glass. Losing myself in just a bit of drunkenness after the horrors of the day feels good, I must admit. I settle into the sleepy fuzziness, just slightly blurrier than the numbness I've felt since seeing Alex's body. "I just think we should have some more evidence instead of a half-baked theory. You also don't want the police ripping open the transi tomb to see if there's anything inside other than a body; you want that to be done with historians at the ready. If you tell them in the morning, you can make sure that the right people are there as well."

I try to formulate an answer but have trouble putting the words together. I am trying to keep focused, battling a cloudiness that feels like more than just a few too many glasses of wine. I turn to tell Wes that maybe he should go, that obviously I need to sleep, that I could use some water, but I am moving in slow motion, my body not responding to the signals I am sending it.

The glass falls from my hand. It is as if I am standing outside of myself as I watch the red stain of wine spread across the white bedspread, a bloom of blood. I see, for a moment, Alex's head in its place.

I try to speak, opening my mouth, but only a croak comes out.

The last thing I see as I slip into unconsciousness is Wes by the window, opening the priest-hole door.

Vale House Manor, November 1536

Agnes decided not to send for the doctor when Philippa's breath became rasping. She had already sent the twins ahead with her servants to the home she had let in London. This was her last duty here, to see the prioress to a good death, to see her buried in the church.

It had been too much for Philippa, Agnes was sure. Watching the priory emptied by Cromwell's men, tearfully hugging her much diminished group of uncertain sisters goodbye as they returned to the homes of families that did not want them. Who wanted to support an unmarriageable daughter? And Philippa had told her that the nuns were given pensions of only one pound a year. Hardly enough to sustain them.

Watching her spiritual daughters leave had killed Philippa more than her own losses, Agnes believed. The prioress herself had no home to go to, having been given to the priory as a child. She knew no other life. She was awarded a meager allowance by the Crown (slightly more than the other nuns, in deference to her position as prioress), and Agnes said she would accept that as rent to preserve Philippa's dignity. But in the end, they both wanted Philippa to live at the manor house.

While at first it was only the smaller convents and monasteries like St. Sepulchre's that were closed, every day they heard of more, and it was clear that the bigger and richer ones were next.

No one was safe.

Philippa's health deteriorated rapidly after the dissolution. She and Agnes had wept in sorrow together when Catherine of Aragon died, broken at Henry's betrayal. They did not weep when Anne Boleyn lost her head but felt the shared recognition that they all were at the king's whims now. Even the woman who had set them on this terrible path.

Philippa grew ever thinner. The last week or so she had barely left her bed. There was not even a priest to call to administer the last unction, but Agnes believed that Philippa would go to heaven with a clean soul. Wiping her brow with a damp, cool cloth, Agnes read aloud the questions that her book, *The Craft of Dying*, instructed her to ask.

"Do you repent for the things you might have done but did not do?"

Philippa considered the question, thinking again of Elizabeth, who occupied so many of her thoughts in these final days. That slight, uncertain girl who had arrived at St. Sepulchre's all those years ago and who over the decade was the cause of so much strife and turmoil. Could Philippa have protected that girl better from the men who used her to their own ends? Would Elizabeth then be here now, alive?

There was so much she might have done but did not do. Did she repent for this? Yes, she begged God's forgiveness.

Philippa turned toward Agnes and, no longer able to speak, nodded as if to say, "It is time." Agnes leaned forward and took the older woman's hands in hers, a crucifix between them. She bent down and kissed Philippa's forehead. As Agnes did so, the prioress closed her eyes and sighed out her life.

She had gone to join her bridegroom Christ in heaven.

* * *

THE BURIAL IN the church was hard to secure. No one was certain how they should venerate the dead, which rites were correct. Agnes understood that Henry's chosen Archbishop of Canterbury, Thomas Cranmer, was making a new prayer book to use for services. It was to be in English, which to Agnes was the truest sign that the Devil had found his way into the country.

She searched out a priest who she knew had his heart in Rome, a Carmelite, and had him perform the funeral ceremony with meager attendants—just Agnes herself and a few of the former sisters who lived locally.

The church was the resting place for many prioresses of St. Sepulchre's, as it was for several members of the Vale family.

They were erased in death.

Agnes did not want that for Philippa. She imagined the church existing fifty, one hundred years into the future. She wanted her great-grandchildren to sit in that church and know the name of Philippa Jonys.

The new church warden finally relented, after much convincing that involved two pounds counted out carefully in silver pennies and groats. More than Agnes would have liked, but it was worth it to let Philippa have a monumental brass inside the church commemorating her burial therein. Agnes had long ago commissioned the art, while Philippa was still alive. The image of her was true, although Philippa had always been in motion and to see her frozen in prayer was not how Agnes could ever think of her. It took more convincing, and more silver, for Agnes to secure the location of the grave.

"This is not the easiest place to bury her," the warden told her. "And it is not near the other prioresses, as is customary."

Agnes removed a small gold ring from her left pinky and placed it in his hand. "This is the place for her. I insist."

Vale House Manor, June 2023, Day 6

It's thirst that wakes me up.

I am dreaming that I am in a desert and there is a stream ahead of me. As I drag my aching body to the water's edge, it disappears. It is a mirage. I am left with a mouth full of hot sand, and hands clutching an unrecognizable dead thing, crawling with maggots.

I struggle to open my eyes, and when I do, I have no idea where I am. I try to stand up and immediately hit my head on the ceiling above me. My arms reach up, out. I seem to be in a wooden box, in total darkness. A nauseating odor fills my nose. A smell of death. I am in a coffin.

I start kicking and screaming, banging my fists on the ceiling above me and the walls around me, ignoring the pain as splinters lodge in my hands and I lacerate them on the wood. Soon my throat is raw, from screaming and the relentless thirst. My now-bruised hands, sticky with blood, throb in pain.

Dizzy, I lie back down and cry.

But then it comes to me: the nasty odor. It's the smell of the dead rat, or whatever it was, mixed with bleach. Only then do I remember the evening. Passing out. Wes at the window.

I am not in a coffin.

I'm in a priest hole.

This realization brings a new wave of distress. Wes *drugged* me.

Did he leave me to die?

My head throbs with a heavy fuzziness that goes beyond any effect alcohol would have. I feel instantly sober and unnaturally slow at the same time. All I can think is that I need to get water and oxygen. Logically, I know the priest hole was built in such a way as to allow for the flow of air—people stayed for days, sometimes, when they were hidden—but the dank humidity of the space coupled with the smell of rotten decay make me feel like I can't get a full breath.

And the relentless thirst.

Need water. Need air.

What did he put in my drink? How long have I been out?

Everything seems blurry, but I know what I am looking for. The exit. I feel around in the dark on the wall until I detect the outline of the door that leads to my room. I push against it with all my might. It doesn't budge. I brace my back to the other wall and push with my feet. It doesn't open.

Wes locked me in here.

Wes. That fucker.

I scream again, pounding on the door with my fists. "Help!! Hello? Help! Officer? Monroe! White! Roger! Charles! Marla!"

Nothing.

It is the middle of the night (I think—I have no idea how long I was unconscious), and my room is slightly isolated from the others as it sits almost at the end of the hallway. I'll just have to wait until morning when someone will (hopefully) come looking for me. I try to think of anything other than the thirst and my bloody hands.

I will be found. I push my ear against the door. Would I hear someone come in?

I am not dead.

Someone will find me. Right?

Breathe. Calm.

I have never been a phobic—not afraid of flying or blood or heights or spiders or open spaces or public speaking. I can breathe myself calm, relax, slow my own pulse.

But now, as I sit in this dark and tight space for what must be the third hour (time is so blurry without a watch or a window that I can't judge how much has passed), claustrophobia is settling in to stay. I don't know if it's the smell of that dead animal, still lingering in the heavy air inside this place, the dust that I can feel crusting on my nostrils, or that my body is touching all four walls of this small, dark container at once.

I am so thirsty. The air is stifling and my mouth is sandpaper-dry. If I ever get out of here, I will never take a glass of water for granted again.

The researcher in me wants to think of all the others who have hidden here, holding their breath, hoping that they are not discovered and that their secrets are safe. But the practical me, the me whose throat is raw from screaming and whose hands are chafed and bloody from pounding on the door to this hole—that version of me doesn't care about the past. I care only about the future. As in, will there be one?

I try not to ask the question that is the only question worth asking right now: Is this how I die?

Breathe, calm.

I try not to think about my thirst and relax as much as possible into the wait for morning. Looking in from the outside, I didn't understand how small this hole actually is. How was it built for a grown man to fold himself into and stay hidden for hours?

I can't stand up, but I muscle my way into sitting with my legs tucked in front of me, cannonball-style, shifting frequently to keep from cramping. Periodically I shout, "Hello!! Help!!" and bang on the door. I am so thirsty and my mouth so dry that my cries are getting fainter, my voice croaking.

Is that how Elizabeth felt? Dreading the noose? Knowing that she had been abandoned?

I begin to have a sense of what people mean when they say, "My life flashed before my eyes."

Tristan and Georgina.

I can see them now with a clarity I have been lacking—teens with one foot in childhood and the other in adulthood. I can almost feel those early days, a baby tucked under each arm in a rare moment when they were both asleep, finding them in the same crib as toddlers (it was usually Georgina who had climbed into Tristan's), the time I came out of the shower to find them both covered in paint (as well as our dining room table and most of our walls) and chose laughter over tears.

Like a movie, I fast-forward to a recent day, after Pete left. My birthday. The twins had turned our small kitchen into a restaurant, Tristan's beautifully written and decorated menu, Georgina at the stove making basically the only thing she knows, scrambled eggs. Both speaking in mock French accents.

This will not be how it ends.

"Please! Someone!" I kick my cramping legs hard in frustration on the floor. And then the floor moves. Just a centimeter, but it moves. Have I broken the floorboard? I imagine kicking through and crashing down to one of the rooms below. Which is the worse way to go:

suffocating in a priest hole or breaking my neck falling through the ceiling? But as I feel around my feet with my fingers, I realize that this is not a crack. It's symmetrical. It's a square. And I can feel a hinge. This is some sort of trapdoor.

* * *

I KICK AGAIN. The hatch opens another inch. What I would do for a flashlight! I can't really see the contours of the door, but I feel around again with my fingers, probing for some kind of latch or handle. Nothing. I do this several times. Kick. Feel. Kick. Feel. I find some reserve of energy I didn't know I had and kick really hard. It moves a centimeter. Finally. I kick. And again. And again.

Then it drops, and the door swings down on rusted, ancient hinges.

I sit at the edge of the hole, reveling in the feeling of letting my legs hang down, of getting out of the crouch I had been in for hours, sitting in a normal position. I welcome the painful pins and needles as the blood returns to long-asleep limbs.

When I have caught my breath and the sensation has returned to my legs, I feel around the frame of the door, seeing whether I can determine where it leads, and discover what I quickly realize are the rungs of a ladder leading down.

I can't see what is below—all is still black—but I hope this leads to a way out. I remember Roger saying that some of the houses around here had two or three connected priest holes, so that the first one would always appear empty when priest hunters, the pursuivants, conducted a search. Clearly this house was one with a double priest hole, a fact that Roger may not have even known.

I feel the spiderwebs on my face as I lower myself down on the ladder, which groans under my weight. Some of the rungs are missing and, after a misstep and near tumble, I proceed tentatively, checking my position carefully before releasing my hands and moving down another rung. I'd guess it is only about ten feet total, but it takes me as many minutes to step off the ladder into a new space, full of so much dust that I must bring my T-shirt up over my nose and mouth to breathe.

Unlike the first hole, which has long been a known feature of this house and an item of curiosity, presumably cleaned out and even used to hide things over the centuries, this space feels like it hasn't been touched for at least a hundred years, if not longer. I can feel a soft layer of dust and dirt under my feet. Even though this chamber is dustier and hotter than the first, I feel like I can breathe more easily. I can stand, too—the whole space is bigger. Big enough for one or two men to stand or lie down. This is a hiding place that would work for days if furnished with water and food. Water. I am still consumed by my thirst.

There must be some way out of here. I know it. I crawl along the dusty floor, feeling for an exit.

My hand feels something soft. I immediately recoil.

Rat.

It doesn't move, though, and there is no smell. I tap the thing with my bare foot and still nothing moves. More tapping, tentative stepping. It must be an inanimate object. Safe to touch. I feel it again with my fingers. It's a cloth package with something inside. I tuck it under my arm and continue crawling along the floor in search of an exit.

This is not how it ends.

* * *

AFTER I HAVE worked the entirety of the floor, I move to the walls. Systematically feeling up and down, hoping my fingers find a groove that signals a door. Finally, after what feels like an hour but was probably half that, I do feel the outline of something small, tiny. Like the kind of door my parents had installed for our fat cat, Boxer. He was too chubby for the regular off-the-shelf cat doors, so my father asked a neighbor who had an impressive woodshop in his garage to make one that accommodated Boxer's exceptional heft.

That's what I think of as I search for the hinge. That I would have to channel the long-dead Boxer and squeeze my (definitely not cat-sized) frame through the space. But that on the other side awaits freedom. It doesn't move when I push it with my hands, but once I apply my shoulder and heave my body against it, the door—miraculously, it seems to me—simply opens outward, and I can feel open space on the other side. I hope it's not just another priest hole. In the dark, however, I can't tell.

I throw my small package through the door and hear a thump. "Hello?" I say, almost in a whisper. All done shouting now, my voice is barely perceptible from thirst, from screaming, and from the dry, dusty air of the priest holes.

There is no answer.

I have lost all sense of perspective, space, and time, but I know I have *descended* from one hole into the other. So, I should be on the first floor. The only rooms I've seen are the library, the dining room, the billiards room, and the kitchen, although there are certainly others that are unused by the guests of the manor.

I try going feetfirst, but my legs quickly hit a wall. I can't conceive of how to bend them properly, which way to move so that the rest of my body can fit. I retract them back into the hole.

Breathe. Calm.

I am almost out of here. My brain is still slow, my head heavy from whatever drug Wes slipped into my wine, though there is clarity that I am safe and alive, even if that wasn't his plan.

I imagine that he thinks I am dead, poisoned, hidden forever in the walls of the manor house. But surely, they would have searched the priest hole eventually? Or would it have taken a rotting, maggoty corpse to draw someone there? Maybe he just wanted me out of the way for a little while? Was he planning to come back for me? Tell someone where to find me?

The questions multiply and overlap in my mind. I can't even think straight.

I put my arms overhead like I am diving into a pool and push, headfirst, through the door a second time. My butt does not want to come through the hole. I push with my hands, wiggling my hips, turning all sorts of ways, and then, finally—*pop*—I am through.

To my dismay, I feel like I am in another cabinet, similar to and slightly smaller than the one in the window seat in my room. Have I just moved from one small, enclosed space into another? Is this some kind of labyrinth of connected holes that has no exit?

* * *

I FEEL ALONG the end of the cabinet, again looking for a door, any kind of exit, now back in a crouch after the glorious feeling of standing in the interim space.

I feel a handle. I pull it, and to my great relief, the door swings easily open. These holes were built with a way out; I knew they had to be. I go through arms first again, but more quickly this time, tumbling out into what I immediately recognize as the billiards room, softly lit by a dim predawn light through the window.

I realize that I have come from beneath the wooden bench where earlier that evening (yesterday evening?) I confronted Wes about Calista. I had no idea what lay beneath it. I lie panting on the floor, not so much from exertion but from the adrenaline that has been steadily building in my body.

I am free.

Taking big gulps of air as if I have come up from a swim where I held my breath just a little too long, I reach back into the cabinet under the bench, its door now obvious to me. I feel around for the package that I had thrown there. After so many hours of trying to wake everyone in the house, now I don't want to wake anyone or—most of all—alert Wes that I managed to escape. As my eyes adjust to the light, I can see the clock on the wall: 4:30 A.M. That means I have been trapped for seven hours. Whatever Wes planned to do while I was in there, I assume he has done it.

I need to collect my thoughts. But more than anything right now, I need water. There's a small drinks fridge in the corner of the billiards room, and I am happy to find bottles of seltzer inside. I drink two straight down and open a third. Thank God. Almost immediately I feel calmer, my thoughts less confused.

I contemplate the police cars parked outside. For some reason, my gut is telling me to do this alone.

I am enraged at Wes. He likely went to find the treasure in the transi tomb and is long gone, but I want to see for myself. Did he mean to leave me there to die? I will have time soon enough to tell the police what I know.

But first, the package. The researcher in me wants to see what is wrapped inside more than the angry woman in me wants to confront Wes. I bring it over to the pool table, where the dawn light meagerly illuminates the center.

Unwrapping it carefully, I see that it's a book. One that I recognize. The thrill of discovery (oh, I felt this thrill so recently, and for the same book!) courses through me.

A marueilous woorke of late done at Court of Streete in Kent.

After nearly four centuries, with every copy assumed destroyed, now I have discovered two within a year. The original owners of this book knew it was contraband, heresy, and hid it away. I can already see the book I am going to write about Elizabeth, the priory, and the Vales.

The last page has an image: the missing woodcut print of Elizabeth. There is handwriting underneath it, but I cannot read it in this light.

I wrap it up and slip it under my arm. I slowly open the billiards-room door, bracing myself for any creak that will come, but all is mercifully quiet. The house is still asleep.

I cross the hall, through the dining room and into the kitchen, which is illuminated by a faint yellow light above the stove. I slip the book inside a cupboard next to the door that leads to the priory. Before I exit, I decide I need a weapon, in case there is a confrontation with Wes, in case he really tried to kill me and tries again.

I take a knife from its block, registering briefly that there is already one missing. Then I silently slip through the door, and head toward the church.

London, July 1540

It had been four years since they moved to London, to a small house that was nothing compared to the manor. Agnes did not like the loud, foul-smelling city, but it was safer to be here, where the community of Catholics was strong and secret. They would stand out too much in Kent.

The messages from the caretaker looking after Vale House made clear that the house was in disrepair, especially after the fire. Still, she paid to have it secured. Someday it would be for the twins when it was safe to go back. And her treasures were there, hiding in their secret places. She waited for that lascivious, infertile king to die. In the meantime, she worked with the other London Catholic families clandestinely, helping to secure support for Mary Tudor, who by all reports remained true to the faith despite her father's attempts to bend her will otherwise. Agnes even paid for now-forbidden texts to be printed abroad and brought to England.

But today was a good day.

Cromwell was going to lose his head.

Everyone knew it, and many were going to watch him die, although that spectacle was not for Agnes. She did not plan to say a prayer for his soul.

Her maid brought the twins in to see her. She had promised them a story. Although she took pleasure in their company, she could not deny that she had been lonely since Philippa's death. Sometimes in the evening, as she read or did her needlework, she conjured the prioress next to her, doing the same. It was the only time in her life she had felt true companionship, especially at the manor house, which had been so devoid of love and affection. And it had been all too fleeting. She longed for the days when they would read together, discussing their shared devotion and heartaches.

Philippa told Agnes that she'd been sent by her parents to the convent when she was just twelve; they had only the dowry to marry her older sister away and wanted to do their duty by the Church. The day they left her with the then-prioress, holding a small donation of books and even smaller donation of shillings, was the last she had ever seen of her parents. But she had been happy with her new family of sisters. Her days as a novice were ones of joy and laughter and pride in her work.

Agnes understood that Philippa's grief at the loss of the priory was so much more than the grief of losing her religious practice; it was her life, her family. In another lifetime, Agnes thought, she could also have been a nun, spending her days in quiet study and contemplation, free from wifehood and motherhood. Of course, it turned out that the nuns were also subject to the whims and greed of men.

The twins settled at Agnes's feet, as they so often did, and she told them the stories of all the saints. The children loved the ones that seemed the most fantastic—Christina the Marvelous, who flew to the ceiling of her church at her own funeral and told everyone what she had seen of heaven and hell; Catherine of Alexandria, who was smarter than all the pharisees and then tortured to death on her wheel.

"Tell the story about the hidden treasure, Grandmother," said Alister. This was his favorite, and she told it often. Margaret liked it, too, but she far preferred the stories about the Holy Maid and what she looked like when she had a revelation and foretold the future. These stories, they knew, were never to be told outside of the shared rooms with Grandmother. Even the stories of the saints were dangerous. They could lose their heads for their faith, like so many martyrs had.

"My little pigeons"—the twins giggled at the silly endearment—"let me tell you about the hidden treasure!"

The children settled in, delighted.

"Once upon a time, in a land not so far from here, there lived a nasty king and his kind queen." Alister made a sour face at the mention of the king. "The queen wanted to use the kingdom's wealth to help the people and save them from an evil demon who was trying to turn them away from the right path of the Lord."

Margaret's eyes were huge like saucers, even though she had heard the story before. "Tell us about the demon, Grandmother!" she said excitedly.

"The demon thought people should worship him instead of God, and he brought a great many to his wicked side." The twins shivered and moved closer to each other. Margaret held tightly onto her poppet. "One day the nasty king died, and the good queen decided to hide her treasure, so that when the people realized the evil demon was not helping them, then they would turn to her for help, and she would be ready. But she was not able to hide the treasure on her own." She paused, knowing the twins would leap in with the next part.

"The fairy godmother!" In unison. Every time.

"Yes, the fairy godmother came, and she and the queen together devised a plan to hide the treasure. They put together many clues for the right people. In books. In brass. In art. In prayer. And one day, when the land is rid of the demon and a righteous angel has taken his place, then that day the treasure will be found. Maybe even you will find it!" This was what they had been waiting for.

"Oh yes, Grandmother! It will be us! It will be us!"

She kissed them and sent them off to bed.

Maybe she would say just one prayer for Cromwell's soul. It was the Christian thing to do.

Vale House Manor, June 2023, Day 6

I walk out the door into the cool early-morning air, still gulping breaths after so many hours of fetid enclosure. It's not yet five, but the sun is already up, so no need for a flashlight. Yesterday was a hot day, but the nightly summer breeze cooled everything down. Now I am chilled in just my T-shirt and sweatpants, shoeless—the pajamas I put on so many hours before, when I thought that Alex's murder had nothing to do with Wes and even less to do with me.

Everything has changed.

My head is pounding. From the drug? Is it still in my system? Am I going to be okay? I imagine it slowly eating away at my stomach, waiting to attack. Don't some drugs work like that? But every minute I am thinking more clearly, my body feeling less heavy and slow.

Only one police car is parked in front of the manor, and I can see from the way the cop's head is tilted back that he is sound asleep. Yellow caution tape surrounds the part of the pathway where we found Alex's body. I walk toward it.

I assume the front door of the church will be locked, but the police may not have thought to secure the side door, the one that leads to what would have been the priory's cloister. It's to that door I tiptoe, hewing closely to the side of the church. The light is on inside, so the leper's squint glows faintly as I approach.

Of course! The squint. I can see inside the church without having to enter. I do not know how long it would take to move the heavy lid from the base of the transi tomb, but it cannot be a quick job. There's still a chance that Wes is there, leveraging the crowbar, trying to get the treasure.

Or he can be long gone.

Either way, the squint allows me to look without being seen.

As I peer through the small opening, I am not prepared for what I find. Yes, the transi tomb has been opened. The bottom part with its cadaver sculpture is shunted off to the side, a crowbar on the ground beside it.

But it is what—or rather who—is next to the tomb that causes me to cry out.

Wes. It's Wes. He is covered in blood, a knife handle sticking out of his chest. He's slouched over, almost as if he has fallen to his knees and then collapsed onto his side. I can't tell if he's dead or alive.

I run to the door—it's open. Not just unlocked. Open. Despite my fury at Wes, the liar, the deceiver, my heart is still tight as I run up to him.

"Wes!" I scream. My voice is barely above a croak, my throat still raw. "Help! Help!" I desperately hope the police can hear me. Wes isn't conscious, but I can see that he's breathing, bloody bubbles in his mouth. "Help!"

"Alison?" A voice at the back door. Marla.

"Oh God, Alison, oh my God, what happened? Is that Wes?" Marla runs to his side.

"Please, Marla, get help. He's dying. He needs help right now."

Marla reaches for the knife, as if to pull it out, gripping it firmly. My thoughts flash back to Jenny's text about Rachel's patient, information given a million years ago.

"No! Don't. It needs to stay in to keep everything together. Please, just get someone!" I can't imagine what she is doing out so early but I send a silent prayer of gratitude to whatever higher powers may be listening.

Marla looks at me strangely but nods and runs off toward the manor house. For what seems an eternity, I hold on to Wes's limp hand with one hand and press the base of the knife with the other, trying to keep the blood from pooling out. Pressure. Aren't you supposed to apply pressure? Normally the sight of blood makes me queasy, but now as I press down I only have a drumbeat in my mind pushing everything else out: *Make it stop. Make it stop.*

Fear and confusion have displaced my rage, and I keep a steady stream of chatter. "Oh God, Wes, I don't know what kind of mess you got into, but just hold on. Help is on its way. Hold on, hold on."

From where I'm crouched, I can see the contents of the tomb. There are remnants of a skeleton, but there is also something else. Something blackened, sinister. With hair. I think it's a skull.

Two skeletons?

I snap my focus back to Wes. There will be time later to ask questions. Finally, I hear footsteps running to the front of the church, doors unlocking. Two policemen rush in, radioing for an ambulance.

"Step away from that body!" one shouts. "Hands up where we can see them!"

"Wait, what? It's not me!" I yell. "I'm trying to save him!"

"Don't make me say it again. Away from the body." I raise both of my hands, one now dripping with blood, and step away. One officer tends to Wes while the other takes me aside and handcuffs me, then pats me down. He finds the knife in my pocket, the twin to the knife in Wes's chest.

He shows it to his partner, who is still attending to Wes. "She has another weapon."

"*Another* weapon?" I say. "I didn't stab Wes! I brought it for self-defense. It's clean."

I watch the scene as if I am standing outside of it, too shell-shocked to object or react. The blood is now starting to gross me out, to make me feel sick. I can feel it coagulating between my fingers as the ambulance arrives and paramedics rush in, administering to Wes and speaking in medical acronyms I don't understand. It is short work before they are taking him out, hooked up to oxygen, an IV in his arm.

Marla comes in with Monroe, who is clearly furious. "Bring her to the manor for questioning," she says. "And make sure someone gets prints off that knife once the doctors remove it."

"I saw her go into the church just seconds before she screamed for help," Marla explains coolly. "It couldn't have been her. Also, you'll find my prints on the knife. I tried to remove it, but Alison stopped me."

"Yes"—I nod—"I did. I heard you were supposed to keep them in so that patients don't bleed out. I swear, it wasn't me."

The officer who cuffed me speaks up. "She is covered in blood," he says. "She has a knife. The same one in his body."

"Take these two back to the house," Monroe tells the officers, glaring at the one who spoke. "Separate rooms. And secure the scene. *Again.*"

* * *

"YOU EITHER HAVE great luck or terrible luck. You seem to have been awfully close to a lot of death these last two days."

We are sitting in the dining room, Monroe across from me at the table, White next to her, silently scribbling in his notepad. The room has been transformed fully into a makeshift headquarters, police computers open and running, the buzz of a walkie-talkie, papers in piles. A small device whirrs on the table, recording our words. One murder and you get some sleepy officers on duty; an attempted second one and you get a command center.

It seems impossible that days ago this was a space of intellectual camaraderie. I can smell the blood on my clothes, and I try to ignore the nausea.

"Can I shower?" I plead, standing up and holding my stained shirt up as proof of my need.

"After questioning," says Monroe, pointing firmly at the seat, "and an officer will be there with you to take all of your clothes as evidence."

"I understand," I say meekly, sitting back down. I feel guilty, even though I know I have done nothing wrong. I understand how people confess falsely. I want to give Monroe what she wants. And get out of here.

"Tell me what you were doing in the church, standing over a body, soaked in blood?" Monroe begins. The recorder is on, White's pen poised over a notebook. Monroe has removed my handcuffs and there is a cup of tea in front of me—a small kindness. I take a sip, and the warm liquid feels like a balm for my raw throat. Everything smells like blood.

"Last night, Wes and I spent some time after dinner pulling out all the clues that we thought we had amassed about this supposedly hidden treasure. I can go over these with you if you'd like, but the result is that we decided that if there had been a priory treasure, the clues pointed to a memento mori—a reminder of death that the medieval people were really invested in—and also a 'mother.' So, we thought maybe the transi tomb, where the matriarch of the Vale family is buried."

Monroe nodded. "Seems like a good place to hide something. So did you and Wes decide you were going to break in there together?"

"No, no! There wasn't any talk of breaking in anywhere. I thought we were getting all the pieces assembled and then we were going to go to the police, to you, but the next thing I knew I was losing consciousness and Wes had put me in the priest hole."

"Wait, what? Losing consciousness?" I can see the alarm on her face.

"I don't know what he put in my wine, but he put something in it. I was drugged. I was talking to him and then I was passing out. And then I woke up in the priest hole."

"Which is . . ." Monroe raises her eyebrows, waiting for an explanation. I can't tell if she believes me.

"Hidden cabinets and rooms to hide priests, from when practicing Catholicism could result in death. This house has one."

"Where is this hole?"

"The entrance is under the window seat in my room."

Monroe nods wordlessly at White, who steps out to speak with an officer. "Hollister is checking on it," he says as he picks up his pen and notebook again.

"Tell me more about what happened," Monroe says.

I explain it as best I can. My confinement. My discovery of the second priest hole and escape into the billiards room. And finally, my—perhaps ill-advised, I admit—decision to go to the church alone.

I do not tell her about the book I discovered, my mind skipping to the cupboard in the kitchen where I squirreled it away. I am so worried that it will be taken, transferred to a police evidence locker to rot.

"Let's talk some more about your decision to go to the church and confront Westley Charney," says Monroe. "Were you hoping he had uncovered the treasure and that you could kill him, take it for yourself?"

"No, no, nothing like that." I can feel some panic rising in my chest again. Is that what Monroe thinks I am capable of? Do they really think I stabbed him?

Monroe leans in confidingly. "Didn't you want to kill him for drugging you? You were sexually involved and then you realized he had been using you to get information about the treasure. It sounds like a crime of passion to me." Although her tone is matter-of-fact, I am alarmed as it dawns on me that I am definitely a suspect here.

"No, honestly, I *did* want to confront him about it. About all of it. I was so angry and confused, but I wouldn't have tried to kill him. Wait, did *he* kill Alex? Do you know if he was trying to kill me?"

Do you really believe he was only using me? Did it all mean nothing to him? That's what I want to ask.

Monroe's face betrays little. "I'll let you know what we know, at least what I decide to share, when you've finished giving your statement. Tell me what you saw in the church."

I describe the leper's squint, the top of the transi tomb, the crowbar. The blood, the blood, the blood.

Wes's body, hunched, fetal-like, eyes closed in an agony-filled sleep. Marla's timely arrival.

I tell it all, an exorcism of the fear and the anger. I still feel sick; the smell of blood is now overwhelming, and even though they swabbed and wiped my hands, in my imagination they still feel slick and sticky.

All the while, White is furiously writing. Monroe is watching me without expression. I have no idea if I am truly a suspect, if Wes is alive, if the treasure has been found.

* * *

"CAN I ASK questions now?" I say, feeling (and probably sounding) both defeated and defiant. I want to know what is going on. I want to go to bed. I want to update Pete and Jenny on the unbelievable turn the week has taken. I also *really* want to take a close look at the book. I want to know if someone was or still is trying to murder me. And I want to go home, to hug my children.

Monroe nods. "I may not answer them, though. And after this interview, you need to report to the ambulance outside so that they can make sure you are okay—draw your blood to see what exactly you drank and if you need more medical attention."

"Okay," I say. "Is Wes alive?"

"Yes. He has undergone surgery. He is unconscious and in police custody."

"Did he murder Alex?"

"He is obviously a prime suspect in Alex's murder since he may have returned to the scene and apparently finished what he couldn't the first time."

"Opening the tomb."

Monroe nods.

"But who tried to murder Wes?"

She shakes her head. "I won't answer that."

"Am I a suspect?" Am I allowed to ask this? Should I be requesting a lawyer? That's what the smart people always do on *Law & Order*: they ask for a lawyer. Does it matter in the UK?

"Maybe," Monroe answers. "We know you were drugged—we found crushed sleeping pills in Charney's room, and it looks like the dregs of the same in your wineglass. It's all gone to the lab for analysis, so we will know more later today or tomorrow, and can match it to whatever your blood will show. But right now, everyone here is a suspect."

"Do I have to stay?"

Monroe nods emphatically. "Yes, you do. Until everyone has been fully cleared of both Alex's murder and the attempted murder of Westley—which may very well turn into a murder charge if he doesn't make it—everyone needs to stay. Especially those of you who would be leaving the country."

I wince at these words. "What was in the tomb?" I surprise myself with this question. I feel like I shouldn't care about anything other than my safety right now. But I, too, have gotten caught up in the treasure hunting—this is more than mere academic interest. I want to see this through to the end. To assemble the pieces the way that Lady Vale had seemingly intended. I think again of the book from the priest hole. Is it the key? Or had Wes and I already figured out the solution and the treasure was found and stolen, lost for good?

"Actually, we were hoping you could help us answer some of that."

She opens a photograph of the tomb on an iPad. There is the outline of a skeleton, but it looks more like dust than anything, although the skull is mostly intact. Next to the skull is not exactly another skull, more like a desiccated head—blackened, as if it had been charred, with the remnants of flesh and hair attached. I remember only now that I saw it when I was willing Wes not to die.

"This"—Monroe points to the first skull and the powdery outline—"is what we would expect in a sealed casket of this age. The bones have decomposed mostly except for the teeth and part of the skull. I imagine this is the original occupant of the tomb."

"Valentina Vale."

She nods. "Apparently. But there is another, more intact skull here, as you can see. We will analyze it for age, but it's been preserved in something. Also, there is no body. My medical examiner says that this head has been severed, and in a rather brutal and unartful way. The ashes of the skeleton have not been disturbed, so I don't think there was anything else in the tomb that was taken. Although everything is being investigated, as I said. So, do you see a treasure here? Why are there two skulls? Is this some sort of medieval practice?"

It's the blackened skull that strikes me. Black. Like tar. "It's Elizabeth Barton's skull," I whisper. "That's a treasure, for sure. But it's not the gems that Wes and the murderer, I guess, were hoping to find."

"Just her skull? Why would that be a treasure at all?" asks Monroe.

"After she was hanged, her head was put on London Bridge as a warning to traitors. Her body was buried at Greyfriars and her head . . . I guess I thought her head ended up wherever traitors' heads go. Some kind of mass grave?" The wheels are turning slowly in my brain.

"So why do you think this is *her* skull?" Monroe presses. "It's not her grave."

"Well, two things. One, it's tarred. It was dipped in tar so that it would remain preserved. All the heads displayed on the bridge were. It was more gruesome with skin and hair—otherwise the birds would pick a skull clean in days. Second, that it is chopped off so badly. It would have happened after her death by hanging. It wasn't a decapitation as a form of murder, but a postmortem removal of the head for purposes of display."

"Do you know of any other heads like this?"

"No, not exactly. Like I said, most of the heads of those who were executed were probably thrown into some sort of mass grave. Maybe even thrown into the Thames. And although we didn't know what happened to Elizabeth's head, we do know what happened to Thomas More's." I can feel myself slipping into professor mode, a welcome comfort after feeling like a victim. I am in charge here, saved by pedantry.

"Yes?" asks Monroe.

"He was beheaded, and his head was also put on a spike, but his daughter must have bribed someone at the bridge, and she recovered it. Some assume the daughter herself was eventually buried with the head. So, we know it was possible. And there were people who would have believed that Elizabeth Barton was a martyr, as they did Thomas More—so the skull would have been a powerful relic if the country was restored to Catholicism, as so many hoped it would be." I cannot deny the frisson of discovery, the very underpinnings of my academic career.

"This was the big treasure?" Monroe says skeptically. "A skull? Hardly worth dying for. Definitely not worth killing for."

I can only agree.

Vale House Manor, November 1554

Margaret did not recognize Vale House Manor when she arrived. She had been just an infant, really, the year her grandmother Agnes moved her and Alister to London, and although the house was rich in her imagination, thanks to her grandmother's stories, the place before her did not match the one in her head.

Alister had decided to stay in London. He liked being around the court. And Margaret sensed that he did not have the same conviction of faith that she and her grandmother shared. He did not really see the difference between Protestant and Catholic, did not believe it was worth risking a life for.

Grandmother. Margaret was not sure she would ever recover from her death. After all, she had been mother, godmother, confidante, guide. Agnes's last act had been to join Margaret with Samuel Pitlock; she assured her granddaughter that it was a good match and that Samuel would carry the torch of faith. She died just days after Mary Tudor took the throne back from that impostor, Lady Jane Grey. Everyone whispered that Queen Mary was sickly and that the waiting princess, Elizabeth, was hale. And Protestant.

Samuel had sent her ahead to the manor. He was staying in London to do some business with the court, to smooth over some of the frayed edges that were beginning to show as the country catapulted from Henry VIII to the child monarch Edward to Lady Grey and now finally, mercifully, to the good Queen Mary. It had been a very confusing seven years since the king had given up the ghost, a time of instability. Margaret hoped that Mary would bring peace, rest, to a people who were not sure what prayers to say, which books to read, what favor they had in the eyes of God.

". . . my Lady Pitlock?" Margaret's eyes turned to the caretaker—what was his name? The man was eager to show her the work they had done to restore the damaged parts of the house, to prove that the money she had been sending had not been in vain. She realized he had been talking and she hadn't been listening.

"I'm so sorry, Mr.—" It was just there in the corner of her mind. "—Charney." Aha. There it was. "I am just reflecting on what a loss this home suffered in the fire. I am saddened my grandmother did not again see this place before she saw heaven." Men were unpacking the boxes and parcels she had in the carriage and carrying them into the manor. Her new home. Her old home.

"Yes, yes," he said. "It was a loss to the entire village, my lady. We loved your grandmother." Margaret knew a lie when she heard one, but she merely nodded assent. "I was sorry to hear about her death." Charney paused. "The builders are here to discuss the enlargement of the manor. That is, if you are not too tired from your journey. We did not realize you were arriving alone, so we can wait until your husband joins you."

"I am quite fine. Thank you. Lord Pitlock will not arrive for several weeks, as he has business in London, so all manor affairs go through me. Let me speak to the builder. I understand we will use the stones from the priory, but I want to make certain the church remains untouched. That it remains consecrated ground. My family is buried there."

Charney nodded. "Yes, your instructions were clear. The house is ready for you, Lady." With that he gestured toward the front door, bidding Margaret to lead the way. She stepped over the threshold and into her new life as Lady of Vale House Manor.

* * *

AT FIRST, THE news that the Heresy Acts had been reinstated gave Margaret some hope. Queen Mary was going to stamp out this stain of Protestantism that Henry VIII had let take hold. As soon as she heard the news from London, she went to the priory church and prayed to God for delivering the country back into his fold.

Mary was setting everything right again. She had outlawed clerical marriage (an abomination!) and restored the Latin mass. Clergy left their families, or they were fined, although Margaret knew that their local cleric had his own children running around the property as he was saying mass.

The townspeople were grumbling about Mary's reinstatement of the faith. Margaret's maid told her that when she went to the market in the village to purchase some fish, the fishmonger had said to her, "I can't believe this queen is dragging us back under Italy's rule again. Doesn't she know we are English?"

And once, when the builders did not realize she was near, their allegiance became clear.

"That Bloody Mary," one said, "she will sell us all to Rome and to Spain. There's nothing English about her."

"She's so sickly. We mustn't endure her long. If she doesn't kill all of us first."

"Elizabeth will be queen soon. She will marry some good English nobleman who will reign as king. We just need to wait."

Furious, Margaret did not send the maid to offer them water in the hot sun, as was her custom. The builders' talk and the way the townspeople spoke about the "papists" who had been at the priory made it clear that the return to the one true faith would be an arduous journey.

Margaret kept hidden the books that Agnes had given her years before, including one that had revelations of the Holy Maid Elizabeth Barton. "These are considered heresy," Grandmother had whispered. "They would hang you for it."

Vale House Manor, June 2023, Day 6

I feel like I am sleepwalking when I am led out to a waiting ambulance where I am examined and poked and my blood is drawn; while I stand outside my bedroom as it's swept for fingerprints and watch as items are carried out in plastic bags; as I hand over my clothes to a female officer who puts them in evidence bags as I stand in my underwear. Finally, I am allowed to shower and feel as if I am slowly coming back to myself. Rubbing some salve on my hands, I notice that they look like they've been paper-cut in a million places. I pull out all the splinters I can with my tweezers.

I've never been so happy to get into a bed. It's now nearly noon, and other than the hours of drugged sleep I had the evening before, this is my first rest in nearly two days.

When I awake, dusky evening light spills into the room. I'm so disoriented, it takes me a while to realize it must be time for dinner. I tentatively make my way down the stairs, driven by hunger, uncertain what people know or have heard. Other than Marla, I haven't seen anyone else from the group since yesterday, and my imprisonment by Wes made everything so surreal. I hear noise in the library and head that way.

"My God, Alison!" gasps Charles as I enter.

He pulls me into a giant hug. It feels so good to be embraced, I bite back a sob. Charles is speaking into my hair: "What an ordeal you have been through. We are all absolutely gobsmacked about Westley and Roger."

"Roger?" I blink, sorting through all the confusion in my brain.

"Oh my, I see you are still in the dark. Come, sit."

The others—Brian, Arjun, Marla—gather around me. I can tell by their strange body language (pats on the back, averted eyes) and stilted, sympathetic platitudes how awkward everyone feels. No one is sure what to say or do.

"Thank you, everyone. Really, I am fine." Of course I'm not, but I don't want them to know that. "Please fill me in on what I missed."

Charles says, "I will let Marla tell you what she knows and what she told the police."

Arjun adds, excitedly, "Priyanka says this is one of the biggest cases this area has ever had!"

Marla shoots him a quieting look but otherwise seems composed given the events of the day and her participation in them. "Well," she begins, "I suppose you have heard that the treasure was a skull. This talk of gemstones"—she waves a hand in the air—"was a fairy tale. It's the problem with folklorists sometimes—they believe their own mythologies." She says the word "folklorists" the way someone might say "satanists" or "Nazis," dripping with disdain. "Roger was unfortunately duped by Westley's fantasies."

He wasn't the only one duped by Wes, I think. "Roger was orchestrating a kind of solution to the puzzle," Marla continues. "He used us—you, me, Wes, Alex. Of course, Roger is all rhetoric and no action. He doesn't like to do things himself." More disdain.

"I realized last night. Roger was not in my bed when I woke up just before dawn." She pauses, adding, "We were lovers, you know," casually, unabashedly.

Even under these circumstances I muster some feigned surprise—"Oh, no, I had no idea"—although most of the others are just nodding.

Marla continues, "Well, we were. So, when he wasn't in my bed, I thought something was amiss. I looked in his room—no Roger—and I went outside to look for him, and that is when I heard Alison shouting from the church." She puts her hand on my arm. "When I found you with Wes and got the police."

"Thank God you did," I say. "I think for sure Wes would have died if he hadn't been cared for so quickly." Why I am so relieved that Wes is alive, I don't know. I'll have to unpack all of my own feelings about these events later.

A flash of what looks like annoyance crosses her face. "He still very well may die," Marla says, "and it sounds like he deserves to after what he did to you. Anyway, I put it all together. Roger, as we know, had told Alex to check out the rood screen. Alex got greedy." She says this while rubbing her fingers together, pantomiming money. "He wanted the treasure for his own, so rather than just looking, he cut the screen. I think at this point Wes may have suspected the transi tomb as the source and was headed there with a crowbar to open it. Wes saw Alex and his desecration of the rood screen and confronted him about going behind Roger's back—although, of course, Wes was doing the same thing. I'm sure he realized that Alex would have somehow blamed him or blackmailed him, so Wes decided to kill him. With Alex now out of the way, Wes went to get the treasure for himself last night. He knew that you knew the transi tomb was also important, Alison, so he drugged you and left you for dead and then went to open the tomb himself."

Something is wrong in this narrative. I know it but can't quite piece it together, my brain still fuzzy.

Marla continues, "Roger always wanted this treasure for himself. He may have brought us in, but he never intended to share it. I assume Roger found Wes at the tomb. Stabbed him to get to the treasure and then ran off back to the manor to play innocent when he realized there was no treasure to be had."

She looks suddenly sullen. "This is what I told the police, and they now have Roger in custody. I imagine we will all be free to go in the morning."

"Are you all right, dear?" Charles says, his hand on my shoulder. "This is a lot to take in for all of us, but especially you. I know you and Mr. Charney had . . . gotten close. And the fact that this touches on your research . . . well . . . it's all a lot to process."

I nod. But Marla's story does not ring true. Several things are wrong with it—for one, Wes was with me when Alex was murdered, but I don't say so. Perhaps after I have had something to eat and a moment to think, I will be able to piece it together.

* * *

Mrs. Bunch comes into the library, balancing a tray of little quiches and warm tartlets on one hand as she pushes the door open with the other. "The police are still in the dining room," she says, apologetically, "so dinner will have to be finger food in here again. I am so sorry."

She places the tray down on one of the low tables, then notices me. "Oh my, Alison, I cannot believe what they say Westy did to you. Is it true?" She takes me in a hug.

I swallow back tears. "Yes," I choke out, "it's true."

"Please eat something, dear." She puts a plate in my hands. "Come into the kitchen to see me if you need anything at all." She leans in closely and almost whispers, "I've hidden the cookies in the cupboard above the teapot so that Charles won't find them again! I had been blaming Alex all week." At Alex's name, her eyes fill with tears but don't spill over.

"Thank you," I manage to say to her, as she turns to head back to the kitchen.

The kitchen. The book. I ache to see it, to go through what I found in the priest hole. I don't want the book taken out of my hands, sent off to some evidence lab, to become part of the story of Westley and Roger and Alex. I want it to be part of the story of Lady Vale and Elizabeth Barton. *That's* the story I want to tell.

Brian walks up as Mrs. Bunch finishes unloading the tray. "Hey," he says softly, "is there anything I can do? I'm sorry none of us saw that coming with Westley."

I smile wanly. This all feels so awkward. I wish people would leave me alone.

"I'm fine. Really, thank you, Brian."

"Well, once they let us go, don't worry about transport to Heathrow or anything. I'll have Princeton take care of it. Get us back to New York quickly. Next time let's stay in America." He laughs, a forced laugh, but I appreciate the effort at some humor, some normalcy.

"You've got a deal." I see Marla standing off to the side, as if waiting to speak with me. "Excuse me," I say to Brian, "I haven't really had a chance to thank Marla."

Marla takes my elbow as she steers me to a quiet corner of the room near the chess table. It's all I can do to grab a mini quiche en route.

"Alison, we need to talk," Marla says, with some urgency, her voice low. "You're the only one I trust here." Marla lowers her voice even more, keeping her eyes on Brian and Arjun, just steps behind me. "I cannot believe that all this talk of treasure was just for a skull."

"Didn't you just say that it was a fantasy? That Roger was misled?" I ask.

"I just don't want anyone else to continue to believe something is here." She looks over at the rest, grouped around the food, lowering her voice even more so that I have to lean in to hear her. "You know, in case Roger had any other accomplices."

Who else? I study our group. Charles? He has proven to be sneakier than I ever imagined, and Roger has known him longer than I have. Maybe Arjun? He's kept more to himself than the others. Brian? I already know his ethics are a little squishy. Would he be able to pull off such a ruse?

I realize Marla is still talking. "If the jewels are here, we can't leave them to rot for another four hundred years. They belong in a museum."

"I agree. That's what I don't understand about what happened—wouldn't Roger or Westley or anyone who found it, if it was to be found, be obligated to sell it to the government?"

Marla sighs. "Yes, according to the Treasure Act. At least for any gold and silver." I am only slightly familiar with England's law that any valuables over three hundred years old need to be bid on by the country's museums. It could still yield the owner of the property where it was found significant sums, but probably not as much as if they sold it on the open market or at auction. "But I don't think anyone willing to kill for these gemstones had any intention of complying with some heritage law."

"I guess not."

"So, do you have anything else? More information?" Marla presses. "The two of us can figure it out, I'm sure."

"Actually, I might," I say, relieved I can share the secret of the book with another scholar, glad to have someone I can trust. "Meet me in the kitchen later. Maybe an hour after dinner so that Mrs. Bunch has time to clean up?"

* * *

I PICK UP my phone, sit on my bed, and get to some long overdue calls.

Pete is the first person I want to reach. I let him know with the barest details what is going on. If it makes the news in the U.S., I want him to be able to reassure the twins that everything is fine. I call Jenny, too, and give her a spare outline of events, not having the energy for more. I just want her to know I am all right.

There is a quick knock, and Monroe doesn't wait for a response before entering my room. "I need to speak with you, Alison," she says. "I'd like to go over some of the allegations that Marla has made and see where you stand on them."

This isn't over yet.

* * *

MONROE TURNS THE desk chair to face me and takes a seat. I move to the edge of the bed so that I am facing her.

"How are you feeling?" she asks.

"Better, but still shaken and confused. I hope this is you coming to tell me I can go home after this conversation."

Monroe smiles ruefully. "No, sorry. Hopefully, we can have this wrapped up soon, and you can get your passport returned."

"Am I still kind of a suspect?"

"Everyone here is still a suspect," she says, "but I think you are in a position to help us figure some things out. More so than the others since you have been at the center of so much here."

"Unfortunately."

"Yes, unfortunately." She pulls out a tape recorder. "White has gone back to the station to get some supplies, so if you don't mind, I'm just going to record this conversation." I can see she's already recording, not waiting for my answer.

"Okay. I have no idea how I can help, though." I feel like I've told her everything I know. She should be talking to Roger, or Wes when—if—he wakes up. They must know the answers.

"Roger has maintained his innocence and has been most cooperative. He has some ideas that we need to follow through on. They may be lies to save his own skin, but they may have merit."

"Oh?"

"I will tell you what he has told us. And tell you what we need you to do in order to close this case, hopefully." She leans forward. "What we need you to do to get you home."

"I'm listening," I say, because it seems like something someone says in this moment, but I feel somewhat outside of my body, wondering how I've gotten here, how I am at all caught up in anything that involves dead bodies and stabbing. And I do, more than anything, just want to go home.

"Roger believes that Westley was working with someone else here at the manor to get the treasure. Initially, Roger had brought Alex and Westley in to help him find it, and claims he had every intention of following the Treasure Act. Indeed, he claims he hoped that it would get a lot of press coverage and perhaps bring some national interest, and money, to Vale House Manor."

"That makes sense," I say. "Roger does like being the center of attention. I do believe bringing money here was his primary motivation. This place needs a lot of work."

Monroe nods. "This plan obviously went wrong. Perhaps Alex thought to take the money for himself. Perhaps Westley. Maybe both. But someone else had their eyes on it, and on those men, and was willing to kill to be the first to find it."

"Not Roger?" He still, to me, seems the most logical one.

"So far, that is not what the evidence supports. We have a primary suspect but very little evidence. This is where you can help."

* * *

THE KITCHEN IS empty when I arrive. I head straight for the cupboard, worried that the book has somehow vanished. But there it is—still wrapped in its cloth, which I now can see, despite its moth-eaten, faded appearance, was once a rich red woven silk. How long has it been hiding in the priest hole? Somehow it survived destruction by fire, animals, water, and any of the dangers that have removed so much of the past from the future's interested eyes.

I sit down at the table and gingerly unwrap the package, scared that the items may disintegrate in my hands. Elizabeth's book. This one, unlike the last I handled, is complete—it has the woodcut print of Elizabeth that I suspected was missing from the final page of the other copy.

The woodcut image is lightly painted with faded colors, although they are chipped in places. The image of Elizabeth in the book is nearly identical to that of the saint in the Book of Hours held by Agnes Vale in the painting at the Beaney. Both show Elizabeth with an open book, crowned by a nimbus of jewels even though she was alive when it was printed.

Jewels just like those in the rood-screen image.

I can now see clearly that all three are tied together—the image in the painting, the image in the book, and that on the rood screen—an attempt at a new iconography for a saint that never was, buried in both body and memory by Henry VIII.

Here, Elizabeth's image is colored in gold (real gold, melted down and brushed delicately on the page, making her glisten). The gemstones are deep reds, blues, and greens. And painted behind her is a structure. A building. It's familiar to me, but I can't quite place it. It is very odd indeed to have something added to the image like this. I smile at the thrill of discovery.

I then turn the page to the other prize, as if I have been forcing myself to wait for it. The last page, with the handwriting. I pull out my reading glasses and turn on the flashlight on my phone, tools to help me decipher the small, unsure hand.

I read the words, breathlessly.

> Added to these revelations of the Maid are two visions witnessed and written by Philippa Jonys, prioress of Saint Sepulchre's in Kent, in the year of our lord Jesus Christ MDXXXIII.

My hands shake as I read. Can this be real? This book contains something written down by Philippa herself? So little survives that was written by women in their own hands. We may not have Elizabeth's second book of revelations, but this may be even better: a prioress writing down the visions of one of her nuns.

I turn the page slowly, wanting to savor the moment before reading Philippa's additions and cautious about the frailness of the ancient paper.

There are three short paragraphs, written in Philippa's small, light hand:

> These two visions were written down in the presence of Sisters Maria, Benedicta, Catherine, in the presence and hand of Prioress Philippa Jonys. This was one of our Holy Maid's true visions where she was outside of herself and could not be awoken. Her confessor, Father

Bocking, was not present. Although we are mere women, we swear this witness.

The first vision:

The ringing has not always been my own, but I am the alarm that sounded. Wielded by men so that the warning could be heard afar. I foresee my own death, the fate of criminals. Preserve what is precious until the day it may be found. I see a day when all will be revealed.

Thc fruits of my labor locked up, hidden away,
beneath Jacob's ladder leading up to the heavens. Someday my clanging will ebb, be silent. And I see when we are all ash, even this place will be ash, long after the stories of my life and yours, my sisters, are written and closed, long after this land has borne a thousand scars for its sins against God. To that day I look, I long, I see the bloodshed that soaked this place and with it these tokens of devotion, the work of women, will lead to a new era. We know not the hour nor the day.

The second vision:

But there is no second vision. This is the end of the book. I can see that a page has been cut out, its edge still attached to the binding. The Vales were willing to take great risks to hide this book and its contents, risking even death as heretics, traitors, if it were found in their possession. And yet, whatever Elizabeth's second vision was, it was perhaps too dangerous to keep. My elation at what I have found is matched by my despair at what is lost. A historian's familiar paradox.

But one more discovery awaits.

When I close the book, the binding buckles in a strange way, and it does not close smoothly. Something is tucked inside it. I shake the book, and an item falls neatly onto the table as if it has been waiting to be discovered.

It is a large key, an ancient one. The kind that I have seen only in museum cases to show how keys have not changed in a thousand years except by becoming smaller.

I slip it into my pocket.

* * *

"ALISON? ARE YOU quite all right? What do you have there?" I have been so engrossed in the book, I did not hear Marla enter the kitchen. I have no idea how long she has been standing there, watching.

"Oh, Marla, it's the most amazing thing. Come see. I don't know why I didn't say anything sooner—right after my rescue—but I was so afraid that Monroe would take this away and I knew it was special. I found this book hidden in the priest hole. It's another copy of Elizabeth's book, with some additions. I believe they are the missing key to so many puzzles."

"Incredible!" Marla says. "What a find." She picks up the book and shakes her head. "You are a magnet for these! After all these years believing there were no copies."

"Look," I say, turning the book to the last page with its painted woodcut. "This was missing from the copy I found in Belgium. It's Elizabeth, for sure, and I think it reinforces that the rood-screen image is also her. You see, the strange jeweled halo is the same."

Marla looks at it closely, pulling the tortoiseshell reading glasses she wears on a delicate gold chain around her neck up to her eyes. "Yes, isn't it? She is always bejeweled. I can see why the legend had grown so clear that there were gems buried with her. And yet, so far, none. Just the skull. For some that would be treasure enough, I suppose."

"Did you have any idea that Roger was capable of this? That Wes was?" I ask, softly.

"Yes and no," says Marla. "We have been lovers a long time." I marvel at how easily that rolls off Marla's tongue. "Over a decade. I knew that he would do just about anything to save this place. Janine and her brothers would just as easily sell it.

"But Roger loves it here. He feels like he was a lord of the manor born in the wrong century and the wrong country. I really believe he conceived of the Consortium so he could playact that role every few years. You saw how much he liked to be the king of this small castle." She smiles in affection. I think again what a beautiful smile Marla has, how it draws you in. "Anyway, I am not sure how far he would have gone. But when Westley killed Alex, all bets were off. I'm sure he would have been happy to have found the gemstones in the tomb, and he was so mad at the lengths that Westley had gone to that he took that knife and plunged it in without thinking. So now he gets no gems, he will surely lose this place—I bet Janine is drawing up the divorce papers right now—and he will have a murder charge." A beat. "Or attempted murder, I guess, although I don't believe Westley has regained consciousness."

I wince. A flash to being in bed with Wes, kissing him, and then to the dazed confusion as he moved me into the priest hole.

"What else does this book have to offer?" asks Marla. I note that even now she, too, is ever the scholar, as I turn to show her Elizabeth's prophecy.

Vale House Manor, February 1587

"The Virgin Queen!" Margaret scoffed. "No one believes that."

The Jesuit priest at her table tried to suppress a smile. Father Edmund was young, barely in his twenties. The journey here had been more arduous than he had planned, and this was the third Catholic safe house to which he had been moved.

"Well, my Lady Pitlock, that is what she has cultivated. Many may not believe it, but they cannot prove otherwise." He gratefully tucked into the food the servant provided. It had been several days since they had been given meat and wine. "Your assistance in this holy war is well marked by the pope himself, and we are grateful for access to this safe house." He nodded to the even younger, quieter priest at his side, whose slight and delicate hands were ripping the chicken on his plate apart as if he had never seen such bounty.

"Father Edmund," Margaret said, leaning forward, "you and your brothers will always find sanctuary here. I am glad that we can offer you rest while you recover from your travel from Flanders and before you go to do your good works throughout this land."

Margaret was in her fifties but had already lived through four monarchs; each one brought a different kind of hope and despair. What it was to live at the whims of others! She had not given up hope that England would again be a Catholic country, brought back into the fold of Rome and forgiven for its many sins at the hands of Elizabeth, but hope was harder to come by these days. She concentrated her attention on her family and on continuing to house and hide the priests who came over from Portugal, Spain, or Flanders, doing their work in secret.

While Margaret did not ever know their full missions, she knew they were all to help their true and Catholic queen, Mary, Queen of Scots, Elizabeth's cousin, assume her proper place.

* * *

MARGARET WAS STILL spry despite her age, and she could easily keep up with the grandchild who lived with them at the manor. When her husband died, her son George inherited the house and property, and Margaret was happy to welcome him with his pregnant wife, Veronica. It was not a love match, exactly, but George and Veronica shared a mutual respect and there was something like love between them.

Quiet, thoughtful Veronica enjoyed sitting at her mother-in-law's side as they needlepointed or read. Veronica who, like Margaret, believed that the country would soon be delivered from Elizabeth, who helped shepherd the Jesuits in and out of the house, doing their good works.

The two recently arrived priests had been in the library saying mass for the women, one of the great benefits to having the priests in the house, when they had heard a horse approach, and they quickly ran to the nursery to hide. It was not much of a hiding spot, but often the officials did not look in children's or servant's spaces. It was the best that they had. They could always claim a sleeping child to attempt to keep prying eyes away.

It was not the pursuivants, fortunately, who were at the door, but their trusted young messenger, Edward. When Margaret opened the door to him, she could see that he was flushed and sweaty from the exertion of his ride.

"My Lady Pitlock," he said, "I am so sorry, but I came without stopping from London. My horse needs water desperately."

"Of course," she said calmly, but with dread at what his next words would be. "You may take him to the stable immediately and hand him off to the stablehand. Please return to tell us your news. I will have some ale for you."

While Edward attended to his horse, Margaret sent Veronica to the nursery to fetch the priests so that they were all in the library together when he returned to share his missives. The news was crushing.

"I am sorry to tell you, my Ladies Pitlock," Edward said, nodding at Margaret and Veronica, "and Fathers"—he bowed quietly to the two priests—"Mary, Queen of Scots, our queen, has been executed for treason at Fotheringhay Castle."

All four of them lowered their heads in prayer at his terrible words, their hopes of restoring a true Catholic queen to the throne severed. "She commended her spirit to God in Latin," Edward continued, "and forgave the executioners their sins. They say her lips moved in prayers for a quarter of an hour after her head was taken from her body. She was a holy beacon until the end."

This news was not good for Catholics in hiding. Elizabeth had already imprisoned and executed those she knew were involved in the plot to overthrow her rule and put Mary in her place. Now she would be looking for Mary's remaining supporters to make certain that they did not live to champion another rival against her.

Elizabeth's men had been getting more aggressive in their searches, too, and Margaret knew that they would need a better solution soon. Every time someone came to the door unannounced, Margaret's heart was in her throat, the thought of the danger she had subjected her family to making her swear that it was over. But just as quickly, the conviction of her faith returned. She prayed she could sustain it now.

Vale House Manor, June 2023, Days 6–7

"This is an extraordinary find!" cries Marla. "A vision in Philippa's hand! What do you make of it?"

"As you know, I really saw Elizabeth as a pawn of Bocking and the other men. I think that is how history remembers her, too. That may very well be due to Henry and his men, who tried hard to discredit Elizabeth before and after her death, casting her as a false prophet and a tool of men the king wanted out of the way as well."

"And now?"

"Now I think maybe she was somewhere in between. She *did* have visions that she believed were true—like so many visionaries—and that the people around her believed, too. Philippa wouldn't have risked writing this down unless it were authentic.

"But at the same time, there is something odd in the way this is framed. She makes sure to note that Bocking was not there. Maybe when he was there the visions were different or more directed by him? And the fact that Elizabeth herself notes her alarm was 'wielded by men.' Did she know she was a pawn? She foresees her own death here; does she understand what led to it?

"And also, the second vision that is mentioned in Philippa's short prologue has been ripped out. Was it too dangerous? Too heretical?"

Marla leans closer. "Does the remaining vision tell you anything different than what we knew?"

"Yes, I think it might. And I think the woodcut does, too." Threads are coming together now, frayed ends I left hanging, knowing I would come back to them. I turn to the woodcut. "Do you see this building sketched behind Elizabeth?" I ask, biting my tongue, letting Marla come to the realization I have.

Marla nods. "A tower?" she asks.

"Yes, a tower we have been looking at for the last week." I point to the kitchen door that opens onto the path leading to the church. "It's the bell tower of the priory church."

"Ah," Marla says with a smile, "so it is. Another clue that Elizabeth's skull was at the church."

I turn to Philippa's writing. "I think it's more than that, actually, Marla. Look at this again."

> The fruits of my labor locked up, hidden away,
> beneath Jacob's ladder leading up to the heavens. Someday my clanging will
> ebb, be silent. And I see when we are all ash, even this place will be ash,
> long after the stories of my life and yours, my sisters, are written and closed,
> long after this land has borne a thousand scars for its sins against God.
> To that day I look, I long, I see the bloodshed that soaked this place and
> with it these tokens of devotion, the work of women, will lead to a new
> era. We know not the hour nor the day.

"It's oddly spaced, isn't it? I would never have thought of it if Roger hadn't found that other acrostic, and this one is a bit more complicated, but the answer is both in the vision and in the acrostic. In the vision she tells us something: 'the fruit of her labor' is hidden away, when her clanging, like a bell, is silent. Up a ladder, or stairs, of course."

I show with my finger how the acrostic works, careful not to touch the paper because I can feel the sweat on my palms, the significance of the moment bearing down on me: "'Beneath': 'b'; 'ebb': 'e'; the two 'long's: two 'l's. So we have the word 'bell.' Then 'To' is both a 't' and an 'o'; 'with': 'w'; and the 'er' from 'era.' 'Tower.' The acrostic is 'bell tower.' We were looking in the wrong place for the gems."

With this I sit back, triumphant, even though my heart is pounding so hard I can almost hear it. "This was so hard to find because there were, in fact, *two* treasures, and the hints pointed to both, and both were probably equally important to the women who hid them. One was in the transi tomb—the relic, Elizabeth's skull, part of a saint that could have refounded the priory—and the other is in the bell tower. I think it must be the gems."

I am very pleased with myself and look to Marla to study her reaction. Is she pleased, too?

"But the clues all pointed to memento mori," says Marla, cautiously.

"Even this one does, with Philippa's ending of 'we know not the hour nor the day.'"

"Yes, but we have forgotten that clocks could also be memento mori; that's why they were so often on churches. The clocks' bells remind us that the hour is always changing and that one of the hours will be tolling our demise."

"And what about all the references to the Mother? Shouldn't that also have led us to the transi tomb? The mother figure of the Vale family?"

"I think that works two ways, too, just like the memento mori. They were very clever; they didn't separate either the treasures or their clues but led their descendants to two places. On the one hand, the clues lead us to the transi tomb and the skull. The mother there is Valentina, the matriarch of the Vale family. On the other, they lead us to the prioress's tomb—the brass cover right in front of the bell-tower door. The mater of the order, the mother of her nuns."

As I say it out loud, I know I am correct. The puzzle has always been twofold.

Two mothers. Two memento mori. Two treasures.

* * *

"WELL, DR. SAGE, I believe you have cracked it!" Marla says, her smile somewhat subdued. "Are the gems long gone, then? I haven't been up to the tower in years, but if I recall it's just an empty room. There is no longer even a bell. Perhaps that is where they were hidden?" She can't hide the disappointment in her voice.

"Actually, I have an idea about that, too. I think it has to do with 'Jacob's ladder,' in the vision," I say, standing, my legs shaky. I feel like I have had ten cups of coffee. "Well, I learned my lesson last time. I will go find Monroe and tell her what I discovered, hand this book in—after I take a few photos of the relevant pages." I pull out my phone.

Marla grabs my arm. "No, no, you mustn't! You are right that they would take this book, and if these treasures are there, they will take the gems, too. Look, the Treasure Act in England would give the money to the Pitlock family, who certainly would give you some reward for finding them. I've seen it happen several times, especially because there's always so much publicity around these discoveries. If the police find them, then nothing will come to you at all. They may not even handle the artifacts correctly and they will be damaged. We must go and find the gems, *then* let Monroe and the others know what we have found. This is too good an opportunity to pass up."

"Are you sure, Marla?" I ask carefully. "This may implicate us in Wes's stabbing and Alex's death somehow. It will certainly make them take a closer look at us when we announce what we have found, if there is anything there, that is."

"I'm sure," Marla says without hesitation. "We deserve to be the ones who find this and reap the rewards. But we can't go now," she says quickly. "There are still too many police around. Wait until they think we have all gone to bed, and that they are babysitting just a bunch of sleepy professors. They plan to let us all go tomorrow, anyway, now that they have Roger."

"And Wes," I say.

"Yes, if he survives," Marla says. "Go to bed, dress in something dark and comfortable, and we will meet back here at twelve. We can always claim a midnight snack if we get intercepted."

"What's your plan?" I ask. I need her to tell me clearly before we part ways.

"We will go see what's in that bell tower while everyone is asleep. We can reveal it in the morning. Shall I take the book?"

"Um, no, I want to photograph it," I say. "Before we turn it over to the police."

Marla nods. "Of course. At midnight, then."

* * *

I AM SURPRISED when Marla meets me in the kitchen in black leggings and a sweatshirt. I have never seen Marla in anything other than pristinely tailored clothing, and here she comes looking like a cat burglar. Leave it to Marla to have the right clothes for every occasion, down to the little messenger bag.

"Tools," Marla says, pointing to the bag. "In case we need to pry anything open or look with a magnifying glass. Also, a torch." She waves a flashlight in the air. Maybe I should have taken some time to consider advance preparation, but I didn't. Marla has it all in hand.

As we head outside, I feel a growing apprehension about being near the places that I now only see drenched in blood whenever I close my eyes. I am glad that we are going directly to the bell tower and not lingering in the nave or outside the church.

There appear to be even fewer police than were here last night. I hope there are more around that we just can't see.

"The police have backed off now that they have Roger," explains Marla, reading my thoughts. We walk quietly to the back of the church, to the door that had been open the night before. It's blocked by yellow police tape.

I pull on the handle, but the door is locked.

"Well," I say, "I guess that's the end of the line. Time to get Monroe—I'm sure she can get us in there if we explain what we suspect."

But Marla roots around in her bag and pulls out a key.

"Oh! Where did that come from?" I ask.

"It's Roger's skeleton key. I know where he keeps it." Marla opens the door quietly, shining her flashlight into the dark space. The blood near the transi tomb has not yet been cleaned up, and the congealed liquid traces the outline of where Wes's body lay; I avert my gaze and we duck under some police tape to walk to the bell-tower door with Philippa's grave in front.

I can't see how I missed it before. The hands in prayer, the eyes of the figure in the brass, looking up. They are all pointing at the bell-tower door. Even the eyes of Elizabeth in the rood screen are upward and to the side, not toward the heavens as I assumed but toward the tower.

The door leading to the tower itself is unlocked. I remember the giddy anticipation I felt, climbing the narrow winding staircase only a few days before with Wes, how he kissed me at the top, my back pressed against the stone. Was it all part of an act so that I would help solve the puzzle of the treasure? It is the only answer I can come up with for what he did afterward. I hear the door click behind us as Marla pulls it firmly shut and my pulse starts to race.

"Don't turn on the light," Marla says as I feel for the switch. "It will light up the whole tower and we will be seen from the manor house."

Marla lights the way behind me as I again make my way up the steep stairs. They corkscrew around and around so tightly that we have to walk at an excruciatingly slow pace, Marla illuminating the path as we climb. I count off the 120 steps in my head.

When we reach the top, I kick the final step. "Do you hear that?" I ask. It is so dark. Marla's flashlight casts a narrow beam at our feet.

Her voice comes out in a whisper. "Hollow?"

"Yes, I think so. And it's slightly larger than the other steps, although they all are so uneven. I tripped over it when I came up the other day. What do you have in that tool bag to pry open the top of the step?" I illuminate the light on my phone, although it isn't much compared to Marla's flashlight. And neither is adequate to the job.

She hands me a crowbar. "Wow," I say loudly, my voice now shaky, "a crowbar! You really did come prepared."

I see Alex's head. Pummeled. Pulpy.

"I know where Roger keeps the tools. Hurry and open this. The longer we are absent from the manor house, the more likely it is that someone will catch us."

"Actually, Marla, I really think we *do* need to get Monroe. This is too much. We could get in serious trouble just for being here—I don't know what we were thinking. I'm going to go back. I'm sorry." I start to stand up and hear Marla rooting around in her bag again.

Then I feel something sharp press into the back of my neck.

"Open it, Alison."

"What are you doing, Marla?" I say, keeping my head very still, my voice echoing out against the cold stone walls. "This is ludicrous."

"Open the step, Alison."

"What are you doing?" I repeat, even louder. My breath is coming faster and more panicked. I try to slow it, to stop myself from hyperventilating.

"I am taking what won't be missed. It hasn't been missed for centuries. No one needs to get hurt here. Now, open it."

"You have a knife at my neck," I say slowly, carefully. "It sure seems like someone will get hurt."

"I like you, Alison," Marla says, pressing a bit harder on the blade. Its point is painful against my skin, threatening to pierce it. I feel like all the blood has drained out of my body; I am cold, clammy, sweat gathering on my palms. "We women need to stick together. The academy is happy to chew us up and spit us out. Listen, we can share what is inside. It will make us both very rich. Open it. I won't ask again." Gone is the warm collegial tone I've heard all week, replaced by a cold, steely resolve.

"I'm opening it," I say, and I take the crowbar from her. I'm still crouching down and speaking carefully. "Wes was with me the night that Alex died. He didn't do it. Did you kill Alex? With this?" I start to feel under the step for a small opening, a place to drive a wedge. I don't dare stop now.

"Oh, you're all so stupid," Marla says. "Roger brought Alex and Wes in on his little treasure hunt. That idiot didn't think to bring me in on it. He wanted the money for himself, for Janine." She says the name with disdain. "I asked Alex what was going on—only took a few pounds for him to tell me. Roger thought Alex was loyal to him, to Vale House"—she laughs wryly—"but he would have done anything for money. I paid him some more to go into your room, take pictures of anything helpful he saw there."

I remember my scribbled notes about the rood screen. Had I sent Alex to his death?

"Are you done yet?" she asks impatiently.

I find a small point of entry and start leveraging the bar. The top of the step is loosening, but not entirely. "Not yet. It's moving, though. There are a lot of nails holding this thing together." I try to distract Marla from my slowness. "Why did Alex destroy the rood screen?"

"He said you suspected it was hidden there. We came that evening and brought a saw and a crowbar—I wasn't sure what tools we would need. It turns out it was the saw. And there was nothing there." Marla pauses. "It was his own fault. He knew Roger would lose his mind with the ruined rood screen, and then it was all for nothing. No treasure. He told me on our way back to the manor that he was going to come clean with Roger. Tell him I blackmailed him to do it."

The stair creaks, and I suddenly can slide the crowbar in deeper. I am getting the leverage I need. "It's coming now," I tell her, scared of what she'll do if I stop. I feel a warm liquid dripping down my neck and can't tell if the knife has drawn blood or it's just my sweat. "That was stupid of Alex, but surely you could have smoothed things over with Roger?" I'm trying to keep her talking.

"Probably. But I don't appreciate blackmail." Marla speaks as if she is lecturing students, explaining the intricacies of medieval wills, demonstrating her superior intellect. "It's amazing what a crowbar swung at the right angle can do." She pauses and pushes the knife in a bit deeper.

I feel a sharp pain, followed by what this time I know is blood trickling down my back. "Don't even think of swinging that one, though. Because this knife will go straight through your neck."

"But you knew we would find his body . . . ," I say.

"Sure, I tried to move it, but even that skinny thing weighed too much for me to drag very far. I was quite sure the blame wouldn't fall on me."

"And Wes?" I ask, flinching.

"Roger called it all off with Wes right after Alex died. He had decided things had gone too far, that it wasn't worth it. That's when I spoke to Wes. He had his heart set on the treasure, and he didn't take much convincing to go along with me. And he was already working you—he said you'd figure out where to look. And you kind of did when you guessed the transi tomb, although you were wrong."

"Why did he try to kill me?" I ask this one quietly. It's the most important one to me, I realize, as I say it out loud.

Marla scoffs. "No one tried to kill you, Alison, we just wanted to knock you out. Get you out of the way for a good long while. You kept wanting to go to Monroe. Tell the police. Wes was sure you wouldn't go in on the plans or would somehow expose us. I gave him my sleeping pills. We figured by the time you woke up he'd be long gone. I'd shift the blame to Roger somehow, and then the treasure would be ours."

"So then why did you stab him?" I ask, swallowing down Wes's betrayal, focusing on saving my own skin. Keep Marla talking.

"I didn't really trust Wes. I knew I could frame Roger for it all, but for that, I needed both Wes and Alex to be silenced. Then the treasure would have been mine, if it had actually been where we thought it was. Wes wouldn't have been found for hours and certainly would have bled to death by then. You ruined that, though."

I feel the top of the stair give way; it pops up like a lid off a stubborn jar. Centuries of dust come pluming up.

"First, hand me the crowbar. Slowly," says Marla, coughing. With each cough, the knife digs deeper into my skin.

In a clear, firm voice, I say, "I am passing you the crowbar, Marla. Please put down that knife."

I hand the crowbar back to her over my head.

This is it. Marla is going to kill me. She is obviously willing and capable.

She killed Alex, and she probably has killed Wes, too.

Now that the stair is open, what will stop her from using that knife? I think I hear the door to the bell-tower stairs rattle below, but I realize Marla had locked it when we came in.

No one is coming to save me. Did I survive the priest hole only to die here?

Calm. Breathe.

"Now, stand up slowly and turn around," she says. "I want you to back into the bell-tower landing and stand where I can see you while I look to see what's in the stair. If you comply, I won't hurt you. Like I said, we can split this money and never have to worry about anything again. I have contacts and I can sell these jewels, quietly, no matter what they are." Marla speaks to me in a controlled way—no panic, severe, as if everything and everyone around her is disappointing. "Now you will have some real money. And I can disappear. We are the only two who know where these were hidden. Everyone else thinks the treasure was the skull. Just don't try anything and we will be fine."

"Marla, please take the knife away from my neck," I say, loudly. "Marla, please. You don't have to do this." Marla doesn't move but presses the knife more firmly.

As instructed, I stand slowly, then turn around.

Now Marla is facing me, the knife pointing at my chest. The same place where I had seen its twin sticking out of Wes. I wonder what story she had told Wes, what he agreed to before she plunged the knife into his heart.

But I have an advantage that Wes didn't. We are on the top of a narrow, winding staircase, and Marla is standing two steps below me.

What had Wes said when we climbed up here?

"One wrong step and you'd be at the bottom with a broken neck."

That sounds about right. I take one more step backward, for leverage, and then I push forward with all my strength.

Vale House Manor, March 1588

Brother Nicholas Owen rapped quickly on the side door of Vale House Manor. He had received Lady Pitlock's message nearly two weeks prior, but he had been so busy in the region. Every English Catholic, it seemed, had found his name and wanted the hidden cabinets he had become so adept at building.

He looked at his hands while he waited for an answer at the laborer's door. They were not the scholar's hands of his fellow Jesuits, hands that held prayer books for careful theological study. No, these were carpenter's hands, like St. Joseph's. Rough and callused, bearing scars from all his tools, his nails and adzes, his riving knives and augers. He was only twenty-four and already had become a master carpenter, having learned at his father's side from the moment he could hold a saw. His parents in Oxford were proud of their three boys—two priests and one lay brother, Jesuits all—but only Nicholas had picked up his father's trade.

Lady Margaret Pitlock herself greeted him, along with her daughter-in-law, Veronica. It was Veronica who had found him. He could work magic in the house, her friend Heloise had said. Make the priests disappear into thin air if a pursuivant came knocking.

"Brother Owen?" Margaret asked as she opened the door.

"No," he said, "Draper."

Margaret expected the alias. "Oh, right, of course. Mr. Draper. Welcome."

"I understand you have a cabinet you need built?"

"Um, yes, that's right." This was also what she had been told. That the man would do a "real" carpenter job for her, and also ply his wares to others in the village for the same. This happened in daytime. And in the night, he would build the more important cabinet, the secret one.

She had heard of a family not far from Vale House who had been caught harboring a Jesuit. They had had their land stripped, their books burned. They were lucky to have kept their lives. Queen Elizabeth was stamping out anything she thought was heretical, any scent of Catholicism. She did not want anyone rallying around another rival as they had around her now-dead cousin Mary.

Nicholas entered the room with his tools, leaving his materials outside, already assessing the house, where they could put its secrets. It was most important that only he and the owner of the house knew where the space was. Any others—servants, visitors, even family—should never be told of its location. He had become so adept at hiding them that some people had called him back to show them the entry again, they were so disguised.

"What should your payment be?" Margaret asked, already heading to the chest in the library where she kept coins for services.

"Only food and lodging while I am here," he answered. "I accept no payment for this work."

Lady Margaret bowed her head in consent, vowing to make sure that he had extra meat and ale while staying in her home.

"Why not show me first where you want the room of concealment?" he said, quietly, even though Lady Pitlock had promised him that it would be an afternoon without servants. "And then we can discuss the cabinetry. It's important that you have something to show for my time spent here. It's the only way I can travel around this country and stay safe. If the Crown knew what I was doing . . . well, I suppose it's only a matter of time until they do, but I would like to help hide as many soldiers in Christ as I can before then."

* * *

IT WAS NICHOLAS who suggested the double hiding place, telling Margaret and Veronica that it was something he had been thinking about trying. This way, if the pursuivants ever found the smaller first hole, they could claim it was just a concealed cabinet, a place for treasures. And the priests could be through a trapdoor and safer in a larger space. He would build a way to deliver food and water stealthily, as Elizabeth's men sometimes would stay for days in a house, hoping to force the men out of hiding.

He spent the first day meticulously going over every room in the house (while also building the decoy cabinet in the library). He thought one of the upper bedrooms, close to the servants' stairs, had enough of a void that two priest holes could be built: one that opened into the bedchamber and one that opened into a smaller room on the first floor that was used to store the linens, silver, and china.

Margaret thought that the double space could even be used to hide some of the heretical books that the family owned, the one or two that had not been defaced to satisfy Elizabeth's men.

Nicholas thought to build a window seat in the bedchamber—another feint for those peering in, asking what the carpenter was creating. Of course, it was also the secret doorway for the smaller priest hole. Because Veronica and George had taken over the larger bedroom that had once been hers and Samuel's, this became Margaret's room.

It seemed fitting to Margaret that her room held the secret chamber. She lay in it after it was built, had Nicholas close the panel behind her so that she could feel its confinement, understand what the priests who had to hide were going through.

It felt like a tomb to her, but also holy.

She marveled at the ingenuity of the concealed space. If she had not known it was there, she never would have discovered it. After that, she never went into a house again without thinking what could be behind the walls, what secrets a house held. And although the hunters only came twice to the manor when there were Jesuits there, they were never found. Holding their breath as they heard the pursuivants' heavy step outside, the priests remained safely hidden away with the dangerous books Margaret's grandmother had given her.

Vale House Manor guarded all of its secrets tightly.

Vale House Manor, June 2023, Day 7

Marla lies in a crumpled heap at the bottom of the stairs. Her body looks like clothes that have been discarded in a hurry, like the leavings of lovers racing into another room.

"Marla?" I am halfway down the stairs, close enough to see the wrinkled mound at the bottom, my meager phone flashlight scanning her form. There is no movement. No sound.

I sit on a step several feet from the bottom, keeping the light trained on Marla's body. I'm shaking uncontrollably. A shake I have known only once before, after my children were born—a body going into shock as it recovers from the excess adrenaline, the trauma, the emotional overload.

Again, an image comes to me of the twins, this time as toddlers, sleeping on me after a party. I hadn't dared move so as not to wake them. For the second time in as many days I wonder if I will ever see them again.

The door to the church rattles more insistently than before. Someone is pounding against it.

"Help!" I scream. I do not want to go down the stairs until I know it's safe. The door groans and strains against its hinges as someone pushes their whole weight against it, again and again. Marla doesn't move, even when the door finally bursts open, nudging her body in the process. Relief floods through me as the light switches on down below.

"That took you long enough!" I shout furiously to Monroe. White stands in front of her, rubbing his shoulder. "I was trying to speak loudly—she had a knife!" I gesture to my chest, where the microphone Monroe had taped to me hours earlier is secured.

"I know, I know. I'm sorry," says Monroe. "We realized that she had locked you in because we tried the door quietly when you were up the stairs. I was worried that trying to bust it down would cause her to panic and stab you for sure. We had no idea she had a key to the church. We didn't think you would get that far. We were ready to break in, though." She points at White, who is panting with his hands on his knees. "See?"

White moves over to Marla and places two fingers on her neck. "She's alive," he says, "but barely. Don't move her. The ambulance should be here any second." Just as he says it, I can hear the sirens.

Monroe steps over Marla's folded body and walks up the steps to me. "Are you okay?" she asks, placing her hand on my shoulder.

I don't cry, but it takes strength to remain somewhat composed. "No. No. No. I'm not." I shake my head back and forth emphatically. "I just pushed a woman down the stairs. And I had a knife at the back of my neck and then at my chest. I did this because you asked me to, and you weren't even here to help me when I needed it." My voice is now hysterical. I can't help it—it has all been too much.

"I'm sorry, Alison. Let's go upstairs to discuss while they attend to Marla." Monroe says this in a calm, low tone, the one you use on a tantruming toddler. Medics have entered the door and are strapping Marla onto a stretcher. I watch for a second and then I will my legs to work, to stop their shaking, and Monroe follows me back to the top of the bell tower.

"I want to see what was in the step," I say. "I at least deserve that."

Monroe nods. In our meeting earlier this evening, Monroe told me why they suspected Marla: That she had been too cool in her responses about why she was out when Wes was stabbed, too easy to turn the blame to Roger. That some of her alibi didn't exactly line up.

When I finally told her about the book I had found in the priest hole, Monroe said I should let Marla know, see how she would react. Would I be willing to wear a wire? Try to get her to confess? I agreed because it seemed so outlandish. Because I thought I would be exonerating Marla, who had taken me under her wing, whose attention was so flattering.

The events of the last hour have been far more terrifying than I could have imagined. I kept waiting for the police to burst in, to save me, but also realized the precarious position of the bell tower, how I was trapped by Marla.

Now, with light flooding the tower from the switch below and Monroe's very powerful flashlight trained on the step, I can see the small chest nestled in the empty space.

I don't ask Monroe's permission as I pull it out. The chest is beautiful, fitting neatly inside my cupped hands. It appears to be gold and enamel with inlaid jewels—garnets and sapphires.

The sides feature etched images—figures of female saints. I can make out Catherine of Alexandria, Barbara, and again Elizabeth, with her jeweled nimbus. Even though it had been hidden in the step for hundreds of years and is covered with a thick coating of dust, I see it's in excellent condition. No water damage. This piece has been safely tucked away, waiting to be found.

I try to open it. It's locked.

Monroe is watching closely, taking pictures all the while. "I need an inventory of absolutely everything in there," she says. "I honestly should *not* be letting you handle it, much less open it, but you're right, it's the least I can do after what you've been through. But these could be of real significance. I reckon even that little chest is important, so once you've seen it, it's in my possession until it can be examined by the National Trust."

"It's locked."

"Well, I guess that's it then," says Monroe. "You can't force that lock open—it's too fragile and too important. We will have to wait until it's in a conservator's hand. Here, give it." She reaches out.

"Wait," I protest. "I think I may have the key. It was in the book. I forgot to tell you about it."

"Sure, you did," says Monroe. But she is smiling.

I reach into my pocket and pull out the key. It's the right size. I hold my breath and slowly insert it, breathing out only when it easily slides in.

I turn it.

It clicks.

I hold my breath again as I open the chest.

Vale House Manor, December 1536

Agnes looked at the small group of books she had pulled out, debating which to take with her to London. Her Book of Hours. A Psalter, well thumbed, with her favorite psalms. It was not much, but she knew she would find a Catholic community in London who would connect her with the book trade there.

The others were easy to leave. Most of these books were not hers, anyway. They were men's books, and all their papers: deeds to land, claims to her dowry, directions as to the inheritance of the manor. There was an additional manuscript of Elizabeth's visions, transcribed by Bocking. She added it to the pile. If owning Elizabeth's printed book was a crime of heresy, owning this one would be treason. It was a risk she could not take, not as the sole provider for the twins.

She picked up Elizabeth's printed book, the one she had commissioned to be painted and colored. The key. She would take this with her. Safeguard it. Agnes read the last pages containing Philippa's additions one more time. The first revelation, in which Elizabeth foresaw her death, would remain. But Agnes was unclear what the second revelation meant and unsure whether she should let the book stay intact.

She read it several times before deciding it was too dangerous—she ripped out the page and placed it in her pocket.

The twins had gone ahead with her servants. Her cases were on their way to the home she had rented in London. But she knew that one day Alister and Margaret would return and take what was theirs. She had hidden the casket well and it could be used for a new priory, a new foundation, a new home here.

She placed the small collection of books in a case and took them out to the waiting carriage.

"I have just one more thing to do inside," she told the driver. "Then we should be on our way." The journey would take two days and she did not want to waste any more time. It was going to snow, she could tell.

One last time in the library. Books and papers that were not hers, in a room that had not been hers, in a house that had not been hers until the very end, when she shared it with Philippa and the twins. All the papers written and sanctioned by men to show how other men owned the property, the land, the treasures. She had learned in the months since John died that the papers were the key. Everyone asked to see them. They had all the information. She had, of course, long ago burned John's will, but there were so many papers. So many records. Everything had to be destroyed. Cleared. So that she could start it all anew.

A cozy fire was still burning in the fireplace, the flames a comfort against the icy winds that were blowing outside. Agnes wrapped a cloth around her hand and grasped the end of a long burning log.

"Goodbye, Vale House," she said. The burning log landed heavily on the pile of John's papers and books.

There was one more thing to add to the flames that were just beginning to smolder: the final page of Elizabeth's book. She took it out of her pocket and held it in her hand, reading its words one final time:

Death awaits me now.
Henry Eight will not rest until he has Six.
Three Catherines. Two Annes. One Jane.
And his voice will ring for centuries.
And mine, silenced.
To only sound once again
Through a woman sage.

Agnes dropped the paper on the fire. She saw its edges start to curl, Philippa's writing turn to black ash. She watched all of the books start to whoosh up into flame. Before long they would reach the tapestries. She went out to meet the carriage.

She did not wait to watch the rest burn.

AUTHOR'S NOTE

Many of the facts related to Elizabeth Barton in this book are true. The Holy Maid of Kent was a real person who was championed by many of the important men of the age, including Bishop Fisher and Archbishop Warham. She had meetings with Cardinal Wolsey and with King Henry VIII. Her book of visions was indeed printed, and an additional manuscript of her visions was written. No copies of either survive (that we know of). Some of the details of Elizabeth's vision I took from the anonymous fifteenth-century text *A Revelation of Purgatory*, and others from letters or sermons describing Elizabeth and what she said.

Elizabeth was always controversial. Thomas More at first believed her and later thought she was delusional and misled (and wrote about this from prison to Thomas Cromwell). Catherine of Aragon refused to meet with her. And Fisher did eventually denounce her. She was executed with her advisor and confessor Edward Bocking and a few other supporters. She was the only woman whose head was displayed on London Bridge as a warning to traitors.

Philippa Jonys was the name of the prioress at St. Sepulchre's, the convent that Elizabeth joined. Some ruins of the priory exist, but its description, location (it was in Canterbury), and the surrounding environs are all fiction. Everything about Philippa (other than her name) is fictional, as is the entire Vale-Pitlock family. I have taken details from several important Catholic families in England during the Reformation and afterward, however. For example, Nicholas Owen was a real Jesuit lay brother who built ingenious priest holes throughout the country and was eventually executed for doing so. I've tried to keep my details as historically accurate as possible and as true to the timeline as made sense for the story, although some events are moved for the flow or storyline (for example, while Elizabeth was hung at Tyburn, the infamous Tyburn Tree would be erected a few decades after her death), and while there were monks killed en masse during the Reformation, these were not the monks at Edward Bocking's monastery. There is much excellent work on Elizabeth Barton, most notably by Diane Watt, Sharon Jansen, Nancy Bradley Warren, and Genelle Gertz.

All of the characters in Alison's life are fictional, but Mrs. Bunch's name and occupation are taken from the story "Lost Hearts" by M. R. James, a Victorian-era medievalist who wrote ghost stories on the side. The Miss Universe pageant and the Society for Classical Studies conference really did coincide in the same hotel in January 2023. But otherwise, any comparison to any real academic I know either in work or manner (hi, medievalists!) is purely coincidental. Although these academics are unwelcoming to Alison, I have always found the field supportive.

ACKNOWLEDGMENTS

After a long day of research at the British Library, I had the good fortune to meet up with Kimberly Hamlin (Americanist extraordinaire) for drinks and dinner. I talked about some of my work on Elizabeth Barton, said something to the effect of "somebody should write that novel," and was told by Kimberly: You should do it. I laughed. And then I did it. When I had enough of "something," I sent it to a few smart people to read, Kimberly included, waiting to be told that it had no legs. All I received was encouragement—so thank you to all of those early readers, especially my mom, Nancy, and sister, Caroline (who've been in my three-person book club for my entire adult life). Kate Coyne was one of those early readers who said, "You may actually have something here," and who introduced me to Kristin van Ogtrop, who I was so fortunate wanted to represent me and believed in the work. And then a gigantic thank-you to Brigitte Dale for taking this novel to the next level, and the team at St. Martin's Press (especially Ginny Perrin and MaryAnn Johanson) for making this novel into something beyond what my wildest dreams could have concocted that first night in London. I feel like I really lucked out with this agent-editor duo.

So many thank-yous and so much love to my friends and family who read this in all sorts of stages (I am sure I am forgetting someone): Buck Brown, Jennifer Crozier, Queenie Mortola Garcia, Tracey Gardener, Bess Hauser, Judith Hauser, Colleen Hennessy, Eric Hofmann, Deitra Mara, Caitlin Monck-Marcellino, Caren Park, Nicole Rice, Anthony Santa Cattarina, Caroline Tiger, Jessica Toonkel, Amy Vanderwal, Nicola Maye Goldberg and the participants of the literary thriller workshop at the Center for Fiction, and my medievalist reading group (Valerie Allen, Glenn Burger, Matthew Goldie, Steven Kruger, Michael Sargent, and David Lavinsky), who read and commented on a few chapters in lieu of an academic piece. Thank you, too, to Eddie Jones for the invite to the Exeter Symposium, which formed the bones for the C.C. (but no murders and much more conviviality).

I've been so lucky to find Jessica Robb, Diane Mines, and Lily Shapiro as my fellow academic mamas writing outside of academia. I love our meetings and readings. Your feedback has been invaluable. Katherine Damm, Bruce Holsinger, and Magdalena Mączyńska, you were the best beta readers a first-time novelist could have asked for and shaped this book in all sorts of ways.

Finally, to my husband, Jeff, who has supported me from the first word and celebrated every milestone of this book, and my fabulous kiddos, Nate and Bee. I love you all so much.

ABOUT THE AUTHOR

Justine Cooper Photography

Jennifer N. Brown is the Dean of Arts and Sciences at Bentley University, where she is also a professor of English and Media Studies, with a specialization in medieval literature written for and by women. She has published a lot on this topic, but *The Lost Book of Elizabeth Barton* is her first novel. She lives in the Boston area with her husband, their two children, and two miniature dachshunds.